Love in Haven

JULIA LAUREN

Copyright © Julia Lauren 2022

All rights reserved.

No part of this publication may be altered, reproduced, distributed, or transmitted in any form, by any means, including, but not limited to, scanning, duplicating, uploading, hosting, distributing, or reselling, without the express prior written permission of the publisher, except in the case of reasonable quotations in features such as reviews, interviews, and certain other non-commercial uses currently permitted by copyright law.

Disclaimer:
This is a work of fiction. All characters, locations, and businesses are purely products of the author's imagination and are entirely fictitious. Any resemblance to actual people, living or dead, or to businesses, places, or events is completely coincidental.

Dedication

For Mom. Thank you for asking me what I was waiting for!

Prologue

Then

Evie

You're just nervous. Breathe, Ev.

This is the one. This is the dress Daniel will see me in when I commit forever to him. This is it. No more hunting on Pinterest in the late hours of the night questioning if I would fall in love with one. No more sending screenshots or links back and forth to my sister or Kyra, because this is the dress to start the rest of my life. I always thought I would want something simple with no lace, bows or fancy shimmering fabric. Whenever I envisioned my dress, it was sleek and perfectly plain. I didn't see myself as an allover floral embroidery kind of girl. Maybe having a different groom makes the dream dress different. As I look in the mirror, the sales associate named Gloria with a bit of a smoker's cough carefully unties the ivory silk-covered buttons on the back of this dress. I realize I have found the dress of my dreams to marry the man of my dreams in nine short months. *Nine.* That was all that was left between me, Daniel, and forever. Daniel would be any woman's dream man and he chose me. My painfully handsome lawyer fiancé and I are ready for our wedding to happen. *No more nerves. No more cold feet.* On my end of course, but I can't think about that now.

Stop, Ev.

A couple of summers going to the weddings of our friends, engagement parties, and fielding questions from those closest to us were over. There would be no more first dates, first kisses to other men, and gossiping to my coworkers. Not that there were many dates before him, but that isn't important. All of the bad invites for first dates and men who behaved like pigs led me to this. When I met Daniel, I had been in a dark place with no motivation to leave that feeling. Then there he was. The one that came along and made all of the horrible memories, lonely nights, and dread go away. At least, he has done his best. The one who picked me up out of my darkness and opened the curtains to let the light come back. The one thing I can't debate is that Daniel is a light. He radiates happiness and even I can admit it's hard to feel anything but joy when you're around him.

"Let's go show the ladies." Gloria stands straight up, lifting her glasses up to her head and she begins moving part of the medium length train from the dress up. I turn around on the worn hunter green platform and think of all the brides who came before me. Ones who cried or yelled. Ones who hated the way they looked. I can't imagine it, because today I feel something that resembles happiness. I wonder for a moment if that makes me superficial. I'm so taken away by watching the way the dress shines as Gloria moves it, I don't even care that I can hear my phone nearby. Not a single text from the office or Twitter notification can tear me away from this moment. I want to remember, because for the first time in forever, I am so certain that everything happening in this moment is right. That life is beautiful and unwavering. Where I am now, is where I was meant to be. I was meant to be Daniel's wife and in New York City. He wants nothing more than to make me happy. Life has tested me once or twice. It has knocked me down, forced me to do things that broke my heart, kicked me to the curb. Now, I truly believe it was to get me to this point. To this statement of mind, in this shop, and in this very dress. The perfect dress for the perfect man.

"Yeah... sure." I take a slow step down, careful not to step on any of the delicate fabric and immediately look back at the mirror to see as much of the back as I can. It really is perfect. It is surprising to me, but every bit as perfect as I could have envisioned. I watch as Gloria makes a few adjustments, adjusting the clamp in one spot, and I try to ignore the warmth that I feel on my cheeks. It can't be that hot in here, but my excitement and nerves are battling for attention.

"We're getting impatient out here!" I hear my mother shout in her thickest southern accent from the lilac-colored lounge on the other side of the boutique's dressing room baby powder French doors. She, my best friend Kyra from work, and my slightly older sister Lexie, joined me for breakfast on the Upper East Side before beginning the hunt for the wedding dress. We talked and talked about the wedding that really isn't that far away. Nine months. Seating arrangements, decor and the music were all a topic of choice. Daniel wants a jazz band and I want a DJ. We've agreed to compromise, just not sure how yet. It doesn't matter though, because we get along so perfectly in every other facet of our lives. I don't care for baseball; he loves the Yankees. I wear t-shirts for loving support. He doesn't mind football, and I grew up screaming 'Roll Tide' at the top of my lungs on Saturdays. He appreciates my cooking and washes the dishes after. He starts the coffee in the morning and I fill up the thermos before he heads into the office. I fall asleep early and he stays up to watch the late shows next to me in our new bed. It just kind of works.

"Okay." I breathe out slowly from my pursed lips and nod as Gloria steps towards the lounge area, pushing the doors open. I barely step into the waiting area before my mother's eyes begin to fill with tears and Kyra jumps up from the velvet chair in the corner. Breathless gasps escape from the three of them that immediately give me a familiar knotted feeling. It puts the last few weeks of anxiety at ease. This is the right thing. "Here it is."

"Oh, baby girl! Everleigh Rose... I swear!" My mother, Nancy, covers her shaking hand over her mouth as I walk out and to another waiting pedestal in front of a three-paneled mirror that catches every angle of this beautiful gown. Gloria takes my hand as I step up, very carefully. I know my mother has read my mind and the look on her face tells me she also knows this dress is the one. Even though she spent all morning reminding me how much I used to say my dress was going to be simple. There is no other dress that is going to elicit this kind of response from any of us. She gave the same look to my sister Lexie when she walked out with the dress she ultimately wore to her wedding. The only difference is she was twenty-two, and she's divorced now with no idea where her husband is. She has one perfect little boy to show for it. It is a great coincidence that I am not one for superstitions or I would be quickly tossing this gown to the side. I don't need any bad omens or to repeat history. "It's perfect. Beautiful, baby!"

"You look so regal." Lexie clasps her hands together and looks over at our mom, who is now dropping tears down her cheeks. "Doesn't she, Mama? Like a princess or a first lady!"

"She does." My mother reaches for her handbag to the right of her feet and pulls a lace handkerchief to dab her eyes with. "Oh, it's so beautiful."

"Kyra?" I look to my friend who befriended me on my first day of work in the city and see that she looks like she wants to burst as she bounces with her hands together. I can't help but laugh as she just lunges forward because everything about Kyra is loud.

"I love it!" She squeals and gives me a mischievous grin as she squeezes my hands for dear life. I know just based on her face right now that I am going to blush. "Daniel won't be able to keep his hands off of you."

"My mother is right there and I won't have any hands if you don't ease that grip up, Ky." I couldn't help but feel a little amused. Still, my peach toned face grows warm, but deep down I hope she's right. "Jeez."

"Well, it's true," Kyra giggles, reaching for her cell phone after she releases her grip on my hands. While I look back at Mama, her smile shifts to something of a melancholy expression. I don't pay much mind to it, because I'm her baby girl. She only has two children and unlike Lexie I don't live close by, so she's had to adapt. Now, I am going to be a married woman and officially more than just her little girl. "You look hot and he's the groom. He's supposed to be all over you. If he's not thinking about banging you somewhere before the end of the night, you're doing it wrong."

"That is the point, isn't it? Kyra's not wrong." My mother stands up and walks the short distance from the plush couch and steps over to where I am standing, gently taking my hands. A much softer grip than Kyra's. For a moment I wince at my mother's response to Kyra, but Lexie laughs and I know I'm just a bit nervous about everything involved with the wedding. Her expression is warm and happy, but I can tell she's feeling all of those Mom emotions you hear about. My smile just widens, because we all know that this is one of those milestones you hear brides talk about. The moment they find the dress and everything starts to come together. In a way this dress will be what it's built around. There are no questions and now. I wish the nine months until my wedding would fly by, because tears are trickling down my face and my mother's too. Even Kyra and Lexie are crying tears that say, *this dress is what made it all come to life.* The love, the heart, and the excitement... it's as if a simple piece of fabric has the power, for just a moment, to fill us with enough joy to last a lifetime. It's fabric that tells a story in my life and will for years to come. "It's perfect."

"Check the detailing." Gloria adds as she adjusts the fabric again, this time fluffing the train out to show just how long it is. Immediately, I make a mental note to tell the photographer to get a picture of the train for my memories and to call around to a few dry-cleaning shops to ask about the process of preserving such a detailed dress. I don't want anything to happen to it. "The beading was done by hand in Italy."

"Italy! That's amazing!" Kyra laughs, shaking her head as she runs her fingers on the skirt. "It couldn't be more perfect."

"I love it." I press my hand to my cheeks as my mother releases my hands and examines the detailing around the waist. "This is it."

"I can't believe how beautiful it is." Lexie joins us in the center of the room as Gloria steps out for a moment. "I wouldn't have looked at it on the hanger and thought it would look this perfect on you. I mean everything looks perfect on you, but this is stunning"

"Thank you. When Gloria brought it in, I wasn't sure." I watch as my sister unlocks her phone again to take another picture. I begin to feel shaky from my nerves and I quickly panic when I realize she's going to get the dress. "Don't let Daniel see it."

"I'm not going to post it anywhere. Although Wade is going to regret ever letting you get away." Lexie rolls her green eyes at me and takes a quick picture of the back of the dress. I give her a knowing glance at the mention of the name and she has gotten the message. I don't want to think about the past. I just want to think about what marrying Daniel will be like. I only want to live working towards the future. "What is Daniel doing today, anyways?"

"He's on his way back to the city." I reply as Kyra examines a wall display of tiaras, bringing one over to me. "He went to a bachelor party for his roommate from college."

"He will have one of those soon. Which means you get a party of your own." Kyra places the tiara delicately on my head, and I can't help but look into the mirror and admire the glamour that it adds to my look. The way the mock diamond's sparkle under the rays of light. "So, should we go to Vegas for one crazy bachelorette weekend or are we going to pretend to be classy bitches and go to wine country or paint something?"

"There is nothing wrong with wine country." I pout, before breaking out a wide grin and Kyra grabs my hand in hope. "But I would say this moment belongs to Vegas."

"Yes!" Kyra squeezes my hand harder this time, but releases it before I can complain a word about it. "I knew you would be up for it."

"I honestly thought she would say no." Lexie says with relief as she dramatically places a hand over her heart. "Mom, we would ask you to come, but we need someone to keep Levi."

"Trust me, I would rather whatever happens in Vegas to stay in Vegas." My mother laughs as Gloria returns with a tray. "Gloria, you've been too good to us."

"I have champagne if you're ready to say yes to this dress." Gloria replies, gesturing to a side of the wall with a built-in bar. "It's here if you want to try a few more."

"I think this is the one." Lexie admits, but I can tell that she's sizing up my reaction to see how I really feel about it. She knows I have the final say, but I give her a subtle nod to tell her that we're on the same page with this dress. "Evie. This is it."

"This is the one." I breathe, running my hands over my

abdomen. My fingers lightly graze the course beading and for a moment I feel so overwhelmed that I think I may be sick. Maybe it's the amount of people in a smaller space, the lack of air flow or that I was so nervous I barely touched my breakfast. I should have eaten more.

"Great choice." Gloria smiles before returning to the bar area and flipping a switch before much to my relief, I feel a cooling air flutter by my face. She thinks of everything, but I am patiently waiting for my nerves to go away. Maybe now, I will truly feel like Daniel's bride. Daniel Preston is everything to me, and I have no doubts about spending the rest of my life with the man who makes me who I am. The man who gave me a spark that I needed to begin living. There is no me without him, and we know that. There is no him without me. Together, we are a team. We're a match. We complete the best part of each other and it's a conversation that we have had many times. Our careers will be our lives for the next few years until he can open his own law office somewhere between his family in New York and mine in Haven, Alabama. We both love the towns we group up in, but neither one of us wants to move directly back to those towns. He doesn't love the small-town life and I need a new start. Then, we'll talk about children. He's on the fence about them and I can't wait to have a baby of my own. It might be the only thing we're not perfectly aligned with, but he's said countless times that he's warming up to the idea. It's a life we both can't wait to move forward with and I can't wait for him to see me on our wedding day.

After a moment of picturing the first moment he will see me, I realize I have zoned out for a bit. Lexie and Kyra are talking in the corner, and my mother is helping Gloria, because my mother can't just watch someone serve drinks or food. She always has to have her hand in the situation. Maybe she's helping, or maybe she's admiring the bar ware. I'm not sure, but

I definitely enjoy looking at the dress in the mirror. "I think I would like to change out of my dress before I risk getting any champagne on it."

"Good idea." Gloria raises a finger before sitting an empty champagne flute on a marble counter space. "Why don't you go back into the dressing room and I will be right in? I just want to grab one more glass, because I believe one of these has a chip in it."

"Okay. Perfect." I smile as she comes up to help me off of the pedestal, lifting the train of the dress so I can hold it as I walk. When she lets go, I am able to make the short walk to the dressing room and close the doors. I need to remind myself to ask Gloria about the lighting in here, because I swear my skin looks flawless under the lights. I know it sounds like I am full of myself when I think it, but it clearly does some sort of magic to make the dress look perfect and make a woman feel confident in the fabric that she's wearing. As someone that works for a skin care company, I know we need these lights in our office. I want to put a note on my phone to bring it up during our next meeting. I know the ladies in the office would be on board.

I pick up my handbag hanging by the ornate triple mirror. When I reach for my iPhone from my black quilted leather bag, I hear a text alert reminder come through the lock screen. It's probably Daniel asking me if I want him to pick anything up from the store before he returns to our apartment. I wouldn't mind a bottle of white wine and maybe some stuffed manicotti from the place on the corner of our street. Although, I should probably be careful now that I have chosen a wedding dress. I wouldn't want to do anything too dramatic to make it not fit on all the alteration appointments and my wedding day. That would be a disaster.

When I finally look at the screen with Daniel and me as the backdrop, I see several missed texts and calls. Frowning, I realize they aren't from Daniel at all. There are numerous texts from members of Daniel's family and friends. Two from his mom. Three from his sister, Jamie. One from his brother Scott. A missed call from his dad, his buddy Colby, and a few others from some numbers I don't recognize. Two voicemails and now another call is coming in from Scott again. It only takes one second before I feel my heart nosedive into my stomach. A car, a semi and one moment for it all to come to an end. One second for the world I know to come crashing down, shattering into a million unfixable pieces.

Chapter One

Evie

Now

There is a split second before you wake up for the day, before any light slips in, and you don't really know what life is. The universe offers a duty-free reset and the anxiety that crept up the day before never happened. For a moment at least. I open my eyes and realize yet again I am in my bed, in my Manhattan apartment, alone. It's my metaphorical Groundhog Day. I wonder if everyone wakes up in the morning and thinks of how ridiculous it is that the day is just here again. The same nine to five, the same wine and routine. How mundane it all is. My day will be filled with most of the same and sprinkled in with little questions of what life would have been like if different decisions were made over the years. The life compared to one of solitude I face when I am in this apartment. It's not like life would magically turn into a whole new scenario when I wake up. I'm never quite sure what I am expecting. Did I expect to be made brand new? Did I expect to feel whole again? 'Again' is the first thought that comes to my mind as my eyes settle to the light.

Whether it's the lightbulb or the city noise greeting me first, the feelings are always the same. Nothing new. No bitterness. Just an ache I never know how to fix. Just an ache that comes in different forms for the last twelve years, made worse in the last four. Every morning as the sunlight creeps in through the custom darkening bedroom curtains, I feel a wave of curiosity about what other people think when they first realize their sleep for the night is over. Is it a sense of repetitive feelings or an excitement for what a new day holds? I don't know that I actually feel either of those. A pinch of anxiety quickly follows my thoughts. *There you are, old friend.* The feeling that something heavy is sitting on my mind and my chest. This morning isn't any different as I roll onto my back, closing my eyes tightly as I debate if I really need to get out of bed. I could work from home or just call in sick and nobody would question it. In fact, they may even welcome it. Sleep makes the days go by faster. It makes the nights come quickly. Quickly to what, I'm not sure. Each night, I fall asleep alone in a bed that's too big for just one person. As I stifle a yawn, I carelessly swat at the nightstand with my other hand until my fingers meet my phone. The screen has been filled with missed messages from a text chain I share with my sister and mother with loving messages, funny GIFs, and random thoughts between the three of us. I shift to my side, noticing the perfectly smooth untouched side of the bed, running my fingers along the empty space. For a moment, I question my life and everything I've done. It's part of the routine. Everything happens for a reason. We all deserve to be happy. I once was told I had a right to move on with my life, but then again, they've never been in my shoes. There is something to be said for love and happiness. Something to be said for your one and only and knowing it rarely comes along more than once, certainly not three times. The people who love you the most just want you to be happy. They offer to set you up with people, ask their sons if they know anyone just to try and show they care. They care, but I don't.

As I finally unlock my phone, it's as if it sent a telepathic alarm to my mother in the deep woods of small-town Alabama, because my phone rings loudly. "Hello?"

"Are you sleeping?" My mother's voice sounds like sweet tea even in the morning, before she drops it an octave. "Are you sick? I told you, Evie. Flu shots work. I told you about..."

"No. I'm not sick, Mom. I just woke up," I candidly groan, falling back into the cream Pottery Barn throw pillows that Daniel once said were way too expensive to just get tossed to the side. "What's going on?"

"I just wanted to know what date you were planning on coming in for your Daddy's retirement party." Nancy Goode was really great at just about everything she did, but planning a party was where she shined and she loved for a party to have a large crowd. Unfortunately, I know where this call is going. She wants me home for more than just the party. She just wants her family together again.

"I plan on flying into Birmingham on Friday after work," I answer, my hand covering my eyes as I prepare for more questions, because she's going to have a lot more to say.

"And let me guess, you're leaving on Sunday?" I hear her dismiss a disappointed sigh into the phone and I know she doesn't approve. "Your father is the only dentist in the town of Haven and he only retires once. Are you sure you don't want to stay more than the weekend?"

"I have a job, Mama. Responsibilities like loans and bills." I sit back and adjust myself up in the bed, pulling my knees to my chest. My mother is everything you would expect an amazing mother to be. She's selfless, a little bit pushy, and the greatest woman I know. She also masters the guilt trip.

"I know. You're a big shot business woman for a makeup

company. We are incredibly proud, but we just miss you," My mother teases and I hear a door in the house close. I know she's probably on a roll getting things done and she's not going to stop while she's on the phone with me. "But even for a holiday, you only come home for two nights at most and you stay home. You don't visit with anyone in town and Libby thinks you don't want to eat any of her food anymore. People miss you."

"Nobody misses me like that, except maybe Libby," I argue, tossing my legs over the side of the bed. Libby was my old boss, but the rest of the town surely doesn't think much about me and if they do, I don't know if it's anything good. "I'll be at the party and to catch up with all of the people in Haven who want to see me."

"Wade is going to be there." There it is. I should have known it was coming. "I'm sure he wouldn't mind seeing you after all these years."

"Mom…" I know she has more to say, but I don't give her a chance to continue. "I will be there Friday evening. I am leaving the office early in time to catch a cab to the airport."

"Darling, you haven't even taken a full vacation in at least four years." My mother reminds me, and I know she's right. She and Kyra were just going back and forth about it a week ago when she called me on FaceTime before we went in for facials. "I just think you could benefit from a few weeks at home."

"Benefit?" I finally stand up from the bed, unplugging the charging cord and discarding it onto the night stand. "Goodness."

"Sometimes coming home fixes the soul." She says as I silently yawn on my way to the walk-in closet and flip the light on. "There is so much that you need a break from and coming home…"

"Fixes the soul," I finish, looking around at my side to try and see if anything catches my attention for the day. There is a dress at the end of the row that I haven't worn recently, so I reach for that to make my morning easy. "Wow, Mayor Mike should put you in charge of tourism."

"Oh, I'm already on the committee." She boasts, proudly and I know I should have known that. My mother gets asked to be on most committees in Haven.

"Of course you are," I smile tiredly before reaching for a pair of nude patent leather heels. "How is Lexie this morning?"

"Levi is keeping her busy already." She explains as I place my hand on a dress resting on a velvet hanger. "He's six and he wants a skateboard. What is a six-year-old going to do with a skateboard? We don't even have ramps in this town and he's too young."

"Dad could build him one with all of the free time he will have now." I tuck the heels under my arm and take the dress out into the bedroom again.

"Skating is dangerous." My mother responds as I shake my head. "I hope she doesn't give in. He's too young."

"Mom." I sit back down on the edge of the bed, before turning onto my stomach. I hate ending phone calls with her. Maybe it's that sometimes I do actually get homesick or it could be the sound of sadness in her voice when I go. "I really do have to go to work."

"Oh, fine." She sighs and knows I have to go, but she's my mother and that won't stop her from making every effort. "Think about coming home for a bit. It would mean the world to your old parents."

"You guys aren't that old." I roll my eyes, running my hand over the pillow sham on the straightened side of the bed.

"Just think about it. It's easier if you decide to on your own." My mother's tone gets softer for a moment and I can tell that she's stopped moving around. I don't know what she meant by the last part, but she goes on with one simple word. "Please."

"I need to get ready, but I'll call you tonight," I say quickly, sitting up in the bed before I can say anything else to shut down her request.

"Alright, honey." My mom sighs into the phone and I feel that little pinch of guilt I know that she likes to use. "I'll talk to you later and just remember we all want what is best for you."

"Love you, Mama." I smile, looking at the clock. I have an hour to get ready for work and get coffee.

"Love you, baby girl," she says softly and disconnects, and I am left here in the apartment once meant for two. The place Daniel and I handpicked together with all of the features we both fell in love with. The amazing laundry space, wrought iron balcony overlooking the city, and luxurious closets. There were so many things to love about this place, but mostly I just loved that I was going to get to share it with him. A place where there was someone else to come home to, to curl in bed and escape the world with. I make my way to the oversized bathroom to brush my teeth and get ready, makeup and all. I have time to get ready, but I'll be using dry shampoo this morning in order to make it to pick up my morning coffee. I run my finger over the engagement ring before briefly taking it off to wash my face. I will put it right back on after. I clear my throat and put my hands on the counter, letting out a deep sigh as I look at the tired woman staring back at me. I'm reminded that at some point in my life, I was happy before my eyes even opened for the day. That I began each day with an immediate assumption of joy. It was a long time ago.

***

I am always one of the first to arrive in the Madison Avenue high-rise for Glam and Simple, with my venti Starbucks coffee, Kate Spade tote bag, and meal prepped lunch. I prefer having the quiet time before the hustle and bustle of the day begins and the office is packed full of people. Before the sound of ringing phones, fax machines and meetings fill the air. However, this morning was briefly interrupted by a bunch of husky construction workers who had come to ask if it would bother me if they started work early. I nodded and said it was fine, but now I regret it. I didn't quite factor in the noise construction came with and I am hoping they have enough courtesy to know the noise would need to be wrapped up by the start of business. They promised not to disturb us too much. Linda would go crazy if she heard this racket, and then the whole office would know about it.

Glam and Simple is the face and beauty baby of Linda Rosen. Linda was once a notorious socialite, but now she's a successful businesswoman who built an empire without her famous sandwich making father. When I joined the company for an internship, I had no idea that one day I would be reporting directly to Linda and consider her a close friend, spending years working for her. Working for a major company was never part of my plan, but here I am. I had no idea either, that I would one day become someone so tied up to their routine that the idea of changing it caused me heartburn. My morning routine was simple. Coffee, pull up the company email, and update the Erin Condren planner that stays in the pocket of my work purse when I go home every night. I made a few notes this morning and sent an email to Cindy in the mail room about some samples that have to go out next week. When I finally close my planner, I can't help but smile at the picture of Daniel and I that sits on my desk. It's from the day he proposed in Time Square and I had no idea that it was coming. Running my finger along the bottom of the frame, I wipe away a speck of dust when I hear Kyra stumble in and throw her stuff on the desk across from mine. "Don't ever let me drink and go home with a guy who takes me to a bar with boobs on the wall. No boob bars. Ever."

"Kane, again?" I ask, looking up from the desk as Kyra tries to fix her disheveled hair in a small compact mirror. I slide over the makeup bag that I keep in my desk and I know she's grateful that I am prepared for anything, including her occasional walk of shame. "Ken?"

"Khoa," she answers. "We met at that new pho restaurant in Battery Park."

"With the neon boobs on the wall?" I question, trying to place what restaurant she's speaking about with the neon sign.

"No, we just met there. We had the date part at the boob bar." Kyra sprays her face with a bottle of rose water before retrieving the eyeliner that I have designated for her. "Linda walk in yet? She can't see me looking this messy. It would only make her judge my dating life even more."

"No. You're safe," I reply, taking back the makeup bag and handing her an extra hair pin that I found at the bottom of it. Kyra isn't a stranger to coming into work a hot mess, but I don't mind helping her get back into presentable shape. "But the samples for your afternoon meeting with the printing press came in and they're terrible."

"Damn." She runs her fingers through her messy waves and slides the pin in just above her ear. "If I have to go yell at Tonya at Bannister Printing again, I might lose it. She cries every time. Are you sure Linda isn't in yet? I was hoping she would tell us about how she taunted the Village People out there."

"It isn't the Village People if they are only construction workers." I zip the bag and put it carefully in the drawer again next to my phone charger. "So Khoa is new. How was that?"

"He is, but he won't be a repeat offender," she replies, opening her bottom drawer and lifting out a black cotton dress. Kyra practically keeps a whole closet in her desk and somehow it never wrinkles. "He asked if he could use my toothbrush."

"Ew," I wince, leaning back in my worn office chair. "And you didn't have an extra?"

"We were at his place!" She notes loudly, turning around and I push my own chair back to stand up. I place my fingers on the rose gold zipper, sliding it up and closing her dress. "Besides, he didn't have a brother. That makes it a hard selling point."

"What's wrong with that?" I ask, pulling her hair from her dress to help her straighten up. "Oh wait...is this a weird threesome thing? If it is, I don't want to know."

"Double dates!" She points out so confidently and she finally turns around, reaching for the extra coffee I pick up most mornings. "One for you. One for me."

"Kyra, as tempting as double dates sound..." I start but she raises her hand up before I am allowed to continue.

"Everleigh Rose Goode. I'm going to stop you there." Kyra stands firmly, a hand up to stop me from continuing. "You could stand to let loose a bit, and when is the last time that you went on a date or even let a guy see you naked? Huh?"

"Kyra, can we not?" I say quickly, before taking a deep breath to hide the annoyance I feel anytime someone tries to send me on a date or get me to 'let loose' in order to fix me. "And before Shirley from reception gets in, I don't need to go out with the new UPS guy either. So please encourage her to stop trying."

"Everleigh, on nights where we don't go out...you go home alone, cook a dinner for one and watch *Law and Order* reruns until you fall asleep." I frown as Kyra, reaches for her phone and unlocks it. "You deserve someone to make you feel special, but more than anything you need to relax. You need to..."

"I had someone that made me feel special," I reply, leaning against my desk as she walks around it. "And I don't need a man to make me feel happy or complete me. Isn't that the whole modern woman thing anyways?"

"Daniel was perfect and he treated you like the queen you

are, but Ev...it isn't about needing a man." Kyra sighs and takes a sip of her coffee. "It's about wanting you to be happy. We want you to be happy. You have an amazing career that women dream of, kickass people who adore and love you but you deserve someone to remind you that you're a woman. To treat you like a woman."

"Like a Khoa or a Kane?" Rolling my eyes, I reach for my own coffee.

"Okay maybe not someone like those two." Kyra laughs weakly, as we hear a bell from the elevator. I wipe traces of my coral lipstick off of the rim of my coffee as seconds later, Linda comes around the corner with her Christian Louboutin heels clicking against the floor and her oversized Gucci tote hanging on her arm. "Morning, Linda."

"Am I interrupting something?" She asks, lowering her sunglasses from her face, before looking me up and down. "Kate Spade?"

"Yes, from that sample sale we went to." I smile, looking running my hand over the skirt of my dress and looking over at Kyra. "And you're not interrupting anything. We were just talking about Kyra's date last night."

"Kane?" She frowns as she waves us towards her office as we grab things for our morning meeting. I look back quickly to grab a stack of samples that came in late last night. "Ken?"

"Khoa." We say together as we follow her across the floor. She's our boss, but also a friend. Our brilliant and sometimes oblivious friend.

"Khoa? That's new." She sighs as we reach the white wooden door which is surrounded by the glass etched walls that surround her office. It doesn't offer much privacy at all and it wasn't so she could watch people work. It was solely because she thought it made her look chic. She slides the key open and reaches for the trash can that the cleaning department emptied the night before and puts it on the floor inside when she pushes the door open. Immediately when we step in, we can hear the drills that work on the other side of her one solid wall. "Oh, good God!"

"I know, they're loud." I wince, before sitting the stack of samples on her desk and we all take a seat around her desk. Usually, we girl talk and catch up, but I have a conference call to be on in an hour and we need to get down to business. I immediately hand her the sample on top, which is the one that I know she most wants to see. "One of these will go out with the May line, we just need you to sign off on one. This is the one with the rose gold detailing and sharp edges...matte."

Linda adjusts her green rimmed glasses and clears her throat, studying the sample intently. "The rose gold detailing was my idea."

"I like it," Kyra grins as we exchange looks. "We also have one with a rounded edge and it looks a bit smoother with a more script-like font."

"Okay..." Linda browses the stack of samples that I had handed her and inspects each one carefully. I watch her, wondering if I will ever have such a talent for understanding detail until she holds one up and smiles. "This one."

"Great." I smile with relief, glad I came with several options with her to choose from.

"Kyra, how is the search for the new Social Media Manager?" Linda hands me the option for the mailer that she has selected and we both look over at Kyra.

"Weak. Girls think just because they know how to use filters, tweet, and post a GIF that they are social media experts." Kyra groans, pulling paper from her folder and sliding them towards Linda. "These are the two newest. I am considering calling them both in for an interview."

"This one went to medical school and dropped out...made her way to the Fashion Institute." Linda says, browsing the resume before handing it back to Kyra. "Schedule the interview. If it goes well, I'll block off an hour later in the week."

"But you're going to be speaking in Milan next week," I remind her, opening the planner and checking the date. "We could do it on Skype."

"Right," Linda nods. "Kyra, set it up."

"I will." Kyra nods as the room fills with the sound of a drill. I look back at Kyra nervously as Linda pushes her chair back.

"Are they planning to do this all morning?" she asks, walking over to the wall and examining it.

"When they asked me if they could start early, I assumed they knew they had to be quiet during the day." I said hesitantly as Linda slammed her hands against the wall at the same time some banging noise began to shake the room. For a moment, I think Linda rests her head before pounding her fists. "But I was wrong."

"Everleigh.." Linda pauses, pulling her hands away and moving them to her waist.

"Yes?" I breath nervously, trying not to look at Kyra who has started to laugh. We both know Linda is quite animated, but we also know where this is about to go. "I know, they aren't supposed to start until after five in the afternoon.

"It's morning." Linda says, pointing at her watch. "Not time for smashing or building or whatever the hell they are doing over there. Let's just finish and we can talk to them after."

"Got it." I nod, opening my planner to today's date again. "I have a few meetings today, but I wanted to get them all done before I leave for the weekend. But I will have my phone with me if we need to tend to more urgent matters."

"You're going to Tennessee, correct?" Linda looks back up, reaching for her pen.

"Alabama," I reply, as Kyra clears her throat and we both

look over at her. "Are you alright?"

"Linda, have you noticed how in the past four years, Everleigh has never taken more than two days off at a time?" Kyra crosses her arms over her lap and looks directly at Linda, ignoring me as I look over at her. I can tell she feels my gaze on her face, because she's tapping her pen against the chair. "Like she has no life ever…that's what we always say. Right, Linda?"

"What are you doing?" I frown, looking over at my friend who is still ignoring my gaze.

"Funny you should mention that." I look back at Linda who winks right back at Kyra. "I was just thinking about that too."

"You winked at her." I say in my confusion as I glance back and forth between the two women. "Why did you wink at her? Why are you guys winking?"

"Kyra and I met for a drink last night before what I assume was her disastrous date with Keith…" Linda explains, reaching for her phone as Kyra doesn't even bother to correct her. "Kyra had recently spoken with your mother and sister and then she spoke to me and it got me thinking, we all really need to unplug and you're the only one who doesn't. Ever."

"It's kind of freaky, really." Kyra breaks her stare from Linda and looks over at me. "Even Greta in testing takes vacation and all she has is an Aunt in Boca and four cats."

"I take time off," I argue, as Linda reaches for her calendar and opens it. "Besides, what does it have to do with anyone else? And why did you guys talk to my family?"

"Because we happen to be your friends as well as your coworkers, and we know you too well." Linda points to a date on the calendar which is tomorrow's date. "You're leaving tomorrow for Alabama. I've already ordered your plane ticket which coincidentally, you have not yet ordered for Friday."

"How…" No, I hadn't ordered my ticket, but there wasn't

exactly an expectation that a ticket from New York to Alabama would be sold out. I've always waited until the last minute to order my ticket home. "Tomorrow...how did you..."

"You left your computer unlocked when you went to the mailroom yesterday." Kyra explains and I feel my jaw fall to the floor at the idea that they would even consider looking at my email. "And you type your phone code in really slowly. It wasn't that hard to memorize."

"You looked at my phone?" I reach for my iPhone and quickly pull up my email.

"I have to admit, I thought that was taking it a bit far, but it worked out," Linda added, waving her finger before poking it back at the calendar. "I had her forward me the confirmation email so you wouldn't find it. I'll send it back to you. So, leave tomorrow."

"And come back Sunday morning," I nod, trying not to get irritated by the invasion of privacy into my phone or the lack of concern they are showing over their actions. "In time for my meeting with the editor of InStyle about the feature we're setting up for you."

"You can join that meeting via Zoom," Kyra says quickly, before Linda begins writing on her calendar. "But other than that, we want you to unplug from work."

"Read a book, online shop...take a walk or do something that isn't primarily work related." Linda's body language and face softens and it is a way I haven't seen her before. She looks almost concerned and for a moment, I feel the urge to stand up and leave the room. "Everleigh, Kyra and I know a lot about you and your past. We were here when everything fell apart."

"But it's been four years, Everleigh," Kyra says again and I realize she may have been trying to ease me into this even before this little meeting. The moment she said 'we,' I should have seen the red flags that this morning was going to bring. "You are in need of a major change of scenery to deal with everything you have been sheltering for four years or to just let loose in a way you can't seem to do here."

"And why can't I do that here? New York is a huge place." I ask, before looking back up at Linda. "If you're really so concerned that I unplug and take time away from work, I will. I won't come in, but I could go to The Met or even upstate. Besides my family, there is nothing in Alabama for me."

"Your family should be enough of a reason." Kyra points out and I know she's spoken to my family. She's been friends with my sister on Facebook since I asked her to be in my bridal party after I got engaged. "But from what I have gathered..."

"You need to get away from New York where his memory and your life is everywhere." Linda cuts in and I know she won't say his name anymore. "And for some reason going home scares you more than being here where the pain of losing him is the strongest."

"Going home doesn't scare me." I laugh, wondering inside of me what makes someone think that. "Did my mother say that?"

"No, not exactly," Kyra said defensively. "But I don't think you've been back there more than a day or two since you moved to New York. I was talking to Lexie, and she pointed that out, and then Linda and I got to talking."

"I think what we're trying to say simply is that you need to go home for a few weeks. I am suggesting it as your friend, but requiring it as your boss." Linda begins labeling the calendar in front of her with the color she uses whenever I take a day off or have an appointment.

"Can you do that?" I ask, trying not to let the anger I feel boiling in my chest show on my face as I push myself up from the chair. "Can you determine where I go on my time off? By buying a ticket?"

"Would you really challenge her?" Kyra says before shrugging her shoulders and I bite my cheek, instead staring out towards one of the windows that shows off some of New York's greatest buildings. "I could help you pack tonight. A month is a lot of time."

"A month?" My eyes widen and I am immediately reminded of how much I could potentially miss in that time frame. Meetings, samples, product launches. Approving PR packages isn't as easy as it seems. "That won't work."

"Linda and I are going to fill in some of the work until you're allowed to log in remotely in a month." Kyra almost offers, but I feel my ears getting warm. "Other than your one meeting, we're clearing your schedule. You can enjoy Alabama."

"You've never been to Haven, Alabama." I run my hands over my face, not even bothering to consider the makeup on my face that it might mess up. "Okay…so a month. I go do some *Sweet Home Alabama*-like bullshit and then come back."

"No…." Kyra says quietly, exchanging a cautious look to our boss.

"What?" I laugh weakly, letting my hand fall to my side.

"As much as I would like you here and back in a month, I was thinking you should work remotely after that for a bit." Linda replies, her voice lowering for a moment, which never happens. "It may give you some perspective and you have been known in the past to bring us some of our best ideas. Inspire yourself and then inspire me."

"Linda…" I turn around to face her, my back to Kyra. "What is it that you're hoping to accomplish with this?"

"It isn't about that." Linda replied, closing the calendar and folding her arms on her desk. "But as your friend, I know you need to shut off this world for a while. Go on a date or don't. Go home, do whatever people do in Alabama."

"Come on Ev…" Kyra pleads, standing up behind me and

placing her hand on my shoulder. "Take advantage of the opportunity. Time off to visit your family, to do something relaxing, and later on work in your pajamas. Give it a chance."

I bite my lip, looking at Linda who is telling me with her eyes that I don't have much of a choice, and then I look at Kyra who I can tell is a little nervous that I may not forgive her. I'm angry, but also not sure that they are wrong. I'm pretty sure I have never taken more than forty-eight hours of time off at once in the last four years. "Fine."

"I knew you would cave." Linda claps and Kyra leans forward, giving her a high five and the sound of a drill begins to fill the room again. "Now since we have to get some stuff done before you leave the office this afternoon, go see what you can do about this mess with the construction."

Linda shrugs proudly and I roll my eyes, turning to face Kyra again. She smiles apologetically and I know she's nervous that I am angrier than I am letting on, and truth be told, I don't know what I am feeling. I pause at the door and look back at Linda and Kyra. "I'll go see what I can do."

"We'll wait." Linda winks at me and I shake my head, closing the door behind me. Once outside the door, I know I am not alone. I am on the main floor of my office and there are so many people around, I don't want anyone to think something is wrong, but I put my hand over my heart to take a moment. The offices of Glam and Simple have always been a safe haven for me. From the moment I started in their first internship program, to my first big job in the cosmetic world, it has been my strongest support system and the one constant thing in my life. It was my life jacket when I needed to escape Alabama and the float I needed to keep me above water when Daniel died. Right now, that float has been punctured and the life jacket has fallen off because I'm leaving the city and the home I shared with the one man who helped me escape the heartache I left Haven with, only to cause me more heartache. I feel panicked as I walk out of the heavy marble doors of the office suite and into a hallway which feels more metaphorical than it really is. I'm being thrown off a cliff with no way to hold on for dear life. Leaving New York to head to the home that nobody except one person knows I ran away from in the first place.

Chapter Two

Evie

Now

The flight into Birmingham was uneventful, but reality quickly set in as my three black Chariot suitcases and two Tory Burch carry-ons became a pain in the ass to drag from baggage claim to the Ford SUV I rented last-minute. I insisted when I called and confirmed my travel plans with my mother that I at least have my own car if I come home for as long as I am. Besides, my dad has an early morning with his last day in the dental office and my Mama's eyesight isn't that great at night. In the event my flight was delayed, I didn't want them out any later just for me. It's almost eleven in the evening and I have fifteen minutes left in my two hour drive to Haven. It's late, I've had a long day, and I feel like I can already taste the sinfully sweet tea and feel the southern air. It definitely hits the body differently out here and for a moment, I feel nothing but peace. I feel lighter. I've never driven from the airport to my parent's home by myself, so with the radio on and the windows down, I am finally spotting the town signs. The peaceful feeling slowly fades and I can feel my nerves awakening.

My stomach rumbles a bit and I wonder if I can make it until morning. If I come home and say I haven't eaten, Mama will unpack the contents from the refrigerator and make me a plate, then she'll join me when I know she's exhausted. I see the flickering sign on the left for Libby's Restaurant where I had my first job and pull into the gravel parking lot. I don't really want to go inside because that's the fastest way to see at least one person I know, but I can quickly order something to go and save my Mama the trouble.

The car has been fully off for a minute and the lights have already gone out, but I haven't moved from the driver's seat. Suddenly, a home cooked meal and walking Mama up doesn't seem so bad. I could do that without being noticed by anyone from Haven. Except it's late and I can do this. The parking lot isn't very full, but the neon sign that reads 'open' is still blinking. There are probably three other cars here and at least one of those has to be someone who works here. Or maybe they are parked in the back. I reach for my black clutch and open the door to get out, my legs aching from being in the car for two hours straight. I suddenly feel overdressed for this small-town restaurant. I'm still wearing my black Ann Taylor jumpsuit and patent leather pumps that I bought a few weeks ago on the Nordstrom sale rack, wondering why I didn't change into something more relaxed. I am way overdressed to go unnoticed in this place. Normally nobody wears anything fancier than jeans if it's not the Sunday church crowd. "I can do this. It's just a diner. You're just getting food. You probably won't even see anyone familiar to you so just go...inside."

When I open the door at the diner, it is as if I am transported into a time machine. Nothing has changed. The mint green paint, the fifties decor and the red rimmed tables are the same. If it were day time, it would be crowded with the people that have come to love Libby and this place, along with a few truckers just passing through on the nearby highway. As I approach the counter, the doors to the back kitchen swing open. Immediately, I know my wish of going unnoticed is not going to come true "Oh my, Evie Goode! I can't believe my eyes."

"Libby." I smile, hands letting go of their grip on the counter as she rushes around the counter to greet me. My chest feels tight, even though I kind of like that I get to see her. She would be the exception to people I want to see. She's like family that I shouldn't have avoided. Libby looks the same, just a tad bit older than the last time I saw her. I wonder if I look different to her, because it's been so long.

"I ran into Lexie at the market and she mentioned you were coming home for a bit." Libby is a petite lady, but she wraps her arms around me and squeezes tight. "Oh honey...I haven't seen you in person since you left after high school."

"I've never really had much time to come home until now." I lie as she pulls away, but squeezes my arms.

"Sometimes we're not ready," she whispers, then steps back and looks me over as if to evaluate my body. "Has New York even been feeding you? I swear for a city with food options on every corner it doesn't look like it is taking very good care of you. That's a shame if I ever saw it."

"You sound like my Mama. She constantly points it out to me." I laugh, but it's true. In a way it's a loving but backhanded compliment about my body. It really just seems to be a southern thing with my Mama. My mother always says it looks like I don't eat nearly enough, even though I just work out regularly and try to eat healthy most of the time. I've lost more weight than I would have ever needed to, but it certainly is for a mixture of reasons. "I was actually hoping to order some dinner to go. I want to save Mama the trouble of having to cook for me at this time of night."

"Oh, of course! I would be happy to make one of my

favorite girls something to eat." Libby pulls away and puts a hand on her waist, measuring me up again. "How about I go into the kitchen and make you something real home cooked. Real fattening and filled with love. On the house as a welcome home gift."

"That would be great, Libby. Thank you." I don't bother to ask for anything specific added on now that I have come inside. The smell of the restaurant has my stomach growling and I can almost taste the home fries that I used to swear Libby did something special to. Maybe it was the salt and grease, but they were delicious. "Is Marv well?"

"Marv? Oh you mean my ex? With that hairline? Wow." Libby laughs and shakes her head at the mention of the trucker she married after he drove through town twice. "I wonder what he's up to. Last I heard from him, he was just going to the post office to get stamps."

"Wow, that must have been some book of stamps." I nod, looking around the old diner. A man sits in the corner booth, probably someone just travelling through if I can read into his trucker hut, another set of headlights pull into the parking lot through the window and Libby is adjusting her apron to fit better when she catches her eye on the window but quickly looks back to me and smiles. "I'll have to stop in more to catch up."

"Please do. I was so sorry to hear about your heartbreak." Libby backs up and reaches for an empty bottle of ketchup as I smile weakly. I'm not a hundred percent sure that it's anything that I want to share the details of, but I know she means well. "I better go get in the kitchen. Let me go make you something nice and then you can head home and get a good night of rest. Sit tight. I won't be too long."

"Thank you, Libby." I smile as she walks into the back and the doors swing behind her, before sliding onto one of the red and silver barstools at the counter. I can feel how exhausted I am, but I reach into my clutch for my cell phone in hopes there is some sort of work email I can tend to before Linda has them temporarily remove me from the office distribution list. Something she threatened to do if she found me working. As I begin to scroll through some of the emails, the bell above the diner door rings. I don't look back because I have found an email I want to catch up on about an ongoing shipping label issue. It seems the wrong packaging was used in some magazine inserts. I should have confirmed them before they went out this morning. I had a feeling that this would happen. The moment I leave the office and hand off some of the things I check on daily, something would go wrong.

"You cut your hair.'" The deep voice forces my body to stiffen, because I know that voice, only I know the younger version of it. I don't know if it's because it takes me back to the last time I lived here in Haven or the fear that if I turn around, I'll have something to answer for. All of these years and I have never been forced to answer to anything for this voice. I finally turn on the barstool and there is Wade Beckett. All six feet and two inches with his ocean blue eyes and naturally tan skin. His shoulders fall in surrender and his hands dangle at his side before he shakes his head. "Damn."

"Wade." I swallow as my skin turns cold and the universe laughs at me a bit as I run into the one person I am truly avoiding on the first night I drive into town. I look around the diner, wishing I was somewhere else or at the very least that it was too busy and loud to hold a conversation with anyone. Even with the few people that are in here, I immediately feel like we're alone. He looks older than when I last saw him, the dark scruff one his face covering most of his cheeks and chin. His once perfectly tamed hair is shorter and messy. He's wearing a flannel worn button down, the sleeves pushed up to reveal ink he didn't have years ago and then there is that scruff on his face. I push a strand of hair behind my ear and straighten up quickly to hide the nerves that are shaking me. "It's good to see you looking so...well."

"Well?" He scoffs and that's all it takes to bring my confidence right back to where it was before he saw me. He shakes his head and I know he's about to say something that might just make this encounter as uncomfortable as I would have predicted. Something that makes me realize there was never going to be some slow, pleasant exchange. He's not acting shocked to see me and there is no warm-up. "Damn. twelve years without as much as a word before you left. No texts, no emails, no visits...hell, I went to New York and stayed in a shit motel to see you and you wouldn't even see me. After a year I stopped trying, but eleven years later I sure am glad you think I look well. Is it the hair? I got a haircut. Actually, I've had quite a few since you left."

"Wade." I push my body up from the seat, trying to ignore the sound of my heart beat filling my ears. It sounds like a drum, beating quickly. "I know you weren't expecting to see me like this."

"Like this?" I wasn't expecting to see you at all." He growls angrily. "You could say that. Don't you think you're a little overdressed for a town so beneath you?"

"Okay, you're being ridiculous and completely unfair." I put my hand up, to cut him off. Maybe he isn't being completely fair, but I came here for dinner and a quick exit. I didn't come here to be chastised by my ex. "You should stop."

"I flew to the city and stayed for a week to try to get you to talk to me. I came a few times and even caught you on your way leaving class and you literally ran into the crowd until I couldn't find you. I sure looked pretty stupid," he says, his tone strong and almost demanding. "Then you just show up in Haven and

"I find you by walking into Libby's as if I should have expected it. Imagine how stupid I feel now. I could have just waited twelve years and bumped into you here."

"I didn't think seeing you was a good idea." I reach for my phone from the counter, locking the screen. "Clearly."

"A good idea?" He laughs before biting his lip, which sends me back to our teen years for just a moment, but it doesn't work on me the way it used to. I think it's lost that charm that it had. "So you just ignored me?"

"We didn't exactly end things on good terms," I shrug, before sitting right back down. I don't want a scene to be made on my first night back in Haven and end up the next day's gossip. I'm not even sure I could say anything that would justify it.

"We didn't end things at all! There was nothing." Wade crosses his arms, before walking up to the counter and placing his hands on the hard surface. "Damn it, Evie. I woke up and you were gone. The other side of the bed where you slept next to me was empty. What the hell? Who does that to someone?"

"Wade…" I shut my mouth quickly, because I'm not really sure that I am ready to say anything. I don't even know that I ever want to say anything more. I wish I could just disappear into the tile and never be seen by him again. "Stop."

"We were engaged, Everleigh!" He groans and uses my full name, his voice raising and I know the guy in the back booth heard it. I twist just a bit to see, but I stop. I don't want this to go on. "Then you were gone and then you were going to marry someone else a few years later. Without ever coming back to end things with me or explain yourself. There were two of us in that relationship and as far as I knew, everything was going well until you ran away."

"Have you been preparing and carrying this anger for the moment you finally saw me and could get this all out?" I snap to quiet the heart thumping in my eardrums. Bitchy, but it's late and I'm hungry and truthfully, I never wanted this meetup to happen. There isn't a single part of me that feels like there is a time or a place where we can talk about this and I certainly won't argue about Daniel with him. I thought of hundreds of things I would say if I saw him again, but I was hoping I wouldn't. Praying I would never have to see his face after what I did to him. It doesn't matter now, but I don't know if it would have mattered then either. "You sure walked in here ready to fire off. Did you have an alarm installed in the event I return to somewhere public in Haven?"

"Yeah well..." He lets go of the bar and walks over to the corner jukebox, but not to admire it. "I came in to grab some food. I would have much rather never seen you sitting at this counter again when I was having a perfectly good night."

"Well, you saw me," I shrug, scanning the place. Looking for any sign that Libby might be coming or heard him walk in. Surely, she didn't miss the sound of the bell. "I can't change that, but you won't have to see me again. I highly doubt I will be out on the town much."

"Yeah, that seems like you." He leans against the jukebox and shakes his head again. "Where did you go, Evie?"

"You know where I went." I answer, but he doesn't understand what he wants to ask or maybe he can't find the words. "New York."

"You know what I mean." His eyes roll and I can tell how angry he is feeling right now. How hurt he was, because of his reaction to seeing me. He has questions that I can't answer, so I hope he doesn't ask.

"I don't know what you're looking for," I reply coldly.

"So you stuck with your side of our plans," he nods before scratching at his chin. He's received no answers about why I left him behind. Why I bailed and why he's still angry. Just as he opens his mouth to speak, Libby comes bursting through the kitchen doors. We both turn around to see her and her shoulders fall. "Evening, Libby."

"Awe hell...I was hoping if you two ran into each other, that I wouldn't miss it." Libby frowns as she gestures to the bag that she is holding before approaching the counter. "Want dinner, Wade?"

"Yeah." He nods as I stand back up from the chair and face the counter. Happy to see Libby again. He steps to the counter, this time by my side as he begins to speak again. "I was just going to pick up a burger."

"Alright, I can get started on that. Evie, I made you some of our chicken pot pie, I tossed in some rolls." Libby says as she walks me through the arrangement of the takeout bag and holds up a slice of pie. "Some of your favorite strawberry pie and some fresh ice cream."

"Thank you, Libby." I smile as I reach for my clutch to retrieve some cash, avoiding any eye contact with Wade.

"It's on the house." She puts her hand over mine and shakes her head. "Hey, you and Wade should just eat together. Get caught up…"

"That's alright. I should get home, Mama is waiting and… it's just better I go." I say quickly as he moves his hand back to the counter. I quickly reach into my wallet and take out two twenty-dollar bills and slide it forward. "A tip."

"Evie…" Libby starts but I quickly hold my hands back in the air before looping the bag of food around my fingers. "You brat. You're just a grown girl now.""

"I missed you." I wink, trying to ignore Wade's gaze that is currently burning through my cheek. Libby is looking between the two of us as I take the food off of the counter and step back. I ignore Wade as he turns around and watches me back up, my eyes focused on the older woman in front of me. "See you around, Libby."

"I better." Libby warns happily, leaning in on the counter as I turn around and push the door open. When it closes behind me, I take a deep breath that I didn't realize I had been holding and the pain in my back from standing so stiff begins to fall off. I was filled with tension and panic when I saw him. I don't even bother to look back, because there is so much about what just happened that I have been afraid of for the last twelve years. Over a whole decade of dread I that I have had for so long was right in front of me. The pain I knew I caused and the anger I felt for finally having to face it has me wanting to just quickly drive away. To leave town and tell my parents I can't ever return. I don't know that I even care what work would do to me and it's not like Linda could actually punish me.

When I finally hop into the rental car and close the door on the Alabama air, I put the food in the passenger side seat and barely wait for the lights to turn on before I put the car into drive. A small part of me always assumed that if I ever saw Wade, he'd act like nothing ever happened. He was such a good man, a great boy, and he wouldn't hold a grudge. Not that he wouldn't have a right to, despite me acting like he was being ridiculous. It had been ten whole years and surely he wouldn't want to show me that it bothered him at all. Except it did. I made a choice twelve years ago that didn't just change the course of my life, it changed Wade's too. He doesn't know that everything I did was to protect him. He doesn't understand why, and to him, I am the villain in his story. I hate that, but it's a role that I spent a long time coming to terms with. I can't help that he held on to his anger. Everything else is on me, but that is solely on him. He won't ever understand why and that was for the best. For him and for me. I found Daniel, and that was what was best for my life, even if deep down there would always be a spot for Wade that I had grown to ignore. A pain masked by a beautiful man who was pulled from my grasp too soon. Just like Wade.

It was a pain I tucked away and learned I could keep it there without ever acknowledging it. It had made it easy to start my life over in New York City. It was a switch that held the connection between my life in Haven and the life I gave to my career. And to Daniel. I feel my eyes water as I make my way through the back of the woods. I don't know what I am doing here. I shouldn't be here, but it's too late to turn around and I'm not sure that I have a choice at this point. There is no going back; he's seen me, and as I pull into my parents' home I see my their bedroom light flip on. They've seen me too.

Chapter Three

Evie

Then

His arms are my favorite place to be. I can't imagine ever feeling this way with someone else and I don't want to try. Even as a little girl when I would play 'wedding' with my big sister, I couldn't imagine that love felt quite like this. Was it supposed to be overwhelming? Was it normal to never feel close enough? Sometimes I don't even fully believe we're two separate people. Tonight, as we dance together to Mariah Carey in his bedroom, I so badly want to tell him what I am thinking. I want to tell him that I know I will never love someone else like this again, but I don't want to move my head from his chest. I press my head against him, breathing in the cologne that I love so much. It's the smell of rosewood, amber and vetiver. I think. Whatever it is, I think I want to smell it forever. He must have caught me, because his fingers slide onto my chin and tilt my head up. "Oh Miss Evie, I'm in trouble and I don't wanna be rescued."

"What?" I breathe, before placing a soft kiss on his lips.

"I love you so much…" He breathes, sliding his hands under my shoulders so he can boost me up so I can wrap my legs around his waist. "We can't stay here right now; we have to go."

"Why? We like what happens when we don't go out." I giggle, sliding my hands around his neck.

"Ev...stop." He laughs, pressing a kiss on my chin before putting me back on my two feet. "We have to get to dinner."

"Wade," I groan, wrapping my arms around his strong waist. "We've been to dinner before...there are still some things we haven't tried in..."

"Evie...don't distract me." He laughs, before pulling away and walking to the night stand. "I am taking you to Libby's for your birthday dinner, because for some reason you didn't want to go somewhere fancier and we're leaving right now."

"Okay but can we just hang out here for a little bit longer because....you're wearing the shirt I like." I wink, trying to inch closer, but he puts a hand up. "And I'm eighteen today, so I am officially an adult."

"No," he says firmly, before moving a hand to my waist and urging me to turn around. "We're going. Ms. Officially an adult."

"You're only three months older than me, don't get carried away." I let him lightly urge me to the bedroom door as we hear the garage door open. His dad is home and Ridge Beckett isn't exactly the easiest man to get along with. "Just...don't fight with him, okay?"

"I don't plan on it." Wade's demeanor changes and I know he was hoping we would make it out without ever having to interact with his dad. He takes my hand and opens the bedroom door. Before we can make our way down the narrow oak paneled hallway, Ridge makes his way around the corner. "Ridge."

"Hey, Everleigh." Ridge wipes at his mouth and the smell of Gin fills the small space. He's a pilot and sometimes I wonder how a man like Ridge Beckett can keep his job, but have so many demons in his off hours.

"Hi, Mr. Beckett." I wrap my arm around Wade's as I feel him tense beneath my fingers. I've known Wade and his father since I was five years old, and for the entire duration, his father has been nothing but an angry alcoholic.

"We're just going to dinner." Wade steps forward, but his father puts his hand up. "Evie, go wait outside."

"I think that's a good idea," Ridge smirks, almost reaching for my hand but Wade jumps in front of me.

"I don't know if…" I begin, but Wade immediately cuts me off and grabs my hand again.

"Go outside Evie." He moves out of the way and pulls my arm forward. "Now."

"Alright." I look back at him as he stares directly at his father as if he's watching for him to lunge towards me. I look back at Ridge who isn't looking at me any longer, but he's smirking right at Wade. I begin to walk faster out the front door, closing it behind me before I quickly walk down the steps. I have seen Wade and his father fight many times, but I've never seen them get physical. Still, I know it does. I know it has been physical long before Wade was big enough to really fight back. Wade always insisted everything was fine, even when we were younger, but as I got older I knew better. I knew that the occasional bruise or busted lip wasn't an accident. When I was fifteen, I came over during the summer to find him sitting on the porch with a black eye. I vowed in my heart that one day, he would be safe. One day, he'd never have to worry about being safe. We've talked about our future many times. He is going to Boston University and we'll meet up every other weekend when I am at school in New York. His father has only promised to do one thing good for him and that is to help pay for college and a place in Boston if Wade gets good grades and a part time job. Once he graduates, he will be free of his father's grasp. Then Wade will have his degree, start his own custom home building business and build us a home somewhere. I'll do something in the fashion or makeup world, but I'll find a way to do it wherever we plant ourselves. When we graduate, we'll decide where to build our home and grow our own family. It seems like a lot, but he's the love of my life. We have carefully planned our life together to account for both of our dreams coming true.

As I walk up to Wade's car, I lean against the hood. I'm pretty sure I just heard one of them yelling. I cringe as I hear more shouting, moving my finger nail to my lips. I know Wade sent me outside to protect me, but I don't need protection. Ridge doesn't have the balls to lay a hand on me in front of Wade. Just as I debate going back in, the front door opens and Wade comes storming down the front steps. "Get in the car."

"What happened?" I ask, walking around to the passenger side door. Wade unlocks the car door and just shakes his head. "Wade."

"Just get in the car Everleigh!" Wade shouts, before getting in and I follow. The door shuts and he curses below his breath.

"What happened this time?" I ask as he looks in the rearview mirror at his cheek. I frown as I notice a red spot that looks like it will be bruised by morning.

"He's drunk as usual," Wade answers as my hand moves to his face.

"Are you okay?" I frown, but Wade locks his seatbelt and moves my hand, before looking over at me.

"Look, he will sober up soon." Wade sighs, before putting the keys into the ignition. "But it's your birthday and I don't want anything to ruin tonight."

"It can't be ruined if I am with you." It's true. I could be alone with him anywhere and my life would be perfect. "We could go to my house."

"No, Ev." He starts as he drives down the driveway. He stops to look both ways, but looks over at me. "This is your birthday, which means it's my favorite day of the year."

"It is?" I laugh and he leans over to plant a light kiss on my cheek.

"The day you landed on this earth? Hell yeah." He laughs before he continues to drive. I have loved this man for most of my life, but he always knows what to say. I hate that he got into it with his father again, but he always knows how to put my mind at ease. "Wanna know my second favorite day ever?"

"What is your second favorite day ever?" I ask, reaching for some lip gloss from my bag.

"The day you grew boobs." He jokes before I swat at his arm, trying to hide the giggle that immediately tries to escape. I don't have a large chest, but he's never complained about it. I'm not sure why that thought came into my mind, but it makes me grateful for him anyways. "What? I'm grateful for those for sure. I learned a lot."

"Yeah...yeah..." I shake my head, but keep my eye on him. He's quiet, but as we stop at one of the few red lights in our town, he's bouncing his leg and twisting his fingers together. I try to ignore it, but I know he has so much going on in his mind. "Wade?"

"Yeah?" He puts his foot back on the gas and stays focused on the road.

"You wanna pull down a side road and..." I tease, leaning towards the middle console.

"Evie!" He gasps, swatting at my leg. "Stop being a horn dog. I need to focus."

"Focus on what?" I tease, reaching for my cell phone and

checking to see if I have any missed messages. One from Wade's best friend Dawson, telling me to have a good birthday and one from my cousin Rachel who lives in Baltimore with her loser boyfriend Ricky. "It's not like driving to Libby's is new."

"It's not, but I'm trying to drive." He takes my hand in his, moving my fingers to his lips to kiss them. "Fun after your birthday dinner."

"Fine." I sigh, watching him drive and wondering how I got to be so lucky. I'm young, but I know people don't always find love right away. It takes people years and I feel so lucky that I met mine so early. "You could stay at my house. My parents will probably make you sleep in the guest house or on the couch, but...."

"Evie, tonight is about you," he interrupts, squeezing my hand as we pull into the parking lot of Libby's, "so eat what you want off the menu, because the calories don't count."

"Birthday calories are zero?" I ask excitedly, knowing it isn't true but I like the idea. "Then I want cheese fries tonight."

"Oh, we're having cheese fries," Wade laughs, putting the car in park. I look around and see two cars. One car is Libby's, which makes me wonder why the restaurant is so quiet on a Friday night. There isn't a game at my school tonight, there isn't a dance or a festival going on and even then, Libby's is usually pretty busy at this time. "Alright, you ready?"

"Yeah." Wade gets out of the car and walks to my side, opening the door quickly. I unbuckle my seatbelt and push my long dark coffee colored hair behind my ears. "Maybe someone inside can take a picture of us, since it's not too busy."

"Good idea." He says, reaching for my hand. "Just don't complain about your hair, I'm telling you now, it looks really good."

"It's not too frizzy?" I ask, running my fingers through the curls as I walk with him to the restaurant.

"It's perfect." He replies, pressing a kiss on my cheek before we walk up the steps. Before he reaches for the handle, he stops and pulls away before he looks at me, his eyes dark and his hand squeezing mine. "You, ready?"

"Ready to eat? Yeah…" I say, but my eyes are narrowing as he looks like he's lying or nervous about something. I want to call him out on it, but his hand reaches for the handle and swings the door open, waiting for me to enter. I walk in and for a moment it looks mostly empty.

Surprise! Happy birthday!

Before I can react, tens of heads jump out from tables, behind the counter and the back of the restaurant. Up front I see my parents, Lexie, Dawson, and Libby. Around the restaurant I see my friends, some of Wade's friends, my sister's boyfriend and some family. My hand moves to my chest, because I'm startled, but I just look over at Wade who has a wide grin painted on his face. "Did you know about this?"

"Did I know? I had a pretty good idea." He teases, before putting a hand on the small of my back and kissing my cheek.

"Happy birthday baby girl," my mama shouts before nodding at Wade.

"Evie…" The way he says my name is so sweet, but it's different. I look over at my parents and my dad is smiling and my mother has her hands clasped together. My sister is clearly taking a video from her phone, so I look back at Wade who has my hand still, but now he's kneeling on the ground. Now, I can feel my heartbeat in my ears.

"What's…Wade." I look back up and everyone is still watching, but then Wade grabs my other hand and clutches it.

"Evie…not many people meet the love of their life when they're six years old, and even less would have the support of their girlfriend's parents on their daughter's eighteenth birthday, but I guess that just proves how lucky I really am. I know we go to college next year, but we already know how to make this work." His voice is shaking as he reaches in his back pocket. "Everleigh Rose Goode, will you marry me?"

"Oh my god," I gasp, looking up at my parents and then back at Wade whose hands are shaking around mine. I can tell he's nervous, but I don't see much else, because I feel like I'm going to burst. "Yes!"

I hear a lot of cheering and I can tell my mother and sister are crying, but I just look right back at Wade who is standing now and wrapping his arms around me. My eyes shift back around the room as my parents and sister walk up to us. My father is the first to speak, but I barely hear him say, "Congratulations, you two."

"Thank you Mr. Goode." Wade kisses me quickly, before turning to shake my father's hand. "Thanks for not shooting me when I asked for your permission."

"Well, thankfully I like you." My dad lightly slaps him on his back as he eyes Lexie. "I like one of the guys my girls decided to settle down with."

"Thanks, Dad." Lexie rolls her eyes and gives me a big hug. "I'm so happy for you, Ev."

"Thank you." I squeeze her back before turning to hug my mother. "Mama."

"He's perfect for you, baby girl." My mom is crying and that makes the tears begin to drip a bit more from my eyes. "What do you think of the ring?"

"I...oh my god." I pull away to finally look down to my shaking hand, because I hadn't once taken a look at the ring he so gently slid on my finger. It's a gold band with two side diamonds and one center one, and then I realize. I look up at Wade and then my mother. "Grammy's ring?"

"She wanted you to have it," My mother says through tear-filled eyes. My Grandmother died last year, but she was so fond of Wade. I used to spend hours in a chair next to her on the porch talking about him and she would always say kind things and tell me to hold on to him. She knew he was the one. I want to find out the story about how Wade got the ring, but I don't know if my heart could take it right now. The same heart that I think might burst out of my chest. "Isn't it perfect?"

"I love it." I smile, looking up at Wade. My future husband, the man of my dreams and the guy I get to spend the rest of my life with. "I love you too."

"You're going to be Mrs. Evie Beckett." Wade smiles proudly, before looking up at my Dad. Their eyes say it all. "Thank you for bringing up such an amazing girl."

"It was all her Mother." My dad jokes, wrapping his arm around my mom. "Just promise to make my girl the happiest."

"I plan to." Wade smiles, pulling me into his side. I wrap my hands around his waist and look up at him as his friend Dawson comes up to give him a high five. I've known Dawson longer than I've known Wade, but they're definitely closer. "Hey man…"

"Mom and Dad…getting married." Dawson replies, before I let go of Wade's waist and embrace Dawson. "I'm happy for you Evie."

"Thanks Dawson." I pat his back before letting go. I have so many emotions running through me, but still try and wipe away the tears that I have in my eyes. "Thank you for coming."

"Dawson, thanks for being here." Wade adds before taking my hand. I look around the room at everyone who is starting to talk and apparently eat the food that is around the room. My mother and sister are talking to Libby and my father and Dawson have started talking sports before I even had a chance to say anything else to him. Wade looks down at me and then runs his thumb over the center diamond. "Happy eighteenth birthday, Evie."

"Thank you," I smile, before watching the way his finger works along my ring. I realize there are other people around here to celebrate with me. To celebrate with us. I realize that it's time to go talk to everyone, but I just want to be alone with him. I want to embrace these moments, because while the details of a wedding and going to two separate colleges in two different states, I know it will be fine. "Should we make our rounds?"

"Yeah...probably." He laughs before kissing my nose and our eyes meet just to soak up this moment again. "I love you."

"I love you too." I smile, before he moves his hand to my back again to guide me throughout the diner. I look around the room at everyone who wanted to be a part of this moment. To celebrate my birthday and watch the love of my life ask me to be his forever. I would have agreed today, yesterday, or even a year from now, but I'm so happy he asked today. The sense of security I feel as we walk to the other side of the restaurant isn't lost on me. He's my rock. I've known him since I was about six years old and it occurs to me now that we met around this time so many years ago. He moved here with his father after his mother passed away. He was a heart broken little boy who immediately caught my attention. From that first day at school, to playing with our friends, to crying because I didn't think he liked me as more than a friend, to our first kiss in the woods behind my friend's Hannah's house. We kissed as a dare, but I told Hannah that night when I slept over at her house that I was going to marry Wade Beckett one day. I was right. As we approach Hannah and a few other friends I hear the door to Libby's swing open and I am sure I am the only one who makes eye contact with Ridge Beckett.

Chapter Four

Wade

Now

When my eyes opened this morning, I had a pounding headache, sweat was dripping down my temples, and my chest felt tighter than ever before. Then the memory of late last night came back. I worked late and stopped in at Libby's to get some dinner and there she was. Everleigh Rose Goode. I didn't need to see her face or wait for her to turn around to know it was her. I just knew. It didn't matter that she looks smaller and her hair is shorter. I know a hurricane when I see one. The world has always felt different with her nearby. That's just how it was with her. The kind of power she used to hold. She could shake things up in my life, just by walking into this town again. Then I came home and nursed half a bottle of Johnny Walker Blue. It's times like this that make me wish I had a dog. Something to come home to when the day kicks my ass. If I had a dog, I wouldn't have needed to forget her. I would have had something else to focus on in my day other than that unfortunate sighting. I had wanted to yell at her, to let her know all the trouble she caused me and her family after she picked up and left twelve years ago.

Six weeks before we were supposed to leave for our separate colleges, I rolled over in bed and she was gone. Only calling her sister twenty-four hours later to let her know that she was safe. I want to grab a hold of her and shake her as I force her to listen about how much it sucked and hurt when she started a new life and fell in love with someone else without a single damn explanation. She has no idea what her leaving did to me. No, that woman in Libby's last night was not the woman I was stupid in love with twelve years ago.

For now, I need to shake off this mood I am in now and get my workout in before I have to go to her parents' house who just happens to be one of my current clients. I need to focus, because chances are she won't come around for me to see her again and I'm not actually sure I want her to. I don't like that she was who I first thought of this morning and the person who left me in anger last night. I hate that I want to know everything about why she is here. That I want to know what went through her head when I first spoke. Her father is retiring, but is she going to be at the party? Surely she knows it isn't a small gathering. This will be the first time in God knows how long that most of the town has seen her.

So it's time to distract myself before I go do some planning at her parents' home. I quickly lace up my Nikes because Dawson is waiting near the large shed outside that I have turned into a backyard gym. I'm not sure what made me want to move back to Haven, but last year I finally bought a full-time residence here instead of the small apartment I was renting on Greenwich Street. I grab two bottles of water from the new garage refrigerator before walking out of the house and down the concrete path. Dawson is leaning against the building, his eyes focused on his watch. "Morning..."

"You look like shit." He pays me no compliment as he stretches and I unlock the doors to the makeshift gym. I toss him one of the bottles before I open the door, not even bothering to give him a look. "What's your deal?"

"Want to hear a funny joke?" I say, walking over to a mat for stretching before I begin some cardio.

"Will I get the punchline?" Dawson says, before heading over to the PiYo box.

"Maybe, because it's more of an observation I made and the joke is just that it happened at all." It makes me smirk for a moment. Just the thought that I spent a good part of twelve years wondering about the girl that broke my heart. The girl that made me a terrible man to date, because now I am the guy that doesn't call back and disappears the next morning before a woman can offer me coffee. "Your mind will be blown."

"I'm on the edge of my seat." Dawson shows his talent for sarcasm as he waits for me to just tell him.

"I saw Evie Goode in Libby's last night." As I announce it, a bit of anger edges in my voice.

"So, she came home for the party," Dawson speculates, but he starts stretching his arms. "That's good, right?"

"In twelve years of her returning to Haven, she's never once been spotted in a store or the post office or even a gas station. She stays in that house and nobody sees her. I haven't come face to face with that girl in twelve years." I see the look on his face when he turns around: guilt. Lexie. It's all I need to know that he knew something. Lexie is one of his best friends and she's Evie's sister. We all stayed close after, even with Evie's absence. He just kind of shrugs and turns back to the PiYo space. "How long did you know she'd be back? Did you think I shouldn't know?"

"I knew they were trying to get her to come home," Dawson admits, before lunging against the box. "They've been trying for years to get her to stay for a longer period of time and maybe this is it, man. I don't know."

I step onto the treadmill and begin warming up. It takes a moment for me to want to say anything else. "Why would she pick now?"

"Hell if I know." He stands right back up, walking towards the treadmill. "All I know is she isn't the most level headed person these days."

"What's that supposed to mean?" I walk, taking my phone from my pocket.

"I don't know." Dawson turns away, walking back over to do his jump sets. "Maybe she's here for a while, maybe she's here for a day, but what good is her being here going to do for you? I saw what happened to you after she left and it was awful man. You nearly flunked out your freshman year up in Boston...took you two years to go on a single date. I think it's best that you just let it go."

"What is there to let go of?" I sit my iPhone in the cup holder of the treadmill and pick up the pace. Dawson is working out as I start running, putting my headphones into my ears. When Evie left, it was hell. I moped around far more than any man with self-respect should. Even in Boston, it took me some time to realize that she wasn't coming back. Even when the idea that she might was the only thing keeping me afloat, it wasn't a good time, but eventually the confirmation of it all set in. She wasn't coming back. not for me. Not for us. So I was going to hold up my end of the bargain and follow through with the life I had planned for myself. I still had goals and here I am, living those dreams I had.

I design and build custom homes for a living in a business that I started and built up myself. It was what I wanted to do from the moment I saw an issue of Architectural Digest at my grandmother's house in Cape Cod. I was just a bored kid one summer and before I knew it, I had a passion. It was one of the things I loved dreaming about with Evie. We knew we wanted to build a big house, with a bedroom sized walk-in closet for her, a bathroom that overlooked the trees and a living room with a huge fireplace. Rooms for our kids. When I bought this land last year, I found that I lack my own original creativity and just started with the original blueprint I thought up with Evie. I wasn't holding on to her, I just couldn't envision anything else in my own home. Maybe it was an absence of creativity or maybe it was just wanted in my home with someone else one day. My chest starts to tighten again as I realize I am sprinting on the machine below me. I lower pace and let myself start to cool off.

"Are you trying to wear the machine down?" Dawson smirks as he hands me my bottle of water. "Aggressive?"

"Just needed a tougher workout today," I pant, patting the handle to the treadmill. "Nothing else."

"Uh huh," Dawson shakes his head, before taking the plastic cap off of his water.

"What?" I groan, wiping some sweat off my head as I move on to the weight bench. I don't bother looking up at him, I just immediately lunge to stretch.

"Look...we don't have to get all emotional and talk like girlfriends or anything, but clearly Evie being here is bothering you." Dawson begins to do some pull ups on the bar and I am left sitting on the weight bar as he begins to lift up. "One..."

"Her being here doesn't bother me." It didn't bother me, but it messed up my night. I don't want to see her again because I don't like that she brings up everything I haven't let myself focus on in years. Immediately I had questions for her last night. I wanted to know things. Things I can't honestly say I would give a damn about if it was anyone else. "I just don't know why suddenly she's home and going out in public. This place clearly wasn't good enough for her before."

"I don't know if it wasn't good enough for her..." Dawson

begins, his voice tapering off as he does five more pullups.

"What makes you think that?" I ask, disregarding the weigh bench to see what he meant.

"Nothing man…" Dawson hops down and reaches for one of the crisp white towels on the rack behind me.

"No… you know something about this." I lean against the wall and deep down, I still don't want to know more than what I do. It doesn't do me any good and it doesn't fix the last twelve years. Still, I have questions.

"Dude, all I know is Lexie said once that guy she was with died…she wasn't doing so well." Dawson shrugged, wrapping the towel around his neck. "I guess something like that can fuck you up."

"Yeah…it can" My voice stays even as the image of her in Libby's sticks out in my mind. I don't know a lot about the man that Evie became engaged to. I had heard bits and pieces over the years. He was a businessman or something. Most of the time when people would talk, I would exit the conversation as soon as I could. The one thing I do know is how much losing someone can mess you up. It was the shame that it bothered me. I felt like a fraud when I was reminded that she moved on and I acted like I didn't care. It felt like a scam to pretend to be indifferent when I knew she was in so much pain. The truth was, no matter how many years later, it wasn't an area where I could pretend to feel neutral. I couldn't make myself hate her. I look down at my hands, ready to shift the subject away from what awaits me. So I do. "So, you going into the practice after this?"

"After I go home and shower." Dawson moves his hands to his waist. "I have a full day of appointments."

"Any old women you have to fend off this time?" I poke fun as I prep the resistance bands, reminiscing about a story he told me about a few older women around town who like to drop in unannounced to bring him a pie or pretend they sprained something. "Any cougars looking for prey?"

"God, I hope not." Dawson begins to squat with a barbell as I wrap the bands around my hands. Working out has become the stress reliever I have needed, and I have a feeling I'll be doing it more until a certain someone leaves Haven. "Mrs. Stelzer drives from an hour away to have me check her blood pressure once a week. A nurse can do it, but she says I have the magic touch."

"Hey, maybe she won't have baby fever," I joke, but move out of the way as he acts as if he's going to lunge at me with the weights.

"You're sick." He winces as I step on the band and begin doing curls. I try to place my focus on the work out as Dawson goes back to doing his. I try to shift Evie from my mind. To put aside all of the things that came back into my head the very moment I saw her. I've been telling myself all morning to shove that out of my head. I don't want the answers to the questions that I have. Not anymore. I've moved on. There is no Evie in my world. Not anymore. That has to be clear. I can't start having more questions about why she is here. I wish her well, but I can't get my mind focusing on her. It took too long to get her out of my mind and for the short time she's been here, she's already consumed it. Mentally, I am blaming it on business. Her parents are my clients. We've both moved on from the life we had known together. From the world where most of the time, it was just the two of us. A world that was burnt to the ground.

Chapter Five

Evie

Now

This morning, the sound of a lawn mower and the smell of breakfast cooking downstairs mixed with fresh cut grass colluded to wake me up. I got home late last night, but my mother mentioned quickly that Levi and my sister wake up early. Even if I wasn't excited or pleased about coming home, I love my nephew and will jump at the chance to see him. He may even be my ticket to avoiding most of the town, although I haven't quite figured out how. I can work out the details later, but as long as he prevents me from running into Wade Beckett. I'm still shaken from seeing that man last night. I get what I did hurt him, but it's been twelve years. If he thinks walking away was easy, he's wrong. It ruined my life. I lost twenty pounds, hardly ate, and cried myself to sleep until a magical man walked into my life. I will never frown when I think how much Daniel saved me. Why couldn't Wade just say hello and be on his way? I was minding my own business, sitting at the counter, and he walked in and notices my hair? Of course I did something different to my hair in the last twelve years.

Just thinking about the encounter yesterday has my heart rate up and my chest feeling tight. He looked good. I wasn't blind, noticing the scruff and the tattoo under the inside of his elbow. He took care. That's good, but my chest is tight. It's a feeling I was unfamiliar with until I first left Haven. When I met Daniel, it went away and started up again occasionally after he died. The feeling of crippling anxiety soaring through my body has left me up at night, struggling to get to sleep. Thankfully last night I was too tired to stay up or I think I may have ended up wandering around town in a sweat. As I put the finishing touches on my makeup, I go to my suitcase and reach for a pair of distressed boyfriend jeans, sliding them on before tucking in a black lace lined tank. I check the mirror and thankfully the outfit doesn't look wrinkled at all. My bedroom mirror is the same one that I used in high school, but it doesn't feel like the same girl looking back at me. I look tired, skinnier than I was as an eighteen-year-old girl, and definitely a lot less fun. I reach for a pair of tan Tory Burch sandals. I'll come back later for my laptop; maybe I'll do some online shopping to pass some time.

"Evie!" The sound of my father at the bottom forces me to open the door to my bedroom. My father, Forest Goode, is one of the most genuine people I have ever met, and today he's working his last shift as the town dentist. He doesn't know a stranger and he would give the shirt off of his back for anyone. "There's my girl."

"Hey Dad," I smile, walking down the stairs and into the farmhouse kitchen. I hear some drilling much like I did at the office and wonder what is being worked on, if my dad is in the house. "Is there someone fixing something here?"

"Uh no..." My father scratches his head before turning to my mother who instantly leans over to kiss my cheek. "I thought your Mama would have told you, we are adding onto the house."

"No," I reply, reaching for a piece of bacon. "From the side garage?"

"Yes," my mother replies, walking to the cabinets just as the back door opens. "They haven't actually started, but he's just out there removing a few shelves to get a better idea of what he's working with and measurements."

"Aunt Evie!" Levi bursts through the door, running and lacing his arms around my waist.

"Levi!" I laugh, lifting him up and hugging him. "Stop growing so fast."

"I can't make it stop." He laughs and I run my fingers over his newly buzzed hair. "Grandpa cut my hair like his in the old days."

"It was starting to look girly," my dad says, taking the syrup to the table as Lexie walks into the kitchen.

"It was not." She rolls her eyes, walking over to give me a hug before patting Levi on the back. "Go wash your hands."

"Fine." He groans as I lower him to the ground and walk over to the window. I don't see anyone outside or another truck, but it's likely at the front of the house. "Grandma?"

"Yes?" She asks, flipping another pancake over so that it's perfectly golden.

"Can we take Wade some breakfast?" As Levi stops, everyone looks at me and my eyes go wide.

"Wade?" I look at my mother who has focused back on the skillet in front of her.

"Mom…" I open my mouth to begin speaking, but I don't know what to ask or what to say.

"Wade is going to be doing the expansion on the house." She says, before sliding the second pancake and a few pieces of bacon onto a plate.

"We've stayed in contact...I thought you knew that." My mother reaches for a small cup of berries and puts it on the plate. "Levi, that is a great idea, now go wash your hands."

"Evie, you can't be mad at them." My sister says softly as she walks over to the coffee pot and begins to pour herself a cup.

"I'm not mad...just caught off guard." I don't know how to feel. A part of me wants to know just how much they have kept in contact and a part of me wants to run out of Haven, Alabama as fast as I can. "So, um...you guys all talk to him a lot?"

"It's a small town." My father says, before pressing a kiss to my cheek. "And he doesn't usually work in town, most of his stuff is in the cities, but we asked him and he was open to working on our house."

"To be honest, I have seen his work and he's the only one we want working on this house." My mother ads, moving out of the way of my sister. "And I can't wait for him to work on this kitchen. He's going to show us some of his sketches soon."

"He's very talented, Ev." My father adds and takes his seat at the end of the table. "Nancy, I'm going to start eating."

"That's fine." My mother sits a loaded plate in front of him and smiles. "You have a big day today."

"Last day before retirement." Lexie adds, walking around the table.

"That's right." I cross my arms, leaning against the wall as I watch my mother return to the stove. "Who is taking over for you?"

"Remember Kasey Blair?" He takes a sip of his coffee, before reaching across the table to grab the sports section of the newspaper.

"Wow." Kasey was a bit of a wild child in high school and once tried to put the moves on Wade. She was drunk and nothing happened, so I honestly never worried too much about her.

"Anyway, this is a plate for Wade." My mother says, turning to me and handing me another filled up plate and two cups of coffee. "Take it to him and tell him not to hesitate if he wants seconds. He can come right inside."

"Me?" I point at my chest, before shaking my head. "No... Lexie you take it."

"Can't…" She shrugs, before sitting down quickly and I roll my eyes at her. "Sorry."

"No you're not," I say, flipping my middle finger up before taking the plate.

"There is a child here." My sister gestures as Levi returns to the room. "And tell me all about it when you get inside."

"I'm six now," Levi adds. "And why does Aunt Evie not want to see Wade? He always asks about her."

"Levi." Lexie shakes her head and shrugs at me. "He's six."

"Wade asks…never mind." I groan, finally taking the plate from my mother. I don't bother trying to think about what Levi said, because after last night I know he isn't thrilled to see me and he probably wants me back in New York as much as I would rather be there. "But Levi if you want…"

"Levi can't help you." My mother stops me and places a hand on my back. "He has to eat before he goes to school."

"And he needs to keep his shirt clean." Lexie reaches for a knife, cutting the pancakes on the plate in front of the six-year-old. "So have fun catching up with your ex."

"Go, Evie." My mother points to the back door and I look at it before my shoulder's drop. She then hands me a cup of coffee, so that my hands are completely full with a plate and two hot mugs. "I made it just how you like. Even with one stevia."

"Thanks," I respond dryly, before walking around the same kitchen table we had when I was growing up. I look back at my mother, who waves me out the door and roll my eyes. I don't want to talk to Wade, so hopefully he isn't out there when I get outside. Right as I remember my hands are full, Levi leans over and opens the door knob. "Oh, I…"

"There you go, Aunt Evie." Levi smiles proudly and my father chuckles, because he knows how much I don't want to go out and find Wade. "Have fun."

"Thanks Levi…" I sigh before stepping outside into the cool spring air. It isn't quite warm yet, but it's tolerable. I can hear the birds chirping from the towering trees that line the backyard, a feature my parents loved when they were buying this house before Lexie and I were born. I look around the backyard and wonder if there is a place I can sit the food where Wade will notice without me having to directly hand it to him. Last night wasn't exactly an ideal reentry to Haven, and I know Wade wasn't thrilled either. I look back at the house where I can see Levi and my mom looking out the window which means I can't just sit the food down and pretend I tried. When I walk around the other side of the garage, I see the black Jeep I saw when I was leaving the restaurant last night and stop in my tracks. Deep breaths. Just drop the food off and it will be fine. Focus, Evie. I take one step closer and nearly run into Wade walking out of the garage. When he notices me, he stops and runs a hand through his hair. "My mom made you breakfast."

"Oh." He looks around, before taking a few steps towards me, his gray t-shirt tight on his arms, where I can see another part of a tattoo. This one looks like the bottom half of the Boston Red Sox logo. Did he just move into a tattoo parlor at some point? "I was just going to my car to grab some tape to mark a few things. For the remodel."

"Right…" I look at the garage space and see that he has been up on a ladder, before seeing Levi's old Playskool picnic table right outside of the garage. "Do you want me to set this there or…"

"You can sit it on the hood of the truck and…I'll take the

coffee for now." He reaches out and takes the French style coffee mug from my hand, before backing up a few steps. "You drink coffee, now? You used to hate the flavor."

"It's kind of a necessary evil at the office." I put the plate on the hood of his truck and shake my head. "Work can get crazy."

"Making lip gloss can get wild, huh..." He nods, before reaching in his driver's side door for a roll of black tape. "Here it is."

"I don't make lip gloss," I glare, and I can tell by the way his jaw is clenched, he doesn't really care.

"Isn't that what Glam and Simple does?" He crosses his arms and waits for me to say something to prove him wrong.

"I work for a cosmetics company, yes, and we sell some lip gloss, but that's not what I do directly. I do PR for a strong, female-led company." I rebuked, my eyes narrowing in his direction.

"Sorry. I didn't know." His hands go up dramatically in surrender. "I don't really know you all that well anymore, so you can see where my mistake came into play."

"Yeah." I turn back towards the house, taking a sip of my coffee. The Wade I know would have never tried to make me feel like less of a success no matter how he felt. Even to his worst enemy, Wade was kind.

"How long are you back for?" He suddenly inquires and I don't walk any further. Before I say anything, his tone gets sharper. "A day? Two days? Or will you be out by lunch?"

"About two months," I specify, turning around as he sits the roll of tape next to the plate of food. "Maybe more...maybe less."

"So what brought you back?" He questions, reaching for the fork from the plate. He doesn't look up at me as he cuts himself a piece of breakfast.

"Dad's retirement party." I take a step closer, but tighten

my grip on the glass mug.

"No... you wouldn't have stayed more than a few days just for that." He shakes his head, taking a bite of a blueberry and pancake. "That's not your thing."

"And why wouldn't I have stayed?" I quiz, because he isn't wrong. He knows that too.

"Really?" Wade shakes his head and begins to walk back towards the garage. "You're suddenly Evie of Haven, Alabama, again? Nah."

"I don't know why you're..." I begin, but he quickly interrupts me before I can continue.

"Are you really that clueless, Evie? Because up until the night before you left me alone in my bed...I was pretty sure that you were one of the smartest people I have ever met." He scoffs, before lifting the tape again. I watch as he scratches his finger, trying to find the start of the fresh roll. "I don't know what happened to you. Maybe it was something you did, maybe it was something I did, but I have never seen someone completely change who they are and bail on their family as quickly as you did."

"I never bailed on my family," I dispute, stepping forward as the grip on the warm mug gets tighter. He doesn't have the right to tell me anything about my family or what I am doing here. "I didn't...I didn't bail."

"Hell yeah, you did." He doesn't step closer, but he points back to my parent's home. "You don't come home, and when you do, you're out just as quick as you came in. Except your family paid a price. I paid a price. Yet no one knows why because Evie herself couldn't come home to even explain it."

"I've paid prices too," I snap, not giving him a moment to respond. He has no idea the prices I have paid. For everyone. He's right. My leaving affected him and my family. Me losing Daniel caused more prices in suffering for me. When I left

Haven, I was broken. Daniel was my reset and I lost that. So I don't need him to say shit about the prices that have paid. "In more ways than one, Wade. You don't know what the hell happened in New York or Haven. You know nothing about it."

"Yeah, well why don't you tell me?" Wade snaps, straightening up. "Or is that one of your many secrets? Since you have so damn many of them."

"I didn't come back to Haven to get in a screaming match with you," I retort, adjusting my cup on the hood of his car.

"I bet you didn't." He puts his hands on his hips and looks around the same property that we ran around as children. Except now, it's patchy, a little wet from the rain and missing that glow I thought it had. "Why are you here?"

"It's none of your damn business why I'm—"

"Cut the shit," he interrupts, putting his hand up before letting out a chuckle that reeks of sarcasm. His hand falls to his side again and I can tell he's angry, but so am I. He doesn't know me. Not anymore. He doesn't have the right to yell at me, but yet he continues. "It's all bullshit. You know it, I know it, and I bet that man in New York knew it too, only he was fine with what he had. Wasn't he?"

Before he can continue, I march up the steps in front of me and before I can think, my entire hand makes contact to his stubbled face. I hit him so hard, I can't tell if the burn on my palm is from my pain or his. He flinches, but other than that, he doesn't even seem to care as I am clutching the hand I hit him with. He just kind of nods and shakes his head again. "Don't you ever throw him in my face! You have no right and you know nothing about him!"

"You're right. Just about as much as I really knew about you." His voice is cold, and I can already see a red spot on his tan skin as I slowly start to back up. I'm not even sure what came over me a few seconds ago. When I turn around to walk back to the house, trying to distract myself from clutching my now very sore hand, he shouts, "So, that's it? You're going to slap me and run away. At least you're consistent in running away."

"Fuck you!" I throw my middle finger straight up for the second time this morning as I keep walking towards my parent's back door. and finally clutch my hands together as the pain to my hand starts to set in and burn. *Damn that hurts.* He has some nerve coming here and trying to treat me this way. He was being an ass almost the entire time I was outside with him and now it just makes me angrier with my mother for setting it up so that I had to take him breakfast. I push the door open to the kitchen and my whole family stops eating just to look at me with jaws open as I slam the door as hard as I can.

"Slam that any harder and I am going to have to have to build a new door," my father jokes, probably looking nervously at my mother. I don't even make any eye contact with them; I just race past the kitchen and stomp all the way up the narrow wooden steps. No words. No more insinuated gestures. Just the sound of aggressive walking on the hardwood floors before slamming the door to my bedroom so hard that one of my high school awards falls to the ground and glass shatters.

"Shit." I curse, turning to the wall where several frames are hanging and my own photo collages take up the most space. There are pictures of my friends, pictures with Wade, and the sight of the lake just down the road at sunset. Moments that became memories and memories that became a painful reminder of my past. I don't know why I never took them down, but as I realize this I begin pulling down the photos, showing no consideration for the tape that is stuck to the blush pink wallpaper that has been up for years. The pile of photos grows on the floor and just as I start to reprimand myself for the mess, my bedroom door swings open and Lexie peeks her head around the door. My eyes return to the wall, frowning at the destruction I have created so quickly.

"So... taking breakfast to Wade went well?" She's not serious given the actual smirk that I can hear in her naturally raspy voice, but still she comes in and quietly closes the bedroom door. "Evie."

"Why didn't you tell me that Wade was going to be spending time in and around the house, while I was here?" I feel my blood boiling as I begin working on another collage, closer to the window.

"I knew you would find a way out of coming," she shrugs, before moving my makeup bag off of my bed and sitting down at the end of the floral comforter. She isn't wrong, given that I was mostly forced to be here. I am sure I would have found a way out of this trip if I had known about Wade. If I had known that the barbwire that I feel like is digging in my skin when he's brought up could get any tighter. She reaches for one of the throw pillows on my bed and pushes it into her lap, before letting out a motherly sigh. "I'm right and you know it."

"Yeah, well you are right." I bend down to pick up the discarded pictures from this side of the room, because the mess on the floor is another irritant for me. "Still. You should have told me."

"Probably, but I didn't. Mom didn't either," she argues, crossing her legs on the bed. She stays silent for a minute before carefully speaking. "Evie, I don't know what happened between you two, but maybe you could tell me and…"

"It's not important," I groan, pushing up from the floor and walking to the wastebasket near the bathroom.

"You picked up and left the state two weeks before anyone expected you to and surprisingly for twelve years, we let you get away with just offering us short answers." Lexie says it as if I don't remember living the entire thing. "Evie, what the hell happened? It's been twelve years and you just came storming in the house as if you just had a fight."

"We did have a fight." I roughly respond as I stare at the damaged wall. "He's just so…"

"He's so what?" She quizzes and tosses her hands up in frustration with me. "Mean...angry...I don't know what happened or why you left, but clearly it had to do with him so what is he? Is he terrible? Was he awful when people weren't looking? You up and left and you never told anyone anything."

"I'm aware of what happened, Lex!" I turn around, my shaking voice gets loud again like it did outside just a few short minutes ago.

"Then tell me! Tell someone!" My sister demands, her hands gesturing every which way as she goes off and tells me what I think has been on her mind for a while. "Is he really just putting on an act that years ago, he doesn't know why you left? Was he playing the victim when he moped around for a long time?"

"I never said he was putting on an act," I deny, pointing my finger right back at her as I see that she's putting up a fight today.

"Only because you haven't said anything at all," she snaps, before crossing her arms. I look out at the window, but I can only see the leaves from where I stand and I think about all of the long talks we used to have, how I could tell my big sister anything and everything. How there were nights I spent alone in a shady motel room in New York before I moved into the dorms at The Fashion Institute of Technology. It wasn't until one day that I couldn't. One day that barbwire latched itself to my skin and never stopped its control. "And I am not leaving this room until you tell me everything."

That drags me out of my thoughts and I look at my only sister before my chest begins to tighten. My hand lifts above my heart and I can feel the room getting smaller because she means it. I know my sister and there is no way that she is going to give up, because she's given me all of my space I have ever needed. For twelve years I have had this secret to myself, and I want to keep it that way forever, except now I feel like I might burst. I'm not sure why. We have all the secrets that can change everything. Only this secret changes nothing. All of the change it brought is done. I've never felt the need to say a word until now. My sister has always asked but respected when I didn't want to talk about whatever happened that summer that made me leave. Now, I look at her and a part of me falls out of the barbed wire that has held me for so long and I sit on my bed, ready to tell her everything.

Chapter Six

Evie

Then

"Evie...wake up." I feel Wade's pillow soft lips on my neck as my eyes blink in some of the bright light in his bedroom. I was deep asleep, but if I ignore him and close my eyes, I should be able to stay asleep in his arms. I turn on my side as he presses his lips below my ear and I smile. Damn. He does know how to get my attention. Still, I'm not ready to get up and if he sees I am tired enough, then surely he won't make me get out of the bed. I remember now that we came in from a day lounging out by his pool and we turned on the television to cool off from outside. Sometime after that I must have fallen asleep, because I don't remember Wade being asleep before me. I always fall asleep before him, unless he drank too much. Then he always falls asleep before me and I usually do something embarrassing to him and take a picture. One time after a cookout at his friend Riley's, I put a little makeup on him. It would be like Wade to get me back for that, but I think he really is trying to get me out of bed.

Still, I am really enjoying my sleep so I just ignore him as he begins to stroke my hair. A few minutes later, he drops on the mattress next to me. I win. It must be about five o'clock, but I'm too tired to get up, so I just curl myself into him as he moves a hand around my waist. He's fighting waking up too, because the room is quiet again and I can hear him breathing. He always says he sleeps better with me in his arms. His breath slows against me and I know he's drifting off again too. I don't know how much time passes like this until I feel myself being pushed onto my back and my eyes flutter open again to see Wade and his messy hair staring back at me before letting out a light groan. "Sleepy head."

"What time is it?" I ask as his fingers run along my side and send shivers beneath my skin. I can't force my eyes open yet as he presses soft kisses along my cheek.

"A little after five." Wade's hands run along my side and most of the time, he'd have my attention, but the sun was strong today and I was up most of the night with Lexie and some of her friends after they got in from partying. Even his kisses can't make me want to get up right now. "Dawson called. He wants to go to the movies, so I need to shower and you need to change out of that swimsuit."

"I'm sleeping," I pout, wincing as my eyes adjust to the light from the window. He must have opened the curtains again, before he got himself out of bed. "Babe…"

"Babe," He mimics, kissing my neck quickly before pulling the covers off. "I promise, we'll go get food and then the movies."

"Why do you think food is going to get me out of bed?" I turn on my side, wrapping my arms around my chest. Now I'm freezing, and I can hear my fiancé laughing because he knows I'm not going to be able to go back to sleep.

"Because food is your favorite thing." He crawls back onto the mattress, and I immediately feel the string on my bikini loosen. He thinks he's slick, but I don't like being woken up from a good sleep. I roll over and put my hand flat on his chest. "Oh, no. There will be no sex for waking me up."

"How is that fair?" He complains, lacing his fingers through mine and placing a soft kiss on the top of my hand. "You like it...I like it. It's a win-win. An activity we can both agree on."

"I was sleeping really well and you took the covers." I explain, looking down at the bed and realizing that he took the comforter completely away. "That's rude. I'm freezing and I could get hypothermia. Maybe I shouldn't marry you or have sex with you."

"Don't say that..." He chuckles, pressing a kiss against my nose, before rubbing his hands along my arms as if to try and warm me up. "Maybe if you put on your dress instead of that tiny bikini, you might feel better."

"I thought you liked my bikini." I lean back on my elbows as he sits up in the bed. I can't help but bite my lip as he steps off the bed. He looks good without a shirt on. Wade works outside at a construction zone in the next town and his tan is perfectly dark and it highlights every line etched through his body.

"I like it better on my floor," he says, before tossing me the sundress that had been lying on the floor. When I finally push myself off of the bed, he's right there with his hands on my side. "We do have some time before we have to go."

"Hands to yourself," I bite, swatting his hand away. "I'm serious. This is what you get for waking me up."

"Mean!" He jokes, leaning over to kiss my cheek before letting go and walking over to his phone. I slide the maxi dress over my body, pulling up the arms before searching for my underwear. A moment later he tosses the small pink fabric at me. "I'm going to hop in the shower real quick, mind waiting?"

"I'll take the dishes you insist on leaving in here to the

dishwasher." I gesture to the old oak desk in the corner of the room.

"Yeah...you should probably get used to cleaning up after me." He laughs as he jumps out of the way, just as I lean over to grab a pillow to toss at him.

"You're not funny." I try to stifle my giggle, but it escapes anyways. I throw the pillow at him, but he dodges it and it just hits the wall. He closes the gap between us again, grabbing my face with his hands. "You really aren't funny."

"You're laughing," Wade grins, before kissing my lips softly.

"Natural reaction from the body." I clear my throat to prevent any more laughter.

"You had no choice?" He said, before kissing my lips again, this time deepening it.

"Nope." I pull away, moving my hands to his bare chest. "Now, go shower."

"Yes, ma'am." He grins, walking towards the door of his bedroom as I go to his desk to grab a few empty plates and an empty bottle of water. He leaves the room and a few seconds after I hear the bathroom door shut. Wade has a way of making me smile most of the time I am with him. He's the perfect mix of boyish charm and sexy grownup man. I can't imagine ever not being attracted to him. I've thought about the days when we're older and he's goofing off with our children and I have to be the serious one. It's a long way off in our life, but it's nice to think about the kind of dad he will be. He's going to be amazing. One time he stopped by when I was babysitting the Norton kids when one of the twins fell and skinned her knee. Wade was right there, scooping her up and holding her as she cried. There was something so innocent about it, but it just made me picture our babies for the first time.

I make my way to the outdated kitchen with the mismatched dishes and drop them in the sink. Then I go to the garage to toss the empty bottle of water into the recycling bin. For a man that makes good money, he sure never put any effort into this house. It's definitely missing a woman's touch. I notice Wade's father's car, but he probably went to sleep like he usually does when he gets home from work. He usually passes out in his room or in the armchair in the front den. I look down at the ground and move to grab the ash tray that Ridge keeps in the garage and empty its contents into the trash can. It's a disgusting habit, but thank God Ridge doesn't do it in the house or I don't think I could stomach as much time as I spend here. As I dust my hands off, I run up the steps and back into the house and close the door to the garage behind me. When I round the corner to the kitchen, Wade's Dad is leaning against the counter, his arms crossed as he looks up at me and I jump. I assumed he wasn't awake. "Sorry, I didn't realize you had come into the kitchen. I was just going to do something with these plates."

"Does Wade have you cleaning his room, because that's his job?" Ridge grumbles, scratching at the back of his neck. "I swear that boy doesn't do a lick of work. No sense in giving that boy chores. He makes the girl do them for him."

"No, I just started cleaning up while he takes a shower." I shrug, walking past him and flipping on the faucet. Mr. Beckett has always been fine to me, but I know how he is. Of every room in this house, the one with him in it is the room I want to be in the least. I begin rinsing water over the first plate as Mr. Becket walks over to the refrigerator. I focus on the mustard stains as they fade away and Wade's father grabs a beer. I wince as the sound of the can opens is met by a sigh and then the sound of the shower starting down the hall is clear. Wade is in the shower and his father is opening a drink, most likely not the first. "I um...do you need me to do anything else? I was just going to load these into the dishwasher."

"No. That's alright." Ridge clears his throat and I can hear him take a swallow from the can of cheap beer he picks up almost every night from the mini mart down the road. I open up the latch from the dishwasher, letting the door fall open so that I can put the dishes in as quickly as possible and get back to Wade's room. He's kind to me, but I also don't try too hard to engage with him, because I hate how he treats Wade. I hate the way Wade tenses up when he's around. "So I guess you've committed to a life sentence."

"I'm sorry?" I blink, tilting my head, the messy graying beard makes it hard to see the expression on his lips and I find myself wondering what Mrs. Beckett ever saw in him. I hope the man that had a wife was better than he is now.

"You're engaged. You're getting married. To Wade." He smirks, then lets out a light chuckle and pushes himself off the counter. "Wow I just aged myself. It's just something people say sometimes."

"Oh," I laugh nervously, before reaching to the next plate. I reach for the sprayer as he walks over to the stove and turns around again. "Yeah, we are getting married."

"Do you know when?" He asks, his eyes wandering out the window above the sink for just a moment.

"We agreed to put aside any planning until we get done with our freshman year." I answer, trying to figure out why he suddenly has sparked an interest in something he's never mentioned before. I return to rinsing dishes when he gets uncomfortably close. So close that I can feel his breath on me." Hopefully, before we graduate."

"You know, it's crazy when you think about it." He sways and I know for sure it isn't the first beer of the night. The water to the shower is still on when I feel his fingers on my neck, then he pushes the braid over my shoulder. My whole body stiffens, but I can't move. My feet don't work. Nothing works. "A girl as pretty as you settling for a loser like my son. That's crazy."

"Wade isn't a loser." I shiver, cringing as I feel his lips on my shoulder. This isn't the first time he's tried something and he knows I'm too scared to do a damn thing about it. It only takes a second when I feel the hair from his face, that I get it together, gather my guts and begin to move. Before I can move, he quickly grips my shoulder with his fingers and I wince at the feeling of his nails. "What are you doing? Stop."

"I'm not gonna hurt you," Mr. Beckett remarks, easing up his grip, but I can still feel the pressure his worn fingers applied to my skin. "I just want you to think long and hard before you make a mistake. Before you choose a man that ends up like me, unless that's what you like. Then I think I could make you happy too. Maybe you could do a test drive."

"Don't touch me." I snap, his hand still on my shoulder, massaging me as I snap at him.

"You're spicy," he smirks, squeezing his hand a little harder on my skin. "Ease up. You might like it."

"Stop. Wade is nothing like you," I bite, jerking my shoulder from his grip. I turn the water off and wipe my hands on the dish towel sitting beside the old sink. "He's smart and he's kind. He has an amazing heart, and he's got a future, and he wants things. Big things. He wants a career and a family that he can make proud. We want things out of this life and we are going to get them together. He's not a bit like you."

"Maybe." Wade's dad begins to chuckle again, moving to stand next to me as I try to focus on the sink. His hands keep moving to my dress, pinching the ruffled fabric in his fingers as I try to focus on the water, pulling away slightly every time his hands come near me. Wade takes long showers and I want to somehow get him to hurry. He's never around when his Dad pulls this kind of stuff. Maybe it's better that way or else he'd probably go away for murder. He finds my snapping back amusing and to be honest, I've never taken that tone with anyone, but I'm so angry that he would call him a loser. Wade is anything but a loser. He's nothing like Ridge. Nothing. He doesn't say anything for a moment as I wipe down the counter quickly. I hear him let out a deep breath and then he speaks. "It's just that I would hate for something or someone to come along and rip that dream away from him. Rip you away from him."

"It won't happen," I insist, before he leans over, sniffing my hair and my eyes close so tight I am sure I could produce tears. I won't let him in.

"It might." He laughs again, shaking his head. "God, you smell like a wet dream. It's no wonder Wade is obsessed."

"That won't happen," I repeat, turning around to face his father, slapping the dress fabric from his fingers. He needs to know I don't want his hands on me. That it feels wrong and if Wade were here, he would be on the floor clutching his jaw. I can't afford to be afraid.

"You came along, didn't you?" Ridge asks, before shaking his head and shrugging his shoulders. "I guess you two have known each other long enough that you didn't just come along, but I think you're going to catch on soon enough."

"Catch on to what?" I pinch my lips together, tilting my head.

"I am paying for his dream. The dream of going to Boston and going to school. The successful career can only happen because I have agreed to pay for college and you don't seem to want to play along." I look up at his father who is now standing directly in front of me, cornering me into the sink. "You see, I seem to be the only one who truly thinks this wild and crazy plan you two have hatched out is utter bullshit. I'm the only one expecting something out of my investment."

"How so?" I feel my cheeks growing hot as I cross my arms

over my chest, he extends his hand, letting the back of his hand graze my skin of cheeks. I can't go anywhere without pushing him. I'm stuck as I pull my head back and he smirks. He's repulsive.

"I don't want to get into too much with you, but let's just say I don't think I would be able to financially support Boston both for college and living if you two go on with your plan." Ridge slides his hands into his pockets and winks at me. "It's simple. I won't pay for college if you two stay engaged."

"Why?" I bite, trying not to raise my voice. I don't want Wade to know that his father is suddenly trying to ruin our plans. I can handle this. Our plans were never a secret.

"Insurance." Ridge decides, scratching at his facial hair. "If I am paying for Boston, all of it, then I don't want any distractions. If you're really planning on marrying him, he has no money for Boston. Dreams ruined. The cause? You of course."

"What are you saying?" I ask, looking to the entryway of the kitchen for saving from Wade, but he's still in the shower. I look at his father and give him a quizzed look.

"I'm saying call it off or Wade doesn't go to Boston." He answers firmly, looking down at me. "If not, there is no Boston. No money. He'll be the same piece of shit he was meant to be."

"So, you're going to take away his money for school?" I hesitate and take a painful breath. "Because of me?"

"No," he shakes his head quickly, throwing his hands up in protest. "I don't like when you word it like that."

"It's what you're saying," I cringe, thinking about how terrible a person must be to punish their own child that way. For a man that I know loved Wade's mother deeply, he's acting and speaking as if he's never had someone so precious to him before. Wade told me how happy his parents were and how his father was a better man when his mother was alive, so why would he want to cause Wade pain. "Isn't it?"

"I'm saying that you can make sure he keeps his college money and future plans by calling off the engagement." Mr. Beckett says this so confidently that I wonder if he even loves his son at all. If he even cares how either one of us would feel if we lost the other. How Wade would feel if he heard this. "You call off the engagement and Wade gets his college money. He gets the money to live in Boston, his car, and he won't have a fear in the world."

"And why can't he be engaged to me?" I ask, my eyes narrowing.

"You complicate things. I'm a successful man, despite how you or my son feel about me." He reaches into his pocket and pulls out his wallet. Before I can tell him that he can't buy me off, he pulls out a check and holds it up. It's a check made out for Wade's tuition. "Wade can't go to Boston without this. There is no scholarship or grant that is going cover it and a loan...well he's a kid. He doesn't have credit."

"I love Wade." I mutter, my eyes feeling suddenly very heavy as a lump that feels like wool forms in my throat. "I'm not ending my engagement to him. We'll figure it out."

"I want my son to make me proud, not be something I am embarrassed by." He says, putting the check back into his wallet. "If he doesn't go to college and build a career for himself, then he's a failure. I won't be proud. It's easy to understand, isn't it?"

"Then why try and get me to break his heart?" I plead, trying to get inside his mind to find out what is really going on. He knows I would never leave Wade. There isn't a chance. "I bring out the best in Wade and he brings out the best of me...wouldn't you want that for him?"

"A man needs to be successful on his own." His father intoned, taking a step back. "He doesn't need to be brought down, he needs to be built up and the only way to truly do that is to see he makes his way to Boston to fulfil the aspirations he has."

"And I interfere with that?" I question him, but he just stares right back at me. "How? You 're telling me that you're going to take away everything he's working so hard for, but you won't tell me why? Is it because he'll be far away and you can't smack him around anymore?"

"That's the beauty of being the one in charge of the money." A devilish smile appears across his lips and I know he's the villain today. "I don't have to give you a reason. You stay with him, he doesn't get Boston. He doesn't get his dream. No Boston, no dream, no future. You'll be at fault. He'll end up a drunken fool."

"Like you," I hiss, unable to stop the tears from forming in my eyes. "That's what you want. You're miserable so you want to ruin his life."

"I'm still willing to give him a future; you'll be the one ruining his life," he counters, putting one hand on the counter behind me and leaning in so close I can smell the beer on his breath. It's consuming my nose as I hold back the tears that are threatening to fall down my face. "Think about it. What happens if he doesn't go to Boston?"

"Get away from me." I wince, pushing past him and grabbing my head. "You disgust me."

"Now, is that how someone should talk to their future father-in-law?" He turns around, chuckling again. "Or is that former?"

"I am not breaking up with Wade." I slam my hands down on the counter, trying for just a moment even to get a grip on the words being spewed at me. "We won't let you do this."

"How are you going to stop me?" He laughs, putting a hand down on the counter next to me. "I mean, if you tell him, it will be a no brainer. He'll give up everything for you. Then twelve years down the road..."

"Shut up." I bite through my teeth and I shake my head furiously. I won't let this happen. Wade wouldn't ever let me walk away and I couldn't ever leave him. This simply isn't an option. "Okay...I don't know why you're doing this, but it doesn't matter. Wade and I can get through anything. You can take all of the money away and we'll still be there."

"Possibly." He shrugs with that arrogant smirk on his face. He contemplates his words for a moment and I know deep down he questions if he's right. He questions if "Or maybe one day he wakes up and realizes that you're just a hot piece of ass he can get somewhere else. He's a man, Evie. He has pride and a reputation. How is it going to look if he gives all of that up to you and at the end of the day, he's working a job he hates with a woman who doesn't look eighteen anymore."

"I don't know why you want Wade unhappy or why you don't like me, but I won't give Wade up so that you can feel whatever power you need to feel. He and I will figure this out if you really insist on putting him through this." I wipe at the ears that have fallen in the moments of my fear, anger and panic and shake my head. "I won't walk away from him and I won't give him up. I can't. I won't."

"Well, the summer is still young." He winks, before walking past me and grabbing for his keys. "And so are you. You have a lot to learn."

"I have nothing to learn from you." I breathe, before he laughs again, shaking his head and walking back towards the garage. A second later I hear the door shut and the garage door open again and my eyes close. No way in hell. That's all I can think as I picture him driving away. There is no way I would give up a life with Wade to please Ridge Beckett and to let him win. There is nothing in this world that would make me change my mind about spending the rest of my life with Wade.

Nothing. He's crazy if he thinks even for a moment, that I would contemplate leaving Wade over whether or not he is willing to invest in his own son. Even if I did, Wade wouldn't hear it. Maybe Ridge will change his mind. Maybe he will think about what he said and realize how absolutely insane and heartless it sounded. A father couldn't do that to his son, that's why he said it to me. It's why he wants me to break Wade. To break us. I can't. I won't. I would never contemplate hurting Wade or myself like that.

"Hey, are you alright?" I hear Wade's voice from the entryway to the kitchen and I quickly paint a weak smile on my face. It's all I can manage. The way his wet hair sticks to the front of his bangs and the way his smile responds to mine, I fall deeper in love with him in that moment.

"Yeah." I lie, moving a hand over my stomach to keep from clutching it. He's dressed in a t-shirt and long shorts, being perfect. I feel ill. "Do you mind if we stay in tonight? At my house?"

"I thought you were okay with us going out tonight." He frowns, stepping forward to take my hand. He presses a soft kiss against my fingers. "Babe, what's wrong?"

"Nothing." I lie again, looking around the kitchen for something to relieve me until I can think of a plan to get us out of this mess. "Can we go to my house? Watch a movie there? I just don't feel very good."

"Are you sick?" His protective hand moves to my forehead, his frown deepening. "Was it my dad? I heard him in here and if he—"

"No…" I move my hand to his chest, blinking back the tears that are threatening to fall. "I just feel tired. That's all. We could just go watch a movie and go to bed."

"On the couch, because it's the only place your parents will let us sleep together until we're married?" He chuckles, wrapping his arms around me and I want to freeze him here. To stop this world from spinning quickly around me.

"Just...please?" I request, realizing that I might sound more panicked than I want him to pick up on and I scramble for more explanation. "I just want to change into my sweats and we can hang out in my room, we just can't close the door when my parents go to bed."

"True." He pulls his face away and winks. "Not that it's stopped us before."

"It hasn't." I force a stronger smile, before tilting my head up to kiss him quickly for good measure. I don't want to let him go and I refuse to ever have to. "Maybe we could stop and grab something to eat or see if my mom is making dinner."

"Whatever you want," he says softly, stroking my back. "Maybe you just need some sleep."

"Probably," I breathe, trying to push Wade's father's stupid voice out of my head. Trying to push the ultimatum out of my head and shift my focus to how perfect this man in front of me is. To how lucky I am to be marrying my very best friend. "Let's go."

"Let me grab my keys." Wade rubs his hands up and down my arms swiftly before letting go, and I wish he hadn't. The sight of him walking out of the room this time makes me need to gasp for air. I turn and grip my hands onto the counter, because I am not sure if I could stay standing otherwise. I take a moment to think over the words that Ridge spoke to me, threatening our entire future like a wildfire in a national treasure. Wade doesn't know that his father is willing to pull everything out from under him, but I don't think that he would be surprised. His father has already inflicted so much pain on him, but for some reason I was surprised. Stupid me. I was a fool to think that he wouldn't try to pull something months before his son was supposed to begin a new life. I should have known better. I curse to myself as I hear Wade grab a few of our things from the bedroom and the sound of the television going off. "Ready?"

"Yeah," I mutter quickly, before taking a few quick paced steps forward, placing my hand on the back of his neck and pulling his lips to me. "I can't wait to marry you."

"I can't wait either." He grins against my lips, moving his hand to my back. "Come on, Evie. Let's go to your house."

"Come on," I say softly, sliding my hand into his before we walk towards the front door. This small house is shrinking on me and I can't wait to be outside of it. There is nowhere I want to be less right now then in this home that Wade shares with his father. I can't ever unhear the words that Ridge propositioned me with, the way he touched me as if it was a threat to show his control. His threat to hurt Wade if I don't first. He doesn't see that hurting Wade, is something I simply won't do. I can't live without Wade Beckett and I don't think he could survive without me. I know he couldn't. From the moment he walked in my life, we were closer than any two people could be. As children, he was my best friend, and now he's my heart. Losing him would mean destroying my entire being. Surely, Wade's father is showing what becomes of a person when they lose the one person they love the most, and I won't do it. I *can't* do it. I would die. Every little piece of me would cease to exist without him and I won't allow it. If it comes down to it, we'll make a new plan until we can get to the life we want. There are options to living a new life, but there is no path to living without each other.

Chapter Seven

Now

Wade

Forest Goode has always been a man that I look up to and respect. My own father and I had our moments, but Forest was a guy that I knew a man should aspire to be like. It probably helped that he raised Evie and there was a time when she was my favorite person on the planet, but their entire family is important to me. Even when my Dad died a few years ago, they got me through despite whatever their daughter felt. Forest took me out on the lake fishing and let me drink beers for hours. He drove me home from the bar when I just wanted to forget the world a few times and Dawson wasn't nearby. He's been a friend and a mentor in my life and tonight, I look forward to helping give him the proper celebration to begin his retirement. I worked with Nancy and Lexie to plan a barn party on their land and all three of us are excited to see it finally come to life after weeks of painting and prepping in our off hours. Right now, I am setting up around the bar I built. I've hired two local bartenders to work the party tonight, but there are still some lights to put in and some hardware. Thankfully the work I need to do in the barn should help me avoid Evie for most of the day. There was a brief moment when I thought our paths would cross as I went in the house to talk to Nancy about some of the plans for the tables, but Evie wasn't around. I haven't seen her since our argument out in her parent's yard and it's probably for the best. We can't seem to have a conversation without her walking out and filling up with rage. I don't know how someone you once were perfectly aligned with can turn into a total stranger. I guess I hoped that if we ever saw each other something would just make sense, and it doesn't. I don't know the woman anymore. She looks mostly the same, but talking to her is like talking to a stranger you have a bad first encounter with. So, I'll stay in the barn as much as I can until it is time to start bringing things in the barn. Just as I use my drill to put the last screw on one of the first light fixtures, I see Lexie and Dawson make their way in, each with a hand on a large cooler. "Hey!"

"There is more ice being delivered, but we had this filled up so we could at least start this off in the ice bin," Lexie says as they approach the bar and I jump in to take her place. "Thanks."

"Lexie's growing muscles," Dawson teased, nodding to Lexie who is holding up her arms. "Look at that gun show."

"Suck it, Dawson." Lexie rolls her eyes, leaning against the counter.

"I mean…." Dawson smirks before winking at Lexie.

"Gross," Lexie rolls her eyes and moves, takes some of the plastic off one of the barstools and we dump the ice into the undercounter bin. "Wade, the caterer is going to be here at four, will the tables be ready by then?"

"Yeah," I nod, looking over to the other side of the room where some of the folding tables are. I quickly count to make sure we have the boxes we need over there. "Dawson and I can get to those."

"If not, I'm sure Evie and I could get them," Lexie offers, tossing the plastic into a giant cardboard box that I have been using for trash and I must have reacted somehow because Lexie puts her hands on her hips. "What? She's an extra pair of hands and she's been cooking in the kitchen with Mama all day."

"Really, you're going to have the Runaway Bride come join the fun?" Dawson groans, before gesturing to me. "I think we should try to go the whole night without a homicide."

"We aren't going to kill each other...well I won't kill her," I insist, although I can't promise that Evie won't kill me. "But I think we can get it done."

"And it's not exactly like she wants to be around us," Dawson scoffs as he leans forward to close the ice bin. "She never came out to see us in the past. She just stayed in that house like a hermit."

"Yeah, something tells me she won't be out here to help us," I concur, letting out a chuckle in Dawson's direction. He nods and begins to laugh too. "By the way, Runaway Bride...that's a good one. Surprised it took twelve years for you to come up with that one."

"It was marinating for a bit," He adds, before rolling up his sleeves.

"Are you guys in high school?" Lexie cringes, before handing me the drill as I return to the ladder where I was putting in some fixtures for the bar. "Does she really need a nickname? I mean, it's childish."

"Come on Lex...you know we're joking," Dawson assures her, squeezing her shoulder. "You can't say it wasn't funny."

"Well, maybe it isn't," Lexie objects, pulling her shoulder away from Dawson's hands. "You know, she's a person and regardless of what she did, she's still human. Maybe she doesn't come around because of what she thinks people call her and think about her."

I watch as Dawson shakes his head and Lexie just begins to work on the next wooden barstool. She seems more annoyed with Dawson than she usually is when he has an opinion about her sister. Normally, Lexie just rolls her eyes and moves along. Sometimes she even joins in when it's harmless or a little innocent fun, but today she isn't. "You, good Lex?"

"Yeah...just not in the mood for it." She looks up, smiling weakly. "There is a lot to do today and if Evie can come out and help here, maybe we should let her."

"You're probably right," I admit. For the sake of her family, I shouldn't take part in the jokes. They've done enough for me over the years and if it bothers Lexie, I should keep my mouth shut. Lexie has been a friend since I was a kid, and I can't imagine being around her sister's ex all this time is easy when we talk about her. Not that we talk much about it anymore. It's been years since we've had a real discussion about it. "So, lets focus on getting ready for the party that is today. A lot of work to be done."

"Fair enough. Where should this box of solar lights go, Lex?" Dawson asks, lifting a brown box from the corner.

"Outside, they need to be set up along the path." Lexie points to the entryway of the barn to the landscaping we did a few weeks back. "There is another box already out there."

"This is a pack of sixty just in this one box," he frowns, examining the box.

"It's a long pathway," Lexie smirks, reaching for a Clorox wipe from the container on the bar. "Get to work."

"You're going to be the death of me," Dawson sighs, shaking his head as he begins to head towards the outside. I watch Lexie for a moment as she cleans off the barstools and examines them. Like her sister and mother, Lexie is a perfectionist. It's one thing the Goode women all have, on different levels. Evie is the most intense. I remember she used to refuse to let loose until she got all of her homework done and her room clean. If she ever learned anything new, she was going to get it right. That was Evie.

I watch as Lexie continues to clean, grabbing another wipe but this time wiping along the bar and I finish with one of the fixtures. I hop down from the ladder and reach for another fixture. "I'm sorry we pissed you off. I wasn't thinking."

"It's fine, but maybe you guys could lay off of your anger towards her," she suggests, a weak smile falling away on her lips before she begins focusing on her hand as it moves along the surface. "It's just...maybe not everything is as it seems."

"What?" I stop, watching as Lexie stops cleaning and her eyes meet mine before her shoulders drop. "What isn't as it seems? Lex, what does that mean?"

"It's nothing," she breathes, but clearly she knows by my face that I want to know more. I do. I want to know what it means when she says not everything is as it seems. Maybe. Maybe it is or maybe it isn't. Still, I want to know. She looks around the bar as she lets her arms fall to her side. "Just lay off of her."

"Okay, you don't usually hear me make too many comments about her." I point out, raising my hands up. "She's your sister and regardless of what happened...I don't have an issue with that..."

"You two clearly fought yesterday. She came inside still angry." Lexie rolls her eyes and then shakes her head. "God, you two couldn't have a civil conversation in Libby's or in the yard. How are you going to coexist in the same town for a month or two?"

"Does she plan on immersing herself into Haven for that time?" I ask, trying to push aside the arguments that have replayed in my head a hundred times since then. "If not, the chances of us fighting again are pretty low after tonight."

"So, please don't kill each other tonight," she pleads as Levi runs into the barn, his face covered in dirt. "Maybe even be civil."

"I'm not going to do anything to jeopardize your father's retirement party," I promise, as I return to unwrapping the fixture. I'm not one to make a scene anyways, but with the eyes of the town likely on us, I don't want to bring too much bad attention into the room. "But clearly, you know something I should know. You said things aren't what they seem."

"I didn't mean to," she admits sheepishly, before hopping up on one of the barstools. "Look, it isn't my story to tell and there aren't any actions I need to speak for. That's up to Evie. Maybe you should try having a productive conversation with her. Maybe if you just talked to her, you two could at least be civil."

"God, Lexie," I groan, tossing a piece of the fixture onto the counter. "I tried that ten years ago. I had to move on."

"But did you? Moving on means being in healthy and stable relationships. You have taken part in none of that and I know that, because you're like my brother." She asks bluntly, referring to my bachelor status. "Because other than the occasional hookup and trying to fend off Kasey Blair, you don't date. If you slept with her ever, please don't tell me, because I would instantly judge you for that one. Maybe you're the occasional man whore, but you've had one girlfriend ever. Evie."

"No, I did not sleep with Kasey," I testify, leaning against the counter. "I'm not looking for a girlfriend if that is what you mean."

"No, that wasn't what I meant," Lexie responds, her hands moving the settle on the bar. "You don't date. You hang out with Dawson and I."

"Levi too," I joke, referring to her young son to which Lexie gives me an obvious, 'come on' look before moving on.

"You don't take girls on dates, and maybe you haven't told

me because Evie is my sister, but you don't tell Dawson either, so I assume my observations are true," she continues, before pausing. "Am I wrong?"

"I'm not interested in settling down," I shrug, being completely honest with her. I figured that was obvious, but I don't mind admitting it. Dating isn't really something that has interested me. I spent too long being stuck on one girl and now, I'm kind of set in my life for the moment. "So."

"Oh, is that because you want to be a wild and untamed bachelor for the rest of your life? Random sex with strangers for all of eternity?" She retorts, before crossing her arms. "Do you want to know what I think?"

I let out an annoyed sigh as I step back up the ladder and reach for a screwdriver. I don't know where this side of Lexie is coming from. She's never pressed me on my dating life before and she certainly hasn't ever made comments about easing up on my anger towards Evie. Not that Evie is a topic that comes up much. "No, but I think you're going to tell me."

"I am," she confirms, nodding confidently as she shifts on the barstool so that she's looking at me. Still. "I think my sister ruined you."

"Ruined me?" I cock an eyebrow, resting an arm on the ladder.

"I do," Lexie nods confidently and leans forward. "I think she was the love of your life and when she left, you decided you were giving up on being the guy you were with her. Wade Beckett was no longer a datin' man."

"Nope. That's where you're wrong." I roll my eyes, turning to hold the fixture in place above the bar. "I'm not carrying a torch for your sister."

"I never said anything about a torch," Lexie puts forth loftily, crossing her legs. "You added the torch. Why is that?"

"You're being a little weird today; did you already break

into Dawson's punch?" I challenge, trying to work with the screws of the fixture. We're still on a deadline, or else I would be right down by the bar, proving her wrong of whatever the hell she's trying to get at.

"Wade, you had two encounters with my sister in less than twenty-four hours and neither one went well from what she tells me." Lexie groans as she boosts herself off of the barstool. "So, maybe don't fight tonight, but also try to put the past behind you…"

"I thought you wanted us to be civil," I grumble, turning the last screw in the fixture. When I am sure the screws don't need tightened, I begin to climb down. I put the screwdriver and turned around to find Lexie resting her head in frustration. "What?"

"Wade, she hurt you and you're a tough guy so you won't fess up, but remember that I know what you went through when she left," Lexie begins, crossing her arms. She's right. I was a wreck after Evie left, but there are a lot of unanswered questions that make my blood boil. "Dawson and I both do, and if there is more to the story then maybe you deserve to know."

"I deserved to know a whole hell of a lot," I bite as I feel my chest tighten, before sliding my hands in my pockets. "Sorry."

"I know," Lexie replies quietly. I begin looking around for more that has to be done before the party tonight, except with everything there is to do, my head is fuller than it's been in a while. I wonder if Lexie really believes a conversation could take place between Evie and I without one of us storming off in a rage. What does she know now that she didn't know over the last twelve years when she would let me vent? Sometimes she needed to vent too and Dawson and I have always been there for that. What she's trying to fix, I don't know. "It wasn't a good time to bring this up."

"Really?" I gesture around the barn, before shaking my head and leaning against the hard tile surface. "You put me in a great mood."

"Wade," Lexie tries to fix this, but I don't give her a chance to say anything else. To make me overthink.

"Lexie, I think we better just get ready for the evening." I don't want to talk anymore about Evie, and I don't want to know why Lexie suddenly believes I should be soft on her sister. I wasn't planning on being anything towards Evie, but she came home to Haven. There are questions that I have wanted the answers to for years, but I know trying to hunt them down now isn't going to do a damn thing. Maybe Lexie does know more or maybe she thinks it's time to move on. I did move on. I moved far away from the idea that I would ever understand Evie Goode. Far away from the thought that Evie would come back to Haven, Alabama and fix the mess she made. The mess she refused to answer for during the last twelve years. Far from the life she was supposed to create with me and far as hell from being the woman I thought she was.

***

It came close, but finally the party came together and most of the town of Haven is in and around this barn. The barn on the Goode property that was only used occasionally and never for the purpose that it was probably originally intended. The Goode's weren't farmers, but that didn't mean they didn't contribute to the town, to the wellbeing for the people of Haven. Forest Goode was celebrating his retirement as the main dentist in Haven and as evidenced by the people on the property tonight, he's seen a whole lot of teeth. Hell, he's my dentist now and he was when I was growing up. The town showed up and for the last two hours, people have been giving speeches, dancing, and talking to Forest and Nancy, who are standing in the entryway. I've been nursing my beer at a table in the corner while I watch them. Two people who built a life that they are proud of and are committed to each other for their whole lives. They're the dream. The life you look at and say, 'I want that.' I know people in town that have said just that. Hell, I said that once. I fought for that once, but if there is anything that I have learned it's that a relationship like that comes along once in a blue moon. It's like winning the lottery and the Goode's have the winning ticket.

I've seen a few people come and go tonight, but everyone is having a good time and there will be a few hurting heads in the morning. Moments like tonight remind me how much I love this town and the people in it. It's a good place to be and if there is one thing I am sure of, it's that coming back to Haven was the right thing. Despite everything that has happened, it's where I am meant to be. Where I am meant to rest my head at night. Just as I reach to take another swig of my beer, I notice a few heads turn as they have been each time Evie walks into the barn. I'm surprised by how many times she's walked in here, knowing she's a topic of interest. Still, she smiles warmly in her parent's direction as her dad hands his beer off to her mother. Forest walks over to her, says a few words into her ear before she shyly smiles and nods. I cross my arms over my chest as she takes his hand and they walk to the dance floor. I don't know why it surprises me, she's always been closer with her parents, but tonight it's almost as if they're a shield between her and everyone else. She's spoken to plenty of people, but they always seem to come rescue her after some time. "She looks good, doesn't she?"

I look up from watching Evie dancing with her father to see her mother sliding into the folding chair next to me, resting her glass of merlot on the table. She does look good. I'm not blind. She still gets my attention, slapping me or not. I smile warmly and nod. "She does."

"I wish she'd get some meat on her bones, though. She was a tiny thing to begin with, but it seems having the world on her shoulders burned more of the fat off," she admits with a light chuckle in her voice, before nudging me and I grin. As a mother, Nancy is as good as they come, but she's funny too. "Really though, I'm glad she's home."

"I know you are," I say cautiously as my eyes return to the dance floor as Forest whispers something in Evie's ear. It takes a second, but she giggles and shakes her head at him. It's a giggle I couldn't hear over the music, but still that sound fills my mind, because her laugh is etched in my brain forever. "You deserve to have her home."

"We can't scare her away." Nancy's voice is soft, filled with concern. I look back to her and she's watching me intently before speaking again as if to beg me not to get into an argument with Evie again. As if to say we all share the power to make the wrong move. Really, it's me. "My baby girl is home right now and while it probably isn't permanent, I want it to go well. I want her to know that she always has a home to come to when she needs it the most and right now she needs Haven. More than she realizes."

"I don't want to fight her. When I saw her in Libby's and at your house, it wasn't my finest moment," I insist as Evie rests her head on her father's chest and Forest smiles warmly under the dance floor lights. He looks content, both from years of hard work and from having his daughter home. She looks tired, but not for the time of night that is. There is something about that moment when she closes her eyes briefly that says she's trying to let go of the whole world, but she can't. Her eyes open back up and for a moment, she sees me looking. I clear my throat and look back at Nancy, who is watching me. "I'm glad she's home for your sake."

"You're allowed to have mixed feelings. Nobody would

blame you." Nancy smiles warmly, placing a hand over mine as we both watch the father and daughter dance. Nancy knows that Evie and I ended, but I've never said a word to her about it. I assume Evie hasn't either based on my conversations with Lexie. I look up to her to say something, but I know better than to begin talking when I don't have the right words. My feelings aren't mixed, they're just a mess of bullshit and I hate admitting that to myself. I hate the guilt I feel for our last two encounters. I hate the guilt I feel when I know her family is so happy to have her home for more than a short window and I can't even settle on whether I'm angry or indifferent. There is still time for her to rush out of town and break her mother's heart again. "It's a lot when you haven't spoken to someone in over a decade. You're not the same people you were when you last saw each other. Well, maybe you are, but she isn't. I still know you to be the kindest boy, with the biggest heart. Just with more muscle and facial hair."

"Yeah?" I question, shifting in my chair as she takes a sip of her wine.. The last two days have been a whirlwind. I grew so used to not seeing her that when I finally laid eyes on her I was filled with everything that had possessed me in the very beginning. The anger, the sadness, and the withdrawals all filled me without an answer to a single question. Evie and her father separate as the song comes to an end and he visibly squeezes her hands and whispers something to her. She smiles warmly before he goes to greet a family that has walked in. Evie walks towards the bar, her head down as if she's trying to repel any attention from coming her way, but revealing the open back of her black dress as she quickly bypasses some of the folding chairs I set up earlier. I swallow the lump in my throat and want to ask her if she's crazy. Men notice that stuff. I'm noticing.

"You still look at her the same way." Nancy breathes deeply at her admission, and I look up at her, her expression no longer cheery but worried. Only I don't know who for. "Maybe, you don't realize it, but you do."

"What?" I mutter, straightening up in the chair before looking around the room quickly. "I don't—"

"I noticed it when she first walked in tonight, but thought maybe it was just the dress. It's a bit more...open than she normally is these days." Evie's mother sits up straight, and looks back to Evie for a moment. "It's not the dress. It's her. You don't look at her a bit different when you're watching her."

"You're wrong." I clear my throat, because she is. I'm looking at Evie the same way, because of who she is. A person. I would go as far as to say, it wouldn't be possible to look at her the same way I did when we were teens. "She's a woman. I noticed her. That's it."

"Oh, she's a woman." A smile forms on Nancy's lips and nods. "But you already knew that."

"I'm not looking at her the way you're trying to insinuate." I roll my eyes, before looking at Nancy who has a smirk on her face. I look down at the tip of my beer for a moment, my finger circling the rim before speaking again. "I'm a man...she's beautiful. I see that. I'm not blind. That doesn't mean I'm pining for her after twelve years. I see what a man sees."

"Alright," she nods, before looking to Evie who is ordering something with the bartender. I can tell he is talking to her and she shakes her head as if to say no to a question. Then her body language shifts, she looks down and he slides her a drink. "Wade, I don't understand what was going on when she left. I still can't get inside of her brain, but my baby girl is a mess. She's broken from the outside in and as her mother I want to be able to fix this for her. I can't."

"If she's broken, she has to *want* to be fixed," I remark, not sure if it's all that helpful. My father was broken after my mother died and he sure as hell never wanted to be fixed. Even at the end of his life when we were doing better, he didn't want to be whole again.

"She does. I know she does. I know you want to be fixed too." Nancy's voice is filled with hope and when our eyes meet again, I see them shining and give her a weak smile. "When Daniel died, she shut herself off even more. That was how I realized that it wasn't just the pain of losing him. It was the pain of every moment since she left town. Every day she spent away and every day that followed after his death added up to that final crack that broke her. She's not an alcoholic or drug addict as far as I can tell, but she may as well be. She's at her lowest point."

"Well, I know what that's like," I pointed out, straightening up in the chair. I then begin scratching at the edge of the sticker of the beer bottle. "That's something we have in common."

"But she put you at your lowest point." Nancy quickly affirms, patting me on the shoulder. "You've both been hurt, but I'm guessing she started it for you. I don't know all of the details, but it doesn't take a genius to know that she's the one who ended things with you, who broke you and left with no answer. Everyone always assumes that I don't know much about the story because you've never openly put blame on her to me. I know better."

"You do?" I frown.

"She hurt all of us in some way that summer, but she hurt you most of all." Her mother squeezes my shoulder before letting go. I look back to the bar and Evie is gone. Nowhere to be found as I quickly gaze around the room. I look back at her mother who just nods at me. "Why don't you at least try to have a calm conversation with her? You two once were inseparable. Despite what happened when she left, you once wanted to spend the rest of your life with my daughter and I don't think you want to end this life years from now being angry with her. That would be a long time to carry that around."

"What if I don't know what to say?" I ask, placing my beer on the table in front of us, before leaning back in the chair.

"Then there is a chance that you'll both be sitting in silence," she says as I look back at her and weakly smile. Nancy Goode is a woman who was always wise then and now. She lets out a light chuckle before she spots her husband and Evie's father walking towards the table. He has an extra pep in his step which could be from the fun or one too many drinks. "Just try. It's all I ask."

"That's all?" I smirk as Forest approaches the table and pats me on the back. "Hey Forest."

"Nancy, I thought you might want to come get a bite from the food tables before sharing a dance with me." Forest holds out his hand to his wife, breaking our conversation and smiling at me. "That is unless Wade officially has grown more charm than me."

"I don't think I could ever have more charm than the man of the hour," I joke, adjusting my posture as our topic of conversation has shifted with Forest coming to the table. "Congratulations on a successful career and now retirement."

"Thank you," He smiles as I stand and extend my hand to him. "Especially since you have been keeping my beautiful wife occupied while I danced with my little girl and talked to some of my former patients. Oh, and for everything you did to make the party come together. Nancy and Lexie were singing your praises as usual."

"The pleasure is all mine," I grin as our hands shake in a firm grip and before he lets go, I pat him on the back. "Now go and enjoy some of that food. I heard the crab cakes are pretty good."

"I plan to." He smiles, before holding his arm out for Nancy to loop her arm in and he presses a soft kiss to her cheek. Nancy looks up at Forest and I see the lightest carefree smile that I used to see from Evie when we were young. I see the resemblance in their eyes. The same dark eyes I used to claim I could stare into for hours, only Nancy's are older. I don't know why I never noticed the insane resemblance before, but as I watch Forest and Nancy walk away, I find myself letting out a deep breath as I look back to the dance floor. Whatever song the DJ is playing is slow enough for pairs to dance to. I see Dawson and Lexie dancing, which isn't unusual, I see Libby and Mr. Hunt from the autobody shop, and Levi and some other little guys running around the barn. It's been a long night and it definitely isn't over, but I think it might be over for me. I reach for my beer on the table, taking the last swig out of it before walking over to the trashcan and tossing the bottle in it. When I turn around, I can see Evie staring onto the dance floor, watching the duos sway to the music. The way her eyes glisten off of the bright lights, I can tell that she's crying. A moment later she wipes the tears from her cheek and I wonder what's going through her head right now. Everyone seems to be so absorbed in the party, they don't seem to notice the daughter of the man we are celebrating looks like she's falling apart in front of all of them. Her head is down now and I can't see her face, but she's still crying. I feel my face turn into a frown and a moment later, she's gone. She is leaving the barn quickly, her head down and again, I don't know where she's going.

Chapter Eight

Now

Evie

One thing I have always loved about Haven, Alabama was the nights when you could look up at the sky and see each individual star for as far as the sky went. Especially on nights with a light breeze and you could hear the birds, bugs, and the trees. The chirps and croaks filling the late May air made it feel like it was all right around you, or good was coming from miles away. It was something about the leaves and the midnight blue backdrop that reminded me how much Alabama was home. I honestly can't remember the last time I took the time to appreciate the dark night sky when I was in Alabama even for a short time. Or anywhere for that matter. Tonight, I can hear the music from the barn and I'm pretty sure people are doing the Cupid Shuffle right now as my father's retirement party goes on without me. I was having a good evening, but then the bartender who couldn't be older than twenty-five hit on me and then I watched several couples who looked so in love dance slowly. I watched the couples sway and I don't know what I got sad for, but I felt my chest get tighter and I stopped being able to breathe. It was like the old wooden walls of the barn finally began to cave in on me and only me. I was being crushed by something in a crowded room, but it was just me there. I couldn't take it so I quickly left, running as I got outside and not caring who saw me. It didn't matter that I couldn't breathe or see clearly. I didn't stop until I got to the pond at the edge of my parents' property. The sky is too beautiful and that just forces another tear to fall. It is troubling to me that I can't watch people dance and not be overcome with sadness. I used to love when I had a chance to slow dance with someone. Daniel would slow dance with me if I begged him to at a wedding or in the apartment when a song I loved would come on, but he always complained that he had two left feet. He was usually good for a dance or two, so I don't know why I'm crying. For a moment, I swear I hear the sound of walking through the grass and my body swings around to look, but there is nobody there. Just trees and the night. For a moment, I scan the land that I can see before opting for the water that has a better view.

Daniel never made it to Haven, Alabama with me. We once went to the Bryant-Denny stadium in Tuscaloosa one weekend to catch a football game. I'm not sure what made us do it except for he came in one Friday and said he bought tickets and we were going. That was the closest he got to Haven. He had offered to come plenty of times, but I always made an excuse that I would be busy or that he would hate it. That wasn't the truth. He would have loved Haven. As a child he loved fishing and camping, and while he had grown into a city guy, he would have adored my hometown. He would have loved that most of the side roads were gravel or covered in dirt, the small-town charm where everyone knows each other and a farm on every corner. I guess I was protecting him. Or maybe I was protecting myself. If he would have come with me, I couldn't hide away from the town that built me, the town I up and left to protect Wade Beckett from losing everything. I couldn't risk my worlds colliding like that. I wouldn't have known what to do, and maybe it was selfish. Maybe it was something I did in vain, or maybe I thought something would change if I ever brought him here. It seems so silly now to hide a whole town from a man you love, because of the man you fell in love with as a child. I know it had more to do with seeing Wade and the chance that if I ever finally came face to face with him, Daniel would be there too, and that terrified me. He'd know I was a coward and Wade would want answers. Wade wouldn't care that Daniel was there with me. He was always so confident and bold and he would have said everything on his mind. I don't think Wade would have waited for Daniel to be somewhere out of earshot to share his mind, and I was afraid of that.

Then there was Wade. I was filled with fear and anxiety over seeing Wade for the first time since I left him that summer. When I left Haven, it was really bad. I remember the missed calls, him calling out for me and the messages from my family begging me to come home. I remember Wade's emails and letters. I remember the messages. I feel sick just thinking of them and knowing that there was so much damage I had created. He pleaded for answers, for something to explain why I did what I did. I remember him even crying into the phone, promising me that he would fix whatever he had done to make me leave and that was more than I could take. Hurting him was something I never wanted but didn't have a choice in doing. I was aware that I had caused pain and it nearly killed me, but stealing his dreams from him? I wouldn't have survived it, and neither would he. I wasn't sure we would have made it through. That was one thing his father had been right about: he may have resented me. So I made the choice to destroy myself and let him eventually move on. I left knowing and believing that I would never recover. Daniel didn't take his place; he just created a spot in my heart. Still, I lived with guilt for so long that I don't know if that guilt went away or if it's just a permanent attribute of mine now. There were so many times where I nearly gave up and ran back to Haven. Times I wanted to stop and just run back to Wade, screaming an apology and to tell him why I tried to leave. I wanted to tell him that he was my home and I wanted the best for him, but that I just couldn't live without him. Instead, I just reminded myself that it was for him. Everything was for Wade even if Wade never understood. Even worse, I was afraid of what would happen if I came home and destroyed his life. I worried about coming home to visit and seeing his face. I wasn't sure if I would feel sad or heartbroken, or worse, imagining Daniel would see my face and know how I felt about Wade. I was afraid of a lot of things. Mostly, I was just afraid of me. How silly is that? How stupid was I? To be so scared of coming back to face the life you left behind. To come back and see the destruction you left in your wake. What was I afraid of?

"Ev?" A quiet and hesitant voice comes from behind me and I jump, turning around quickly to see Wade stepping through the green, coming out from the small path that connects to the other part of my parent's land. It's like deja vu for a moment, the way that voice echoes in my brain. I can't really see his face, but I know that it is him. My hand is still on my heart as I take a deep breath, attempting to conceal how startled I am, but my heart can be felt on my hand. Wade stops in his tracks, holding a hand up as if to stop me from panicking out loud. "Sorry, I didn't mean to scare you. I wasn't even sure if this was where you would be."

"Shit." I take a deep breath as my eyes close for a second, dropping my hand. "You just caught me off guard. I wasn't expecting anyone out here."

"You're crying." Wade looks around as if he isn't sure if I really was out here by myself. As soon as he sees it's just me, he steps forward.

"I'm fine," I sniffle, using my knuckle to wipe some of my tears. "I was just out here and something from the trees must have gotten in my eye."

"You were crying in the barn too. When you were watching the dance floor," he adds as he starts to walk closer but stops after a few steps. "When you were watching the couples dance. What's wrong?"

"That's ridiculous," I deny, avoiding making any contact between our eyes. Although I am sure he finds my denial more ridiculous than my actual crying.

"It isn't if you're upset," he remarks sadly. "Besides, you forget I once knew you the best. I know when you've been crying."

"Alright. I've been caught." I breathe, my eyes avoiding his direction. We're still alone and I don't know why he's opted to come find me, but I don't have the energy for another argument with him. I'm too tired to put up a fight. There is a familiarity of him standing here. "I'm fine. You can go back."

"Ev...I don't think you're fine," he admits, sliding his hands into his pockets and he shakes his head as if he's given up something. He looks uncomfortable, but persistent. Like he's caught me in a lie and maybe he has. "Look, I don't know why you're here beyond your father's party, but I don't just forget the old things I know about you and I can tell you're not fine."

"Am I that obvious?" I nervously cross my arms, shifting on my uncomfortable feet.

"I think you might be to me," he admits, taking a few more steps forward. He doesn't make eye contact with me; he just leaves his hands where they are and looks out at the pond. "It's funny, really."

"What is?" I frown, facing the water again. He's standing by my side, but it's like having a stranger next to me.

"That I recognize when you're not alright." He begins as if he's fully aware of the irony. "I don't recognize much else, though."

"Look, if you came out here to yell at me again, you're wasting your breath." I begin, but he quickly puts his hand up and I stop when he begins speaking over me. "I'm too tired for it."

"God, Evie, I didn't come out to fight with you," he groans, rubbing his temples as if to say being this close to me inflicts pain. "I'm just checking if you're okay. You looked really upset in the barn and you still look pretty upset. I was trying to make sure you weren't going to run off or something."

"It's nothing," I lie and bite the inside of my cheek, taking a deep breath through my nose and forcing a smile onto my face. "You didn't need to come out here. I got a little upset. That's all. I don't need your help."

"Okay. If that's all, I will go." His signs and his hands return to his pockets and he turns away, taking a few steps. With his face in the other direction, I look at him as he starts to walk away, but he stops and looks up at the top of the trees. The crickets that hide somewhere in the ground and trees are chirping and the occasional bellow of a frog are the only noises we can hear between us as he stands there, not looking back. "You know what? No."

"No?" I repeat quizzically and he turns around with his hands on his hips. I feel my arms freeze at my side, watching as he begins to walk this way.

"Why were you crying?" He asks, but his voice sounds angry. Like he's holding in rage that might burst from the seams. He's lost that concerned look on his face that he had moments ago and I think if I say the wrong thing, he might snap. "Damn it, Evie."

"I thought you didn't come out here to fight with me." I scoff, stiffly standing as I keep my shoulders back.

"I didn't, but there was a change of plans." He clarifies, speaking over the crickets that fill the air. "I'm only going to ask you one more time. Why were you crying?"

"Do you think this is actually going to get me to confide why I was upset in the barn?" I frown. "Demanding I talk like a fugitive."

"What the hell is wrong with you?" He snaps, stepping towards the pond. My tears have begun to dry up and I sense his tone is only getting stronger as he rubs his fingers over the hair on his chin. "I asked you what happened that made you leave, you don't answer. I ask you what is wrong, because you're visibly upset and you don't answer me. Why did you even come back to Haven? And don't say for your father's party unless you're going to leave in the morning."

"I'm not leaving in the morning," I mutter, watching as he gears up for his next attack. He seems ready for me to say something that will fire him up. "But you already knew that, didn't you? I saw you talking to my mother. I'm sure she's still telling everyone that I am here for a while."

"Yeah, well I'll still be impressed if you're not gone by morning," he quickly responded, bending over to pick up a flat rock out of the Bermuda grass. "I know you're aching to be out of the county line at least."

"Don't tempt me," I bite back, placing a hand on my hip as I watch him skip the rock across the water. It stops a few feet out from us, the ripples weakening behind it. I want to say something about how he used to do it, but I don't. "Are you done chastising me yet?"

"I'm not chastising you," he denies, searching around the

grass, making no eye contact with me. "I'm just tired of you being selfish while everyone else pays the price."

"Selfish?" I whip my body around, facing him again as he reaches for another tock. "You think I'm selfish?"

"Ev, what would you call what you've done?" He raises his voice again, skipping the rock the same distance as before. My body starts to heat right back up again as the word selfish echoes throughout my brain. "You up and left, showing no regard for anyone else. You left your parents who were already sad about sending their baby girl off to the crazy city, you left your friends, Lex...me."

"So that makes me selfish? Selfish was the last thing I was!" I shout, my finger poking into my chest as I realize my blood is boiling and I may have finally snapped at him. "You have no idea why I did what I did! If you knew, the last thing you would think I was is selfish. I did what I had to do and I paid prices for it!"

"I don't know why you did what you did because you won't tell me! I know nothing about the prices that you have paid, but I sure as hell know what I paid." He points out onto the water, as if our whole past is playing out on the surface. "I had a right to know if you were going to make a decision for our relationship. I should have been the first to know."

"It was twelve years ago, Wade!" I shout, before putting my hands on each side of my head. "We were kids!"

"No... I don't buy that." Wade shook his head, the veins in his neck looking like they're trying to escape as he yells. "There are a lot of things you could say, but how young we were wasn't the reason. Maybe you freaked out and got cold feet, but I still don't see you pulling what you pulled over that."

"It wasn't easy then and it isn't that easy to explain now," I sigh.

"Try me!" He demands, crossing his arms firmly over his

chest and I flinch. He's mad, he's looked angry at me each time that he has yelled at me but as he continues speaking, the hurt that I caused is evident in his face. Even behind all the facial hair that covers the bottom half of his face. "Because I don't care if it was a year ago, twelve or twenty. I was owed some sort of answer and maybe call it rumination, but I still think I should get one. Seeing as I was supposed to be your husband one day, I had a right to know if you didn't want to marry me."

"I did want to marry you!" I shout, the urge for denial rushing through me. It was never about that. Not that it provides any explanation, but the need to let him know that I wanted to marry him overshadows any need to shut him down.

"Bullshit," Wade snaps, pointing his finger at me and I'm aware of how firmly he's standing over me. "If that was the case, you would have stuck to the plan. We had a solid plan that accounted for every speed bump."

"No it didn't, Wade." I insist, running my hands through my hair.

"That plan accounted for us being able to get married by the time we finished college!" He argues loudly and I feel my heart beating faster.

"No it didn't!" I shout.

"What the hell does that mean? There was no way we..."

"We didn't account for your father, Wade. We didn't plan for him, okay?" I snap and my eyes go wide, immediately wishing I could take the words back from my lips. Maybe it was the look on his face or maybe it was the feeling that I couldn't take back what I had just said, but my eyes began to water again. I feel like I may have just done more damage than I did in the twelve years I went in silence, but I would give anything to take the words back. His hands fall to his side and he looks puzzled. "Shit."

"What do you mean my father?" His brows pull together

as he looks at me, completely puzzled. "Everleigh!"

"I was never supposed to say anything." I lament, trying to turn around to walk back to the house, but he quickly puts his hands on my elbow, holding me in place. I can't run away and even if I could, my feet don't feel much like they are working. "Shit. Shit. Shit."

"Everleigh." He lets go of my arm, as if he trusts me not to move. I'm frozen. "What does this have to do with my father?"

"I never wanted to hurt you. I didn't know what else to do!" I scream, as if the lid just exploded off a pressure cooker. Debris ready to fly. "I did all of this for you, Wade! But I can't tell you any more than that."

"Yes you can," he insists, gritting his teeth as he tries to stay calm. He's still mad, but maybe something has stabilized. His expression has softened, but I'd have to walk past him to get away. He wants answers and he's going to get them. I just know it. "Everleigh, what does this have to do with my father?"

"I can't," I shake my head furiously. I can't tell him. Wade runs a hand through his hair and cursing to himself as I take the chance to step by him.

"Everleigh! What happened?" He snaps, grabbing my arm again, but this time his grip isn't as tight as he lets out a deep breath and lowers his voice. "Please, tell me."

"Wade," I mutter, looking down to the ground as fight back the urge to cry or let the tears fall, because I'm not so sure that I can say the words. I can't say what has haunted me for the last twelve years.

"Please," he breathes.

"He was going to take away Boston. Leave you with no money to go to college..." I divulge and let out a deep breath. Wade releases my arm from his grip. I don't know how long we stay there, because he doesn't say anything. We're just quiet and the ground no longer feels comfortable below my feet. "I'm sorry."

"Shit," he whispers, turning to face the trees. He says something else, but I don't know what it is. He should just say it. It's out in the open now.

"I'm sorry, Wade," I repeat. It is all I can manage to say, realizing that there is no comfort in saying the words after twelve years. I felt relief when I said them to Lexie. There was a pressure that I felt that kind of relieved itself when the words escaped my lips, but this hurts. Everywhere. Especially when I look up to find him still facing the trees. "You could at least say something."

"I can't," he admits, his hands falling dead to his side. He looks at me as I wait for anything to happen, but I don't know what. He looks me up and down, before he speaks again to break the silence. "I just...I can't talk to you right now. I have to go."

"Wade," I breathe, stepping forward. I can't take it back; he knows now. He knows what started all of this. He doesn't know the details yet, but he doesn't need to. His face tells me that he knows all that he can take right now. He knows more than he actually bargained for. Maybe he had another idea in his mind of what happened, but his body language shows he's defeated. That his father got just what he wanted. No matter how it happened, his father won. "Please."

"I can't. I just can't Evie. I have to go," he says in disbelief, sliding his hands into his pockets as he looks down at the ground in confusion. I watch as he starts to speak several times, but then he begins to walk away, towards the same path he came from. For a moment he stops where he stopped before. He wants to say something. I know he does. Instead, Wade Beckett keeps walking. Away. Into the trees and out of my sight. Leaving me along with the wilderness, only accompanied by the crickets and frogs that I used to find comfort in. Now I just feel alone. I'm reminded of how broken I am as I begin to cry, turning to face the water. I wish I could get away, take everything back and never return to Haven. To where I could further dig in the hurt I caused. I wish I hadn't told him anything. I had never planned to. The secret would die with Ridge Beckett and me. Being the villain allowed me the distance I needed to live my life, but now I can't help but think of how disappointing this all is. I think I preferred when he just hated me for leaving when there was no explanation. He's gone. He has his answer.

Chapter Nine

Wade

Then

Everleigh Rose Goode was God's gift for something I did right in this life. I'm not sure what, but that girl is my end all be all. It's hard to pick my favorite thing about her because I love her so damn much. Evie is my first and only anything. She's the first girl I kissed, the first girl I ever made love to, and the first and only girl I will ever picture having a life with. She's the only person I've ever told I loved. The way she rests her head on my shoulder when she's sleepy, the way she whines when she's hungry or the way she smiles when I touch her. Anywhere. I can't get enough of her. She should be illegal, because I'm pretty sure this girl is my drug and I'm an addict. She's also my biggest teacher. There is so much I learn from her and not all of it is physical. No, this girl is so much more than meets the eye. She's intelligent, silly, and has a zest for life; sometimes I'm just trying to keep up. She's beautiful, every inch of her, inside and out. The dark hair, the creamy skin, and the freckles should have been an indicator that I was in trouble. It feels like a sin to love someone this much and in a few weeks, we're going tour separate ways to college and I can't get myself to come to terms with that. I'm not ignorant to the fact that it is going to be our biggest test yet and I think Evie knows the same. She's been really quiet the last few weeks. Constantly and carefully stroking the engagement ring. She won't admit it, but she's emotional about leaving, and sometimes I just catch her zoning out, miles away in her mind. When I ask if there is something wrong with the ring, she responds only to tell me that it's the thing that makes her happiest. It reminds her of me even when she's not with me. She takes it off to shower sometimes but always keeps it close by. She said it's her safety net, except she's still quiet and nervous. It doesn't scare me, because to be honest, I'm full of thoughts too. From the moment I met her, I've never been away from her for more than two weeks. When her parents would take the family on vacation, I would sit home and count the days until she got back. Now, I'll be counting for a bigger window of time until we can get together. We've worked everything out so the longest should maybe be a month or two. Still, I'm aware that it is a lot. We're young, but we know what we want. She doesn't need the stress. New York is a big city and she's constantly worrying that she won't be able to be as successful as she wants to be. She's crazy to think that. She's brilliant and she loves makeup. I might be biased and I know nothing about it, but I know already she's good at it. I mean, I really know *nothing* about it.

Right now, it's late. I'm watching her sleep after she drifted off during an old episode of *Friends*. She's wearing a new blue sundress that she tells me is eyelet fabric and ruffled sleeves that I wouldn't care for, except she looks beautiful. She's like an angel. She turns onto her back, her hand moving up to her forehead. I can't help but touch her, sliding my hands along her side and pressing my lips to cheek. "Hi sleepyhead."

"Hi," she smiles, her eyes closed as she stretches beneath

my hand. She hasn't quite woken up, but her other hand moves to the back of my neck. "Can't sleep?"

"Can't stop looking at you," I admit sheepishly, pressing a kiss to her jaw.

"Dork," she giggles, reaching for my face and pulling my lips to hers. She smells amazing, like something sweet but that isn't always as innocent as it seems. That's what I love about her. She's delicate, but she also is strong and wild. "Love you."

"Love you, too," I smile against her mouth, lowering my hand to her thigh. "Wake up."

"Are you going to make me food?" She asks, her hand moving down my back. "Because I am starving."

"Of course you are," I roll my eyes, pulling my hands off of her, because it won't get any further until she eats. "You already had dinner."

"But I haven't had a snack, Wade," she laughs, giving me a lopsided grin as I take her hand. "And if I don't have a snack before I go to bed, I could starve and if I starve, then I could die and you wouldn't want me to die, right?"

"All because you didn't get a snack?" I ask. "I don't think it would kill you if you went like nine hours without eating. Seems a bit extreme."

"But would you want to risk it?" She tiredly quizzes as she sits up in the bed, fixing the strap from her dress that had fallen. "Dead, Wade. From hunger."

"I am quite attached to you," I beam, as she extends her hands and I pull her up, pressing a soft kiss to the top of her wrist. "Fine, let's get you a really good snack."

"I don't ask for much." She winks, the first ornery wink I've seen in a while. I can't help but grin as she stands on her tiptoes to press a kiss to my cheek. "Also, dessert would be good."

"Isn't a snack a dessert?" I frown, walking to my bedroom door. She stops and glares at me. "What?"

"Are you crazy? A snack is a snack. It's sustenance. It's protein or some carbs but it's not dessert," she explains, stopping in the doorway of my bedroom. "Dessert is specifically sweet and maybe sometimes mixed with salty, but always part sweet."

"So, your fruit bowls are…" I inquired, crossing my arms.

"Sustenance," she confirms, pushing her hand onto my arm and urging me out of the way. "Let's go."

"Bossy," I tease as I lead her through the hallway. As we round the corner, Ridge is headed in our direction. I try not to make a sound out loud that makes it clear I don't want to see him, but Evie tenses up immediately. She's been doing that lately sometimes. Maybe it's because she hates that my Dad and I fight or it's because she's nervous about everything changing. I wish he didn't remind her of that. "Ridge."

"I'm Ridge today, not Dad?" My father slurs, before nodding at Evie. "Everleigh Goode…Good ole' Everleigh Goode."

"Hi Mr. Beckett," she says in a voice much quieter than normal, looking down at her feet. Everleigh doesn't normally do that, but she has when she's spoken to my Dad over the last few weeks and it leaves me with an ache in my chest. She's so nervous and stressed, that she doesn't meet his eye and I know she's worried something might explode between us.

"Great, just heading to bed." He sways, grabbing onto the wall. "And things for you?"

"They're good." She breathes, crossing her arms and still avoiding his gaze.

"We're just getting something to eat," I say, pushing past him and Everleigh follows. I ignore the way he stares at us as we walk to the cabinet.

"Well just let me know if you need anything or to tell me something. Just gonna go watch Sports Center in bed." He offers with glazed eyes and stops. "You too, Everleigh Goode.

My door is always open. Y'all know where to find me."

When I turn around, my father is still staring at Everleigh who is now staring down at the counter, her fingers playing with a leftover receipt from Piggly Wiggly this morning. She doesn't say anything and she doesn't look up, leaving me to look up at my father who is still staring. "We get it. Goodnight Ridge."

"See ya," he shakes his head before walking out of the view of the kitchen, Evie looks up, her face serious, but she doesn't say anything as I go to the cabinet and grab a bag of Tostitos and some cookies I bought from the bakery. As I reach for a stack of napkins, Evie goes to the freezer to grab a tub of ice cream, before opening the refrigerator to grab a bottle of salsa. I watch her for a moment pause as she stares at the shelf, before closing the door. Then she turns around and nods towards my bedroom.

"Are you okay?" I hesitantly ask, taking a step forward.

"Just...let's go to your room," she swallows, stepping ahead of me and walking towards my room. The room isn't far away, but she steps quickly to cover the distance from the kitchen to my room.

With my hands full, I follow her down the hall and she pushes my bedroom door back open again, her eyes back on the ground. It makes my chest tight, knowing how scared and nervous she is for our lives to change so I don't say anything. I just sit the food on the bed as she closes the door. Then I turn around to take the items being held up in her shaking arms. When I grip the ice cream, I notice she's got tears in her eyes. When she knows I have noticed, she shakes her head quickly and I toss the ice cream and cookies on the bed. As to tell me she's upset at all. Except I know better. I know her better than she knows herself. "Ev..."

"Let's run away together." She blurts out, before with her red eyes, a sob escapes her lips. "Out of Alabama. We don't need it here."

"Evie...what?" I can't help but trail into a smile, because the very words coming from her mouth have never even crossed my mind. They haven't crossed hers either.

"Wade..." She begins to cry and shakes her head again, reaching for my hand. "I can't...we don't have to go to school. I'm serious. Let's go. We can take my car. There is more space for more things in my car and we have the money from our graduation parties and work. We could get a small apartment somewhere and start over. Just us."

"Evie...you're scared," I say softly, reaching for her arms.

"No...no..." She shudders, pulling her hand away and tears stream from her face, the mascara dripping black from the corners of her eyes. "We could get out of here. Tonight. Let's go somewhere together. Away. We don't need New York or Boston. We could go to Florida or California and get married and just work hard at some jobs we find there. We could go to a community college in a few years and just be together. We don't need Boston or New York. We don't need them."

"Who?" I wonder, but she doesn't stop to answer me at all.

"Please." Evie begs, clasping her hands together. "We don't need anyone. We just need each other. I only need you. Just you Wade. Please."

"Evie," I try to reach for her hand, but she begins to pace, her hair swaying with each movement. "Calm down. Babe, you're just having a freak-out about everything. It's going to work out."

"Stop! You're going to try and tell me that it's okay but it isn't. Wade, we could pack bags and just leave. Together, please leave with me. Please." She cries and I realize she's working herself up so much that her face is red. "We don't need Boston. Please leave with me. Please let's go. I have a bag...we could leave. Now."

"Evie, you were fine a few minutes ago," I frown, sitting on the edge of the bed as she paces in front of me. This is by far the worst of her panicking about school and she's never mentioned not going. I know she's just overwhelmed and something about this evening triggered her anxiety.

"This isn't fine." She turns around, grabbing my hand out of my lap and pulling. "Come on. Let's go. We can leave. Fuck it all. We don't need the plan, we just need each other. We can go to another state, get married in a courthouse. I just need you. You're all I need. Tell me I'm all you need."

"Ev...you know you're all I need." I breathe, trying to rub her hand as she attempts to pull away but I won't let go. "I realize this is scary, but it's going to mean amazing things for us."

"It's not scary...it's not," she cries, pleading with me as if I hold the key to something she wants. As if I am controlling her future and I don't know how to make her see everything is fine. "Come on."

"Evie," I breathe, pulling her back to me, she moves onto her knees. "Baby, what's wrong? Is it the distance? We can plan more weekends together. Are you worried about me being somewhere else? You know you don't have to worry."

"No... I trust you but please... let's go. Please." She whimpers, grabbing my wrist, but I move my hand to her hair, slamming my lips to her forehead to comfort her. To find just a second to give her solace from whatever is triggering her panic. "Baby... please. This is our last chance. We can go and get out of here and it won't matter. It's our chance."

"Chance for what?" I ask, her head falling on my knee as she cries. I put my hand in her hair, rubbing her head lightly. "Babe...it's a big change. College isn't going to be like Haven where we see each other every day, but it's going to be worth it."

"Please...I just want you. I just need you. Shit..." She just cries and her sobs start to slow down, she doesn't look up at me as I start to rub her back. She's making herself tired, her cries becoming labored as she occasionally begs 'please' followed by another sob. It breaks my heart, but after a few minutes she begins to slow her cries. Finally, she looks up at me, her face a mess and red, cheeks tearstained and pushes her hair from her face. Some of those dark strands stick to her face. "Wade, is Boston and the program really everything you want? Is it the one thing you want most?"

"The only thing I want more than Boston is you," I smile, pressing a kiss to her forehead. She doesn't smile and her shoulders fall. The tension falls out and she nods at me as she wraps her arms around herself. A moment later she pushes herself up off the ground and sits next to me on the edge of the bed she was sleeping peacefully in a little while ago. I wrap my arm around her shoulders and she lets go of some of the tension in her body. "It's going to be okay. When it's all done...we can build the house we want...wherever we want. I'm not going to pass up the opportunity to make our dreams come true."

"Right. Dreams." She breathes, wiping at her eyes again and I press a soft kiss against her temple. She's hiccupping on her tears every few seconds, but she's not hysterical. I would be lying if I didn't say it freaked me out a little to see her so upset. The idea of her being upset bothers me. The truth is, I was expecting it in a way. For her to be upset about us being apart, but I know it will hit me too. When she leaves for New York on the same day that I leave for Boston, it is going to kill me a bit. The only excitement I have, is that we've already decided we will study on the webcam together. Just so I can see her face, before I go to bed. She shifts in my arms, looking up at me. "Can you tell me about the house again? Please."

"Yeah, I can do that," I respond, standing up to go to my desk. I have a book of all of the magazines we've clipped pictures from for our house, of sketches I have made to show everything that we want. We've spent hours cutting out pictures in the town square while we lay out on a blanket, passing images in the halls at school and lying under the stars by the pond on her parents' land, sharing our ideas. This house book is compiled of everything the two of us want so badly. I sit back on the bed, this time against the pillows as she crawls back, resting her head on my shoulder. I open it to the first page, pointing at the first picture. "Okay...so this will be our front door, but I want to put some windows above the door, it will help bring in more natural light in the entryway."

"And we're painting it navy," she adds, her fingers delicately stroking the picture that shows a floral wreath on the door.

"It's up for discussion," I laugh, kissing the top of her head. I look down and she's closing her eyes tight, tears still slipping out as if she's trying to imagine it and I decide to force a smile by skipping a few pages, opening it to a full page spread of a walk-in closet. "Here, I think this will be your favorite. Wall lined shelves for your unnecessary amount of clothing and shoes, with a dramatic chandelier on the ceiling. Of course, we'll have to pick out a rug and maybe an ottoman. Then a vanity built into the wall by the window for..."

"Natural light," she finishes my sentence, opening her eyes finally and looking at the picture. Normally she'd start mapping out where she'd hang her sundresses and how she wants a drawer dedicated to sunglasses and rant about how makeup storage is just as important as clothes, but she's quiet. I think she notices that I have picked up on it, because she paints a weak smile on her face, looks at my lips and speaks. "Your dream is to do this. To build custom houses and you're going to be really good at it, aren't you?"

"Yeah," I smile, trying to hide my excitement about my dream career, because she's so sad. I try not to think about the nights where I am going to have to go to bed without even kissing her once during the day. That alone is an agonizing thought, let alone weeks at a time. I stroke her hair and kiss her head again, lingering there. "And you're going to kick ass in New York, right?"

"Yeah," She swallows, closing her eyes and nuzzling her head in my neck. "I am."

"And we can still plan out the house; it has to be perfect," I chuckle, tapping my finger on one of the images she's previously cut out for a paint color that she said would complement the closet.

"Go back, I want to see all of the pages," she instructs, moving her hand from the page. "I want to see everything about the house."

"There is nothing to worry about." I assure her and feel her conceding to everything as she stays beside me. She's exhausted and I know if she wasn't, she would still be pacing. Her hiccups slow, but she's still tense. Evie needs to sleep and she needs me next to her. She'll sleep over tonight. I'll keep her safe, happy and she knows she's loved by me. She knows we're going to be okay no matter what. Deep down she knows that and it's my job to keep her up when she's feeling low about this. I know her and I know I bring her peace. Just as she brings me peace when I need it the most. We're a packaged deal, but we know the next four years will test us. Still, there is nothing that can break us. At the end of it all, we'll have gotten where we wanted together. We'll be stronger than ever and ready to start a life. Tomorrow she will wake up and everything will be bright again.

Chapter Ten

Now

Evie

Unlike most of the town of Haven, when I woke up this morning, I wasn't met with the feeling I was going to die from drinking too much. No, my feeling of death came from spending most of the night crying quietly in my old queen-sized bed and if that didn't make me feel pathetic enough, I couldn't tell what I was crying the most for. The look on Wade's face when he found out his father had everything to do with me leaving? Or was it the betrayal I felt to Daniel when my admission came out? He knew nothing of Wade and when I confessed somewhat to Wade, I felt like I was confessing something to Daniel too. He knew I had a high school boyfriend, but I just skimmed over it as if it wasn't important. The truth was, I couldn't handle reliving it. Now, I felt guilty for both Wade and Daniel. So I had to get out of the confines of this house, get a cup of coffee, and clear the mess that was my mind. I quickly did some light makeup, tossed on a red maxi dress, my beige Tory Burch sandals and packed up my laptop. I needed to do some kind of work, even if it wasn't for Glam and Simple. I'm allowed to handle one meeting tomorrow and then I am cut off. I have to do something. I don't know what yet, but I will think of it. I was off to get that coffee from Magnolia Gray's, a small cafe that opened my senior year. It's no Starbucks, but I remember enjoying it and as it turns out, Haven has WiFi now. Barely anything in the town has been updated except for a few boutiques and the local pool.

Now, I'm sitting outside of the cafe, in a blue and white wicker patio chair with an iced coffee and my laptop on a full battery as I try to brainstorm something to fill my time. I've already filled my Kindle with books I need to read, but I can't just do that for a month. So, here I am, out of the house and seemingly on display for the citizens of Haven to see. Fortunately, thanks to the hangovers, it's pretty quiet in town and I imagine I have a few hours of uninterrupted time. I actually feel a bit brave being out here, but I pretty much saw everyone and their mother last night, so I think I can handle sitting outside for a few hours. I scroll through my personal email which doesn't seem to be overwhelmed and practically drool over the Kate Spade and Uncommon James emails of new arrivals. This is another thing I can't 'only' do while I am here. I can't only shop. Although it would be easy. I haven't gone summer shopping, so I click on one of the links and add a belt with blue and red stripes to my bag.

"Everleigh Goode!" I hear a voice that makes my eyes cringe as I look up from my online shopping cart. Kasey Blair with her platinum Barbie blonde hair is stepping onto the sidewalk with almost-Barbie Price Canon following right behind her. I don't have a problem with too many people, but I do have an issue with Kasey and her minions. While it was never a situation where I was picked on, she did want to do a different kind of picking on Wade. Not that it matters now. "Well, Price. Look who we have here."

"Hello Kasey," I smile, leaning back in my chair and remembering my manners. She's wearing a Ralph Lauren collared dress and carrying a bag she surely bought at one of the boutiques. It's my style, but given my opinion of her, now I hate it. "Hi Price."

"Hey Evie," Price waves, sliding her sunglasses up onto her head as Kasey keeps hers on. She's always been sweet to me, but I don't get what she sees in Kasey other than they both have babies the same age now. "How are you?"

"Fine," I smile, reaching for my coffee.

"It's so nice to finally have you in town again," Kasey releases a Cheshire cat grin. "Isn't it, Price?"

"It is," she responds, eying Kasey.

"Wade never mentioned you were coming back, I thought that was something he would have told me." She babbled, before letting out a forced laugh. "I am going to have to get on him. You know men, they don't mention anything."

"Well, Wade wasn't aware that I was coming back for a visit," I comment, before taking a sip from the straw, keeping eye contact with Haven Barbie.

"Oh," she utters with defeat, before smiling again. "Well, Wade and I have been spending a lot of time together. He's quite the charmer."

"He's remodeled her bathroom and helped her with her pipes," Price states, before pushing her hair back and a look comes across her face that she feels maybe she shouldn't have said anything. "I mean...realigning some pipes for the remodel. He recommended a plumber. He didn't touch her pipes."

"I bet he did," I retort, feeling my own southern twang slip out. Internally I cringe at the idea of Wade being with Kasey. Not for another other reason than how pathetic and desperate she acted around him in high school. It's shameful, really.

"Oh, don't be jealous Everleigh," Kasey dismisses, holding

out her hand with a big sparkly rock. "I'm married to a man who owns a few ice cream shops around Alabama and a few outside. The best vanilla swirl on this side of the continental United States."

"Not jealous," I assure her, sitting the coffee back down on the table firmly. The liquid splashing up onto the lid, preventing any spills. "He's all yours. My pipes are fine."

"I'm sure they are," Kasey quips, flaring her nostrils. "Well, we won't disturb you anymore. Price and I just wanted to get a low-fat chai before our mommy group meets at her house. I'd invite you, but well...you're not a mom."

"Have a good day, Kasey," I force a smile, waiving my fingers at the two women in front of me. "You too Price."

"Bye Evie," Price smiles weakly, waving her hand again as Kasey just tosses up a hand and waves her fingers, before reaching for the iron black door handle and pulling it open. The girls disappear inside, but not before Price gives me one more apologetic smile. Not that she needed to, Kasey is a bitch. I knew that. It wasn't new information and she always had an eye for Wade and while we were never overtly nasty to each other. Wade was mine. Back then. She knew it, but my knowing it was all that mattered. I never fought too hard about it because Wade never made me feel like I needed to. It probably didn't help that I got into FIT in New York, but she didn't. She's clearly bitter.

It isn't long before the two girls from my past left the coffee shop and I was without interruption again. I have been staring at my laptop without doing much more than adding a few items to my shopping cart. Two belts, one handbag and some oversized sunglasses later, I still don't have any ideas. Not being able to do my job sucks because it's my hobby. It has consumed my life for the last four years and even a bit longer than that. I love the industry I work in, regardless of the assumptions that are made. When you tell someone that you work in the makeup and fragrance industry, you sort of get an eyeroll. What they don't realize is that there is chemistry and other difficult classes are involved. It wasn't easy, but after I left Haven, I threw myself into this world. I love it. I love everything about makeup products, but contrary to what some people would think, it isn't a job for airheads and bimbos. It actually takes business skills, hard work, and determination. It's why I make great money and am able to keep the apartment that Daniel and I shared together. It also helps that I got a lump sum from Daniel's family, asking me to go my own way after he died. I don't understand it, but I chalked it up to thinking I was a reminder of what they had lost. So I can't for the life of me figure out why I can't come up with a good idea to pass the time that also has to do with the job that fuels me. The one thing that has kept me going for the last four years.

I pick up my phone to see a text from Lexie asking me if I want to go out to a bar next week and tell her maybe. I say maybe, because if I say no right now, she'll just say something about how I need to let loose. I respond to a text from Kyra telling me she has a date with a guy named Kane tonight, and I remind her about her track record with guys whose name start with the letter K, and then respond to a text from Linda asking how I take my acai bowl. She's finally going to the place I have been telling her about for months. She then asks me if I prefer spinning class or Pilates since I do both. I tell her Pilates, but then she wants to know why I don't prefer spinning. I wonder how my boss thinks she will do without me in the office for all this time. It's not like I only do work stuff for her; she's a sucker for trying out things that I have suggested. She says I am her lifestyle guru, which is kind of amazing seeing as they spent a good amount of time last week telling me that I had no life. I finish up a text to Linda before putting my phone down to stare at the screen again. My coffee is almost gone, but I can get another. I just need something to fill my time here. Instead of trying again, I push the wicker chair back and go inside the shop to order another coffee. That only kills a few minutes before I push the door open and return outside to see Wade standing over my table, his hands on his hips. "Don't you know it's risky to just leave your things unattended. A laptop is expensive and easy to steal."

"It's Haven," I state, trying to remember if I have ever heard of any major theft. It wasn't exactly the crime capital of the world.

"It's common sense," he gripes, waving a finger to his head, a condescending reminder to use my brain. I don't recall his arrogance being such a strong trait when we were teenagers.

"What do you want?" I probe, pressing my lips together. He looks up at the sky for a moment, squinting at the sun before he looks back down at me with a wrinkled nose. "I want answers. To everything you started to say last night," he answers, adjusting his navy Boston Red Sox hat. He shifts on his feet, before leaning forward and closing my laptop, sliding it under his arm. "Come on."

"What are you doing?" I groan, trying to step forward with it, but he just turns his body a bit. "You're going to hold my laptop hostage?"

"You can have it back, but I want to talk," he replies, holding a hand up. "Let's go for a walk."

"Wade," I glare, before looking around the square. There still aren't a lot of people out around town and Wade is persistent. I said more than I wished I had said last night. It didn't mean I wanted to talk about it. I wanted nothing more than to leave it in the past and pretend it didn't happen, but then we got to talking again and I made the stupid choice to blurt out the part about his father and it was downhill from there. Now, he's staring at me and he won't stop coming to talk to me until he has those answers. "Did you come looking for me?"

"No, Evie," He shakes his head, before gesturing across the street to the hardware store. "I was coming to pick up a light fixture I ordered for my hallway. I saw you sitting out here before I went inside, and when I came out your stuff was unattended. So I figured I would watch it until you came out."

"Heroic," I roll my eyes, before taking a sip of my fresh coffee.

"Will you just go on a walk with me?" He requests again, but his body loosens up as if he's trying to make it sound more appealing and less like he's angry with me.

"I'm not carrying all this stuff on a walk," I gesture to my bag. It really isn't much to carry at all even with the laptop, but I'm not sure I could handle telling him anything else regarding our past. "Maybe another…"

"We can toss it in my Jeep, and I actually have more concern for your stuff so I'll lock the doors." He cuts me off, reaching for my bag and planner before turning to face the street. He waits for two old cars to pass by, before gesturing me over to him. "Jaywalk with me."

"Wade…" I stop and he looks back at me. He's not going to change his mind and I guess a walk can't hurt me. There is something about Wade and seeing the hurt in his face last night that makes it seem like the least I can do. It doesn't mean we're friends, but maybe I can at least feel better at some point about how I left things. He takes his sunglasses that are hanging off the blue t-shirt he's wearing and slides them onto his face. "Fine. Let's go."

"Very good," he nods, crossing the street and I follow him, stopping when we get to his car. He unlocks the car and slides my stuff on the passenger side floor, noticing my sunglasses hanging on my purse. He grabs them and holds them out to me. "You're going to want these."

"Thanks," I hesitate, before letting out a deep sigh. "At least my stuff will be in your car if I go missing and you've dropped my body somewhere."

"You should probably drop a piece of hair in my truck for good measure." He quips, winking at me as I slide my glasses on. "You know, for evidence."

"Let's just go, since you're a comedian," I remark, dropping my arms to my side and leaving him there as I walk onto the sidewalk in front of the hardware store, sliding my phone into my pocket. "I wouldn't want to take up too much of your time."

"I appreciate that," he replies, sarcastically. He locks his car, before putting the key fob in his pocket and joining me on the concrete. As I walk a few steps ahead of him, I can hear him take a few long strides to catch up with me, but he doesn't say anything right away. I'm thankful for that, because walking next to him doesn't seem so overwhelming in the silence. If anything, it feels familiar and almost light. As if there weren't mounds of frustration and anger between us. Maybe, it's the silence or maybe it's the weight of what happened last night. The idea that he knows a little bit of why I left. Maybe it was last night that took a little bit of the pressure off my chest. I don't feel like an elephant is sitting on my chest when I am around him. That doesn't last for long. "You're going to have to start giving me answers, Evie."

"I told you—" I begin to defend myself, but he stops me as he begins to speak a level louder than me.

"Evie, for the last time, cut the bullshit. It's me," he cuts me off, not letting me finish my sentence. We stop on the sidewalk and face each other. "I'm not asking for an apology or for you to feel bad about what happened. Believe it or not, I know better. I just want the truth. I deserve that much. Hell, I deserved to have a say in my own life."

"There isn't much else to it," I lie as I scuff my sandals

along the pavement to walk faster ahead of him. We're across the street from one of the state parks and I'm grateful we can at least walk there and not in front of everyone.

"Yes there is and you know it," Wade shuffles to catch up, lightly gripping my elbow. I get ready to yell at him, but then an oversized pickup truck zooms past us and I realize he was just stopping me from getting pummeled by a truck. "And try not to run into oncoming traffic, because people might assume I pushed you."

"You want to," I growl, as we step down onto the street and walk across the way to the park entrance which is towered by pine trees that have been growing for centuries. When we make our way across the street, we start walking side by side again, passing by the park sign. The park goes on and has another town on the side of it, but it's big enough to get lost in if you don't know where you're going.

"Can we start actually talking now?" He questions, rubbing his hands together nervously and I wonder if he's worried about what he might hear.

"Fine," I say, nervously looking ahead as we walk. For a few more minutes, we just walk along the path. I know he's waiting for me to say something, but I don't know that I can. Twelve years have come and gone with moments that have lived in my dreams, haunted me and also brought me some of the best moments of my life. Life isn't great without a little bit of pain, is it? "What do you want to know?"

"God, Ev," he stops, taking his baseball cap off and scratching at his eyes. I can see his hair is flattened under the cap, but he just puts it back on and moves his hands to his waist. "You said we didn't account for my father and that he was going to take the money for Boston."

"Then you know what happened," I counter as I try to turn back towards the entrance, but he grabs my elbow again. "You know, you're really going to have to stop doing that."

"That isn't the whole story and you know it," Wade argues, letting go of my arm and pointing towards a bench just a little bit further. We start walking again, the birds chirping up in the trees is the only real sound that surrounds us now. There aren't too many people walking the trails this morning, it seems. When we reach the bench, I sit first on one end, but he stays standing. I don't know if it's because he's nervous or just doesn't want to sit next to me. "Talk."

"Okay," I say defensively, twisting my fingers together as I avoid his gaze. I don't even know where to start, but somehow the words come. "A few weeks after you asked me to marry you, I was at your house one afternoon and you were in the shower and I had started to clean your room or something. I had found some dishes and I took them to the kitchen to clean up and your Dad came in and we started talking. He was talking, mostly."

I stop for a moment to try and read Wade, but he's just rubbing the back of his beck and staring down at the ground as I talk. A part of me feels like I might be sick and run out of here, but I can't. I know I can't. So I just begin again. "He um...started getting too close. Trying to kiss my shoulder and..."

"Evie." Wade stops, running his hands down his face. "Did my father... did he..."

I look at him strangely for a minute and then I know what he's asking. He's worried about what his father did to me. "No. He didn't. He tried to pull something a few times but he never... no. He um...I think me turning him down made him angry."

"Shit." He waves me on cautiously to keep speaking. "Talk."

"He wanted me to know that you would probably end up like him and I told him that he was wrong, that you were a better man than him." I explained, wanting to melt into the bench to get away from this moment. "Then he said he didn't think he could give you the money for college if we stayed engaged. He said I put your dream career at risk and when I asked why he said it was because he didn't think he could pay for college if you were with me. Something about insurance."

"Insurance?" He cocked an eyebrow, his face still stern as he watched me. "What did he mean by that?"

"No money, no Boston, which meant no career," I bit my lip, shaking my head as I pinch the bridge of my nose. I can practically smell Ridge Beckett and whatever brewery he crawled out of that day. "He said he was still a successful man and he had the power to take it away, basically. He said I complicate things. He felt you would get distracted and embarrass him. Wade…"

"How could you have stopped me from being successful?" He snaps as if he's asking me for the answers.

"I don't know, but he was ready to cut you off. To take everything financially supporting you," I mutter softly. "I complicated matters and if the money was taken away, he reminded me that I would be the reason you didn't get to go to college. He just wanted to make you miserable, Wade."

"What did you say to him?" Wade snaps, before I can even react, he raises his voice. "Evie, what did you say to him?"

"I told him no," I bit, acknowledging his volume before pressing my back into the bench. "I told him that we would find a way to make it work. We didn't need him. I thought that would make him snap out of it eventually. Or maybe when he was sober, he'd realize it was wrong."

"But he didn't?" His voice shifts, I don't know when it changed but he sounds like he wants to believe his father changed his mind. Like he wants to believe this isn't how it happened. This isn't how I left.

"No," I shake my head and bite at the edge of my thumbnail, a habit I had as a child that my mother worked so hard to groom me out of, but it's the only thing that stops my eyes from forming the tears it wants. I can't look at him anymore, because if I do, the tears will fall. Wade doesn't say a word, he just kind of stands there as if he's trying to think through everything. As if he's trying to decide what to believe and playing out our past, looking for something.

"You could have told me," he interrupts the silence and I look up at him, dropping my hand to my lap. He rubs at his facial hair for a moment, before dropping his hands as something clicks in his mind. "You...fuck."

"What?" I ask nervously, his hands moving to the back of his head. He just keeps cursing to himself as he takes a few steps away from me and doesn't look at me. I look back down at the fabric of my dress, finding a small imperfection of thread that has lifted and focus on that. I don't know what is worse, the fact that he finally knows or the fact that I have finally said it out loud to him. Telling Lexie had been a relief, but then she kept pleading for me to tell him. I wasn't going to. It could have died with me, but then somehow, he was able to get me to tell him and I'm not sure when it happened, because I was pretty sure we were only yelling at each other. "It's fucked up, I know."

"That morning when I woke up and you were gone...fuck. That is what that was about." He starts to talk, but then just trails off. Then he swiftly turns around. "You tried to do something the night before. You begged me to just leave. You wanted to run away together. You knew..."

"What?" He looks as if he's seen a ghost for a moment, an empty stare comes across his face as he tries to think back on that night. "Wade."

"After we saw my Dad...in the kitchen...you went into my room and started begging me to leave with you. Is that why? You thought that was the only way?"

"It was the only way," I shrug, my eyes burning.

"Bullshit, Ev! It wasn't the only way and you know it! I would have left with you in a second if I knew why," he snapped, poking at his chest, his face turning red. "I would have packed my shit up and gone in a second, but instead you made a choice for the both of us!"

"You would have resented me!" I argued, before quickly lowering my voice as a man I didn't recognize jogged right by us. "Wade, I asked you if you wanted that more than anything in the world and you said something along the lines of next to me it was what you wanted most."

"You came first!" He claimed, before dropping his hands to his side and looking around to make sure he wasn't making a scene. "Ev...you always came first."

"But I would have been the one thing holding you back from designing the homes and the program in Boston. Boston meant so much," I reminded him, toying with the Stella and Dot bangles on my wrist, twisting them every which way. "When you said that I was the only thing more important, I knew I couldn't be the reason. I knew that I was going to have to leave, because neither one of us would have been happy in the long term. I did what I had to do."

"Don't throw that shit at me, okay? You did what you wanted and made a decision for me. It should have been my choice, and *you* would have been my choice!"

"Excuse me, but did you think this was easy for me?" I begin to fume, my face getting warm as I push myself up from the bench. "Did you think I wanted to end anything with you? Do you think sneaking away and not telling you, ignoring every call, text, email, or visit? Do you think there weren't a million times that I didn't want to just tell you everything? Wade, we both had dreams and if those hadn't come true, you know for a fact that we wouldn't have been okay with that. Boston was the program you fought to get into."

"There were other programs," he argues, waving me off as if he's done with me, but then he just keeps speaking. "Do you think that I wouldn't have been willing to take the long way around to get to where I wanted to be. You may have felt I would have resented you, but I had a right to know what was going on and what those risks were. It was my father making demands of *me*. You had no right to keep that from me. What he did to you and what he threatened...it doesn't matter. It would have been you. I would have picked you and taken the long way to my career. Do you think that would have meant more to me than you? Do you think I would have regretted you for a second? No Everleigh, because you were who I planned on spending the rest of my life with. Instead, you wrecked my life! You made a choice for me that impacted me much longer than it impacted you!"

"There you go again, just assuming this was easy for me to do. Like it didn't destroy me." I bark, clenching my jaw. We stop again, as an older man runs by us. The moment he gets far enough away, I go in again, this time with no regard for anyone that can hear me. "I was miserable! I was ill over it! So don't sit here and act like you were the only one who was hurting or that I just ended it, because I wanted to. It ruined me."

"It ruined you? Great, because even after years of not knowing, imagine how I feel when I find out my ex-girlfriend was practically violated by my father and made a choice that she deemed right for me." He states angrily, a vein in his neck straining as he steps forward. I've never seen Wade so angry. "And in the end, it wasn't the choice I wanted."

"But you wanted the career you have now and I would have been the only thing standing in the way of that!" I protest, throwing my hands in the air. "You know yourself, that Boston was the dream. When I asked you that night, I knew I couldn't do anything else. I had to let you have that. That is what you wanted most. That is what you wanted..."

"You were the only thing I wanted!" He snaps, before letting out a tired sigh and running a hand through his hair.

"Shit Ev...none of it meant anything without you. I wanted a career, but the moment you were mine...none of it meant anything without you. It was just a job. You were what I wanted. I could be flipping burgers or working in a bank...that wasn't what was important."

"I'm sorry!" I concede, throwing my hands up. I don't know what else to say or do. I don't think if I could do something, that it would fix the pain I have caused. "I tried to find a way out and I tried to get you to run away with me, but you didn't listen!"

"I thought you were just nervous!" He argues. "Like anyone would be in our situation, you didn't tell me the real reason why! If I had known, I would have chosen you."

"When I realized how much it meant to you...I couldn't do it. I couldn't make you give it all up so I did the only thing I knew I could do. Did you think I would have been able to just break up with you? To look you in the eyes and lie and say I didn't love you or that I didn't want to marry you? Wade, I couldn't. So I left, because that's the only way I could do this and have a shot at surviving," I admitted, pushing my hair back behind my ears as I struggled with him knowing the truth now. Now he looks hurt, but still angry. As if he wishes some of what I said, could be put back in the chest that held the truth. "I made it a point to not ask how you were when I spoke to my family, because I couldn't handle it. For twelve whole years, I was miserable over it."

"But you were able to move on, weren't you?" Wade prodded as he acknowledged Daniel for the first time since our last fight that his name came up in, but this time there is a bite to his tone, one that seems like he's trying to make a point. A point I realize I don't want to address. "It wasn't too hard."

"No." I shake my head, my breath heavy as I realize his anger is shifting. I should have expected this anger to shift. "Don't make this about him."

"I'm not making it about him," Wade insists, almost out of breath from all of the shouting before waving his hand at me. "I'm making it about you."

"I think we're done here," I decide, standing firmly in place as he begins to shake his head and laugh. For a moment the laugh reminds me of him, but when he was younger. When he was my world. I don't know what is going on in his mind anymore, I used to be able to read him, but now he's a mystery to me. Now, he's taking a few steps away, walking towards the forest as he mumbles something, but I can't make it out. "What was that?"

"Of course, we're done here," he chuckles dryly, throwing his hands up in the air before marching right back to me. "Because you always get to decide. You decided when our engagement was over, when any of our fights are over. Let me ask you this. Do you always make decisions for everyone else or is it just me? What about Daniel? Did you make decisions for him or was I just special?"

"You're an ass!" I shout as I purse my lips, raising my hand, bringing it down hard enough against his face to feel the burn I put on his cheek. I fight through the instinct to grasp my hand and acknowledge the pain I feel as he puts a hand on his face. He examines his hand for a moment afterwards as if he's checking to see if he's bleeding. "Don't ever bring him up! Say what you want about me, be mad at me. Don't talk about him, ever!"

Instead of saying anything arrogant or yelling at me for slapping him, he just drops his hands to his side, letting out a tired sigh. His face doesn't look angry anymore. He actually looks a bit sad. Maybe it's the damage to his pride. Maybe it's the realization that what he said wasn't right. That it was mean and ugly. It doesn't matter. Not to me. I just don't want to be here anymore. I 've told him what happened and I don't need to say another word. Before I can keep walking, he opens his mouth. "Evie, I deserved that."

"Yeah, you did," I agree, dropping my arms to my side, rubbing my fingers together nervously. I glance around the area nervously, praying there wasn't anyone that saw me slap him. It doesn't look like there was anyone in the direct vicinity and I'm grateful. The last thing I need is the town gossiping about an argument with Wade that got out of hand and I managed to slap him. Even if he did deserve it. Now though, we're just standing in front of each other and I can't make eye contact with him. I'm too angry, too upset. Angry and upset with myself. Angry at him for bringing Daniel up.

"Ev..." He begins to say my name in the quietest his voice has been since before we entered the park, but I can't stand to hear it.

"No," I say quickly, shaking my head once, before turning away from him. I march quickly, biting back the tears that threaten to fall. The anger and the hurt that we both feel, stretching the distance between our bodies. As the distance grows, the tears finally fall again and I feel a mix of disgust with myself and pain for the three people involved in this moment.

"It wasn't easy to get over you, Everleigh," he announces as I stop, frozen by his words. I squeeze my eyes closed, trying to ignore my name on his lips. "I'm angry because...hell I don't even know now. Except, I know one thing. You leaving was the worst thing to ever happen to me. I don't care if I sound weak for admitting it and I know it doesn't matter, but you leaving...it ruined me. I just wish you would have told me. I wish I had known, because I would have chosen you and I wouldn't have resented you. I knew it when you came to me that night, begging me to leave. I knew even if we had run away, we still would have made our own dreams come true, even if it took longer. I would have rather done that with you. The money, Boston...I would have picked you. I just want you to know that. It was a long time ago and I just thought you were nervous, but that's one thing I can tell you. If I had known the truth, it would have been a no brainer. It would have been easy. It would have been you. No questions. No regrets. Just you."

The first tear that successfully makes it down my hollow cheek feels like fire on ice. It could make me shatter until a million little delicate pieces at any moment, unable to reassemble myself. Unable to be reassembled at all. He doesn't call out for me; he lets me be. We're just two people with the past out in the open with no way to split the blame. It was all me and I know it. I chose to use my power for him, for what I believe was good. Boston came and went; New York did the same for me. We have the lives we wanted, mostly. We're simply two people who once saw the other as their whole world, now strangers. Two angry strangers with nothing but now settled dust between us. Alone.

Chapter Eleven

Now

Wade

I fucked up. I may be a hard headed dumbass, sometimes oblivious and a lot arrogant, but this was nothing other than me being a complete dick. Evie was once my whole world and then she wasn't. I spent time getting over her then agreeing with myself that if I ever saw her, I would be the 'better' person. I had spent so much time figuring I would never come face to face with her, that when I did, I found a way to make it worse. Then in a split second I made sure she'd never want anything to do with me ever again. Not that I blame her and not that I ever thought things would change between us with the way they are now. Things now are ugly and hell, I don't know what this is. Maybe I didn't deserve what she did twelve years ago, but I deserved that slap in the face. Not that it hurt, it actually didn't hurt that bad, but telling her that would have likely earned me a kick in the balls and that would have led to some pain. No matter what had happened between us, I never should have made that last comment about her dead fiancé. Shit. I never met the man and when I first found out she was seeing someone, I wanted to punch his head in. Even though I had moved on by all accounts, it felt wrong. It felt like she was still mine and he had no place during all that time. I kept it to myself, telling nobody else that I was feeling that way, because I had gone on to assure them that I was over her. But then when I found out he had died, I felt sorry for her. No matter how mad I was, I would never wish death on anyone. It still meant she was hurting and that was an unbearable thought which led to a pinch in my chest. Which made what I said a real dick move. She told me why she did what she did and after all of these years, I should have just shut up and accepted it. She had been hurt by this too. Instead, I ridiculed her for it, mocked her, and made a dig at a man who isn't even alive to defend himself. It was low. My father is dead, but he should have taken the brunt of my anger. So last night, I came home and paced around my house, wanting to kick my own ass, only stopping to drink from my whiskey glass. This morning I paid the price of my intake. I met with Forest and Nancy about the addition to their house, settled on plans all while feeling like I was going to die right there at their kitchen table. I think they knew it too, because Nancy kept trying to fry me up some breakfast and Forest was pushing the coffee on me. Thank god they know me, otherwise I am sure I would have discouraged them somehow from doing business with me. Forest just kept chuckling every time I looked a bit green.

    The rest of my day has been filled with errands for the business and checking on one of my sites right outside of town. I have a great group of guys who work for me and do amazing work. The best part is, I can trust them on our job sites while I handle other business. Still, when I visit a site, I put myself to work. I can't wait to get home and shower and maybe—just maybe—unwind for the day.

    I have a text on my phone from Dawson asking if I want

to go for some drinks, but I'm not in the mood. There is another text from Kasey Blair asking if I could help her measure for shelving and that definitely is not something I want to do. I hate to admit it, but I think Kasey is looking for something more from me. I'm dumb apparently when it comes to Evie, but with Kasey I know what she's doing. She's been doing it since high school and since Evie arrived in Haven, I've been getting three times the number of texts and calls. I mean, she has a husband. I'm not really looking to make trouble with her. We had a brief close encounter a few years after Evie left and I shut it down quick. I didn't sleep with her, but I felt guilty about how far we did go. Evie was gone and I was still worried somehow she would find out. I wasn't wrong to do what I did then, but thinking back I wonder why it filled me with guilt. For so long that girl had a hold on me and after yesterday, I think she still might. Hell, I think I know she still does. She had a right to slap me for what I said about him. About the other man she gave her heart to. She had a right to be hurt.

I also have a right to be angry with her, but her words about my father keep replaying in my head. What he did to her, what he said. I have so many questions that I don't want the answers to. He put his hands on her, threatened her. I didn't need to know anything else. Where we were now, didn't matter. Knowing she was put in any position to be scared fueled me with rage. I knew what he was capable of. I'd seen the way he looked at her sometimes, like she was a piece of meat at the butcher and I ignored it. He was a pig. I knew my father well and while we mended a lot of our broken fence in the last year of his life, that man could do a lot of damage. She didn't say everything I am sure he said. His words were often ugly and insulting. He would call me names, push me around and claim my head was in the clouds when it came to her. I can only imagine the seething distaste that came from his mouth. Words I would have never wanted her to hear. Words that would scare an innocent girl away.

This Jeep is too small for me right now, as I stop at the last red light right before Haven. I roll the windows down, trying to let in any extra air I can. I'm angry at my father, for getting to her. I had a right to know, so I'm angry at her for making a choice for me. I was perfectly capable of making the choice myself. It should have been my choice. Not hers. He should have threatened me. Not her. It should have never been up to her and he knew that. He knew what he was doing. He knew the choice I would have made. Knowing this is where we are, because of him makes me angry. I slap my hands down on the steering wheel, stopping as another car pulls up to the light next to me. Thank God for the green light that comes, because I press my foot on the gas and speed through the stop sign only to have to put my breaks on quickly for someone that is moving too slow. When I do stop in time, my empty leather work belt flies into the floor and I look down instinctively. "Shit."

The laptop and bag. The things I offered for her to put in my truck so that she would agree to go on a walk with me. Her watered down and melted iced coffee in the cup holder. I had been too busy to really take notice of it before, but leave her to find a way to make my mind return to her even when I don't want it to. I let out a tired groan before I quickly check my side mirror and switch lanes, ignoring whoever blared their car horn at me. I make the turn down the road the Goodes live off of just in time, speeding down the road before I have the idea to slow down and stop on the side of the road. It's her bag. The contents of her life are in this bag. At least that's how it used to be. I open up the white purse, unsure of where to start or why I am even looking in the first place. There is a smaller green leather bag that I unzip, it's just a lot of makeup and maybe a small bottle of perfume. Then there is her planner, I open it but it's just dates and stuff about meetings. There is a packaged tampon. I quickly drop that back in and see that it lands on a small white satchel. For a moment, I leave it there as it's too small, but then I grab it. It's made of velvet, tied tightly so you can't just slide your fingers to see if there is anything in it. I feel on the fabric, there is something round and hard in it. There is something else I can't quite make the feel out of. There is something else in there; I think it's paper. That's when I quickly loosen the attached strings, opening the back up and pulling one of the contents out on my hand, my heart stopping. It's her grandmother's engagement ring. The ring I gave her when I proposed. The ring she held onto for comfort in the weeks leading up to her leaving, the ring that made her think of me. My heart is pounding, thinking maybe she brought it back to return to her mother, but when I pull the other item out, I know that isn't true. It's a cognac leather bracelet that belonged to me and the first item I ever gave her as her boyfriend. We were inseparable and one day between classes in school, she stuck out her bottom lip and said she'd missed me. I carelessly and quickly kissed her, giving her this wrap around bracelet I had on my wrist. It's in this bag. With the ring I gave her. A symbol of the love I gave her. I look in the back and pull out a folded-up piece of white paper, wrinkles all over it as I unfold it. It's a white envelope, but my name is written right on the front. I slide my finger under a lifted piece of seam, but stop myself. I don't know what I think is in this envelope. It has my name on it, so maybe at one point or another, I was supposed to read it. Maybe I am supposed to read it now. I start to reach for the open flap, but an aggravating feeling of guilt comes over me again. Reading this behind her back isn't going to help a damn thing. Especially when I take it back to her and she sees I have opened it. I carefully trace the wrinkles with my finger, before urging the envelope folded the way it was before, slid it into the little satchel and slid the delicate pieces in there too. I return it to the purse and toss it back on the floor. It's not doing me any good to look through a purse and I'm pretty sure I learned back in high school not to look through a woman's purse. I learned that lesson from Ev in a much more relaxed circumstance. I'm confused. Not sure why she has it in the bag. Is she returning it? Has she been carrying it? Hell, it doesn't matter. I just get so frustrated, I punch the wheel of the car again, much harder this time and wince at the pain that sears through my wrist. I definitely hit the wheel too hard this time and I know added on from the residual hangover I feel, I'm going to regret this too. "Shit."

After waiting for a few minutes, I finally put the Jeep in drive and make the way down the two-lane country road again, driving at a much more reasonable speed. I'm still angry, but I don't have it in me to drive with the rage I had before. I have so many more questions, but this damn bag is cutting off the air in this vehicle, so the moment I see the mailbox that is at the end of the driveway, I turn probably too quickly, narrowly missing it. The driveway to the Goode family home is long, but when I make it to the top, I see Forest on the front porch, writing in a small book. It's probably one of his crossword puzzle books. I stop just short of the garage area on the side of the home so he sees me, hopping out and closing the door swiftly behind me.

"Hello there, Wade," Forest looks up, waving his pin. "Seven letter word for an illegal baseball pitch?"

"Spitter." I answer quickly and he chuckles sheepishly, waving his book. "Where is Evie?"

"Backyard with Levi and Lex." He gestures, before he begins to write in the crossword. I nod appreciatively, and make my way around to the passenger side to retrieve the purse and laptop. As I pick it up and close the door, I'm fully aware again of how much it smells like her. Even though it's been a long time, she still smells the same to me. It isn't perfume, it's her. I don't know how crazy it sounds, but I hold the handle in my sore hand, ignoring the pain in my wrist that I am pretty sure is swelling up and put the laptop in my other hand. I hear Levi laugh just as I come around the back and see him running with a squirt gun away from the patio. Lexie is sitting on one of the wicker benches, a magazine in her lap with a glass of wine, but I don't see Evie.

"Wade!" Levi shouts, dropping the squirt gun and running towards me. "Wanna shoot the gun with me? I have another in the garage and it shoots really far!"

"Not now, bud," I smile, patting him on the shoulder. "Maybe next time."

"Levi, why don't you go get ready for your shower?" Lexie straightens up, closing the magazine and discarding it to the side.

"But it's still light out," Levi wines, pointing up at darkening sky. He wasn't wrong.

"But if you want to watch Iron Man before bed, you have to have a shower first." She reminds him , before her eyes change and I frown. Whatever look she just gave Levi was some sort of magic, because his shoulders drop in surrender.

"Sorry, Wade," Levi bleated, shaking his arms out dramatically. "I have to go! Mom told me earlier, I could watch a whole movie!"

"Well, you better go," I laugh weakly as Levi takes off for the house and leaves me there on the patio with Lexie.

"Nice purse," she points to my hand with a smirk on her face. "Not really your color, though."

"Funny," I respond dryly, giving her a weak nod. "Evie left her purse in my car. Can I leave it with you?"

"Because you don't want to give it to her yourself?" She guesses. Before I can answer or step forward to give her the bag and run, the back door opens. Evie is in the doorway, her dark hair flipping as she looks down, to check something behind her before she steps out. Her long pale legs are shown off by the short black one-piece outfit she's wearing. I'm sure there is some sort of fashion term for an outfit that appears to be one piece of fabric, but has shorts to it, but it looks good on her. The woman has had legs for days ever since I have known her and I've never stopped noticing. Lexie must see me looking, because she gives off an obvious throat clearing noise which forces Evie to look up.

"Sorry Lex, I was having issues getting the bottle open but..." Evie stops as she closes the door behind her, her own shoulders falling as she realizes I am here. She wants to duck back inside. I can tell. Except now she has mine and Lexie's eyes on her and she isn't quite sure what to make of it. "Wade."

"Wade wanted to return your things. Not sure about how he got those," Lexie smirks suspiciously and stands up, before turning around and reaching for her wine and phone. "We can talk about that later."

"You don't need to go anywhere, Lexie," I assure her, my eyes still on Evie who is nervously ringing her fingers together, looking between the two of us. She doesn't make eye contact, but she doesn't look angry. She looks nervous. "I was just going to drop these off."

"No no," Lexie says quickly, walking over to Evie and nudging her in the arm, "I need to go check on Levi anyways. You two should probably talk."

"We've already spoken. He said what he needed to say" Evie offers up nervously, before looking down at her hands then back up at me. "Unless..."

"Actually, we should talk," I assert, before looking away from Evie for a moment. Her narrow brows give away just how uncomfortable she is and for a moment I fear she's going to reject me, so I just look at Lexie, my eyes pleading with her.

"I'll leave you two," Lexie says, before quickly rushing up

the steps and into the back door of the home. I don't know if that is what I had in mind, but now I am here alone with Evie who isn't running. She isn't leaving. At least not yet. Not that I wouldn't expect her to. She didn't deserve what I said to her and that just keeps repeating itself in my head as she stands here looking nervous. I was a dick and as I look at her, I feel worse about it and the throbbing wrist I have feels like a bitter payback for that. The door to the house is closed, but Evie looks nervously back at it.

"I know you want to leave me out here," I announce, before holding out her purse and laptop. She doesn't say anything, she just gently takes them from my hand, frowning as she looks down at how close our hands are.

"Your wrist is swollen and red," she observes, before quickly placing the items on the nearby patio set.

"Yeah, it's nothing," I lie, discarding the pain as I slid my hand over my facial hair, letting out a deep sigh. She just crosses her arms, eying me cautiously. "Listen, Ev. I don't want to fight with you."

"Wade, you've said that." She starts, her thin fingers combing through her hair.

"Stop," I put my hands up, shaking my head before I let her continue. "I know I have said that and every time before, we end up yelling and not talking and I end up being a complete dick. I've had a right to be angry with you, but what I said about...I said some things that were wrong. I said things because of how I felt about what happened. Just because I felt that way, doesn't mean it was fair. Not to you. Those things were in my car and I wanted to bring them back. I also want to apologize. I wasn't the only one this situation hurt. I didn't think how it could have hurt you too. I didn't think about a lot of things."

I stop for a moment, but she doesn't say anything. She just shifts nervously on her feet, tapping her hands together. It's a nervous habit she's had her whole life and for a moment, I see the young girl I could look at for hours. She wants to say something, but she doesn't. I don't think she knows how to start or maybe she doesn't know what to say. Maybe she's too nervous around me, which hits right in the gut. No matter how mad at her I am or was, I don't like her feeling that she's not comfortable around me. I'm realizing how wrong it seems. It's not like I have made it easy for her either. "Evie, I'm sorry. You didn't deserve a lot of the things I have said the last week. I've been feeling bad about how I treated you, but before today I didn't really bother to think about anyone's feelings other than my own."

I wish I could read her mind as she slides one of her hands into her back pockets and she lowers her eyebrows. She's right in front of me and nowhere close at the same time. I don't know what is going on in her head or mine for that matter. She's watching me and then a frown comes across her face. "What happened to your hand?"

"What?" I frown and her hand gestures to my wrist. I know what she's talking about, but I didn't realize I was clutching my hand, because of how much it hurts. It's actually quite swollen now and I know I can't say, I punched the steering wheel with my wrist, because of her. "Oh, I just hit it at a site today. It's fine."

She eyes me, her face turning suspicious. She looks at her purse for a moment and her shoulder's drop. I look away from her quickly, so that when she glances back, our eyes don't meet. I don't know what she's thinking. I wish I knew what went on in her mind. Then, before I can wonder any longer, she calmly says, "Come on."

"Come where?" I frown, looking back at her as she holds her wine glass in one hand and begins to walk towards the back door. I watch her as she stops and looks back at me.

"Inside," She gestures, before stopping because she notices that I am hesitant to follow. "Your hand needs fixed up, or do you want it to get worse?"

"Oh," I frown, looking around. I don't know if I was looking for someone to confirm what she said, but we're alone out here. She begins walking up the steps again to the back door and I finally follow, watching the way her legs bend with every step. I push my hand on the door as we walk into the house I've been in a million times. Somehow, it feels different with her here. It's been so long since I've walked in the door with her right there walking with me. I look around, for traces that she's been here. Everything is normal, except she's in this kitchen. "Where is your mother?"

"At some town group. Honestly, I think they're just all gossiping about Hannah Mayfield. Apparently she moved to Ohio and got pregnant by some business man who already has a wife." She responds, her voice a bit casual as she opens the freezer and pulls out an ice pack. I swear I hear a hint of Bama in her voice. I guess she has sounded more like a city girl to me and I hadn't noticed if any of her old twang was there. She grabs a dish towel off the stove and wraps it up, before handing it to me. "Put that on your wrist. For the swelling. Twenty on, twenty off. When you go home, you can just put some ice in a Ziploc bag."

"Thanks," I say, taking the icy cold block from her and wincing as I touch it to my hand. I look up to catch her staring at my wrist, but when she knows I have spotted her, she walks to another cabinet.

"So you just hit it somehow at a work site?" She asks, her voice suspicious as she reaches for a bottle of Tylenol. I don't say anything for a moment as she opens the bottle, dosing two of them out and handing them to me, before walking to the refrigerator.

"Yeah, on a steering wheel at the site," I answer, stammering to come up with a story that doesn't have to do with her. She looks at me for a minute and smiles, as if she's unsure of how that would happen. I clear my throat and nod, holding the ice pack up. "Thanks for this."

"It's nothing," she breathes, twisting open a water bottle and handing it to me. I put the pills in my mouth, before taking a swig of the water. She's turned to the counters, digging through one of the side drawers. I'm silent watching as she searches through the drawers, before going to a cabinet under the sink and she pulls out a metal box with a red cross on it. "Here it is."

"What is that?" I frown as she sits it on the counter, opening it up and searching in the box.

"We should wrap your hand, something for compression to help it heal up. If it gets worse you might need to go see a doctor," she states, retrieving a bandage and pushing the box away. I just look at her, my mind frozen as she steps closer. She must catch me staring, because she looks up nervously. "What?"

"Nothing," I comment, glancing away. She's not comfortable right now, but I can tell she's trying. She doesn't make eye contact with me as she takes my hand, laying it down in front of her on the counter as she begins unrolling the bandage. I'm staring and I know she can feel my eyes on her, but it's like seeing a ghost. I haven't taken much time since she's been here to just watch her. To see if I see that person I knew. She's focused as she lifts my hand and her skin feels warm against mine, but she just tightly wraps the fabric around my hand. "Did they teach you first aid in fashion school?"

"That summer I went to camp. In Oklahoma? I had to work a couple day in the medical cabin." She corrects me, before firmly pressing the bandage into place and letting go, before resting her hands on the counter. She bites her lip, moving nervously, but then stops. "You knew that."

"I forgot. It was so long ago." I recall as she closes the first aid box before walking to put it back where she found it. She turns back around, before dropping her hands onto the end of the counter. When our eyes meet again, I shift in my seat, unsure of what to do next. "So uh...thanks for taking care of my hand."

"You should probably take it easy on that hand for a day or two," she advises, before reaching for a dishcloth that has been discarded on the counter. She immediately begins picking it up and folding it, focusing on the fabric as I watch her. She has something on her mind, but I don't know if she has anything to say about it. Eventually she just shakes her head and starts to speak. "Just so it doesn't get worse."

"Yeah, I will," I agree, knowing full well that I may not sit too still. I struggle with that once I arrive on the site of a project and love to get my hands dirty. Then again, I didn't really hurt my hand at a project site. I got hurt because she was on my mind. She has filled my brain since the moment she marched back into Haven with her high heels and perfect legs. Getting hurt at work is a harmless lie I've told to keep from her that she's why I hit the wheel. I slide my hand off the counter and take the ice pack back to the freezer. I won't leave the house with it, because I know I won't remember to bring it back.

"Just have Kasey or whoever check on it," she shrugs, before looking up at me.

"Kasey?" I frown, looking back at her. She's got one hand on her hip as she bites her lip back. "There isn't a Kasey or whoever in my life. I'm single."

"Oh," she utters as she looks down at her hands. "I wasn't exactly sure and Kasey mentioned that you have been seeing a lot of each other."

"Kasey is the same as she was in high school," I roll my

eyes, stepping forward for a moment. "Desperate for attention and apparently still jealous of you if she felt the need to bring it up."

"Not sure about her being jealous," Evie murmurs, dropping her hands.

"I think she might be," I wink, even though I want to kick myself for it after. I feel the urge to tell her that I am single, that there has never been a steady girl in my life since her. That I have sworn that concept off from my life. I'm not with anyone. At all. Regardless, she seems to know it's not her business, because she looks more nervous than the moment she was helping me wrap my hand. "Thanks for my hand."

"Of course," she smiles weakly as if she's trying to remember something. I want to ask her what is on her mind, but I don't want to ruin this interaction. I don't want to force us into fighting or yelling, because having even one moment with her where we aren't hating each other, feels familiar. "Thank you for bringing my stuff back."

"No problem," I shrug, following her to the door. As I watch her walk, she seems so much smaller than I remember. Maybe I'm noticing more today, because she's just wearing flip flops and isn't standing in high heels, but she feels so much smaller when we're this close. I think about giving her a hug, but then I remember everything that we've been through and how I don't know how to read her anymore and decide not to try, although I am curious what it would feel like. "I'll see you around."

"See you around," she smiles, before opening the door. I brush past her, for a moment I think her hand comes close to grazing my arm, but it hasn't. Her touch was electric and maybe it wasn't anymore, but I felt the warmth of her skin being near mine. I get to the bottom of the stairs when I hear her. "Wade?"

"Yeah?" I turn to look up at her, one of her hands moving to her back.

"You um...you didn't like...go through my purse, did you?" She quizzes, shrugging her shoulders, and for a second I see a bit of fear. "I mean..."

"No," I deny, shaking my head. I see a bit of relief wash over her face and she smiles again. "Why? Should I have?"

"No," She responds quickly and maybe she doesn't know that I can tell, but she's thinking. "You know, New York isn't the kind of place that you can just leave your purse. The chances of someone returning it are one in a million. Not that it's a bad place, it's just a lot more people."

"Yeah, well you're not in Manhattan anymore, Dorothy," I smirk, and she rolls her eyes before I slide my hands into my jean pockets and head back to my car. She plays it off like she's annoyed at the tease, but it's the first time I have truly seen one of those smiles that used to make me forget all reason. Just a hint of the girl I knew when I was young. I turn away quickly and begin walking to my car. I don't want to look back, because the look on her face has probably faded away and for one second, I want her to be the girl I remember. The girl who took care of my wounded hand was a little bit like the girl I was once madly in love with. The girl with a smile to make me break every rule. Even if that girl is a distant memory, I realize just by living it that, I would give anything to see that smile again.

Chapter Twelve

Now

Wade

It's been a hell of a day. Between a gas leak at one of my job sites that put us behind an already tight timeline and the constant inconvenience of Evie crossing my mind, I was exhausted. I want nothing more than to watch television and head off to my bed, but Dawson asked me over to catch the baseball game and have some pizza. I was going to say no, but honestly if I went home my mind would wander before I went to bed and that wasn't any good either. There were a million reasons why I needed my mind focused on something else and my ex-girlfriend just happened to be one of them. My hand has been doing better, not as swollen, but I have a nasty bruise from where my hand met the steering wheel. A few people asked about it and I blamed it on a construction job around my house. I just put up some shelving in my downstairs bathroom, so it came to my mind quickly and ended any questions I got about it. The truth was, I had been an idiot to punch my steering wheel, but a bigger idiot for being such a dick to Ev. Then when she saw it and I blamed it on work, she very quietly stepped in to take care of it. Forgetting everything to try and prevent it from getting worse. In her parent's kitchen, she went into action and it was the closest and calmest either of us had been since she left Haven.

I didn't hate her skin touching my skin. In fact, I think I crave it again. The way her fingers worked to inspect the bruising from where I was swelling and the way her hair smelled as she bent her head over my hand. All the things that, deep down, I was wondering were answered. I want to kick myself and talk myself down from it. Down from wanting to see her again, down from wanting to know if just for a moment things could be the way they were before. I want to kick my own ass and I know in order to get this sorted out I need to say something, but I don't know if it's the right time. I'm not one to open up and share my feelings, but when I do it is to Dawson. It's kind of an unspoken thing between the two of us that if we need to talk, the other is there to listen. We've seen each other through our worst and he knows the most about my history with Evie. He also has his own opinions, and I am not sure I can change his mind.

"Want any more wings?" Dawson interrupts my thoughts and I look up as he holds a narrow white Styrofoam box up.

"No, I'm good," I decline, turning my head back to the game as the announcers inform everyone that there is a weather delay. "This game isn't going to be over anytime soon. I'll have to catch the rest at home."

"Fair enough," Dawson reaches for a wing, sitting the rest of the box down on the same coffee table he has had since college. Even with a successful career, he lives like a frat boy. I look back to the television, watching as a team of guys bring a tarp onto the field, quickly covering the diamond the best as they can. "Hey, did you hear about—"

"Evie Goode is messing with my head." I blurt out abruptly

as I jump up from my seat, my hands moving to my hips. I'm in just as much shock as Dawson as I realize the words escaped my subconscious. I just knew I liked being around her, no matter how mad she made me. "And I think she's one of the most difficult people I have ever met and there is absolutely no reason why I should even be thinking about her, but her hair smells so good."

Dawson sits back, dropping the wipe that he used to clean his fingers on the dirtied paper plate in front of him as his jaw falls a bit and he leans back. "Shit."

"Yeah, I know." My finger slides into my belt loop as I begin to pace and I don't know whether I should just start talking. All of my anger towards Evie is all twisted and I'm not sure why I can't get her out of my head other than I must still have some sort of emotional connection to her that I never let go of. That's beyond humiliating enough.

"You do realize she was your fiancée and then just one day decided to ignore you for twelve years," he relies as casually as possible. "I mean that's crazy. She's hot, so I get it, but you dodged a bullet."

"Yeah?" I query, before turning around. "What if I told you everything I know now? That maybe I had a reason to not be mad at her and to have to rethink everything about the last twelve years? Even for me, it's a little weird."

"What the hell does that mean?" He probe's crossing his arms and leaning back into the couch. "She ripped your life apart."

"My father ripped my life apart, Dawson," I say with a tired sigh, realizing I don't feel angry at anyone except my father and maybe myself. Regardless of how my relationship had improved with my father before he died, he tore the life I had apart. He knew what he was doing and he knew it would lead me down a road of hell. "He was behind all of it!"

"What?" Dawson stopped, turning his head towards me. "What does Ridge have to do with it?"

"He put her in a position where she felt she had no other choice. He used everything he was going to pay for, my entire future, as a threat to her," I explain, clenching my jaw at just the thought of Evie dealing with that. I was so protective of her and I couldn't have saved her from Ridge. "The rest of the story doesn't matter. He did this. He used her and made her scared."

"Scared?" Dawson looks at me, shaking his head a little. "Run far away from here scared? It's Evie…"

"He was going to take away Boston, my car, my tuition…" I start, massaging my wrist that had been in pain, but then her fingers touched and I felt some sort of relief. Dawson would mock me if I told him that I think being close to her has healing powers. I want to mock myself, until I want to be angry again when I remember what happened to us. "He told her it was us or my future."

"Wait, why did he go to Evie? That seems like an unnecessary step," Dawson questions as if to find every possible reason for why we've been blaming her. "Why didn't he go to you? He could have just told you that he was going to pull everything away."

"Do you really think it would have been a question for me?" I ask him, because to be the answer is obvious. I can tell between us, we're both confused by it. Even if I have had time to think about what Evie told me, it doesn't sit with me any easier. It doesn't make everything wrapped up and closed away. Dawson knows exactly what my choice would have been. I don't need to tell him.

"But she didn't pick you," Dawson notes, looking thoughtfully up at the wall across from him. A concerned look comes across his face as his body shifts. "Or maybe she did, just not in the obvious way. She did what he wanted."

"I guess it depends on how you look at it," I counter, running a hand through my hair. "I mean, she thought she was giving me school, a place to live...the career I wanted. Hell, she begged me the night before she left to run away and I didn't do anything other than laugh it off as if she was just nervous."

"So, she had to choose your future. One door you get it all, one door you get it all and lose it all at the same time. Damn," Dawson scoffs, before shaking his head. I can feel a rage trying to grow inside me that I feel anytime I think about what happened. The same one that made me want to hit my steering wheel. "She chooses you, and you don't get her. She chooses you and she doesn't get you. We spend the next twelve years with anger and dislike towards her. He made her the bad guy. No matter which way I say it out loud, it sounds messed up."

"Sounds pretty fucked up if you ask me," I growl, trying not to raise my voice. I can feel my blood pressure rising as I reach for my bottle of beer. "He was behind everything and I didn't even know it. When we were finally on good terms, he still didn't tell me. He made me think she just left. He talked about how he knew she wasn't up to the task of being with me. He said he knew she was weak and I believed him. Even when he was dying, he kept it to himself. He knew she was the most important thing, the one good thing I really had."

"Son of a bitch," Dawson groans and pushes himself up from the couch, reaching for the pizza box. "If that is what happened, it's fucked up."

"Dawson..." I start, watching as he walks towards the kitchen. I give him a moment, but when he doesn't say anything, I keep walking. I follow him as he walks in and turns a light on, sitting the box on the counter. "It happened."

"Look, your dad was a piece of shit. I don't want to piss on his grave, but we have to lay the facts out here," he insists. I can tell he's not trying to be an ass, but ask the real questions. The ones I don't want to ask. The ones I would ask him if he were in my shoes. "He wasn't a great guy, but how sure are we that Evie is telling the truth?"

"You don't?" I ask, sitting my beer on the counter. Dawson rubs his chin and I can tell that he's thinking intensely about what I told him.

"I do think that's the truth, and that's what's so fucked up," Dawson grumbles, leaning against the cabinet. I can tell he's angry at my father, filled with a toned-down rage, because there is nothing we can do to address it. "It screams Ridge Beckett. It actually makes me feel a little dumb that none of us dared to think about it over the course of the years. Still, why didn't she say something now?"

"We came face to face a few times, she eventually spilled it." I shrug as I walk around the other side of the counter. "Made it a little easier to get things out in the open."

"Easier or you two just finally decided to top using screaming as your form of communication?" He replies with the edge of sarcasm I know him for. Dawson has heard about every fight so far, but I had left out a key part of it. Knowing what my father did left me with a lot of anger and questions that I needed to sort through, because nobody else could answer them for me. Not even Evie. "Lex and I thought one of us was going to have to report a murder at some point."

"It would have been due to her killing me," I admit, laughing weakly when I think about the slap I received for being nothing short of an ass. "And I may have been deserving of it."

"That isn't surprising at all," Dawson agrees with a dry chuckle in his voice, but a heaviness of concern in his voice is evident. "Well, what now?"

"What do you mean, what now?" I question, looking up at him as he sips from his beer.

"A few minutes ago, you blurted out that she's messing

with your head," he inquires, taking the rest of the pizza over to the refrigerator. I think about his question, knowing the way I reacted to having her so close to me and the way I couldn't stop smiling like an idiot when I left. Seventeen or in my thirties, she still has power over me. "So if your dad fucked everything up so I can see how that would change things a bit, but she still left and you still went twelve years without speaking to each other. Are you ready to let her off the hook?"

"You think I should leave her on the hook?" I quiz, because I don't know what he's trying to say. I know it's been twelve years. I know what I went through. "Stay mad at her?"

"I don't know," Dawson hesitates. "Being angry with her doesn't really seem all that fair anymore, but she was still gone. She had time to come back. She didn't and now she has a different life. She was engaged to another man."

"She moved on," I remind him, but the aggravation of that statement sears through my chest. I know defending her is right, but it makes none of it easier. It makes a familiar pain come right back. "I hate it, but what was she supposed to do? Sit around and be miserable until my dad died and then come back and hope I didn't find anyone either?"

"You didn't," Dawson reminds me with a weak smirk across his face. "But that's because you've been love sick for Everleigh Goode and just rolling out of random women's beds to conceal it."

"I have not been lovesick for her," I object, thinking back to a time when I could finally feel normal after her. It isn't a secret with Dawson that I went through a tough time, but I still made life happen and got used to the idea that she wasn't coming back. I had a new normal.

"You were engaged to the girl the moment she turned eighteen," Dawson argues as he begins to head out of the kitchen and I follow him again. "You haven't had a girlfriend since."

"That doesn't mean I was pining for twelve years." I roll my eyes in his direction as I sit back down on the sectional sofa. "I just haven't met anyone I wanted to start a relationship with."

"And you built the exact house the two of you always talked about." Dawson has me there and he knows it, because he's grinning like an idiot. Like a lawyer who released the smoking gun. "No teenager and his girlfriend plan a house from pictures of magazines and then it still gets built after they're no longer together. Does she know the house exists?"

"No and I didn't build it for her," I debate, but inside he has a point. It's the very house we planned together, with so many unfinished touches, because I don't know what all of the right colors or finishes are. There was a time where I wondered what she would think of it, but then I stopped. Now, I wonder again and I think Dawson is on to me. "I needed a place to live."

"Uh huh," He nods, the satire booming in his voice. "If you wanted a place to live you could have moved into a place like this. A one room, modern bachelor pad. Instead, you built a five-bedroom, three car garage house overlooking miles of land and a pool. You built a home for a family."

"I did not," I deny it quickly as I think about the three years it took for the house to become complete. It had been mostly a side project that I hired workers for when I knew it would fit into the company schedule between other jobs. This house was one of my favorite projects. "I build a lot of houses. I just happen to have built this one to live in."

"A small bedroom right off of the master to overlook the front yard? That's a nursery my friend." Dawson informs me before taking another sip from his almost finished beer. "You have a house built for a family, but you haven't had a second date since Everleigh Goode."

It's a house," I counter, with a light drop in my shoulders. "Not a metaphor or a plan. Just a house. Made of wood and nails and drywall. It doesn't have meaning. I build a ton of them."

"Even with Ev back in Haven and on your mind? Not a bit of meaning?" Dawson asks the question in a way that tells me he doesn't need the questions answered. He already thinks he knows what is going on in my mind. The truth is, I don't know what is going on in my head. It's all a mystery even to me. The one thing I do know is that of all the women I took on one date and sometimes spent the night with never held a candle to the girl I had first loved. I look back up at my friend as he's revved and ready to continue talking. "Because if I recall you searched all over Southern Alabama to find the right shade of navy to paint the front door. I didn't even know there was anything other than just navy. All for that damn front door that just happens to match the book you made with Evie."

"Your point?" I groan, thinking I am heading towards calling it a night.

"You know what my point is," Dawson glares. "She's back and you're already fueled with want for her, but you're not thinking about the time lapse. The stuff that has happened and putting what your dad did into consideration, doesn't change the fact that you might not be the same people you were before."

"We probably aren't, and I'm not saying I know what to do about it," I admit, running my hand through my hair. "I don't."

"Look, I know it's confusing and I'm not saying you two shouldn't talk," Dawson speaks, his tone softening even for him, "but, Evie has been through a lot with that guy dying and from what Lexie tells me, she just hasn't taken everything so well. She's not the same girl you used to chase around town."

"I know she's not the same," I stress quietly, almost as if I don't want anyone else to hear. I begin thinking about the girl I saw in Libby's. Somehow smaller than before, distant and defensive. I knew then and there she was different, but some things were still the same. I knew that, because I know the old her and see the woman she is now. "I know things happened that changed her."

"Okay," Dawson holds his hands up in front of his chest. "I'm just saying keep that in mind. She's got a lot of heavy baggage it seems."

"Yeah," I laugh weakly, thinking about how Dawson was right there filled with hurt and anger with me all of those years. He seems to understand that the narrative has changed, and with Lexie warning us to ease up on her, I can tell he feels like I might not have my head in the right place. Maybe he's right or maybe he has it all wrong. I don't know. I'm feeling as confused as the day she left right now. He is right about one thing. Everleigh lived a different life in New York and that has also helped shape her into who she is now. I take a deep breath, rubbing my hand over my wrist for the thousandth time, before Dawson reaches for the remote, unpausing the television. "What?"

"You're so far gone already," he shakes his head, crossing his leg over his knee as his attention faces back to the game. I stare at him for a minute, before looking at the television as the game resumes. So far gone. I think about it for a moment and want to put my face to my palm, because I don't know if he's wrong. I'm not sure if he's right, either. She's filled my brain since that night in Libby's, but so much comes with that—the baggage that he says comes with her. It's the one thought I try to push from my mind every time. She lost the man she was going to marry after she left my world. It was when she truly stopped feeling like my Evie. It isn't a competition, but I feel an immediate defensiveness that she was mine first. I was her first everything and I wanted for years for her to be my last. I don't like thinking about Evie loving someone else or being heartbroken over another man. It feels wrong in every way and it always has. I remember downing a bottle of Jack Daniels after learning about him for the first time. I remember waking up in the back of Dawson's truck. Her meeting someone was the sign that I had lost her for good, or so I thought. I hate that she was in any pain and I'm sure he was a decent man, but it doesn't stop me from feeling a sense of competition when I think about it. I try not to think about what it means as I pinch the bridge of my nose and try to get her out of my head. I wish there was a switch or a button I could trigger to get her out of my mind so none of this would be a question. Evie's been behind some of the best and worst moments of my life. I know I'm confused. The only clear thought I have is that a part of me wakes up when she's around. A part of me that had shut down a long time ago. I felt it in the diner, fighting in the park and her backyard, but I can't figure out how to turn it off. I can't figure out if I want to.

Chapter Thirteen

Now

Evie

It's the first full weekend that my father has been fully embracing life as a retired man and instead of relaxing he has talked Levi and I into riding with him to the hardware store. He knocked on my door this morning asking if I wanted to ride with him and my nephew so he could stop at the hardware store. Since he knows he will get roped into talking with a few of the men about town, he added that I could stop at some of the smaller boutiques and antique stores. I'm missing the shopping aspect of being in New York and I know Levi likes hanging out with my dad and the guys in the store, so I agree. It helps that it would be a nice distraction from the thoughts racing through my head after my talk with my mother that resulted in more confusion and frustration for me. I haven't really slept since. My mind is full of thoughts about what I should have done, what I need to think about, and how the hell do I get my life back. I quickly got dressed and joined my two favorite men in my dad's truck. The windows are down, because when my dad does handiwork he likes to drive the old pickup he's had since before

I was born. It doesn't have a working air conditioner, so my hair is whispering in the breeze until it rolls to a stop in the parking lot at the back of the hardware store.

"Grandpa, can we get ice cream after this?" Levi says from the middle seat in the back and I question if the backseat of a vintage truck is actually that safe.

"Maybe," my dad chuckles, reaching into the never used ashtray for his wallet and sliding it into the front pocket of his old Levi's. "Are you and Aunt Ev gonna rat me out to your grandmother?"

"I won't. Promise," Levi celebrates, clapping his hands together before stopping and leaning on the back of my seat. "You won't, right aunt Evie?"

"Heck no," I laugh as Levi raises his hand to give me a high five. "But I want two scoops. With chocolate sprinkles."

"Me too! Lots of sprinkles." Levi bounces as I open the car door, stepping out and I smooth out my navy paisley print pants from the ride over. Levi pushes the front seat forward and hops onto the ground, but can't stop bouncing around. I look up to catch him and my father staring at me. "What?"

"Why are you uptight, Aunt Evie?" Levi looks up and I look up at my father as my jaw falls. "Is that why you always fix your clothes?"

"Oh, damn," my dad chuckles as my jaw drops. Levi looks so innocent as he looks between my father and I. "Levi, son. It seems you haven't learned how not to ask a woman a question."

"Who told you I was uptight?" I frown, reaching in the truck for my handbag and cell phone. When I have them, I come around the front of the truck with my dad. "Did your mother call me uptight?"

"It wasn't my mom," Levi says proudly as he skips a few steps ahead of us. The bounce in his step shows me just how unconcerned he is and my father looks like he wants to laugh.

If it isn't Lexie, there is one, maybe two people, I can assume would say that about me. At least in this town.

"Who said it, Tanner?" My dad asks him, adjusting his old Alabama Crimson Tide baseball cap. He

"Wade," Levi laughs, digging his foot in the gravel of the parking lot.

"When did Wade call me uptight?" I question, crossing my arms.

"I asked if you would go ride on the four-wheeler, but you said maybe later. He said, 'Tan, don't expect her to, because she's very uptight. Then he said you have a stick where the sun doesn't shine, but he didn't know I heard that part. He took me on the four-wheeler after that, because you wouldn't."

"What? I am not uptight. I had just taken a shower and... he shouldn't have said any of that," I frown as my father begins to chuckle loudly, clapping his hands together. "Levi, that isn't a good thing to say. Don't repeat that."

"What does having a stick mean?" He asks innocently, and my father's laugh turns into a full-on cackle and I send him a glare. "Why is grandpa laughing so hard?"

"Dad," I groan under my breath, as Levi returns to walking ahead of us. "This means Wade is teaching him things shouldn't. Things that aren't good. That's...adult humor, right? You can't laugh to encourage it."

"Everleigh? I'm going to be real frank with you." My father takes his sunglasses. I bought him two Christmases ago and puts them over his eyes as he takes a few steps ahead of me to meet up with Levi. He looks back, lowers his glasses a bit so he can see me. "You're uptight these days."

"Forest Goode!" I gasp, trying not to let a smile come across my face. My father has always tried to tell Lexie and I the truth and maybe I am uptight, but there is a smirk that comes across my father's face before he laughs and runs a few steps closer to the hardware store. "You better run!"

"Go buy some shoes, you don't have enough of those," he teases, opening the door to the hardware store as Levi laughs and runs inside. My dad stops, holds a hand to his ear and says, "Oh no, Ev! I think I heard there is a dress emergency down on Dixie. You better go make sure."

"You just go inside," I glare before he disappears inside, and I begin walking around the front of the store. The hardware store that my dad prefers has been in business probably longer than my father or anyone in this town has been alive. It's one of the truly small businesses that has outlasted all the other big box retailers that have popped up in bigger towns nearby. A lot of the men in our town like to frequent there on the weekends so they put an ice cream shop on the other side of it. Kind of a smart idea.

The first boutique I spot is the one I have wanted to visit since I came into town, but coincidentally has been closed every time that I have been here. I open the old oak door and step inside. I'm immediately met with the small of eucalyptus and mint and small pink chandeliers are hanging every few feet. I run my fingers along a rack of scarves, my eyes immediately catching on a light green one on the end.

"Welcome to Hilly's" A small petite brunette with a navy headband comes around from the black marble checkout counter with a dress on a hanger. "Have you been here before?"

"I have not," I respond, smiling as she stops in front of me. "I have come by a few times, but y'all have been closed."

"Y'all? So you are from around here?" She giggles, before shaking her head. "Sorry. I didn't mean to call you out. I just tend to recognize most of the women that come in here."

"I am from Haven, but I live in New York now," I respond, trying to shake off the slight twang that came out a moment ago. "I guess some habits die hard."

"You're Nancy and Forest's daughter!" She exclaims, a hand popping on her hip. There is a slight bounce in her as she makes the discovery and I can't tell if I am put off by it. It's hard to know what people in this town might think of me. "I have heard so much about you."

"That's probably not good," I wince, thinking of the possibilities of who she's spoken with before me. God, if Kasey has briefed her on me, we're in trouble.

"Only good things. Promise," she says, before marching across the floor to hang the dress on a sale rack. "I am open Saturday through Tuesday from ten until seven, closed Wednesday, And then open from noon until six on Thursdays and Fridays. I'm taking a business class at the community center and Hilly, the owner, doesn't really want much to do with the shop. We have a few teenagers from high school that work here part time, but I still can't leave it open as often as I would like right now. Maybe next year."

"It's a beautiful shop," I say, looking around the walls. It really is. It is clear she spends a lot of time caring for her company and even more time shopping for the right pieces. "I'm Evie."

"Harbor." She extends her hand and gives mine a light squeeze. "Harbor Finn. I'm from Baton Rouge originally."

"Nice to meet you," I smile warmly. Another customer comes in the door so I smile warmly and begin to shop around, admiring the detail on all of the pieces. I try on a few and settle on a set of dark denim overalls, a gray moto jacket and some color blocked tank tops. I also grabbed a pair of sandals, a maxi dress, and a few accessories for good measure. When I walk to the counter, I also spot some bracelets and grab one for me, one for mom, and one for Lexie.

"All set?" Harbor walks back to the checkout taking the items that I have slid on the counter.

"Yes, thank you," I smile warmly as she begins to scan the items. I'm impressed by the shop and know that I could find more things I want if I looked around, but I want to be able to check out some more shops before I have to meet up with Levi and my dad again. My eyes catch on some orange makeup sponges in the corner and I toss a few packs on some of the clothes she hasn't scanned yet. "I'll take these as well."

"Have you tried using a makeup sponge? Life changing," she asks, reaching for a white paper bag.

"Yeah. I actually work for a makeup and skin care company back in New York. Our makeup artists use them a lot," I add, before taking my wallet from my purse. "It's a game changer."

"What company?" She asks, wrapping the bracelets in some white tissue paper before keying in a few buttons on her cash register.

"Glam and Simple," I respond, handing her my credit card. Her eyes light up and I smile. "I work in PR."

"I love the lash serum. I swear by it," she claps, fluttering her eyes. "It's made a true difference."

"I'm so glad," I smile, making a note to remember that people out in Haven do actually buy high end beauty products, despite what I recall from growing up. I used to think it was a far-off wish to meet someone who liked makeup and fashion as much as I did. Lexie didn't mind it, but she wasn't as dedicated to it as I was. She was more into sports and riding horses. "We have a lot of things coming on the market in the next year."

"I can't wait," Harbor grins, handing me a receipt and pen. "Women are such a vital part of the retail industry and makeup brands know that. It's just that sometimes we miss out on stuff here in places like Haven, simply because we don't know what is out there and all of the focus is on big cities."

"Yeah...you're right." I feel a thoughtful grin spread across my face as she slides my bag across the counter. I like Harbor and I like her shop. She's refreshing and I think if I were to talk to her more, we would be friends. If I was someone who would be spending more time in Haven, which I am not, Harbor has real southern charm and great style which is evidenced throughout the shop. "I'll stop back in."

"Please do," Harbor smiles warmly before she starts to get to work behind the sales counter and for a moment, I am reminded of my days working in the shoe department at Macy's. I used to work as much as I could during the school year and full time after to be able to afford a room the size of a closet so I wouldn't have to come home in the summers. I walk towards the door, looking back around the shop before I step outside. Harbor's point about companies focusing on big city life is kind of true. Maybe not Glam and Simple specifically, but it means we could be doing better at something. I can't think of a way we have specifically thought about people who are living in the middle of nowhere or in the suburbs. We think of makeup, which makes us think of fashion, which makes us think of a city. I make a mental note that maybe this is something I should bring up when I am finally 'allowed' to start working again from my computer. Once Linda feels I have spent enough time away, I will rush back to the city and do something with this. Not that I haven't been enjoying Haven, but I am not eager to stay longer than I have to. Except I don't even know when I am 'permitted' to go back to New York. So far Linda gets mad when I ask about returning to work, threatening I stay out of the office for a year, so I opt to leave her alone for now.

That nostalgic feeling hits me as I walk by the hair salon where I used to get my hair done for all of the school dances. I remember sitting in the chair as one of the hairstylists would work on me and I would daydream away about the moment Wade would see me. How he would look at me later that night under the dance floor lights. How he would stay by my side, even though he hated dances. He would always suck it up and make them the best nights out. Speaking of the devil, I spot Wade leaning against his Jeep as he examines his phone, scrolling through it. For a split second, I consider ducking right inside the hair salon, but then I remember what Levi said and I am given some fuel. I go from wanting to avoid him, to wanting to slap him right across his pretty face again. So I'm going to confront him and see what he has to say for himself. If he thinks he's so funny, he can explain. I look both ways, holding my purse and shopping bag close. "Wade Beckett!"

Wade looks up, examining to his left and right, before he looks straight ahead to see me crossing the street. When he does, I swear a small smile tugs at his lips as he slides his phone into his back pocket. "Hey Ev."

"Don't smile at me!" I shout, before stopping halfway through the street to let a car pass. "We need to talk!"

"About?" He asks, the smile vanishing from his face.

"You said I was uptight!" I shout, making it to the other side and come face to face with him. Or more like face to chest, since he's taller than me. I kind of forgot how much taller he was than me and I wonder if I am even intimidating at all when I am mad at him. "To my nephew."

"Ah shit." He looks around, before grabbing my elbow, but I pull it away. "Ev…"

"Don't 'Ev' me," I point, before planting my hands on my hips. Our eyes match up for just a moment, but I look away quickly. "And don't touch me."

"Sorry," He puts his hands up in front of him, realizing that wasn't how to calm me down. It's a nice day out, so there are people all along the sidewalks, visiting the shops and driving by. "Levi told you I said that?"

"Of course he did," I bite, dropping my arms to my side as he towers over me. "He also said that you didn't know he heard it, but that I had a stick somewhere."

"Shit. Alright," he laughs briefly, before sliding his wrist across his face. "Okay...I really didn't know that he heard me say that part. I was going to take him out on the four-wheeler but I told him to go ask his mom. I didn't realize he was still there."

"And that suddenly makes it okay? Because you didn't realize he heard you? And you said I was uptight to my nephew." I groan. "I was nice to you. I fixed your hand and you said I was uptight. You said I had a stick...that isn't even appropriate for a kid to hear."

"Are you concerned about Levi hearing it or are you concerned that I am the one who said it about you?" He asks, crossing his arms as he looks down at me. I don't say anything to that. I don't know what he's trying to imply. Of course, he shouldn't have said that to my nephew.

"What is that supposed to mean?" I question as he leans back against his truck and models his stupid smirk on his face.

"You know, you come over here and you're being pretty uptight about someone calling you uptight," he proudly responds with that little look still on his face. A look that used to work wonders on me. "You're kind of proving my point."

"I'm not proving anything, Wade." I roll my eyes and continue my rant. "You told my nephew that I was uptight because you're still mad at me, and I don't appreciate that. I wouldn't tell Levi anything about you."

"It has nothing to do with me being mad," Wade counters as he looks up and grabs my elbow, this time pulling me closer to him. Immediately I see red when he does it. He's testing me.

"Don't touch me, Wade!" I shout, pushing his chest away from me. "I told you not to!"

"Ev, I was pulling you out of the damn road before you got run over!" He points down the road where I see an old van speeding off. *Shit.* I lower my head for a moment in embarrassment, feeling the immediate need to calm down. "God...Ev."

"I didn't...sorry," I say; my cheeks warm and I feel my face turning rose red as he looks around to see who exactly heard us a moment ago. I feel a little bit like an idiot and an ass all at once. Also feeling a bit relieved I wasn't flattened a moment ago. "I didn't hear or see it."

"Get in my Jeep," he demands, reaching for my arm again. I want to yell again, but I'm feeling a bit stupid.

"Hell no," I look up, pulling my elbow away again without acknowledging that he is ignoring my request, which I can tell irritates him. Only not because I am fighting him, but because he looks lost on what to do with me. He doesn't know what to make of me yelling at him so publicly after all these years. Maybe it's because I took care of his wrist the other day.

"Because I would like to not have to stop you from becoming roadkill right in front of my eyes. They cops will blame me as your ex," he barks, pointing to the road. Wade waits for me to say something, his free hand moves to the driver's side door and he clicks it open. "Also, I don't think we need to risk members of the town hearing us every time we try to have a discussion."

"Fine," I respond quietly as he releases my elbow from his hand, even though he wasn't gripping it as hard this time. Granted, I wasn't about to get plowed over by Scooby Doo's van. He lets out a sigh of relief, before I walk around to the other side of the Jeep and he follows me. I stop and turn around quickly. "This is your car. Why are you coming to the passenger side?"

"I was going to open the door for you," he sighs, the annoyance growing in his voice and for a moment I contemplate telling him I won't get in the car. Instead, he just gestures to the side and I let him follow me to open the door. "I don't remember you always being this impossible."

"Chivalry is dead in New York City." I cross my arms as he opens the door to his jeep, letting me duck under his arm to get into the empty side. For a moment it feels familiar. It feels weird to feel a bit like it's deja vu, but when I sit down in the Jeep, I put my purse and bag on the floor in front of me then exchange a glare with him. "My phone shows my location."

"Good to know," he says before slamming the car door shut. I put my hands on my lap, looking around the car nervously. Not because I worry he would pull something. I know better. I'm nervous because this is going to be the most confined I have been with this man I have avoided for twelve years. We're going to be mere inches from each other with no easy escape. These walls keep us limited. When he closes the door after sliding into the driver's seat, he puts the keys into the ignition, but turns down the radio. "I thought you might want the air on instead of sweating to death in here."

"Thanks," I hesitate, watching as I twiddle my fingers together. He lets out a deep sigh, checking his phone before placing it in the center console.

"I called you uptight," he confirms. He lightly taps the steering wheel. "And I did say you had a stick up your ass, but I didn't know Levi heard the stick part of that. Either way, I probably shouldn't have said it."

"Yeah, I know." I look straight ahead. This car is confining with the only view straight ahead is the view of the Volvo and the town ahead of us.

"It's just Ev...I don't know what to make of you. Of you being here, of being around you." His voice changes as he begins massaging his wrist. I look up and his lips are pierced together and I assume he's thinking. Trying to share what is on his mind. Wade has always worn his heart on his sleeve, but I can't read him the way I used to. At least, I don't think I can. "I really don't."

"So that's why you said I was uptight? Because you don't know what to make of me?" I question.

"No," he answers quickly and shakes his head. "I said you were uptight because I think you're uptight."

I look up at him and he has that stupid smirk on his face again. I try to find the words, but my jaw drops from my top lip and I can't help but let out one 'ha' before I can say anything else. "I am not uptight. I had just cleaned up for the night and gotten comfortable when he asked to use the four-wheeler."

"Forget about Levi and the four-wheeler for a second and tell me the last time you let loose and have fun," Wade requests, cocking his head to look at me. "Tell me."

"I go to bars with my friends in the city. We have wine and food and sometimes we drink a bit more than is good for us," I respond, trying to remember the last time I had a bit too much. Come to think of it, I am pretty sure the last time I had a little bit more than usual, Daniel was alive. I catch Wade staring at me and then he just shakes his head again. "What?"

"I wish I didn't know you so well, Ev." He slides a hand over his mouth as he lets out another sigh. He lowers his brows as he looks down at his hand. "Even after twelve years. I can read you like a book that I wish would close. There are things I recognize, but then there are things that tell me just how much you've changed. I wish I didn't recognize any of it, but I do."

"How have I changed?" I blurt out the question and immediately wish I hadn't asked it. I know I've changed. I began changing the moment I stood in that old kitchen with his father and never looked back.

"Really? The hair, the clothes, your whole... the way you carry yourself," he chuckles, looking over at me with the same eyes he could give me in high school. The ones that usually said he was sure of something or maybe about to make a point. "You're here but you're not, Ev. You're so serious now. It's like if you open up for even just a second, you might reveal something that would leave you vulnerable. So you walk around with this guard over you that keeps you from getting too close to anyone. Because whatever you've been through, you don't want to get hurt again."

"And what do you think I've been through?" I ask as I turn my shoulder to lean against the passenger seat, looking down at his hands, a cross tattoo on the base of his thumb I hadn't noticed before. I assume it's for his mother. He once told me she had a small silver cross that would hang from her necklace.

"I know he died," he acknowledges, shifting uncomfortably in the driver's seat. "I know you didn't eat or sleep much for months after he died. That your family was worried that you would need to go to the hospital. Hell, it scared me just hearing about it. Anyways, I know he was in some sort of…"

"Daniel," I say softly, the echo of saying his name burns briefly in my throat. "'He' has a name."

"Evie," He blows air through his lips, stiffening his back. "I know he has a name and I don't intend to disrespect the dead. I'm sure he was a great guy, but that didn't make any of that time any easier on me. It doesn't make what happened with us any easier and when I say his name all I think about is that he got you and I didn't. That nothing I could have done would have gotten you back here to me."

"I'm sorry," I frown, pushing out the thoughts of what Wade may have felt in the weeks after I left. I've never tried to think about it and maybe it's because I know he was trying to get to me and shutting him out was breaking me. Everything I did was for him, but deep down I knew I was hurting him. I don't want to think about what he was dealing with, about what he felt, because I am certain it would be too terrible to imagine.

If he felt even a quarter as terrible as I did, seeing him like that would have destroyed me. It still might. "I am. Wade—"

"I'm not finished," he says quietly, weakly lifting a hand for a second. "I can't put myself in your shoes and promise that I would have done the opposite of what you did. I want to believe that I would have, but if someone held your future in front of me I don't know what I would have done. Your happiness was the most important to me so maybe that means something. I don't know what, but it has me trying to see this differently. I'm trying to understand."

"You wouldn't have done it," I quietly dispute, before biting the top of my lip. He wouldn't have. I'd never thought about it before, but Wade wouldn't have left. "Your father knew you wouldn't give me up so he had to come to me. He knew what we were capable of. Alone and together. He knew who would be weaker."

"Maybe, but given what I know about the last few years, you aren't weak," he shrugs, before looking out his side window. He balls his fist but lightly hits it against the steering wheel. So light it doesn't make a sound, but he stops and wraps his hand around it for a moment. "I want to believe the Evie I knew is still there. The one that loved to dress up, but two seconds later had jelly on her dress."

"I still always manage to wear my meals," I inform him. Our dates always ended in laughter right at the table, because I would make it most of the way through before I took a sip of something or leaned forward or even dropped a piece of food on me to mark up a perfectly good outfit.

"Some things never change," he teases, before a thoughtful look comes to his face. "You know, we used to have so much fun. Whether it was just hanging out in my room, your parent's house or if you were just trying to catch up with me when you heard I was on my way somewhere."

"I'm still me, Wade," I assure him, looking over at the steering wheel that his fingers are wrapped around. "But you have it all wrong. You were catching up with me."

"Nah," He chuckles, the grin breaking the bittersweet expression on his face as he remembers our younger days. "You must be remembering it wrong. If I recall I once left without you on the four wheeler and you chased me all the way down to Libby's, albeit an hour later in a soaking and very see through white dress."

"Yeah, because you shoved me off the dock and into the pond." I argue, as I remember that day from the summer after our junior year. It had been a blazing, hundred-degree day and I hadn't been in the best of moods. Still, I was a teen girl who just wanted to spend time with her boyfriend and somehow ended up in water. "And I left the pond ready to kill you, so you better be grateful that walk gave me time to cool down."

"Oh I am," he grins as his eyes give away just how nostalgic it is. "I thought there was going to be one less man in Haven that night."

"You came very close," I recall, my eyes settling on the dashboard as I replay the night in my head. In one deep breath, one memory in particular comes to light and I unintentionally burst into a giggle I feel as low as my stomach. "Oh God."

"What?" He looks up, the beaming smile still at the corner of his lips. It widens after a moment, which just makes me stop laughing and begin smiling too. "You can't just start laughing and not tell me why?"

"Remember the stunt you pulled to get me to talk to you?" I ask him as he thinks to himself for a moment and his eyes go wide. This only forces the belly giggle to come back, which sits heavily on my chest. Yet I can't stop laughing as he begins to shake his head. "You stood on the counter at Libby's and told everyone in the restaurant to take pity on you, because your girlfriend was going to dump you."

"It worked, didn't it?" He gives me a pure dimpled smile and looks away from me for a minute. I'd be lying if I didn't say that smile still works. It still has some effect on me, but in this moment the weight on my chest disappears. I didn't realize I missed it until just now.

"I was young and stupid," I cross my arms as I bite back my grin, looking out my own window to avoid staring at those cheeks.

"I like to think we were young and unshakeable," Wade says quietly as I look out to the sidewalk. Unshakeable. An older man walks by with his small dog on a leash and for a moment I just want to focus on that. Although my brain could care less about what my eyes are looking at. It's like it doesn't register beyond the initial recognition of what I see, because my mind is focused on who I am in this car with and the word *unshakeable*. Young was a given, but were we unshakeable? Then he says something, breaking my focus away from the dog and his owner. "Boundless."

"Boundless?" I frown, trying to repeat the word in my head after it rolls off of his lips.

"We had what most people fight their whole lives for and at the end of the day, we had each other. No stupid fight or difference was going to break us, and we'd have figured anything out together." He takes a deep breath, looking away from me, but now I can't take my eyes off of him. "We were indestructible."

"Were we?" I ask, before shaking my head as I dispute his explanation. Clearly the last twelve years and my choice was an indicator that he was wrong. "Because look at where we are, Wade. We're trying in a jeep as we try to sort out anything to understand how we got to where we are. That's not boundless, it's not even progress."

"Yeah, but you're still in my Jeep." His breath is light but a reminder as our eyes match up again. I can feel the tension in my face wanting to melt away as he just looks at me. Almost hopeful that I haven't pushed the door open and thrown myself from his vehicle. "You haven't run from Alabama. Yet."

"Yet," I affirm with a bit of humility in my voice as I push a strand of hair away from my cheek. "There is still time."

"That there is," he smiles, before looking up the road. I see his eyes trail to the hardware store. I'm sure he knows that is where my father and Levi are at the moment, because he takes a deep breath and rests his head back on the seat. "So, what is it you plan on doing with however much time you have left here, Evie Goode?"

"I don't know, but I need to find some idea to return to New York with," I sigh, looking away from his eyes for a moment, staring back at the damn Volvo when I smirk. "And maybe work on getting that stick out of my ass."

"Oh, really?" He chuckles as he turns in his seat, facing me. "Wow."

"Then maybe I won't be so uptight," I grin, before winking. Winking? Of course I did.

"Well, if you need help with that, just let me know," he offers, before returning the teasing wink. I roll my dark eyes to which he holds a hand out in question. "What? I know removing a stick can be very difficult."

"So kind of you." A weak giggle escapes my lips as he grins widely. "What?"

"It's nice to hear you laugh. I missed that sound." He lights up and speaks quietly as he looks a little sheepish and his cheeks flush. It's hard to see on his tanned skin, but it's there. It's like I've been in a time machine that only takes you back, but everything looks the same as you do now. The way his eyes smile, but soften. I've seen the look a few times today, but right now it's the first time I feel like we both know something feels different. Still, the same. He must notice that something is going through my mind, because he straightens up in his seat like he wants to change the subject. "You should probably get back to your dad and Levi. Or resume your exploring of the town shops. Someone might get suspicious if you don't buy up all the shoes."

"Yeah..." The mood in the car suddenly deflates at Wade's hands. I didn't mean to be, but I was starting to feel more relaxed and like things were actually okay for once. Like there wasn't some ongoing battle with Wade to get the last word in before someone storms off. Usually me. "Levi wanted some ice cream so I should go make sure he gets it."

"Tell Forest he should buy you an extra scoop," Wade adds as I put my hand on the door handle and click it open. "You earned it."

"I might," I grin, reaching for my purse and the bag of clothes I bought and then put my hand on the car door. I feel strange for a moment, like I am about to get caught for something I shouldn't have been doing. As if talking to Wade was a transgression against something else.

"Hey Ev?" Wade's voice interrupts my thought as I push the door open.

"Yeah?" I stop, just as my foot touches the road before I can slide my body out of the car.

"Dawson, Lex and I go get drinks usually every other week. Most nights it's pretty tame," he announces, but stops for a moment as he looks back to the road and nods. "If you wanted to come. You should come. Next Friday."

"Okay," I bit my lip nervously as he delivered the invitation. For some reason that seems like a huge step from him hating me. Still, I'm not quite sure what to say or how to respond. "I'll see what I have going on."

"Yeah, you do that," he smiles, reaching for a pair of his

sunglasses from the visor. "And tell your Dad my guys and I will be there in the morning to start the demo of the side wall in the garage."

"Okay. Next Friday." I step out of the car, my mouth still slightly upturned. I look at him for a second, before pushing the passenger side door shut and turning on my feet quickly to break eye contact. I begin to take a few steps, but I feel acutely aware of how I walk. Am I walking fast or too slow? Am I walking in a straight line? Do I look like I know where I am going? Why don't I know how to walk? How does someone just forget how to walk like a normal human being. When I get to the corner of the sidewalk, I look back. Wade is still in his car, but he's looking down at his phone. So he's not watching me contemplate the right way to walk and I feel an edge of tension ease from my body, but now I am wondering when exactly I lost my mind. Talking to Wade is just like talking to an old friend. He knows what happened in our past and we were able to have two real conversations without either one of us storming away angry. That's why I'm smiling. He's right. I've made progress. *We've* made progress. Not that there is a 'we' in this world anymore. There isn't. I don't care what my mother says, I don't still love Wade in the way she seems to think. I love him as a part of my life. Just as Daniel was a part of my life, I experienced love on two beautiful occasions. I've been giving myself such a hard time, that I never really considered I could be friends with him. I don't know that I could have been his friend before this. I don't think I would have ever been okay to be alone in a car with him or to laugh with him before now. Maybe it was finally getting it off my chest or maybe it was growth between the two of us. Maybe it's that I am essentially being forced to stay in Haven and I've found it as a way to pass the time. Whatever it is, something has changed. Or gone back. I'm not sure, but if I can stop trying to talk myself out of it, I am going to see him at the bar on Friday night. We're friends and as his friend, he should be able to know that I am still fun. We used to spend hours together laughing and talking and doing so many other things that made us forget about the world beyond the two of us. A part of me wants to know if at least some of that world is still there.

Chapter Fourteen

Evie

Now

I can't remember the last time I ate food until I literally couldn't fit another bite into my body. It makes me question my agreement to go to Libby's midday with Lexie, but I am glad to be wearing some Lululemon leggings. Little bits of a strawberry milkshake, a burger, cheese fries and a soda sit in front of me and I feel like I might burst. Not from happiness. I might actually physically burst into a million pieces overeating. Not to mention the number of people from the town who have taken their time to either stare at me or come up to make conversation. Then there is Libby who, while I love dearly, keeps not so subtly hinting at me moving back. I think I told her at least three times that wasn't on my radar, no matter how good it felt deep down to be on my home soil. Alabama just hits differently and does something for the soul. I can't deny that. The nostalgia hits at every corner of this town. I also can't deny that New York is where things seem to be for me. I have a job that is stable and I don't mind doing. By any definition, it's a dream job. I don't know that it's something I want to do forever, but it's a great opportunity. I work with friends and I am really good at it. I have a beautiful apartment and pieces of Daniel are there. There isn't much here for me in Haven, even if it does have some of the people I love most. Even if being here takes an edge of pressure off of my heart. Even if I feel like I can actually breathe for a change.

"I think I might actually die," Lexie gasps, a hand moving over her stomach before she takes a sip of her cookies and cream milkshake.

"Then why are you still eating?" I groan, my own hand floating over my distended abdomen. The sounds of ceramic plates hitting the metal counter's fills the diner, but I am pretty sure I could fall asleep in this very booth.

"Because it's so good," Lexie sighs, falling back against the booth. "All the calories and greasy goodness. I don't know why I haven't pigged out here in years. I usually order takeout or just stop in for a quick lunch with Dawson or Levi."

"This is a feast," I gesture. At this point I can't even find an empty spot on the table. "This is…how did we do this in high school?"

"Right?" Lexie frowns, lifting up a discarded napkin and tossing it onto an empty plate. "I don't remember feeling this way after stuffing our faces back then. I remember eating a ton and then going on about our day as if nothing happened. Now I have a food baby!"

"Maybe this means we're old now," I tiredly sigh as I watch one of the waitresses walk by with a plate of onion rings. Immediately I feel a look of disgust come over my face at the thought of eating anything else. "I may never eat again. I may go back to my bedroom and sleep until next week."

"You can't sleep that long, you have to be awake to go to the bar tomorrow night," Lexie remembers, her tone pepping up as she leans back. "Wade told me he invited you."

"Yeah...I've decided not to go," I speak quickly, lightly drumming my fingers on the linoleum tabletop.

"Yes you are," Lexie demands quietly, looking around the bar and then focusing on me. "You and I haven't had a night out in forever and we need a night at a bar. *I* need a night at a bar."

"So go with Dawson and Wade," I shrug, despite knowing that response won't satisfy her. "Isn't that what you would normally do?"

"Ev," Lexie's face falls and for a moment I think she seems like she's not surprised. Instead of arguing, she does what Lexie does best. She keeps talking. "You and Wade haven't killed each other yet and from what I gather, you two have even been getting along. So what can it hurt?"

"There is nothing to hurt," I exhale, straightening up in the red booth. "I just don't think it's a good idea."

"Why? Because you might have fun?" Lexie asks abrasively. "Or because you might find that you still have fun with Wade? That you two still have chemistry?"

"Lexie," I object, but she doesn't seem to care even as I reach for a French fry, just swirling it across the plate.

"I'm just going to say it," She begins, tossing her hands up to just blurt out what is on her mind. "You and Wade still have the hots for each other whether you recognize it or not. There are major feelings still there."

"What?" I gasp, as she arches her eyebrow. I want for her to laugh or say she's joking but her face doesn't change and she doesn't say she's kidding. "That's ridiculous."

"Why is it ridiculous?" She asks, as I find my hands clasped together, one finger lightly grazing the engagement ring on my left hand. The one I don't take off except to shower or wash my face. "Ev, you told me why you left. You didn't end things because you were over Wade and you didn't date Daniel because you were ready to move on from a bad relationship. Now you're back at the scene of it all and the man still holds a well-lit torch for you."

"No he doesn't," I shake my head, despite how Wade has been acting since he learned why I left.

"He hasn't had a single girlfriend since you left," Lexie debates, before sitting back. "I mean he definitely didn't take a vow of celibacy, but he didn't move on from you no matter how bad you broke his heart. He may have screwed a ton of..."

"Can you not?" I jump in, holding a hand up in disgust. I don't want to think of the women Wade spent his time with. It gives me a nauseated feeling that I don't care to analyze. I'm sure if I took it to a therapist, they would have the pen and paper ready to go. "I don't need to hear how many women Wade has stuck his junk into."

"So you're jealous?" Lexie inquires, her voice quiet, and I am grateful for that respect.

"I am not jealous," I deny, although I don't want to admit it. I feel a little bothered by it. I have no right, but I do.

"Yeah...okay," Lexie rolls her eyes, before clutching a cup of water on the table. "He never slept with Kasey, but not for lack of trying. On her part. That girl will spread like butter for anyone when her husband is out of town."

"Lexie!" I gasp, looking around the small-town diner. "You can't just say that."

"Sure I can. My point is, that man won't date anyone. I used to think it's because he just didn't want to get heartbroken again, but that isn't it." Lexie explains almost proudly. "I figured it out when I was eavesdropping on you two in the kitchen and in the backyard that night. When he brought you your purse. He's still in love with you."

"No he's not," I deny, pressing my finger onto the diamond of my ring as Lexie looks at me as if I'm crazy. Maybe I am.

"He is. It's painfully obvious," Lexie affirms, crossing her arms. "And that's okay. I mean maybe you guys are meant to be together. Endgame or whatever people call it."

"Lex, I'm not really looking for anything," I admit, pulling my finger away from the ring Daniel gave me in front of hundreds of people. "I don't want anyone new."

"I guess that's a good thing Wade isn't new, huh?" Lexie's face softens and I know she really wants something to click for me. She wants me to be happy and believe in love again. I respect it. I do. I've struggled to have the conversation with myself. It's a combination of knowing I may have blown it and the heartache that leaves me unwilling to bother. The idea of having already hurt two men, sits on my chest in a way I can't explain other than to try to breathe beneath the weight. "Ev, you don't have to be looking for something and it's not like anyone is trying to set you up with some blind date by having you go to the bar with us. We just want you to come hang out with us and drink. If you happen to have a great time, well then it was worth it. But Wade...you know he's a good one. Hell, you were going to marry the man after he proposed to you in this very diner. The question was never if he was the right man for you."

"Lex," I utter softly, running my hands over my head, my elbows on the edge of the table. I can't explain the knot as it forms in my stomach, not from the food but the overall anxiety of this conversation. I hate the part of me that thinks about that boy I fell in love with. How he is a man now and it's hard not to notice. It's human nature, I remind myself. For a woman to notice those things. "I'm not looking for anything."

"Then don't look for anything," Lexie shrugs casually. As if it shouldn't be anything to feel pressure about. "Go out with us, drink and let loose. If you have a good time with Wade then you have a good time with him. Just see how it feels."

"Lexie, I don't know..." I groan, massaging my temples as

I try to run it through my head.

"Tell me you're not at least a little curious." Lexie seems so confident, that it makes me take a deep breath. I have this overwhelming feeling that letting the idea even come to my mind is in some way wrong. That maybe it's tempting fate or worse, an admission of guilt. Guilt of moving on or shrugging off the guilt I feel for what I did to Wade in the first place. "That if he told you up front how he really felt, you wouldn't at least want to know what life could be like."

I try to think about it for a split second. If Wade might really feel something besides bitterness or anger about our past. Before I can respond to Lexie, Libby comes marching to the table. We asked her for the check an hour ago, but I know she isn't coming to kick us out. "So, do you like the milkshakes? We use organic milk now! It's only a seven-cent difference with my new supplier."

"They were so good," I smile warmly, handing her my credit card. She tries to put a hand up, but I push it towards her. "I am paying this time. Don't argue."

"Still stubborn, I see," Libby sighs, taking the card from my hand and sliding it into her faded black apron. "I better see you guys in here more."

"We'll come in more, but I don't know how long this one is staying," Lexie responds, gesturing towards me and I can only let out a light breath. I don't know when I am leaving, but I have to admit I feel a bit clearer headed in the country. It reminds me of why I had planned on moving back to the country after college. That plan went out the window quickly after Ridge Beckett interfered. "Unless you've decided to listen to Libby and move home since we started eating."

"I will make sure today isn't the last day I come in for food," I speak quickly, hoping that it's enough that they don't push me any further.

"Alright," Libby responds, lightly nudging my arm. She slides a pen over her ear and shakes her head. "Let me go check on the kitchen, then I'll ring out your check."

"Thanks Libby," I smile before she walks away, and I lean back.

"We all just miss you," Lexie says softly, leaning over to squeeze my hand as it rests on the table. She pulls her hand back as I smile warmly. "I see Mayor Mike just came in and I need to ask him about making an appearance at summer baseball for Levi's team. You mind if I step away real quick?"

"Go for it," I reply as Lexie slides out of the booth and makes her way to the other side of the familiar diner. I look around and see quite a few faces I recognize and a few I don't. Some are surely guests that popped in on a break from their journey through the interstate. The truth is, I know I feel more like myself in this town. I'm home here. But I don't know that I can leave my life in New York. I don't know that I am ready to look at life outside of the small bubble I've created. That of course makes me weigh what Lexie said. That she believes he's still in love with me. I don't know if that's true, but I saw the hurt when he learned what his father did. It was as if that crushed every theory he had about why things went the way that they did, and I was okay with him hating me. I was. I was prepared for it and spent years living my life on the very idea that being the villain was best for him. The real truth was that once I saw him, it made it more difficult to make the truth out of a lie. I wasn't prepared to deal with the familiar feeling of being in his presence and those emotions weren't lost on me. It was painful and it made me cold towards him. It was the cost of keeping a secret. It made it too hard to be around him, but now he knows. I didn't want to tell him and I had planned to go to my grave with that truth, but seeing him along with the coldness was going to bury me alive.

I look over at Lexie who is surely now in a deep conversation in the corner with the mayor and his wife. I've missed being the sister she deserves to have. She got the short end of the stick too. My whole family did, and I feel the guilt from the price they paid. I feel the guilt to Daniel, but something inside of me for a moment, allows me to make a decision. I can go to the bar for a drink or two. My finger instinctively massages the engagement ring on my finger. It's a dead end of promises that I'm the only one keeping. Still, I don't know that I can take it off just yet. If anything, to just hang out and have a drink with my sister and Dawson. Who I personally think need to work their own crap out, but that's a whole other situation. The anxiety I feel about being around Wade Beckett and alcohol isn't lost on me. I know I have enough self-control to avoid doing anything stupid, but I'm still nervous. So much so that I briefly consider backing out.

Chapter Fifteen

Now

Wade

I've worked my entire life to be nothing like my father, but it seems the one thing I inherited was his need to get up early and be productive through the work day. It's the need to get things done as soon as they need to be done. After I moved back from Boston, I became very strict about my morning routine. Today was one of those rare days where I broke away from that and was running late from the moment I woke up until I left the job site. I probably would have caught up on time if I had skipped my workout this morning, but something told me that I needed to burn off some steam. I'm pretty sure it's the energy I would have spent thinking about tonight. I have told myself a million times that Evie probably won't show up tonight. It would be too much of an opportunity for her to be vulnerable. People drinking around her, their inhibitions lowered, and chances are conversations would come up. She wouldn't like it. It doesn't matter about the time we spent talking in the car and how I kept looking away because all I wanted was to look right at her. Right at the dark eyes that used to control me. For the first time since she came back to Haven, she looked like the girl I was in love with as a teenage boy. That smile where her nose crinkled up used to set my world on fire and for a few minutes in my jeep, it felt like we were young again. Like hiding out in my jeep was hiding out in my old truck, breaking curfew to get a taste of her lips one more time. Only I didn't taste them, I wouldn't have. I'm not even sure I want to. Her contagious laugh eased any of the tension I had. Even when she called my name from the other side of the street and stormed in anger, I didn't see a stranger. I saw that girl I used to pass notes in the halls at school or admire on summer days at the pool even though she was mine. She isn't mine anymore. She isn't anyone's. So when I asked her to join us at the bar, I knew I was taking a risk. Maybe it was a risk of pushing her away amidst the progress we had made. If you could even call it that. I got a smile I didn't even know I was trying for and when she walked down the street, the Jeep started to feel the way my house does. Too big.

Then there is one more minor detail. The invitation to the bar for tonight. I think that's the closest I have come to asking a woman to go somewhere in years. I wasn't even asking her out on a date because we've been there and done that. My style these days tends to be finding a woman at the bar and it's usually someone just passing through. It seemed like the right thing to do when I regularly hang out with Dawson and her big sister. It's a small town and it seems to me like Evie might need to escape the life she lives. Even if she doesn't want to and we were her old crew. When I texted Dawson and Lexie, I was surprised that Dawson didn't have some jackass response about it. To be honest, he's been more laid back since I was a bit more open with him about Evie once I told him what my father put her through. It seems that it changes the narrative a lot. So now, she might be at the bar. Or maybe she won't be. Lexie hasn't said anything since I told them and I am running late. I know from

Dawson that he is there already and Lexie had texted him to say she was on her way. No mention of Ev. I'll know in a few minutes, because as I run down the stairs of my house, I grab my keys and wallet from the table by the front door and head outside. After working all day at one of my sites, I was already rushed when I came home to shower and change my clothes from the dirt covered ones I had on earlier. Evie or no Evie, I don't go too many places covered with dirt, drywall, and sweat.

The Timekeeper Bar is just down the road from my house, so it doesn't take me more than three minutes to get there. When I pull into the parking lot, I see Dawson's pickup truck and Lexie's car parked next to it. Just as expected. I turn the keep off, before hopping out and locking it behind me. It looks like a slow night at the bar, which should make for a quick first trip to get a beer. I pull open the worn red metal door and walk inside. Some old Hank Williams plays as I head straight to the bar. The bartender is tied up with another customer, so I turn away to look for Dawson. I see a few people I recognize, but finally see him and Lexie at a table against the wall. Just the two of them. No Evie. That's okay. I try to swallow the disappointment that I feel, but the relief I feel from the tension that I didn't realize had been in my shoulder's begins to fall off. "Wade?"

"Yeah?" I turned around quickly to see that Evie had come up to the bar when I was looking around. Somehow I missed her with her hair pinned up. Beautiful. I quickly stand up, a grin spreading across my face. "Hey stranger."

"I was just coming back from the restroom and saw you come over here," she gestures to the hallway behind her. I do something stupid: I look her up and down and pray she doesn't notice. She looked momentarily at the bar, so I think I am safe. She's wearing jeans with rips on the thighs and knees and a black top that just goes low enough with some sort of lace. "Are you getting something to drink?"

"Yeah, what do you want?" I ask, turning back to the bar to break my eyes from trying to look back down. I wave and the bartender comes down to us.

"Sorry about the wait," he offers, before swinging a towel over his shoulder. "What can I get you?"

"Can I get a bottle of Landshark and Ev, what are you having?" I ask, taking my wallet from my jeans.

"Oh um...I'll have the same," she smiles, placing a hand on the bar as she turns back to me. I hand my card to the bartender before looking right back at her. "Thank you."

"It's nothing," I shrug, before leaning against the bar's surface. "So you came."

"I did," Evie takes a deep breath, using her finger to push one of the curls out of the way. She looks nervous and I almost want to tell her how happy it makes me that she came, but I don't know if she would like hearing that. Heck, I didn't even realize I was happy she was here until I saw her. "So um...you're building the custom houses and all that now, right?"

"I am," I nod, reaching for my phone as I decide I want to show her my home. The house she inspired. "I actually want to show—"

"Two Landsharks." The bartender slides two bottles between us and hands me my card. "Close the tab?"

"Keep it open," I nod, sliding the card into my wallet as Evie takes a beer into her hand. I slide the wallet into my back pocket. I click my phone off, because I realize it isn't the time to bring up my house or anything that we had once planned for our lives. She's just a girl in a bar right now, she's a friend and nothing more. I don't know what came over me, but it might have something to with those jeans and that top. "We should join Lexie and that loser Dawson."

"That loser is your best friend." She rolls her eyes as she begins to walk away, towards the table. I grab my beer and follow her, making a quick glimpse at her ass as she walks away. When I look up, Dawson has a smirk as he's watching me when we approach the table. "Look who I ran into."

"Wade!" Lexie jumps up and gives me a hug and I realize she already smells like Malibu rum. Lexie doesn't really get out too much, because she's a single mother, but she's always excited to see Dawson and me on these nights.

"Hey Lexie," I hug her back before releasing her, then slide onto the chair near Evie. "You didn't bring Levi? Who else is supposed to keep us all in line?"

"I tried, but apparently hanging out with his grandparents was more exciting," she jokes, before waving over to the waitress. When the tall blonde walks up to the table, she winks at me, before turning to Lexie. Normally I would have eyed her up and down and Dawson gives me a 'what gives' hand gesture that I ignore. I'm not interested tonight. "Can we get two rounds of Fireball for the table?"

"Fireball?" Dawson winces as the waitress nods and leaves the table and Evie's eyes go wide. "Who are you trying to kill?"

"I'm trying to get my sister fucked up," Lexie chirps very matter-of-factly and proudly as she pushes at Evie's drink towards her. "Drink up."

"I'm drinking, but I am not getting drunk like you seem to think." Evie picks the bottle up and puts it to her lips, but I look back down at mine instead of watching her.

"Oh, yes you are or else I have failed tonight," Lexie exclaims, pointing right at her sister. "As a big sister and as a human."

"Dad made Lexie some concoction of things he found at the store when he went instead of Mom," Evie informs us. "So she's had a head start on all of us, because I refused to try it."

"Well, guess that means I'm driving the ladies home tonight." Dawson leans back in his seat, placing his phone on the table. "Since you plan on drinking like your senior year again."

"I'm a mom. I rarely get to have fun," Lexie jokes, before finishing the last of the rum and coke in front of her. "And my sister needs to loosen up, but what about the shots?"

"Since it has been decided by Lexie that I will be staying sober, I humbly hand them over to Evie as a coming home present." Dawson sighs proudly, leaning back in his chair. "Welcome home Ev...please don't throw up in my car."

"I don't think you'll have to worry about that." Evie raises her head confidently, before holding the beer bottle in her two hands. "I'll be on my best behavior."

"I believe you," I nudge her arm, winking as she looks up at me. "Just remember later, that Dawson had little faith in you."

"Your friend is an idiot," her eyes give me a wink back and then quickly takes another sip of her beer.

"I haven't left!" Dawson throws his arms up which makes Evie laugh. "God, it's like high school."

"Oh! Speaking of high school, Evie is wearing jeans from high school that she found in her closet." Lexie points out, before sliding her empty glass to the center of the table. "I wouldn't let her wear the jeans she brought. They were so stiff looking."

"They were not," Evie rolls her eyes, before taking another swig from her beer.

"Ev, everyone knows you have the best style of anyone in this state, but you dress like you're on the streets of Manhattan most of the time," Lexie explains as the waitress returns to the table with the tray of shots. Evie looks annoyed, but I think she might be trying to act like it doesn't bother her. The waitress sits the tray down and walks away as Dawson sits a few in front of Evie. "For example, you wear a dress like no other. I mean, you're perfect, but you're dressed for the Hamptons, not Haven."

"Because that's where I probably intended to wear them

when I bought them," Evie groans, reaching for a shot of the dark amber liquid, downing it within seconds and wincing as the liquid hits her throat. "Oh shit."

"Down the hatch, Goode," Dawson chuckles, holding a fist up. Although both mine and his jaw falls as Evie reaches for the second one and downs that quickly, before grabbing for her beer and coughing. "Oh shit."

"Everleigh Rose!" Lexie gasps as Evie coughs and I try to hand her the bottle of beer. "Chase it."

"God!" She grouses, her fingers wipe at her lips before she takes another sip of her beer. "What the hell is that?"

"I just got my truck detailed," Dawson groans, clutching the bill of his baseball cap in his hands. "Lexie if anything happens…"

"She'll be fine," Lexie nudges him, briefly resting her head on his shoulder before looking up at me. "Besides I am sure that Wade would gladly take her back home and his interior is leather."

"Oh, he doesn't…" Evie starts as Lexie takes a shot for herself.

"I can make sure she's safe and good to go," I offer, interrupting Evie which I realize is a pet peeve, but I don't care. I don't think she's paying attention though, because she's already moved on to Lexie and her shot.

"How do you drink that and not cough?" Evie questions her sister as Dawson pushes the shots that were set in front of him towards Evie. A part of me wants to tell him to stop, that she's tiny and probably doesn't need anymore, but I know if I say it she'll just get mad. She'll make a comment about me needing to mind my own business or mock me somehow.

"It takes practice," Lexie laughs. "It's not a Cosmo or Chardonnay and for that I am sorry."

"Is it supposed to make your face feel warm?" Evie glares

in her sister's direction, taking a deep breath as the two shots sit in front of her. She takes another sip of her beer and eyes the liquid suspiciously.

"It does," I confirm as seconds later, she keeps putting her fingers to her face to feel her cheeks. "You warm?"

"It makes everything warm," Lexie winks, before sipping from a glass of water that I am sure remained untouched until now. "Tingly too."

"I didn't need to know that," Dawson gripes as he leans back in the chair. He watches Lexie intently and then bursts into laughter, which then makes Evie laugh. I still love her laugh and for just a split second I feel seventeen again. Watching the most beautiful girl in the world and wishing I could do this forever. The way her laugh ignites something in me and how I could watch her for hours and I don't think I would get tired. Some things don't change apparently. I pull myself away from my thoughts, because I know in a way it's wrong. I just don't know why until I catch that Dawson has been watching me. "Hey, I'm going to get another beer. Wanna join?"

"Uh, yeah," I say, watching as Evie bravely holds her head high towards her sister, before taking another one of the spicy shots. That is three. Three shots of Fireball for the small woman to the left of me. I push my chair back and sit my almost empty beer down as Evie looks up at me. I don't know how well I can read her anymore, but her fingers pinch at her earring as she frowns. "We'll be back."

"Okay," She nods with a weak smile, before looking back at Lexie.

I follow my friend to the bar, making a note to ask for some more water for the table. I don't know what Evie's tolerance of alcohol is, but I know her size and I know the amount she's consumed in a small window of time. I also know I'm watching her far more than I should and so does Dawson, because when

I get to the bar and reach for my wallet he turns to me. "Listen man, I was joking about my car if she gets drunk. I can take her home."

"What are you talking about?" I put my hand up, looking back at the table as Lexie answers her phone.

"Look, I don't care if anything happens between you two, because that's between you two and honestly...never mind." Dawson stops and looks back at the table. "But you're looking at her and—I don't know what this says about me for noticing—but you look like you want her."

"I don't want her," I deny quickly, looking back at the table where she's digging into a small black bag. "I don't know. She's just Evie."

"She's not '*just* Evie'. She's different now and that isn't completely her fault, but she might not be the same woman. A lot has changed," Dawson sighs as he looks back at me. "She's damaged now and you aren't exactly a man who takes a woman on a second date these days. Just as you don't need to end up screwed up after her again, she doesn't need someone to screw her up even more."

"Okay, first of all Evie isn't just any other woman. I'm not going to screw her up and I'm not trying to do anything other than maybe be her friend," I try to insist, but before I can assure him that I am just being civil and getting along with her, Lexie begins walking over so I have to hurry. "It's nothing. We're just catching up."

"Just be careful...for both of you," he says quickly, turning towards the bar to see where the bartender is currently. Before we can flag him down, Lexie interrupts us as she clutches her phone in her hand. "Lex."

"Hey guys, my Mom just called and said Levi is really not feeling well and running a temperature," Lexie groans, sliding her phone into her pocket. "Dawson, can you take me home? I don't think I should be driving and Ev drove us here."

"Of course," Dawson frowns, leaning his back against the bar. "What's wrong with my buddy?"

"It's probably just a bug he got from a birthday party he went to last weekend. A few kids have been sick since," she sighs, running her hands through her hair. "I'm sorry. I feel terrible because I think Evie is kind of bummed. I think I had finally gotten her to loosen up a bit."

"Why don't you guys go check on Levi and I will hang out with Evie for a bit?" I suggest, ignoring the expressions looking back at me. Both of them are unsure of what to think. "I mean, it's one of the few bars in town, so it may be an opportunity to catch up with some people if the crowd picks up. I'll make sure she's well hydrated and stays out of trouble."

"No, get her in trouble. She needs trouble," Lexie jokes, before giving me a hug. She squeezes tight and whispers in my ear. "Just, please try to actually have fun together. She needs it. So do you."

"Alright, let's go close our tabs," Dawson instructs before I can respond to Lexie as she lets go. He eyes me suspiciously as he puts his hand on the small of Lexie's back to lead her out of the old bar, but he gives me a nod as they walk towards the other end of the bar. I look back at the small table we all shared and see Evie watching them leave before she looks at me, her eyes narrowing in confusion, so I just approach the table and pull out the seat across from her. "Dawson took Lex to check on Levi, so it's just us."

"They were my ride," she points to the door, her finger waving. "I was supposed to ride with them after I took my four shots. I took four shots."

"That quick?" I question, looking at the table to see Lexie's shots gone, the four empty shot glasses in front of Evie and the two that Lexie bought for me. I've done the math and by looking at her, that's more than enough. "Yeah Ev, that's a lot in a short period of time."

"It's kind of funny, because after the first three I couldn't really taste number four," she frowns, tapping her face, before sliding the two shots that I never drank in front of her.

Are you going to drink those?"

"No, but you shouldn't either," I caution, as she holds up her pointer finger, waving it down to one of the shot glasses. She pulls it in front of her protectively. "Ev."

"I'm good, Wade," she states, gesturing to the empty shot glasses before trying to reach for a full one in front of her. She still has it mostly together, but her words are starting to slur a bit and I think it's time to slow it down, still she seems adamant that she should take another shot. Four. Four for the tiny woman in front of me.

"I can't stop you, but you don't have to prove that you're not uptight," I point before shaking my head and sitting back in the chair. I wouldn't normally try and stop someone from doing what they want, but I am going to prevent her from feeling like her head is caving in when she wakes up tomorrow. "Then I am cutting you off."

"Fine," she scoffs, scowling at me before she picks up the shot glass and swings it back like a pro. This time she doesn't race for another drink, but claps her hands together. "I think Fireball is powerful."

"I would agree," I confirm as I slide one of the untouched waters at the table over to her. "Have you eaten?"

"I had a big breakfast!" She replies as she takes a gulp from the water, some of it dripping down the front of her shirt. I briefly put my head in my hands, wondering how I am going to deal with this woman in front of me and how I am going to keep myself from wanting her. Spilled water and all. "Shit."

"You are going to need to eat something before we call it a

night," I reply, shaking my head. Slowly I can see the alcohol start to set in, because Evie's smile just gets wider and her eyes have a certain shine to them. She looks happy. The happiest I have seen her look since I first saw her that night in Libby's. She doesn't seem all that bothered that Lexie and Dawson have left, which means she doesn't seem to mind being around just me. Something about that makes me feel better about tonight, about the fact that I really think I want to be around her. "We'll grab some burgers on the way home or I can cook something up for you."

"Cheese fries with bacon and ranch." She waves her hand at me before reaching for a napkin. "But I can walk."

"You're not walking," I insist, clasping my hands together on the table. "But if you want cheese fries, you got it. You get whatever you want."

"I can't feel my cheeks. Can you feel your cheeks?" She asks, shaping her hands over her porcelain skin. I want to tell her to be gentle, but her hands are delicate too. "It's like sparky."

"Cinnamon whiskey will do that to you," I mumble as she looks around, twisting every which way. "What are you looking for?"

"I think I want another beer." She frowns, lowering her hand again.

"I think you're good, Ev," I remark as I push the water towards her again. "You've had four shots of Fireball and a beer. For a small person who doesn't go out and have fun very much, I think that's enough."

"I have so much fun, Wade" She groans, sliding her hands on the table. As I relax into the chair, I smirk when she dramatically grabs her phone. I don't know what she's doing, but she's typing frantically before I hear ringing and she has the phone on speaker. I try to ask her who it is, but someone answers before I have gotten her attention again. "Kyra!"

"Everleigh?" A woman answers with a bit of an east coast accent.

"Am I fun?" Evie asks loudly, putting her chin on her hand as it rests on the old table. Her other hand holds the phone. "I'm fun right?"

"Oh," The girl on the other line hesitates as I lean forward and rest my arms on the table. "You're fun in a lot of ways. Why?"

"Just please tell Wade how much fun I am," she demands, her voice getting loud as the table next to us looks over. I try to tell her to lower her voice, but there is no point. The alcohol is hitting and as she waits for her friend to respond she takes the very last shot on the table. Six. I didn't even get a chance to stop her, but that is six. We need to leave. "And just so you know Fireball is...it's evil and great. It's like Big Red gum and Makers Mark."

"You've never had Fireball?" The woman on the other end gasps. "Oh my God, are you drunk? Evie, when was the last time you...oh God. You're drunk."

"Not yet," Evie responds, swatting her hand at me as I just sit there and watch. "Tell Wade that I am fun and not uptight."

"Evie, you're a fun coworker and you plan really good brunches, but you don't really let loose. Hence my shock," Kyra hesitantly responds through the phone as Evie's shoulder's drop. "Wait...who is Wade? Is Wade a guy?"

"Doesn't matter," Evie frowns, hitting a button on her phone to hang up the call and sliding her phone across the table to me before she waves nonchalantly. Evie looks a little defeated, but that doesn't stop her from bouncing around in her seat. "My face is so...it's falling asleep and now everyone in here is just everywhere. Cheese fries."

"Yeah, you're drunk," I sigh, standing up from the table. I push my chair in and walk to her side. I pick up her purse that she's since discarded to the chair next to her as she stands up and sways a little bit. "Easy there. It's hitting you quickly."

"Shit," She giggles, grabbing on to the table as I wrap my hand around her arm. I look up and shake my head, trying not to laugh as she steadies herself and takes her purse from my hand. "Okay...okay."

"You good?" I ask, before letting go. She's much steadier after the shock of standing up and I realize of all the firsts Evie and I had together, I've never seen her drunk. Sure, we snuck a couple beers, but we never got drunk. Maybe tipsy, but this is Evie *drunk*. "I am going to close my tab and what do you say we get out of here, pick up some food, and I will take you back to my place to eat it?"

"Hurry, I'm starving," she nods confidently, leaning against one of the wood poles in the bar. She then points to the restroom sign and says she'll be right back, but I watch her until she disappears into the hallway before making my way to the bartender. I don't really know what I think the rest of the night will be like, but my only goal is that she's safe, fed and not hating herself in the morning. There is a lot of potential that she might, even with my best efforts. The girl downed six shots of whiskey in a short amount of time and I think it might have been to prove to me that she wasn't uptight.

***

As I pull down the long dirt road to my house, my ears are filled with Evie mumbling the words to Miranda Lambert and I'm not even sure she knows the song. She's gone from the shock of the whiskey hitting quick, to full on intoxicated. It's no secret at this point and she wouldn't be able to hide it if she tried. Thankfully, she's enjoying herself as she holds the takeout from Libby's on her lap. The car smells like burgers and I'm pretty sure Evie is sneaking an occasional fry from the bag. The windows are down and I don't think I have seen her look this carefree or happy since she came back to town. She just keeps closing her eyes as she sings, letting the breeze land on her face as I drive down the road. She doesn't even care that she fell flat on her ass as we left the bar, gravel getting into her shoes. I helped her to the passenger side and took her shoes off, cleaning them off before putting them back on her feet. All she cared about was getting her cheese fries and the fall was slowing her down. I don't even think I have laughed this much in a while. To see her grinning constantly was like fuel to a fire and it makes me feel like I could do anything. She's just that powerful. I always knew that, but I missed it.

As we pull up the driveway, her eyes go wide as she sees the house. I start to feel a little tension in my chest as I realize she's going to see a life I have started to build. We haven't talked about me much, because I haven't wanted to let the conversation head that way. I was so focused on getting answers from her that I haven't told her I have a house that is a constant work in progress. I stop the car in front of the house and as we hear the car wind down, she looks at me. "Wasn't this the land that the old Tenant barn was on?"

"It is," I nod, pointing towards the house. "We tore down the big barn and I turned the smaller one into a gym. I refinished some of the wood and actually used it throughout the house for shelving and a few odds and ends. The rest I sold."

"Wade Beckett built himself a house. From a barn," she exclaims, pushing her door open. I quickly grab the bag of food from her lap as she swings her legs over to get out. "With great wood. Good wood..."

"You don't know what you're saying," I mumble under my breath as she giggles to herself, before opening my door quickly to try to make it to the other side of the Jeep. By the time I get over there, she's already running up the sidewalk towards my front door, thankfully without any faceplants or tripping on the steps. I stop on the sidewalk for a moment as she looks back at me. I knew she was short, but she looks so much smaller than I had imagined she would look if I was coming home after a long day. An image I had tried my best not to picture over the years. Evie standing on the front porch of the home I built. The home she inspired every inch of.

"Hurry," she waves.

"You do in fact need food, because you smell like Fireball," I chuckle, shuffling up the steps. She opens the screen door and knocks on the navy wood door.

"I'm starving, Wade," she whines as I slide the key into the lock, pushing the door to the house open. Every time I walk in, I think of the hours of work and lumbar that went into building this house. I think of the hours I would stare at flooring and wonder what she would have picked, before settling on a darker wood for the floors, but Evie doesn't notice anything. She just begins looking around, twirling in every direction. "Your house is so big."

"I wouldn't say it's big." I look around, at the mostly empty space and rooms that are visible from the front of the house. I have a mirror and an old oak entryway table I find on the side of the road and fixed. She's focused on her food thankfully and doesn't seem to notice the blue color I picked for the front door or the paned windows above it. "It's big for one person."

"Kitchen!" She claps, taking off towards a light I must have left on when I came in from work. "Did we get ranch?"

"Yes, I got you extra ranch," I answer, flipping on another light over the island as I meet up with her in the kitchen. Evie is running her fingers over the granite counter tops, looking up at the cabinets as she circles the island. She looks like she wants to say something, but I see her swallow and sway a bit. "What?"

"Do you cook?" She frowns, before stopping at one of the barstools.

"Sometimes," I shrug, taking the food out of the boxes as she sits, immediately pulling the box of cheese fries in front of her. "I'm just one person so usually I pick food up. Can you cook?"

"I'm actually a really good cook," she says as she stuffs a fry into her mouth. "I took a cooking class with my friend Kyra because she was trying to hook up with this guy Kyson that was teaching it, and we went every week until she found out he was gay. Then I just kept going for a while and then started trying to cook on my own. I make a mean lasagna."

"Mean?" I laugh as she dips her fries in ranch. I take a bite of the double burger in front of me, before walking to the refrigerator to grab two bottles of cold water.

"It means really good," she rolls her eyes, before taking one of the waters from my hand. "I mean, really good. I just always have to throw some of it out, because I can't go through all of the leftovers. I mean, I'm just one person and I live alone, but I still shrink the recipe. Lasagna is meant to be big."

"It is," I agree, watching as some ranch drips onto the corner of her mouth. I take a deep breath, leaning forward to wipe the sauce off of her. I stare at it on my finger and quickly suck it off my finger. It tastes just like ranch, I tell myself. Nothing more. "You're sloppy."

"Because I am drunk, maybe?" She quizzes and throws a hand up, before picking up the burger in front of her. Evie opens her mouth wide, taking a huge bite as her eyes go wide. I'm in trouble. I can feel the warning light flashing red in my brain. I knew trouble was coming when she sat in my Jeep the other day. I was beginning to suspect it in the moments I was talking to Dawson about her. I don't know what is going through my head, but I know I don't want her to leave Haven.

It's an insane thought, but she's sitting in the kitchen of the house I built and she's the only woman I've ever brought back that wasn't Lexie when Dawson is here or the woman I once hired and fired in the same day as a decorator, because there is only one woman whose taste has ever mattered to me. "Wade!"

"Yeah?" I answer, jumping out of my own head. Evie is sitting in front of me, holding a burger in one hand and a cheesy French fry in the other. I watch as she looks between the two items, trying to decide which one to eat next. "Ev, you said my name."

"Oh...right! Are you drunk too?" She asks, stuffing the fry in her mouth as her eyes go wide in surprise. "I knew we should have taken an Uber."

"Definitely not drunk," I smile weakly, before walking around the island. I pull out the barstool next to her and sit down as she slides the box with my burger in it in front of me. "Ev, I need to ask you something."

"What?" She asks, taking one of my fries as she turns in her chair. Her eye makeup has smeared black below her eyes and her hair is falling in several places and is pressed against her face a bit, but I know why to me she still looks perfect. I know why I have to ask questions right now. "Ask away. I am an open book."

"Why did you take those shots tonight? I mean I understand one or two, but that doesn't seem much like something you would do. Six, really?" I ask, pushing a curl from her hair from her face. The drunken smile on her face falls and she looks down at the counter, her fingers grasping at one of the grease-stained takeout napkins. She takes a deep breath, her eyes refusing to meet mine. "Ev..."

"I don't know how to be around you. I don't...I can't...I don't remember how to be around you or me. Like what to do with my hands or how do I stop walking like an idiot or.... and my head and how do I act when I am here?" She concedes, rambling on before pushing her hair away from her face and adjusting her top. I start to try and say something to help her along. Something that makes sense. To tell her that I am having a hard time too, but she puts her hand up and lets out a deep breath. "It bothered me when you said I was uptight. A lot, but I think it bothered me more because it was true. I don't know how to have fun anymore and I realized that when Lexie...that stupid sister of mine was pushing the stupid Fireball and it was strong and then I realized I didn't have a plan. I always have a plan and I'm organized. You should see my planner. I'm so organized, Wade."

"I'm sure you are," I laugh weakly, as she covers her eyes with her hands before breaking into laughter. I worry for a split second as she swings her head forward, but she just folds her arms and rests her head on the surface of the island. I place a hand on her shoulder, urging her back up. "Ev, if you were nervous, that's okay. I was too."

"No, no, no," she groans as she lifts her head. Evie hops down from the stool, running a hand over her cheek. "Don't say that. You can't say that."

"Why?" I ask, arching my eyebrow as she paces back and forth. I know she's trying to avoid really talking to me, as if she's realizing she might say something she'll rethink in the morning. "Evie?"

"Because! We can't both be nervous," she insists.

"Why can't we both be nervous around each other?" I quiz her as she stumbles, grabbing onto the counter.

"Don't get smart," She demands, before bursting into giggles again, this time she leans into the counter before she straightens up, fixes her top and begins to open a cabinet. "I need to look at what you have. So don't get smart with me."

"I won't," I hold my hands up, removing my smile even though I want to laugh at her. I also look for a nearby water bottle, because something tells me I need to start pushing it or she's going to hate me.

"You use paper plates? You live here!" She gasps, taking one of the disposable dinner plates out and holding it up. She bends it and tosses it on the counter before she looks at me with disgust. "This! You have a house now. You're supposed to have glass plates. We're adults now. This isn't a college boy's hookup house! You have granite! Granite people don't kill trees I don't think."

"I also use plastic forks and spoons," I add as her jaw drops dramatically and she slams her hands down. "Sorry."

"You're posing as an adult, Wade!" She shouts, pulling open a drawer and lifting a plastic spatula that I think I bought and used one time. "Well at least you can flip pancakes, but your fork might break."

"I can make pancakes," I stand, walking around the oak kitchen island that I finally spent months debating what color to paint it, before I just opted to put a protective coat on it to finish later. Evie puts the spatula back in its place before turning towards me. "I can make you pancakes in the morning if you want."

"No, pancakes are serious. Pancakes are a couple's thing and you're trying to distract me from figuring you out. Wade, we're in our thirties. You need real kitchen stuff and painted things and furniture," she lists, clutching her hair in her fist as she looks around in confusion. "I literally have no life, but I have silverware and real plates and I know I have no life, because my mother and my friends and my boss all made sure I knew I had no life when they made me come back here. I'm a train wreck and you don't have silverware. Or real plates."

"Am I a train wreck too?" I ask as I put a hand on my hip, my other one pushing the same curl from her face. As drunk as she is, I think she has some sort of train of thought that she's trying to follow to make sense of things in her head. Either way, I am along for the ride. "I'll be a train wreck with you."

"I'm a train wreck," she points her finger into her chest, before shaking her head quickly. "You're Wade and you just don't buy real house stuff. Do you even really live here or is this just a house you rented and now you're really a sociopath or something."

"I don't think I'm a sociopath," I joke, putting my finger to my chin as she pushes another drawer shut. "Maybe you could help me pick stuff out so it looks more like an adult's house."

"No," She shakes head rapidly, before clutching her head and wincing. "God, for someone that builds houses, don't you know it shouldn't be moving."

"What shouldn't be moving?" I ask, as she puts her head down in her arms and lets out a groan.

"The kitchen," She grumbles, lifting her head. She looks a bit green, any signs of the goofy drunk fading away. I reach for a bottle of water and place my hand on her back. It reminds me of the time I took her home and she came down with the stomach flu the same night. Her parents let me sleep outside her bathroom door and care for her throughout the night. It took a week before Evie was back to herself after that. "I hope you build things for people better than this."

"Me too," I chuckle as she straightens up, swaying a bit. Evie kicks her shoes off quickly and just waves it off as one lands a few feet away. "I can't have my houses moving while people are in them."

"It could be bad for business," she nods slowly as I hand her the water. "You'll get better at it though."

"Thanks for looking out, Ev," I watch her take a drink of the water, a small bit of it dripping down the front of her before she puts it down and wipes at her mouth. I let go for a second, just to tighten the lid and then I take her hand. "I'm going to put you in my bed upstairs and I will take you home in the morning."

"You only have one bedroom?" She frowns as she points upward. "Really, Wade?"

"There are bedrooms, just no other beds." I point out, looking over at the food. I'll pack it up after I get her settled, *if* I can get her settled. "You can sleep in my room and I will sleep on the couch."

"How clean are your sheets?" She asks, as I finally lead her by hand towards the back stairs. "I mean...you're a single guy."

"My sheets are clean and since you may not remember this in the morning, I don't let women sleep in my bed," I admit as we reach the bottom of the stairway.

"Huh?" She looks up, before falling backwards, my hand pulling her to me and my other one moving to her back.

"Never mind." I sigh, scooping her up. For some reason, I thought she wouldn't feel this light. Not that she was heavy or anything before, she just feels different. Not as familiar.

"I could walk. My feet are still there, I can see them," She points, her head drooping against my shoulder. The smell of whiskey sifts up to my nose and I try not to react, because she's looking right at me. "Wade, why are you carrying me?"

"Look, we're already upstairs," I ignore her, putting her down on her feet as she turns around, opening her arms wide, before bending her hand and poking her nose with her finger. "What are you doing?"

"I could pass a sober test," she replies confidently, before a smile appears across her face. One of those where her eyes squeeze shut and the grin goes from ear to ear. It used to be my favorite sight. It was when I knew she was really happy. I don't know if she's really happy now, but that smile shifts something that I try to ignore. "I bet you couldn't."

"Walk," I shake my head, unable to hide a foolish grin before turning her by her shoulder to face the hallway. "I really should be filming you for you to remember."

"You can't film without my permission and you don't have it. Consent is everything my friend," she responds back as I follow her to the end of the hallway before I lean in front of her and open the door to the large master bedroom. I flip the light on and she stiffens. "Your room?"

"My room," I repeat, setting the water bottle on the nightstand. Evie pulls her phone from her pocket and sets it there too. I remind myself to text Lexie to tell her that Evie is okay. I'm sure it won't be worth having her wake up the whole house to take her back and I'm not quite sure she feels that great. I open the top drawer and pull out a bottle of ibuprofen. Evie is going to need to take two before she falls asleep so I portion it out and hand it to her. "Take this."

"I don't feel bad," She frowns, draping her legs over the side of the bed as she takes them in her hand. As I watch her, I can tell that something has crossed her mind, but she's trying to hide what might be there. "Not sick. Really fine."

"And let's keep it that way," I speak and Evie looks up at me, blinking rapidly. I feel like she's studying my face or trying to read what she really thinks is going through my mind. Only the blinking tells me she's struggling. Thanks to whiskey. Everything tells me to leave the room now. That I don't know what will come through my head if she keeps looking at me with those eyes. I will once I get her settled. I'll leave the room and not look back. I reach behind her head, taking her dark hair and pulling out the piece that is holding her hair back, letting it fall to her above shoulders. Then she runs her fingers through it. "All better."

"Yeah," She breathes as I grab a pair of shorts and a Crimson Tide t-shirt. When I look back, Evie has already taken off her top, her black lace bra immediately catching my attention. As breathtaking as she's always been, I don't stare. I swiftly toss the clothes on the bed without looking and keep my back towards her. "I have clothes on."

"Great," I acknowledge her with relief and turn around. She swims in the oversized University of Alabama shirt as she rolls up the Adidas athletic shorts a few times to keep them from falling down. Her focus on the shorts takes her attention briefly away from her balance, because Evie just stumbles before climbing back onto the bed.

"Lookin' right at home, Goode," I chuckle as I reach for her clothes she's discarded. The smell of her perfume fills my nose in the lightest way and I place them on a chair in the corner before coming back to her.

"Roll Tide," She raises a fist weakly, before looking up at me and singing. "Rolllll...."

"Well done," I clap before I grab her hand, squeezing it. "You're a true Alabama girl."

"Remember that big elephant you got me for my fifteenth birthday? The one with the Alabama shirt?" She asks as I feel my eyes go wide and she looks confused. "What?"

"His name is Big Al," I remind her before forcing a look of disgust. "You forgot his name. I take it back. You're not a true Bama sweetheart. You didn't remember the name of the mascot, Ev!"

"No I didn't!" She insists, her voice loud, before she legs out a drunken laugh. "No...I knew it, but my head didn't say it. I mean my mouth didn't. I knew that was his name."

"Big elephant? That's what you called him. He's just an elephant to you," I laugh, falling back onto the big bed and clutching my stomach. "Wow. I'm hurt."

"Wade! I knew his name," she whines, lazily slapping my arm.

"Okay, fine," I surrender, turning on my side as she struggles to sit up with balance. "What about the elephant?"

"Ass." She rolls her eyes dramatically before falling back against the pillow. I ignore the way her toes hit my arm as she stares up at the ceiling, talking expressively with her hands. "He's in my closet at my parents! In the very back. I saw him and he looks the same. He hasn't aged a day. I forgot about Al…"

"Big Al…"

"Big Al!" She shouts, kicking her legs in annoyance. I hear her mumble something incoherently, before she bursts into giggles as she tries to speak. "Whatever. He's in the back of my… what was I…oh my closet. Just back there. Like a sad…um…"

"Elephant," I offer, lifting my head to see her. "Drunk girl."

"Yeah, I think," she nods. Evie stays quiet for a moment as she lets out a labored sigh. I look up at the ceiling, my eyes focusing on the ceiling fan I installed about a month ago. It's funny how I wouldn't have imagined I would have Everleigh Goode drunk in my bed in my thirties. It's the furthest apart we've ever been in the same bed. It sounds a little cheesy for my taste, but it's true. It's the best way to describe it, because I'm not really sure how I feel about it as Evie lets out a groan. "God…"

"What's wrong?" I look over, as Evie is shaking her head. I can't get a good view of her face to tell if it's a look of nausea or something else. "You good?"

"No…" Evie shakes her head, running her hands over her face. I sit up in the bed, noticing the corners of her eyes are wet and I wonder if Evie is about to be that girl that begins to cry when she's drunk. I've never seen her drunk, I remind myself again. This is a basket of surprises. "I shouldn't have done it. I… this is how I ended up here."

"Fireball usually makes you regret things," I laugh lightly, looking up at my master bath and thinking I might need to rush her there. I jump off the bed, kicking myself as the bed shifts.

"Wade," She whispers, her voice full of sadness. I almost don't hear her, but she looks up at me with tears in her eyes. "I messed up. Bad."

"Are you sick?" I frown, reaching for her hand as she closes her eyes tight and pulls away from me. "Ev…"

"I loved him, I swear I did." Evie lets out a breath that sounds like she's been holding it forever. "I did. That wasn't… I'm not lying. I really did love him."

"Ev, you don't have to explain," I mutter, feeling a little bit smaller than I did a minute ago. "I know you moved on. That's in the past and we're good."

"No, I have to…I loved him. So much, but never as much as you. Never as much." My stomach flips as Evie opens her eyes, staring straight ahead towards the wall. I don't know what to do now, whether to leave and let her fall asleep or to stay and listen. I don't know how to move as she tries to explain something I don't think I can understand. I just know she's trying to speak and all I can do is stare at her as she asks for me to listen. "I told him I wanted to call off the wedding."

"What?" I quiz, my chest unexpectedly clenching as she speaks. The big master bedroom gets a little smaller around us and I wonder if she knows what she's saying. I wonder if she knows who she is speaking to. "Evie."

"Stop…I'm trying to think." She swats at nothing, sliding one of hers under the pillow to press it closer. She swallows back the tears and closes her eyes even tighter than before. Stopping the tears. "But…when your Dad died I wanted to come home, because I knew it was safe to. I wasn't happy he died, I mean I'm not a sadist. I don't even know if that's the right word. I just knew I wanted to be home. You. Wade was my home. You were my home, but I loved him too. I wanted to come home. I just didn't love him the way he...and now he's...shit. God, I can't think right now. This is all my fault."

"You wanted to come home," I repeat quietly and move to sit on the edge of the bed, because no matter how physically strong I am, my legs are feeling a little weak.

"He was angry. Really mad" She stammers, her voice shaking as she tries to explain this to me. "He wasn't home. Wade was home. I said, 'I don't want to get married', but he told me to focus and said I was crazy. I told him not to call a woman crazy. Who does that? I mean maybe if you're mad. Maybe I was being a little crazy. I shouldn't have listened. Maybe he was right. I don't think I know. My head is spinning because the room...not important. I was wearing a wedding dress and then I had convinced myself he was right and then he was dead, because I wanted to leave. My fault. Always my fault. Damn it. Stop moving the house."

"Ev..." I hesitate, looking down at my hands. I'm a strong and steady man. Few things make it hard for me to stand tall, but my hands are a little shaky right now. She's crying to herself and I don't really think she's thinking too much about what it means. I don't know what it means. All I know now is I'm pretty sure Evie wanted to come home. She wanted me. She knew she wanted me, but she waited until this moment to tell me. Drunk, it doesn't mean much. I remind myself that drunk people aren't the most reliable with their words. I know that better than anyone. "I think maybe, you should just go to bed."

"Wade...I think now you know. I...don't know why I told you. Just...talk," she whimpers, drunkenly crying as I stand up from the bed. She tries to sit up, but I just turn around and reach for a blanket that I had hanging over the edge of my bed. "No...listen."

"Ev, just go to bed," I roll a knitted blanket one of the older ladies in town made for me and reach for the lamp to turn the light off. She's drunk. She might have an idea of what she has been saying, but I know in the morning it may hit her differently. It's already hit me what she said. "Just sleep it off and drink water when you can."

"Wade..." She groans, throwing her head back on the pillow. "I'm confused right now."

"Yeah...me too." I let go of the blanket, crossing my arms over my chest. I don't know what else to say to her, so I just walk towards the door, neglecting anything I could have wanted to grab out of the room before I left. She has water and pain medicine, she's near a bathroom. She'll be fine. She doesn't need extra help. She'll be fine. I hear her mumble something just as I step over the threshold and into the hallway, quietly closing the door behind me. I couldn't stay in the room any longer as it got smaller. Words and things I had once been shamefully weak to wish for from her for years being admitted as if they weren't a big deal. Knowing she had at one point planned on being mine and giving up everything without any consideration of where my head was. That at least four years ago this could have possibly been a different story. I haven't had anything close to as much as Evie had to drink, but I think I feel just as confused and distorted as she does right now. Like the world was flipped off its axis and is rolling haphazardly around. Just like that I'm filled with more questions. Ones I don't think Evie ever intended to answer. It was clear she was still hurting and she wasn't sure who she would have hurt the most by her admission.

I should have left the room sooner and never looked at the goofy familiar smile, because right now I'm not sure I will sleep much if I am replaying all the words in my head throughout the night. I never should have sat on the bed with her or maybe I should have taken her right home after she ate. She wasn't in any danger. She would have been fine. I kept her here for my own selfish reasons, which I realize now. Not sure what I was expecting, but I wasn't expecting her to tell me what she had. As I clean up the kitchen, I splash some water over my face because it's the only thing I think might shake this pain I have in my chest. Pressing my hands to the counter, I try to replay her words in my head. I only find myself filling with more confusion that isn't helpful. Throwing a dish towel on the counter, I make my way into the living room to ready the couch for sleeping even if there won't be any of that. I'm embarrassed at how much I know will be running through my head tonight, and it's not just because the woman that ruined me is asleep in the room of the home I had once wanted to share with only her.

Chapter Sixteen

Evie

Now

It just takes a moment to feel the warm ray of morning on my face and my eyes hesitantly blink open a few times, clearing whatever fog I have left in my eyes and look up at a paned window with the light streaming through. Then I wipe my hand over my face, cringing when I realize that my mouth feels like sandpaper. I sit up in the bed, but it isn't mine. It's more comfortable than mine, with really nice stuffed pillows and a comforter that I could only wish I had. It gives me a brief ache for my empty bed in Manhattan, but even this bed feels a little bit better. A light drum in my head causes me to take my hand over my forehead, pushing the hair out of my face and I smell stale alcohol that I am certain is diffusing from my pores. I'm hungover. In a bedroom that I don't think I shared with anyone else, because I am in the middle of the bed and sideways which means my drunk ass carelessly slept in this bed and anyone else surely would have been miserable sleeping with me. I look around the room again, but I am slowly piecing together the night as my eyes go wide and I slap my head over my forehead and wince. I'm in Wade's room. My hand drops and I immediately collapse back against the pillows, pulling the cloud-like comforter over my head in humiliation. I slept in Wade's bed and pieces of the night are starting to return. I laughed a lot. So much that my cheeks actually hurt. I think I fell at some point, but I don't remember when. I just know my ass hurts a little. Then something hits me and I sit up in the bed quickly, but I can't put my finger on it. Guilt waves through my chest and I am trying to think of what happened last night. I didn't fight with Wade. At least I don't think I did. I remember Lexie and Dawson leaving the bar because I wasn't that drunk when they were there. The stupid Fireball hadn't hit me yet. I slide out of the bed, stumbling back against the mattress for a second. I'm a little wobbly, so I reach for the bottle of water that I remember Wade sitting down for me. The liquid is a welcome relief against my throat and I down half the bottle. I pause as I sit the water back on the nightstand, my fingers tapping against the surface for a moment before I gaze around the room. I'm wearing an oversized t-shirt and gym shorts that have been rolled over, my clothes from the night before tossed on a chair in the corner. I try to think through the night again, wondering what exactly could be causing me this feeling. I get out of the bed again, this time a little steadier than before. I don't feel queasy which is good, but my head does hurt a bit so I stop and reach for the bottle of ibuprofen that I remember Wade giving me last night. I take two out of the small white bottle and put them in my mouth, groaning at the dry feeling again before I finish off the bottle of Ice Mountain. It's a little bit better as I look around the room, with mostly neutral colors and dark furniture. There isn't a lot of substance, no frames with pictures or throw pillows. The bathroom is pretty simple too. It's beautiful, with a large window and a clawfoot tub. I close the door behind me, looking at the two sinks and light granite on the counters. This house is pretty new and I'm pretty sure Wade designed it. It just feels like a very Wade style which I don't think I could explain. It's a feeling. I come face to face with the mirror and cringe when I see mascara smudge under my eyes. I quickly lean over the sink, splashing some water and wiping at my eyes until I've gotten the smeared makeup as best as I can. Then I pull my hair down, running my fingers in it and sliding the rubber band onto my wrist. I'm not sure I smell that great since I can still smell the liquor, so I quickly peek in the top drawer and pray there is some toothpaste. Then I do something I haven't done since I was a kid who slept over at a friend's house and forgot their toothbrush: I put some on my finger and brush as well as I can, using two rounds of toothpaste. I step back and realize I look like some of the girls back in college that would sneak back into the building early in the morning to avoid being teased for the walk of shame. The only reason I even saw them was because I haven't always had a great time sleeping since I left Haven and would give up and study in the common areas sometimes. Back then I thought they were living quite the adventurous life, but now that I have seen myself, it is not a look I'd repeat.

 I step back out into the bedroom and see Wade hasn't come to find me yet, but I'm not surprised. I don't think this is comfortable for either one of us. I quickly swap out my clothes for the ones I wore last night, pleased to find the clothes don't reek of alcohol. It's just me. I shake out the clothes he lent me and look around for a hamper. I didn't notice one in the bathroom which is where I would have thought to put it, but maybe Wade puts his in his closet or just tosses them straight into the laundry machine. That would mean he would have to walk naked across the house sometimes and I quickly shake that familiar image out of my head. I decide to opt for checking the closet, opening the door and I'm immediately stunned. The closet isn't just a walk-in closet. It's the size of a bedroom. I vaguely remember noticing the size of the home last night, but I didn't really explore it. I focus for a moment, sure that Wade isn't coming before I step in. The laundry basket is the first thing I notice and I discard the clothes, but the room has my attention. This wasn't just a walk-in closet, this was custom. This was a dream. My dream. I push away any thoughts that one day another woman will walk in and it will be hers.

Nancy Goode would shake her head at me right now because she always taught me that snooping was wrong, but I still walk further into the room. Every wall is covered with antique white wood shelves, some for hanging clothes, others for shoes. There is an island of drawers in the middle with a dark wood surface. I run my hand over it, noticing that every inch of this room is perfect. The molding throughout the room accents everything else, including the vanity built into the wall by the window. I feel a frown cross my face as I walk over to it, my bare feet a little cold still against the solid dark wood floors. A vanity with the window for natural light, but there are some bulbs attached above it. I flip the switch on, then off again and step back as I feel an ache in my chest. My fingers rub firmly over my heart as I back up. I feel like I recognize this room, but I've never been here before and we didn't come in here at all last night. The room is reminiscent of a dream, but not just mine. It's practically out of a book and I run my hand along the vanity to make sure it's real. As the familiarity of the space begins to return, it finally clicks about last night and what I said. I told him I almost left New York for him. I almost left Daniel. He knows, and maybe he just thinks I was rambling nonsense because I was drunk, but it's the truth. The truth I never wanted anyone to really know. A truth that had woken me up many times over the last few years in a panic. Now I am in a room that I think means more than being just a closet. I know I have to check if there is one last thing. My eyes gaze up at the ceiling

Love in Haven

and there is the large gold leaf crystal chandelier. Dramatic.

"I found it in a shop in Nashville," Wade's voice interrupts my suspicions as I turn around, facing him as he leans against the frame of the doorway, his hands in his pockets. His cheeks are a little pink, a frown drawn at the corners of his mouth. "It took me six months and earned me a lot of airline miles, but I found the best one I could to match the picture. Thankfully this guy in Mobile could tweak it a bit and now it's here."

"Mobile." I swallow, looking around the room at all of the details before squeezing my eyes tight. We had a book; this is the closet. "What color is the front door?"

"You know what color the front door is," Wade replies, flipping the light switch and the chandelier lights up beautifully alongside the daylight outside. I swallow as the lights on the shelves come on too. "It wouldn't be anything but navy."

"You built the house. Our house," I falter, my heart rate speeding up as he uncrosses his arms from his chest. "From the...you still have it?"

"Yeah." He straightens up before walking over to the center of the room, carefully sliding out one of the doors in the center of the room. I feel my body stiffen as I see the familiar book with tired binding come out and he places it on the wood top. "It's a little worn, but I still have it."

"You still have our house book. Oh," I breathe, stepping forward to look at the book. It's torn a bit on the seam, the color on the cover is faded, and I can tell there are little rips in the paper throughout. It even looks like it's been a bit dirty over time. I wonder if he can tell how stunned I am. It's been ages since I've even thought of this book and what it once meant. I'm filled with questions that I don't know I want to ask. "It's dirty."

"It's been to a lot of construction sites and planning meetings," he begins, stopping and letting out a deep sigh. He sits it down in front of me and my hands fall to my side. It sits in front of me as if I don't know if it has the power to burn me. "I didn't change a thing in the book, but there were some things we didn't put in there and some things that aren't finished, because I don't know what I want the color of the kitchen island to be or what colors to put in what rooms or what furniture accents the—"

"Why?" I inquire, my legs feeling weak, I run my fingers along the cover, sliding my hands through the middle of the pages and flip it open. On the first try I open it to the pages we created together for this closet and I'm amazed I instinctively knew where to open it. It's a capsule, a time machine into everything Wade and I. "Wade, why did you build the house?"

"I wasn't planning on it, initially," he admits, pinching the bridge of his nose before he places a hand on my arm, urging me to turn to face him. When I do, he's tired. I can see the bags under his eyes, the way his hair is disheveled and he likely would have shaved this morning based on the stubble. "I tried to draw inspiration somewhere else, but at the end of the night I would sit down with that book and that's the only house I had in my mind. That book would feel like more of a home for me than any of those houses I built or walked through with a stiff realtor."

"Right..." I confirm again, filled with wonder to know what it feels like. The familiar feeling of home I once knew, replaced with the feeling of being alone. The walls are getting closer as he drops his arms and crosses them again. Putting that distance between us. It's needed, because that book is a magnet to our past. "Does it?"

"Does it what?" He asks, dropping his arms as he runs a hand over the book.

"Feel like home?" I question, nervously rubbing my fingers together as the pain in my head begins to seize thanks to the pills. I don't know if I want to hear what he has to say for the fear that I'll be envious or even hurt.

"I don't know," he shrugs honestly and I watch as he debates in his head, what he wants to say. "I only had one plan for my life and some of it I couldn't control. I stuck to what I could, because no matter how much I tried, I could never envision a different one. The house, it's great, but empty. I don't know what I was expecting, but it feels so close to being home without being one."

"You live here, right?" I frown, my heart pounding.

"Yeah," he scoffs, flipping a page in the book, but I don't think I can look. "I guess so."

"What does that mean?" I ask, finally brave enough to look down at the page, just a few pictures of closets we must have tossed in the book for extra ideas. I'm overcome with relief that it's not a page dedicated to any other rooms. "You guess so?"

"I don't know, Ev," he sighs, looking down at the book in front of him. He slides his hands into his hair, before letting out a labored sigh and stiffening his body. "What did you mean last night?"

"What?" I freeze in front of him, the room definitely closing in. I think back to last night, how moments ago I recalled my admission to him and wished I had kept myself quiet. I remember the look on his face, the one he has right now. One of confusion, maybe a bit of anger and a lot of hurt. "I don't know…"

"Evie, don't play dumb. Not anymore," he grumbles, one hand resting on the surface of the drawers. "I don't deserve it."

"I'm not," I lie, watching as his face changes to one of annoyance and I know he wants answers. I can't lie anymore because of the stupid Fireball. "What do you want to know?"

"You said you wanted to leave him, Ev." Wade stops and shakes his head, turning for a moment. "You wanted to come back here."

"Wade." I want to tell him he's wrong, that it's not that

simple. Except he isn't wrong, but it really wasn't that simple. He wouldn't understand why I couldn't. Why I stayed, has nothing to do with him. "I couldn't."

"Just tell me the truth. Did you really want to come home? Did you really want to return to me?" He asks, his voice is firm but I look away from his face. I don't recognize the look on his face. "Don't lie."

"Wade..." I start, but stop when I see how filled with pain his eyes look and the dark circles below them. It's gut wrenching and maybe it's the feeling of the room around us, but I've never seen him look this way. Ever. The look of built-up ache and hurt. The damage I have done, becoming crystal clear. I'd never had to face it before. I wish I didn't now, but one thing is clear. I can't lie. I can't deny it to him, he doesn't deserve it. He's right. "Yes, I did."

"And he convinced you to stay?" He asks, rubbing a hand over his stubble.

"He thought it was just cold feet," I tell him, inhaling. I'm flooded with guilt as I remember standing in our New York apartment, telling Daniel that I didn't want to go through with the wedding. The moment I ruined everything.

"Was it just cold feet?" He asks, his hands moving to his waist. "You were just nervous."

"No," I respond honestly, feeling ashamed as I remember the hurt on Daniel's face, even more ashamed by the way Wade is looking at me now. "But I loved him too, Wade."

"Were you in love with him?" He questions me, making my stomach chest tighten again. "When you told him you wanted to call it off?"

"No...yes. I don't know," I breathe, hating myself as the word spills from my mouth. The pain Daniel must have felt when I said that, was something I couldn't imagine. Still, I find myself wincing as I realize how it could have hurt. How in that moment, telling him had filled me with sorrow, but also hope that I might have had something waiting for me. Something to return to. "I had realized I wasn't in love with him the way I wanted to be a long time before that. I just kept thinking it was something that would return."

"Are you...were you still in love with me?" He asks and when I look up at him, I realize most of the color is gone from his naturally tan skin. The edges of his jaw are firm and I wonder if he realizes how tight he's holding his jaw. It doesn't matter. I don't know if I can have the courage to answer his question, without feeling I have betrayed someone else. "When you told him? After...seven...eight years?"

"Wade, please..." I begin.

"Evie, it's a yes or no question!" He raises his voice and I have come to realize I don't like it when he yells. Not at me anyways. I jumped when he did and he must have noticed, because he takes a deep breath and continues quietly. "Just answer the question. Please. Were you still in love with me when you tried to leave?"

"Yes," I answer softly, lowering my head. The room has gotten smaller, less air to breathe between the two of us.

"You did?" He breathes, and I can tell he turns away from me. I still won't look up, because I'm not sure I can look him in the eye after this. Not after I admit that I loved him, waiting on the moment that one day I would feel like my love for Daniel was stronger. I feel Wade shorten the distance between us, our bodies just inches apart, before the back of his hand lightly caresses my hair. I look up, ready to apologize but he doesn't want to hear it and he's too close for me to think of words anyways. I can smell the leftover cologne and coffee. I nod, confirming his question before I look at his full lips. Nostalgia or maybe it's deja vu, but my head stops working. "Evie..."

"Yeah?" I swallow, before his hand slides to my neck, just behind my ear as if it was still a front row parking space just for him. In just seconds, he slams his lips into mine and I'm taken aback, but I don't resist. I'm not frozen, but I can't think. The only voice in my head tells me not to move. Not to fight it, because I don't want to fight. Nothing to stop the walls of this closet from closing in on us. I don't know that I want to do anything as he lightly presses his lips over mine. A puzzle grabbing at that missing piece. I let him do it, but he pulls his lips from mine a moment later, my breath gone. When I open my eyes, there is no real distance between us. My chest is pounding as my ability to think goes out to the window and I slam my mouth against his, leveraging a hand on his chest. For just a moment, it feels like all of my anxiety and all of my trouble has stopped as I let him slide his tongue into my mouth. Like someone has lifted the weight that wakes me up in the middle of the night or takes a smile away, away from me. Then they drop it, heavier than it was before and there is a small voice inside of me that creeps up to tell me I'm selfish. That this is wrong. That the relief I felt was temporary and criminal. That I'm causing pain. The one voice that tells me to push his body away. The one that tells my hand even as he deepens the kiss, to slap him across his face. "Oh my god."

"Okay..." He pulls back, stunned as he moves his hand to his cheek leaving a hand on my side that I didn't realize was there before. "Sorry, did I do something?"

"You can't kiss me," I gasp, stepping away and running a hand to my hair. "Oh my god. I can't kiss you. Stop."

"Okay." He looks at me strangely as his arms fall to his side. "I'm sorry."

"No...Wade." I can feel the waves of panic growing in my body as I realize what just took place. A line drawn that I just stepped over. The way I feel like the ceiling flew off of the room when it happened. The way the nagging voice in the back of my mind reminded me how wrong it was. How the peace I finally felt, was a betrayal in more ways than one. "I need to leave."

"Alright, but did you have to slap me?" He groans, putting his hand on his face. "Once was enough."

"Sorry," I apologize as the guilt continues to build, because my instincts are clearly murky at the moment. "I just...we shouldn't have done that!"

A sadness and disappointment spreads across his face as I pull myself even further away from him, clutching my tangled hair in my hands. I try to ignore it, because I know it was wrong. I know it was just the moment fueled by memories. "Don't do this."

"Do what?" I snap, before rushing towards the bedroom I slept well in last night, but I feel his grip on my elbow. That fuels something in me, because I pull myself away. "You know I hate when you grab my arm like that!"

"I'm sorry, I know," he breathes, releasing his hand as he lets go and I rush out of the closet. "Where are you going?"

"Home!" I huff, ignoring the palpitations as they become quicker. More powerful. I simply don't dare meet his eyes. I rush to the steps, no longer admiring every small detail of this perfect home. I can't look at it anymore, because the moment I said 'home,' I saw his eyes sink a little more. Instead of saying something to make him look less hurt, I just rush down the solid wood steps, nearly slipping as I reach the bottom but the grip on the banister saves me. "Damn it Wade! The wood stairs aren't safe! You have to cover them with something unless you want to kill someone and what if I... You know what? It doesn't matter. They're nice stairs but they're slippery. Slippery doesn't mean safe, Wade!"

"Alright, Ev," he sighs in surrender and I know I am being loud and ridiculous, but I think I might be having a panic attack and I need to get out of this house. The walls are no longer coming in closer, they're crashing down on top of me, and soon

I won't be able to get out from the rubble. I pull the front door open and step onto the deck and the morning air hits me right away. "Here, I put them by the front door."

I turn around and Wade is there holding my discarded shoes up in his hand with the reminder that I won't get far. He gives me a tired smile, one that says he's sorry. I know she shouldn't be sorry. I should be sorry. I should be filled with regret, the one feeling I don't seem to have right now. I'm sure it will come in, like Miley Cyrus on an actual wrecking ball to remind me of how badly I have screwed up. I could have prevented all of this. I reach up, taking the shoes and walk over the post by the steps to gain my balance as I use my feet to slide into the shoes.

"Let me get my keys," he offers, sliding his hands into his pockets.

"I can walk." I respond quickly, forcing my confidence even if my mind is still feeling a bit light from the kiss, despite the panic. My heart rate has slowed a bit with the fresh breeze, thankfully the heat hasn't hit yet. I quickly run down the steps, stopping in front of them as I look around. I recognize that this is the Tenant farm land by the old Barn and the windmill, but I realize I don't see any other properties. I forgot how far apart some of the homes in this town were.

"Really? You could make it home maybe by dinner or I could get you there in three minutes," he huffs, gesturing down the road. I turn back around and he drops his hands from his pockets, letting out a deep sigh before walking back into the house. "Stay there."

I see the screen door swing behind him and I want to leave. To just start heading for the two-lane road and not look back, giving him the hint that it isn't a good idea for the two of us to be around each other. What I did was wrong. Getting drunk and letting Wade put me to bed wasn't right. Even if it felt like the weight of the complicated world I live in had been moved off of my shoulders the entire time his lips were on mine. Even if it didn't feel like it was long enough. It came falling right back, pushing down to remind me of why I am the way I am.

Before I can weigh any more of how wrong it was, Wade returns holding up my purse and his keys. I take my leather bag from him before quickly getting into the jeep when he unlocks it to avoid him opening the door for me. I don't want him close to me because of how whole I feel when he is. It feels wrong in a way I don't think I could put into words. Like a ring burning a married woman's finger. Still, I want to feel safe again. I want that weight off my shoulders. It won't happen again. Feeling temporarily safe from my own head, wasn't worth the price of someone else's pain. Dead or alive.

Chapter Seventeen

Now

Evie

My childhood bedroom overlooks many acres of land in the backyard, and when I was little I used to pretend I could see old gray brick castles just past some of the trees in the forest. I'd imagine I was sitting in my bedroom, in my family's castle, wondering if the people living in other castles were doing the same. Maybe a guard was passing the time from one of the towers, trying to count every doe and fawn that skipped across the land. I had a whimsical imagination about a world with fairies and magic spells. I lived for it. Only it wasn't real. It was just countryside Alabama, so there were no mysterious castles in the woods that my parents' house was built on. There were no fairy godmothers who could make everything perfect and no genies that could grant me three wishes, reminding me I couldn't wish for three more wishes. If there were, what would I have wished for? Now I don't know, and that's the guilt that fills me. Still, endless miles of dark green trees and water meant a child's imagination could run wild and a thirty-something year old woman could stare out at that wilderness for however long she needed to. Or at least until it went dark. Which it was right now, but it didn't stop me from looking. The lights in my parents' yard and the little bit of light from the moon in the stars only give me a short viewing distance right now. I've been mostly in the house for the last few days, because it's been raining and to be honest, I haven't felt like being a topic of discussion for people. I haven't felt like running into Wade. So I've written down every random thought that I hope might lead me to some sort of good idea that I can take back to New York with me. A list of ideas based off of everything Harbor said in her little shop that day. There has to be something. I miss the city. It lacks the same natural view that Alabama has, but the city has its own charm to it. The lights and tall buildings and the option to do something at any time has a certain allure to it. Still, this Alabama air might be winning my heart at the moment. It's been amazing for my skin and maybe even my mind. I feel like I can think a little bit more clearly here. Or at least I can hear my thoughts. Not that I couldn't in New York. It's just different. Daniel isn't everywhere I look. My guilt over what I had done, breaking his heart and never trying to mend it before he died. Someone else is everywhere and I can still feel his lips on mine. I look down at the pen in my hand, which has written nothing down on this new piece of paper. I close it up and sit it to the side, pulling my knees to my chest. It's a little after nine, but I'm not quite tired enough for bed. My father went to bed an hour ago; he's taking Levi fishing early in the morning. Lexie is watching some reality dating show downstairs that will probably be over any minute. I'd go join, but I don't feel much in the mood for it. When I look back out at the window, hear a knock on my door, before it cracks open and my mother pops her head around. "Hi."

"I was just closing up everything downstairs and decided to check the dryer." She comes in, holding a stack of clothes that I recognize. "I folded these for you."

"Thanks," I smile weakly as she walks to place them on the end of my made bed. She looks around my bedroom, before frowning at the walls. She looks around at my room, noticing the changes I made abruptly the other day. "I did some redecorating."

"You took most of the pictures down?" She asks quietly and points to the wall where some of the photos had previously been placed. "I don't think I have seen the walls with this many empty spots since you were little."

"One too many faces looking back at me," I admit, lowering my legs on the floor. She takes another look around the bedroom, before walking over to join me on the bench by the window.

"You've always loved sitting here. I remember when your Daddy built this. He said you loved your window and reading so you deserved a spot especially for those things," she reminds me, her Alabama twang deepening with each word. "He said you were his wanderer."

"I think he was right," I sigh, nostalgically trying to remember the day my father came into my room, measuring the spot to start the project. How he was trying to focus and I talked his ear off about anything that was flowing through my mind that day. "I think it might be my favorite spot in the house."

"You sure it doesn't have anything to do with the fact that Wade could sneak in through this window?" She asked, cocking an eyebrow. My jaw falls slightly and I still feel a bit like I've been caught, even years later. "Oh honey, you think I didn't know? I didn't at first until a week before you left. I saw his sneakers fall from the window when I was in the kitchen. By that point you were eighteen and you guys were so upset about parting ways at the end of the summer."

"You let it slide," I say quietly.

"That was before I knew you were going to up and run away to New York a few weeks early," she admits, giving me a knowing look.

"Mama..." I begin, but she knows that is one of the many things I feel terribly about. My decision didn't just affect Wade, it took me away from my parents and put a decent amount of strain on our relationship for a while.

"It doesn't matter anymore," she insists, but I struggle to think about how hard it must have been on her. To wake up one morning, not know where your daughter is gone until she calls you from her cell phone, in another state and begs you to understand and not ask questions.

"Still, I wasn't thinking clearly," I add, though I am not sure if that would make it hurt less. Of course she's moved on, but I imagine it still burns to relive.

"I know who you were leaving and it wasn't your parents. You and I got past my issues with your decision a long time ago," she shakes her head, before reaching for my hand. "But baby girl, we have to talk."

"We do?" I question, looking down at my hand that she has a hold of. I don't want to talk about the things I think she wants to talk about. I don't like talking about Daniel or missing him or how he was the one person that made me feel inside, that what I had done was right. Without my choice, I never would have met him.

"Sweetheart, you are a beautiful young woman in your thirties with a whole life in front of you. I won't say anything about the clock that is ticking. You're a modern woman and it isn't like my day where it's a race against time," she starts, and as much as I want to roll my eyes at the biological clock reference and tell her to stop, I know it isn't an option. She will keep going. She's my mother and if she wants to talk about something, we're going to talk about it. I don't have to cooperate. Even if I don't say much, she has no problem doing all the talking. I mean all of it. "And I think you're punishing yourself by not getting back out there."

"Out where?" I quiz innocently, unwilling to give her the satisfaction of having the conversation without having her say what she's really worried about. She wants me dating again, like everyone else. I am back in Haven and I know where her mind is. It's on weddings and babies.

"Sweetheart." My mother lets go of my hand, shifting to face me. I see in her eyes that she wants to have a talk that is tough. One that will challenge me and make me talk about the things I don't want to talk about. "It's been four years since Daniel and none of us can begin to imagine the pain that it has caused you, but you're still young."

"So it is about a clock?" I quiz her, my natural defenses coming up for attention. I get ready to make some strong, independent woman comment, but she knows that and she stops me before I can continue. Before I can make a case for her leaving me alone.

"Is mom about to talk about your biological clock?" The door pushes open and Lexie slides into the room, quietly pushing the door closed behind her to keep from waking my father and Levi.

"I'm in my thirties and I need to get out there," I respond dryly, looking back at my mother and shrugging. "Go on, Nance."

"Your age has nothing to do with it other than it's a marker for how long you've been holding onto all of this guilt. Daniel would not want this for you. Lexie, your father, and I don't want this for you. You should be happy, not living a life full of regret and hostility towards yourself," my mother attests with confidence as I am met with a burning that sparks me right in my chest, but I don't want to show her that. Lexie pulls my old desk chair over to us, sitting down and holding her glass of wine close. Neither one of them know that Wade and I have kissed. They just know I fell asleep after he tried to sober me up with food a few nights ago. I won't admit weakness in the face of my mother or anyone else who thinks I need a third shot at love. I want to show her that I am okay, that all of this wasn't necessary. Still. She seems pleased with herself. She knows me. "Daniel has been gone for over four years and he was a wonderful man. He loved you so much, but don't you think it's time to discuss moving on?"

"Mom, if this is one of those talks where you try to boost me up and convince me to join a dating site, it isn't worth the time. Lexie is more of the dating app kind of girl," I groan and Lexie just sips from her glass, having heard this all before. From Linda and Kyra, my mother, Lexie, the woman who does my hair, and just about anyone who finds out I haven't dated since my fiancé died. Imagine if they all knew about Wade. "I'm not interested."

"It's not one of those talks," she assures me, taking a deep breath before she looks at me with a wrinkled brow. "This is one of those talks where I tell you I know more than you think I do. A talk where I come in here as your mother with as much as I have figured out over the years, as much as I have been told, and then I try to sort out the rest."

"What?" I solicit, confusion washing over me as I watch her tighten her oatmeal-colored cardigan over her body. My eyes shift to Lexie, but she's just following along as she waits for my mother to speak. My stomach twists nervously, because I realize my mother looks painfully nervous which isn't like her. She's bold and strong willed. She doesn't ever seem hesitant like she does now. Like she's ready to burst at the seams. "Mama."

"We know you didn't really have a choice in leaving Wade," she admits, leaning back against the window. A look of pain creeps across her face and I know she's telling the truth. I look back at Lexie who just shakes her head at me in confusion, confirming that she never told our mother anything. Still,

Mama knows something. It's in her eyes.

She knows. There is no hiding it anymore, even as the nausea creeps into my body. There is no longer a secret in this family. I can feel it weighing over all three of us. "We know what Mr. Beckett did. About how he threatened you. We know what he put on your shoulders. He shouldn't have done that. It was wrong, Everleigh."

"You what?" I gasp, shifting away from her on the old padded bench as I reject the idea that my mother could have known and never said a word. There is no way. No way she could have known what he had done to ruin everything. Lexie is the only person I have told after all of these years. She swore she wouldn't tell. "You knew what? I...What do you mean? How?"

"It was a few years after you left Haven. You and I were getting along just fine, but I was still hurt. I am a mother, after all. Anyway, it was one night when we were leaving Libby's and Ridge Beckett showed up drunk and smelling of gin of course, falling every which way. He was completely belligerent. Thankfully, your father convinced him to let us take him home. I drove the truck back, your father drove him in our car," she begins to explain, her eyes wandering out at the window. She doesn't want to look at me, but I look at Lex. Her focus is now on her hands, twisting them nervously. Everyone knows. I don't know if she's worried that I am angry or if she knows there is no way to avoid hurting me. She has gone on for years, acting oblivious to my distance from Wade. I don't even know what thoughts have filled my mind, they're all battling for front and center and then something clicks. Lexie knew. They all knew. I want to cut her off and make her get to my questions, but I don't know where she's headed with this. I look at Lexie again, she just shakes her head apologetically. She wasn't shaking her head to deny telling my mother, she was trying to get me to stop the conversation. "We got him inside and he told us what he did. Not knowingly of course, he just kind of slurred it out and your father and I were stunned. I was sick over it."

"So, you knew?" I immediately stand up, sliding my hands over my face. I look back at my mother and sister. Lexie is staring down at her hands and my mother looks like she wants to keep telling a story, but I don't know that I can listen anymore. They held on to a lie. I feel a heavy urge to fall and to destroy something at once.

"Your father and I wanted so badly to tell you we knew, but you were in the early stages of dating Daniel and you were finally so happy. When we would talk to you, all you could do was talk about him. Some of the color had finally come back to your face and when we spoke to you, you were filled with life again," she pauses, but I don't say anything. I don't know what to say, I just put my hands on my hips and stare directly past her. The words of her admission piercing through me. I'm not sure if I am angry, hurt, or both. Could she and my father have helped me? She knew what Ridge Beckett had done to get me to go away. "We thought long and hard about whether or not we should tell you, but at that point, we weren't sure if you would have changed your mind and we loved Daniel too. You were so young when you made that choice. We love Wade, but Daniel was amazing to you. He brought you back to life and you were so invested, there was no right way to bring it back up."

"So that's why you stopped being so mad about me leaving? Because of Ridge and that I met someone. So it didn't matter?" That's all I can manage to ask her, my mind filled with the conversations over the years. "I found someone else? I moved on...so you never told me you knew what he did to Wade and I? You could have helped me!"

"You could have told us," Lexie interjects, before the look of regret comes over her face.

"You knew! You came up here and asked me to tell you

what happened after all of these years and I did!" I raise my voice at Lexie in a way I haven't done since we were fighting over sharing a bathroom in high school.

"I didn't know as much, but found out a little when Wade's dad died," Lexie defends, gesturing out the window. "I wanted to tell you, but I figured it was better if you told me."

"What would have changed? Daniel was perfect for you during that time. He was a perfect match. It was like you were dying and he saved you," my mother softly replies and ignores Lexie's request, delicately placing her hands on her lap. The lump in my throat forming feels like it might take the last of the air I have left. "You loved Daniel and you were his soulmate."

"You don't think he was mine?" I quiz back at my mother, noting she only said that I was his. I open my mouth to speak, but Lexie clears her throat, forcing us to look at her as she moves to sit next to my mother on the bench by the window.

"No. I don't." Lexie crosses her arms as she speaks so confidently. "Because other than the moment I saw you in a wedding dress, I didn't believe that you wanted to get married. At least you weren't ready."

"Lexie..." I object, but I can't form a coherent argument in my head as I look at my mother. "You can't be serious?"

"I thought Daniel was the best thing for you after Wade. That's why you two were perfect. You were truly fueled by the idea of love and the love you had for each other. We loved Wade, but we loved Daniel too. It was never possible to distinguish one as better for you than the other." My mother's face shifts as she tries to explain her feelings, but sadness washes over her face and I know I don't want her to continue speaking. I can't hear this. Her words make me nauseous, placing a lump in my throat that won't shrink no matter how hard I try to swallow it away. "I don't want to change anything about your love for Daniel. I wanted him to be my son in law. He was a part of this family.

"We just always wondered what would happen if you gave yourself the chance to see Wade again," Lexie quietly utters, trying to gesture for me to sit on the bed. "Evie, I saw the way you two looked at each other last night. The way he looked at you. You guys were in high school again."

"What is that supposed to mean?" I ask, my voice shaking as I feel my eyes grow bigger with concern. Wade and I got along, that is all. She and my mother know nothing of the kiss that took place in the master bedroom closet of Wade's house. Sure, I'm sure she knows something about the meaning of the house, but it's a house. With walls and rooms that Wade created. "Well!"

"I think what your sister is trying to say is that you might..." My mother's voice trails off and I watch her bite her lip for a moment and I glance at Lexie while she ponders what to say next. Neither one of them seems to know who is going to speak next. My mother lets out a tired sigh, rubbing at her forehead. "I guess I'll just say it."

"Say what?" I rasp as my mother and sister look between each other. Maybe they're making sure that they're on the same page without saying a word, but I can feel the anxiety hitting. Silence is filling the air of my small childhood bedroom and the sound of my nerves pounding are all I can hear. No whimsical interruptions come to rescue me from the quiet. "Hello? Say what?"

"You're not over Wade," my mother concedes, almost crossing her arms tightly over her chest in frustration. As I struggle to bury heated frustration I have in my chest. They don't know anything about what I feel. "And you feel guilty about it."

"But you shouldn't!" Lexie blurts out, her arms out in front of her and maybe it's because she can sense that I can feel myself getting angry. For the first time ever, instead of sad and heartbroken about everything that transpired over the last twelve years, I'm mad. "You were forced to move on without ever getting closure, and you two were inseparable. You were meant for each other and whether it was a year, twelve or twenty, you were denied any chance you had to see it all the way through. You don't even know what life would have been like if Ridge hadn't done what he did."

"And every relationship deserves the chance to see it through, even if it's just for closure," my mother says encouragingly as I put my hands to my head again as I can hear a weak ringing in my ears as my mother goes on. The kind of ringing that makes you feel anxious and you wonder if it was always there or if the room is just too quiet. I know she is waiting for me to try and say something to prove that her words are getting through to me, but I have nothing. She wants to know that she's magically gotten through to me and after twelve years, she's fixed her damaged child. Both her girls were damaged by love, but only I have made it an art. The air in the room is thick and I wonder why the temperature keeps rising. "And I just think maybe you and Wade have some things to talk about before you can really move on with the next phase of your life."

"Both of you, because I think Wade still..." Lexie adds confidently, her eyes wide. I don't know how much more I can take as my hands press against my eyes. "Ev..."

"Can you both just stop talking? Just shut up!" I wince, shaking my head. I'm somewhere between tears and rage and my breathing quickens. "Stop!"

"Sweetheart, what's wrong?" My mother asks apprehensively, but I turn away towards my old dresser. I don't know where to start, what to say, or if I should kick them out.

"I can't think," I gasp as blood drums in my ears, my hand moving to my chest as the tightness becomes too much. Too much to hold onto. I can feel my hands shake as I struggle to steady myself. I've only felt this a few times, but before I can get a grip or store it away, I feel hands on my shoulder and I'm pushed to sit on the edge of the bed. I feel my head shaking 'no,' but I can't seem to get the words out. "Stop."

"Ev…" Lexie's arms wrap around my shoulders as my mother kneels down in front of me, her hand moving to my face. Their mouths are moving, but the ringing is too loud. Too abrasive. Lexie runs out of the room really quick, returning and throwing something into my mother's hand. Cold. The ringing stops suddenly and I can hear them talking. "Evie."

"Oh, Everleigh." My mother strokes my head with a wet washcloth and I pull my head back as the cool water meets my skin. "Calm down."

"Breathe, Ev." Lexie squeezes my arm, her other hand rubbing my back. I can see the concern in her face, but I still can't breathe. The weight of the last twelve years is sitting on my chest. The moment my lips broke away from Wade's, this panic was brewing. "Say something."

"I'm a terrible human being," I reply softly, staring blankly down at my hands. When I am sure I can't panic any more than I have, I look up at my mother and sister. "Just stop trying to make sense of everything. Stop trying to fix me. Even when he's dead, I hurt one of them. I can't be fixed. Ridge may have started it, but I'm doing just fine setting it all on fire."

"Everleigh, we're not trying—" My mother begins to speak, but she stops when she's interrupted. The strongest voice in the house interjects itself, breaking the glances between us.

"Everything alright in here?" I hear my father and see him when the three of us look up. He's in the doorway, eyes wide and tilting his head in the room. "Our show starts in ten minutes Nance, wasn't sure if you were coming."

"Yes." My mother stands, stiffening her body. "I'll be right there, Forest."

"Alright then," he says suspiciously, eying the three of us again. He mumbles something under his breath before letting go of his clutch on the doorway and leaving as quickly as he popped his head in. I place my hand over my chest, taking a deep breath as I try to remember a grounding technique I learned from a therapist I visited once about six months after Daniel passed. Right now, the joke appears to be on me.

"Everleigh, we just want you to be happy," my mother insists, looking back at the door to confirm my father has retreated down the hallway. "I'm sorry, honey. We just wanted you to be happy. You seemed to be..."

"Okay, this is enough. You've just given me a lot of....just, no more. Alright?" I plead and stop her from finishing, planting my hands firmly into the mattress. A million thoughts are racing through me and I don't have it in me to handle any of them. Not right now. "Just, please."

"Fine," Lexie breathes softly, standing back up from the bed. I think I've drained the air from the room, bringing them down with me, and I feel a little ashamed by it.

"I should probably go in with your father anyways," my mother states, her voice tired but still full of guilt. "Sweetheart, we thought we were doing what was best for you at the time and we all knew there could be consequences. Just know, no matter what, we love you."

"I know," I mutter, without a doubt that my family would try to do what was best, but that didn't stop it from stabbing me right in the gut. I want to be angry. I'm not. Mom leans over and presses a soft kiss on my forehead before pushing some hair from my face and letting out a weak sigh, as if she just doesn't know what to do with me. Then she kisses Lexie's cheek and makes her way out of the room. Lexie follows, but stops, nodding at our mother and closing the door. She didn't leave the room, but watches the door for a moment, before she turns around to face me with her arms crossed. "What?"

"What happened between you and Wade at the bar?" She quizzes me, as her thoughtful expression fades off of her face. "Why aren't you answering?"

"What do you mean?" I answer, watching her walk across the room. Her jaw clenches and her eyes are narrowing in on me. Lexie knows. She knows something has happened, but I let out a deep breath before lying. "Lex, nothing happened."

"You're a shit liar, but you've been in a weird funk since you came back from that house," she scoffs quietly before shaking her head at me. I look down at my feet, the worn UGG slippers that I have had for a few years now are the only thing I let my eyes focus on as she sits back down on the bed. The mood in the room changes, because Lexie seems to have pushed the thoughts from her own head. "Everything is going to be okay, Ev. You...so much has happened in twelve years, but for a moment I wish you would stop blaming yourself for everything. You're not some horrible person who ended up in this mess. You ended up here, because you were and are a good person. I wish you saw that."

"I appreciate you saying that, Lex." I wipe at my face, pushing myself up before she can do something like put her arm around me to assure me I'm not something I already know that I am. The thing is, they've worn me out. More than I could do tonight, staring out into nothing. "But, I'm exhausted."

Lexie looks displeased for a moment before letting out a defeated sigh. She's not going to fight me anymore. At least not tonight, which right now feels like enough. "Fine."

"I appreciate you and Mom, but I really just want to be left alone now," I tell her, leaving no room for the discussion to continue. "I'm not mad. I swear, but I just want to go to bed. I really need to be alone. You guys did what you did for the right reasons, but it's still a lot to process."

"Okay," she concedes, nodding weakly, before I cross my

arms. I regret the colder gesture, but I feel moments away from panicking again as a chill fills my body. Lexie gets up, pushing a strand of hair behind her hair as she walks towards the door. She stops for a moment, looking back over her shoulder. "I don't ever doubt that you went through hell. In fact, I know and saw how all of this broke you, but it broke him too. Neither one of you are the same. So...take that however you want."

I open my mouth to say something as she looks away, opening the door, but I have no words. Nothing to tell my sister. Like a coward, I don't tell her what happened between Wade and me. I don't tell her that I think she's wrong or that I understand why they did what they did. This whole thing put everyone in a terrible position. I refrain from that now I wish I had said something. I don't tell her I regret Daniel, because the truth is I don't. In fact, I miss him. So much it hurts, and I truly wonder if we would have worked our way through it all. He believed in me. He believed in us and maybe I had it all wrong. I don't tell her I never gave myself the chance to see the pain this caused Wade, because it could have killed me. It's probably true, I never actually stopped loving Wade Beckett. I just managed to fall in love with another man for a little while. I close my eyes tight as she closes the door and I fall back against the mattress, covering my face with my hands as I inhale deeply. Exhaling as I drop my hands to my side and stare at the ceiling. The confliction running through my mind, as I settle on the very fact that loving two men was wrong. Maybe it's possible. I fell out of love with Daniel when I realized I couldn't get over Wade, but could I have fallen back in love? Would Wade have eventually left my mind? No. I don't think he would have and there is no way of knowing if Daniel and I would have worked ultimately. I'm more confused than ever, only feeling the stabbing pain of being reminded Daniel is gone and the feeling of confusion. Pure confusion.

Chapter Eighteen

Wade

Now

One thing they fail to tell you when you're building houses or working on a renovation is what your client will be like through the entire process. There are some you can pick up on what you think they will be like from the first meeting. Then there are some who turn into the absolute devil. I have had some great clients, and then I have had clients that on several occasions nearly had me ready to throw the plans on the floor, refund the money and go running. Ones that made me think it wasn't worth it at all. Most clients are great, but great is an understatement when it comes to Forest and Nancy Goode. They let me do my thing and they feed me at least one meal during the process. The other night, Forest stopped me on the way to my truck with a plate of hot off the grill burgers, some sides, and a slice of chocolate cake. I've gotten used to them feeding me over the years, because they always seemed to find a way to bring me some sort of dish at least once a week. Now that I am working on their home and building a new kitchen, they're spoiling me. I should tell them it's unnecessary, but they wouldn't listen.

Thank god we're building a new kitchen before we move on to something else. I don't think I'm ready to part with the constant food. Nancy is an amazing cook and Forest is a champion of the grill. Haven's Summer Fair has a grilling contest that he has won several times and the town knows the spot on the podium is for him. I've definitely gotten used to this. Even today as the family visits a zoo a mile away, there is a plate with my name on it to take home for dinner. The guys from the site have already left, and I'm here just finishing a few things up before I head home.

They've always made me feel wanted, even if I stayed away for a while after Evie left. They sent care packages to Boston, even coming to visit a couple of times, and I think about how I tried to keep my guard up around them. I think deep down, they wanted to see if I had answers. Now, those things don't matter. They are the closest thing I have that resembles family. They are the ones who make me realize family isn't just blood.

Evie has been noticeably absent, which makes me feel guilty. It makes me question if I should leave the Goode family behind. Anytime I walk into a room and she's there, she finds a reason to rush out before I can say a word to her. Some days I don't see her at all. She just hides out upstairs or goes into town and sneaks out when she knows we won't come face to face. She's avoiding me, and I don't know that I blame her. I don't know what to say about what last happened between us. I don't know if we should talk about what happened or blame it on some stupid missed emotions. We shared a kiss that, for a moment, made it seem like time never passed. Like I was a teenage boy, sneaking into her room, because I just needed to taste her lips one more time. It was just for a second, before she pulled away from me. Before the look of panic covered her face, but failed to hit me. I didn't for a second feel the guilt, despite how confused I was. She had been in love with me while loving another man too. I have a lot of stereotypical masculine pride, but that burned deep inside. I rub my hand over my chest, trying to toss out of my mind the thought that in their most intimate moments, maybe she knew she was in the wrong place. In the wrong bed, in the wrong arms, with the wrong man. Twelve years of living with the wrong choice. I decided to call it a day, turning off my drill and putting it down on a sawhorse. I unplug some of the equipment and make my way around to the back door, because the garage door isn't accessible at the moment. Stepping inside, the house is quiet and a little dark due to some closed blinds. Still, I flip on the light over the kitchen table and head to the refrigerator. Before I can open it, I hear a large thud come from the upstairs. "Hello?"

I walk towards the kitchen stairway, waiting for a response and I don't get one. Then I hear more shuffling coming from one of the rooms, but I know the house is supposed to be empty. I kick off my work boots real quick, still trying to be mindful of tracking anything onto the carpet and dash up the steps. I can hear the movement around Evie's room and as I get closer, I hear her shout out a few curse words. I didn't know she was home, but I use my knuckle to knock lightly on the door. "Ev?"

"What?" She groans, but doesn't sound nearly as startled as I thought she would. Then I realize, she probably knew I was here. Hiding in her room, making sure she didn't have to interact with me.

"You good?" I ask, lightly pushing the door open. Evie is on her knees by her bed, cleaning up a bunch of makeup products from the floor. I step into her room, which immediately reminds me of a time capsule. with the absence of all the pictures that used to hang on the wall. "I heard something fall."

"I knocked over my train case from the desk," she gestures up to an open laptop. I watch as she puts piece by piece, carefully in the storage piece. "Makeup went flying."

"You know, it takes longer if you go one by one. You could just toss it all in there." I advise, watching her lift her face up, a death glare painted across it that says she has her own system to all of this. I take a few steps into the room, the old floorboards creaking below. She looks like she's contemplating saying something smart. Instead, she just goes back to the pile. I debate walking out for a moment, but don't. There is too much on my mind and as much as I shouldn't, I want to be around her. An opportunity to show her that she doesn't have to be afraid of being around me. I walk further into the room, taking a seat on the side of her bed. The same bed she had in when we were so much younger. "It's a little bit like a time capsule in here."

"You didn't really think Nancy would get rid of any of it, did you?" She asks, checking the back of the item in her hand. She bites her lip for a moment, tapping the packaging on her wrist before sliding it into the case. "She still has all of our baby teeth in her top dresser drawer."

"That's a little weird," I laugh weakly, trying to think for a split second if my father was ever that sentimental. "Although I remember one time you took a fallen eyelash from my face and made me make a wish so…"

Evie pauses for a moment, her mouth opening slightly as she shakes her head and tosses her finger towards the door. "No. Get out."

I glance at the bedroom door, examining the nostalgic symbol of the past we shared together. I used to stare at that door, praying the footsteps in the hall wouldn't bust in and catch me in her room. Sometimes in the afternoon, sometimes in the middle of a summer night. "Remember when your dad caught us in here napping?"

"Yes," She rolls her eyes, squinting at the bottom of a piece of plastic. "Thank god that was all we were doing."

"I think if it was anyone else, he would have pulled out the shotgun," I chuckle, looking back to try and read her, but she's back to focusing.

"Oh, he definitely threatened to shoot you more than once," she comments, and I feel my face fall. Her dad loves me. When I was a nervous wreck at eighteen, asking her dad for permission to marry her, he was overjoyed. I must have been silent for too long, because she looks up so casually. "What?"

"Your dad loves me," I comment, but she's managed to make me hesitate. She looks up with a smirk I haven't seen since we were teens. "He does."

"Wade, he was still a man with daughters," she declares as she shrugs her arms. "Did you not think you were ever a guy he should completely worry about? I mean yeah, he loves you, but you and his daughter were all over each other, completely enamored and in love. He wasn't constantly coming down to the basement to check the air filter, he was doing hand checks."

"Hand checks?" I frown and she arches an eyebrow. I nod, because I realize she's saying he was making sure I wasn't doing anything salacious with his daughter. Then as I remember what being alone with her a lot of the time was like, I smirk. "Well...sometimes we were doing things with our hands."

"I thought I told you to get out," Evie breathes, but her cheeks are a light pink. She reaches for a tube of something that I hadn't noticed I was twisting around in my hand. Her fingers touch mine when she pulls it away from me and slides it back into its place. I feel my shoulder's drop, wondering if I have made a mistake, but I don't give up.

"Your dad wouldn't have shot me," I insist, but she gives me another look. I can tell she's moderately annoyed, but I don't want to leave this room. I can't leave this room right now. "He may have kept his eyes on me, but he loves me."

"Wade," She sighs, scratching at her forehead as she drops her other arm to her lap. "Why did you even come up here?

Was it to stress me out? To mess with me?"

"I assumed nobody was home and heard something from upstairs," I shrug, reaching for one of her many makeup brushes. "What? I wasn't going to just leave and maybe leave a robber in your house."

"Wade, it's Haven," she insists confidently, holding her hand out, but I ignore it and flip the thin brush in my hand. "I don't think there has ever been a robber here."

"Not true," I debate, pointing the brush at her and she snaps it from my hand quickly. I watch as she lightly spins the brush over her fingers, I assume to fluff it out a bit. I close my eyes tight for a moment because I know she isn't looking at me, and I find myself wondering if she was this passionate about makeup before she left. I force the thought out of my head, willing myself to remember my teasing her. "Someone stole the Cole's goat that won first place at the state fair our senior year."

"Okay...one goat robber in the entire history of Haven," she admits reluctantly, shaking her head. She begins to organize the makeup, but she must realize that I am watching her, because she lets out a tired sigh. "It's hardly a town riddled with crime."

"You're probably right about that," I joke, taking a small pink sponge and tossing it in her direction. It falls into her lap and she catches it, just tossing it right back at me, before searching around the area where she's sitting. She's looking for something, still avoiding any chance that our eyes might meet. I know her. I know that she doesn't want me to see those dark grayish-blue eyes. She gasps weakly when she finally finds a gold tube that was almost completely under her bedside table and grabs it quickly. I watch as she pops the lid off and examines it, she knows exactly what she's looking at. I just think it's pink lipstick. She sees colors for what they really are. "So, what were you doing up here before the train case incident?"

"I was trying to throw some ideas together...for what I don't know," she answers, sliding the tube of lipstick next to some others, before pressing her hands on both sides to even them out. "I figured since I am not in the office, I should at least try to come up with something to go back with."

"New York," I nod with a big breath, reminding myself that her visit isn't permanent. More signs that her presence here is messing with me. A reminder that she has a life that has nothing to do with Haven. "So, have you come up with anything?"

"I don't know." She sighs, clasping her hands in her lap before shifting to sit against the wall. "I met Harbor, she owns a boutique in town and she was nice. We really got to talking and she said something that got me thinking. I just don't really know what to do about it. I think I want to do something else. I think I might want to do something on my own. When I was in school, I thought cosmetics was the only industry that I wanted to break into. The thing is, I really like fashion. Shirts and bags and all of it."

"Then do something on your own. Branch out into something where you can work with all of those things," I shrug, and she looks back up at me. This time she looks completely puzzled. "What?"

"It's not that easy," she answers, before going back to picking up the makeup. "Great ideas don't just come out of thin air and... I just have a lot of other things to think about."

"Well, what are you working with?" I ask, sliding down onto the floor and sitting against the bed. "I can help."

Evie looks down at the makeup for a moment as she visibly begins thinking to herself. Maybe she's figuring out the nicest way to kick me out of her room, maybe she's wondering if she wants to leave. Or maybe she's wondering if she can trust me with her thoughts. Still, she nods and looks up at me with the eyes, I have never been able to forget. "You don't know anything about makeup. Or women for that matter."

"I think I know women just fine," I smirk, but she continues to look unimpressed. I decide for my own entertainment, to push my own luck for just a moment. "I'd think that would be pretty memorable about me."

"You are just..." Evie stops, her hands falling into her lap as she shakes her head. She tosses a tube of lipstick into the train case before gliding her finger above her eyelid. "What are you doing? What is any of this?"

"What do you mean?" I frown, watching as she pushes herself up off of the ground.

"You kiss me and then you just..." I watch as she puts a hand to her small waist and turns around, her face turning red. "What?"

"That is not what happened," I toss a hand in front of me and hop up quickly from the ground. "You kissed me."

"Oh. Absolutely no way," Evie objects, shaking her head. "I wouldn't have done that."

"Yet you did," I try to remind her. I remember it perfectly. I'll be honest. What happened the morning after the bar is kind of a blur in my head, but I really know I would not have just kissed her. Not after her drunk admission. Not after her twelve-year absence. What I do know, is that none of that stopped me from kissing her back. It doesn't stop me from wanting to kiss her now. She's like something you taste and can't quit. It's like being an alcoholic and having a drink for the first time in years. "In the closet, you leaned into me."

"I did not!" She denies, crossing her arms firmly. "We were in your closet and you kissed me. First!"

"Technically our closet," I tease, watching as her frustration builds. If I have learned one thing since Evie returned to Haven, it's that she doesn't appear to keep it cool easily. She doesn't like confrontation, not when it comes to me. I think there is something about me that scares her. In the same way I think she might scare me."

"Excuse me?" She gasps, taking a step back. "Yours."

"I could have cared less about the closet. I would hang my clothes anywhere. Hell, I would be just as fine tossing them in a pile in the corner." I argue, referring to the book that we had made together. The pages carefully curated. The book that has done nothing but haunt me. "The closet was all you when we planned that damn book out."

"I didn't ask you to build that for me!" Evie groans, her hands moving back to her hips as her annoyance quickly begins to grow. "You could have built a smaller closet. Nobody asked you to build that house. I didn't even know you were building it!"

"You're right." I hold my hands up in surrender, before dropping them to my side. "I didn't have to build that house. I could have built just another copy of a mediocre home I have built for someone else. I could have built a small closet and put another door on that house. Any other color than one of the hundred variations of navy."

"Then why didn't you?" She questions apprehensively, biting her lip.

"I don't know," I answer, scratching at my head and then sucking in a deep breath. She stands across the room, and when our eyes meet, she moves hers to look wards the other window in her room. The one I never came in through because I would have had to walk right in front of her parents' bedroom. It takes a moment for me to interrupt the silence with words I can't take back. "You could have come home."

"Wade…" She says softly, but then looks down at her hands, her fingers twisting nervously. Evie shakes her head before speaking again. "It wasn't that simple."

"Maybe you didn't feel like you could. You could have

when my Dad died or sometime over the last twelve years. I... we would have figured it out. We can figure it out," I start, looking at her but then quickly looking away from her, because I need to speak and I need to do it with whatever reason I have in my head. Reason doesn't exist when I look at her. "You said you wanted to come home. That you loved him, but that...Evie, *I* was here. That story, the one between the two of us wasn't over. It wasn't my father's story to write."

Evie lets out a shaky breath and for a split second, I wish I had left the room after finding out that it was just makeup that hit the floor. I knew something was changing, that every bit of anger I had felt when I saw her in the diner was shifting into this panic to keep her from disappearing again. A curiosity to discover who this woman was. A desire to be next to her and now I can't stop myself from trying to understand this.

"You could have come home at any time." She still isn't looking at me, but she isn't stopping me from talking either. I remember a time where I wouldn't have looked for her guidance to talk to her. For her permission. She was just a part of me. I look at her bedroom door, before looking at her. There is this brief warning, that I could leave or fight for something I may never have in front of me again. "Maybe you felt you owed something to Daniel, but you wanted to be here and you wanted to be with me. I don't pretend to understand but—"

"Wade." She softly cuts me off before I can continue, her eyes welling up as she shakes her head and braves on with speaking. "I meant what I said about wanting to come home and it's true. I didn't love him the way I loved you. It wasn't magic or some sort of painful passion, but I loved him. Differently than I loved you, but I still cared about him and I still miss him. I miss him every day. I can't diminish that or pretend he was some sort of rebound. I can't let you think that he was just a replacement. It just wasn't the same love and I should have told him that, but he died loving me more than anything in this world. Not that he was always perfect, but that doesn't matter now. You need to know even if I was ready to end it, that doesn't take away how I feel about that relationship and it doesn't take away the guilt. It's still painful. No matter how wrong it was. I know even if we had ended it, he would still have been one of my very best friends. He wanted to fight for me. He will always be someone I mourn and miss. I don't regret everything about him, and will live the rest of my life with him being a huge part of my heart. Even when I knew where I really wanted to be."

"With me. At the end of the day, you didn't want to be with him. You wanted to be with me," I cut her off, maybe from a bit of jealousy that I feel guilty about or the realization that I may have lost control of my own head. The only thing crystal clear is that the woman in front of me is the most beautiful person in this world and I miss her. I miss her heart. I miss the way she used to get mad at me or the way she used to scrunch her nose when she didn't like something. So much that it physically hurts me. I know it hurts, because it's a pain I have had every day for the last twelve years. I miss everything about her, and she's right in front of me, fighting with herself to stop crying. "It's where you should have been the whole time and you know that. Everything you said, means you knew where you belonged. Maybe he was the most amazing man to you, but it didn't matter because you knew you should have been right here with me. That you walked away from our future out of fear that you could destroy mine. But you know what? Ev, it doesn't matter. It really doesn't."

"Ev," I continue, stepping closer until I am right in front of her. Close enough to touch. She won't look at me, instead bowing her head. This isn't her. Everleigh Goode doesn't look away from people. She looks life head on and so I remind her, lightly pinching her chin in my fingers and tilting her head up. "Hey..."

She doesn't at first until my hand touches the side of her face, pushing a strand of hair behind her ears. The dark hair I used to run my fingers through. Her umber eyes divert back to the window and I begin to slide my fingers away, but then Evie's hand moves over my wrist, almost pushing it into her cheek when she looks back, closing her eyes tight. "I don't like the doorknobs."

"What?" I ask, my thumb stroking her cheek, my stomach tightening,

"The doorknobs in the house. They were supposed to be a dark bronze. Not black." Her lashes flicker open and I'm gone. I'm still a victim of Everleigh Goode. No wiser than I was as a teenager. My fear of the worst has crumbled into nothing and I place my other hand on her shoulder, pushing her to the wall and slamming my lips against hers. For a split second I question if I may have hurt her or gone too far, but she doesn't stop me. She lightly kisses me back before her hand moves to the back of my neck. I'm reminded of my favorite taste, a familiar feeling I can't put into words. Both familiar and new. When I hesitantly pull my lips from hers, her eyes examine my face, studying my lips before she bites her own and nods. Subtly, but clearly. We can't turn back now and we both know it as Evie slides the too-big-for-her sweater off her shoulders. Twelve years doesn't mean anything right now. I slide my rough fingers under the straps of the ruffle sundress that is the only thing left shielding her from the world. *It looks much better on the floor anyway*, I think to myself. I clench my fingers into a fist, before opening my hands again and pressing my lips into hers.

Chapter Nineteen

Evie

Now

I remember the moment I met Wade Beckett. I was a little girl with a toothless grin, shy as could be and completely curious about the boy that had just moved to our town. He seemed sad. That was my first thought. When the teacher introduced him to our class, he was shy and weakly waved his hand. He looked eager to sit down where the attention was off of him. When he did, it turns out that his desk was right next to mine. It took two full days for him to open up to the table of kids, but what got him to break his shyness is what took me by surprise. When this kid Rick who moved to Gulf Shores in the fifth grade began picking on me, Wade stood up to him so quickly. We were best friends from that day on. It wasn't until we were older and hormones came into play that I realized Wade Beckett was more to me than someone who hung out with Lexie and I after school. Years of friendship to young lovers was nothing short of a kismet encounter. Then one day it was gone. Replaced by fear, hurt, and guilt. I want to hear a voice of reason, someone telling me to walk away. That this can only lead us somewhere bad, but I don't hear anything. Not a sound. Not a reminder that this will all go up in flames.

At some point, I must have dozed off as I look at my bedside table. It's a little after six and for a moment I forget that I'm completely naked under these blankets, until I feel a finger tracing along my shoulder. Wade. The thing is, even if I had completely forgotten, I would know. Being next to him is a different kind of familiar. A different touch. I turn over in the bed, immediately met with a soft kiss that I don't reject. I don't want to. "Hi."

"You fell asleep immediately after round two," he smirks, before pressing a soft kiss to my forehead. "I guess some things haven't changed."

"It makes me sleepy," I say, stretching my arms over my head, before placing a hand on his bare chest. This is the first time I have gotten a good look at the tattoos. "And technically it was round three."

"I stand corrected," he chuckles, kissing the top of my head. I run my finger along a tattoo that I have seen peeking from his shirt before. This is the first time I am getting a good look at it. It's the Boston skyline around the Red Sox logo.

"You got a Boston tattoo?" I quiz, tracing my finger around the permanent ink.

"I was drunk, but I think it turned out," he laughs, as I pull his other arm up and point to the cross that I already recognize. "For my mom."

"Like the necklace," I whisper, then point to one down his side. "This one?"

"Just some lyrics I found," he admits, weakly coughing into his fist. I run my fingers up and down the words. *A mountain so high, it broke through the sky.* I don't know the song off hand and I don't know exactly how Wade has picked all of this ink out. "I've acquired quite a bit over the twelve years."

"Did they hurt?" I ask, running my fingers over another. A clock that I know has something to do with one of his favorite books as a child.

"Nope," Wade grins proudly, even if I believe he's lying. I just roll my eyes and let him continue. "I'm tough."

"Of course you are," I giggle nervously as I prop my head up with my hand. "So um...I know I..."

"Ev, this doesn't have to go anywhere," Wade offers, his voice low. I feel a dull stab in my stomach as he says it. So far I don't regret what just happened, but for a moment I wonder if we've just let our emotions get the best of us. Twelve years of no closure. Except, I feel safe and protected in a way I haven't felt since I left him. "I don't want you to freak out."

"I'm not freaking out," I lie, looking at his lips. I can't help but remember all of the times I've looked at those lips in my life, thinking of how perfect he was. I tilt my head, pressing a soft kiss to him before he laces his fingers with mine. His fingers are worn, a little dried out, and for the first time I can tell he really works with his hands. "I don't know what's happening in my head, but I'm not freaking out."

"That would make two of us," he weakly laughs, kissing the top of my hand before he examines our fingers intertwined. I feel a wave of nerves wash over me. I am freaking out a little. Maybe it's panic or regret. Although surprisingly, I don't think I want to have any regrets at this moment. Maybe it's because he's always felt like home. I feel safe even in the presence of my anxieties. Or maybe it's because for the majority of the twelve years I was gone, I was craving this very feeling. Craving what it felt like to be back in his arms. A place I had never wanted to leave despite a small knot in my stomach. For a moment I want to acknowledge there is nothing better than this. I want to pretend like my time in Haven isn't temporary or that I won't always be haunted by guilt. "I'm taking Levi fishing next weekend."

"Fishing?" I quiz, looking up at him as my chin rests just above one of those tattoos. His fingers have unlaced themselves from mine as he pinches between his eyes. I feel a faint smile paint itself across my lips, because I know this to be an old tell of when he was nervous about something.

"Dawson is going with Lexie to some sort of outdoor concert, and I told Levi I would take him fishing," He explains, his fingers lightly grazing my shoulder. I can feel his chest rise and fall as he sucks in a deep breath. "You could come. I could teach you to fish or something."

"Wait." I frown, lifting my head and pulling the sheet tighter to my chest. He moves his hand off my back as I sit up in the bed and eye him suspiciously. "I know how to fish. You know I know how to fish."

"When is the last time you cast a line?" He asks, holding his hand up as if he's bracing for me to hit him. Which is possible. "I assume you've forgotten."

"I have not," I groan, tightening the blanket over my breasts. "I could put a worm on a hook and get a catch much faster than you. Still."

"You were never faster than me," he remarks defensively as I lean over, bravely pressing a kiss to his cheek before sitting back up

"And don't give me pity kisses," he groans, turning his face before I grab his chin, turning his face to look at me and he starts laughing. "What?"

"So you admit I'm still going to be better at fishing than you?" I tease, ignoring that growing pit in my abdomen before I softly kiss him. "Even after twelve years."

"Are you going with us or not?" He laughs, running his hands up and down my arms. "Gosh, Ev."

"Fine, I'll go." I debate in my head the number of reasons this is a bad idea, but for now I want to put that voice to bed.

For a moment, I want to remember and maybe learn again what it's like to be wrapped up in my own little world with Wade. "But you can't be moody when I do better than you."

"And you can't fish in one of those frilly dresses you wear," he says, sitting up on his elbows, eying the fabric that is covering my chest. "And sensible shoes. Do you even own a pair of tennis shoes?"

"Of course I do," I respond, but I actually wonder if I have any in my closet from years ago. I don't recall tossing any tennis shoes that I wouldn't mind getting dirty into any of my bags before I left New York. There is a good chance I'll be driving to the next town over to hit a Target or Finish Line. I won't tell him that though. Before I can say anything else, he slides a hand behind my neck, pulling my lips gently to his. "I will wear sensible shoes."

"No dress?" He says, kissing the corner of my mouth. Then placing another soft kiss against my lips.

"Levi will be there, I have to wear something," I giggle against his lips, I move my hand to his chest, to push him back on the mattress, but I am interrupted by the sound of a car outside. I look at the old clock on the bedside table. "My parents are home."

"Shit," he groans as I jump off of him, pulling the sheet with me. He sits up in the bed, but I don't look back at him as I rush to the other side of my bed to search for the dress he discarded on the floor. I finally find it, piled perfectly where I stepped out of it. I look back at him, sitting with his hands behind his head as he leaned against the headboard. "What?"

"Find your clothes!" I groan under my breath as I hear the car doors open outside. "You can't stay naked right there."

"You're panicking," he comments, pushing himself to the edge of the bed as I toss his roughed-up jeans towards him.

"Can you just get dressed?" I beg, pulling the straps of my

dress. "I would prefer nobody see you without your pants on."

"Gonna get jealous?" He laughs, sliding his boxers on before reaching for my hand and pulling me to him. He quickly places a kiss on my wrist, before looking up with me with those eyes. I can't get caught up. I can't get caught. "Hey…"

"What?" I groan, pulling my hand away quickly before I run to my bedroom door and turning the lock. A part of me wants to go back to him. A part of me is angry that my feeling of comfort and being safe has been interrupted. I haven't heard the door to the house open, but I begin lowering my voice as I run to the mirror and run my fingers through the messy hair I'm looking back at.

"Are you okay?" He asks as he buttons his jeans and I look back at him, abs still on full display. I take a split second to appreciate that this man's body is a work of art. Built by Greek gods and I remember feeling like it was just for me when I was a drooling teen girl. He's still beautiful, but somehow now it's even better.

It isn't until the sound of talking from outside begins that I really begin to panic and break out of my trance. I find his shirt on the floor by the dresser so I pick it up and toss it at him. "Put this on. Hurry."

"So don't answer my question," he sighs as his abs disappear and he adjusts the worn gray t-shirt. The ecstasy I was feeling is killed now that he's put his body away, but I hear the tone in his voice. I don't know if he's filled with doubt, but I don't dare let him know that I am scared. Maybe he already knows, but I just turn around and give him a weak smile. He's everything I could have ever wanted and more. Yet somehow it doesn't seem like there is enough of an argument that this could be a steady thing.

"I'm going fishing with you and Levi." My voice is quiet, but I lean down to the floor, grabbing his shoes and pressing them against his chest. "But right now, I need you to put your shoes on so I can go and speak to my family and they don't realize we just had sex in my childhood bedroom."

"This isn't the first time we've had sex in this room," he offers with a grin and there is no longer a sign of letdown on his face and taking the work boots from my hands. "Remember when Lexie—"

"No," I gasp, putting my finger up, before he sits on the bed and begins to put those shoes on. "You can't distract me. My family is downstairs! Do you really want them to know that you and I just rolled in the hay?"

"The hay? Is this the sixties?" He chuckles, sliding the second shoe on. I can feel my panic taking over as I hear Levi running down upstairs so I quickly wave my hands to urge him to move faster.

"Can you please just hurry?" I plead, rubbing my fingers under my eyes to try and blend the mascara and eyeliner that had smudged. He can see my panic growing, because his face softens. "I need to get downstairs.

"Okay." He stands, his hands moving to the front of his body in defense but he quickly drops them as he comes to me. I could turn around and leave, but I just wait as he stops in front of me, pushing my hair behind my ears. I remind myself that this is how I lose all reason. He gets too close, touches me...looks at me. When he lightly kisses my cheek, I feel my cheeks turn warm. "Let's go."

"What?" My eyes go wide as he reaches behind me for the doorknob and I press my ass to the door to shut it quickly. "No way. You can't go downstairs with me."

"Why not?" He frowns, pulling his hand back and I give him a look that makes him get defensive. "I have to get downstairs. I can't just hide in your room all night. Unless you want me to wait up here for you and then we could...""

"No," I bite through my teeth. "They will know we were

in my room together and have a million questions."

"Well, what do you want me to do?" He quietly mutters, looking around the room.

"Go out the window!" I murmur, pointing at the window by my bed that I used to sneak him in through as a teen.

"Are you kidding me?" He asks as his voice lowers as if he's just making sure that he heard me right. "How old is that wood out there? I don't think your parents will..."

"Please," I plead, before deciding to leave him to it without argument. I stand on my tip toes and press a soft kiss against his lips before he can say anything else. "I will make it up to you."

Before Wade can argue or even sneak out, I step into the hallway and quietly close the bedroom door behind me. I don't know how I will make it up to Wade, but I already miss his lips on mine. That's a thought I will have to deal with later as I descend down the old back steps of my parent's house. "Aunt Evie, why is your makeup so black around your eyes?"

"Oh," I jump a little when I see Levi, a red baseball cap still on his head. I wrap my arms around the little guy, playfully putting his cap down. "I was playing with some makeup and I tried something new. It's not very good."

"Grandma always tells Mommy that she made pretty girls who don't need much makeup," Levi says proudly as I kiss the top of the baseball cap that smells sweaty from being outdoors. "Grandma tells me that too, but she loves when I send her makeup samples."

"I heard that!" My mother yells from the kitchen as I round the corner and see my mother putting on a pot that I assume is for sweet tea. "Hey baby girl."

"Hey Momma," I smile, but she doesn't look up. My father is at the table with Lexie, who is eying me suspiciously. I give her a look that says we can talk later. Dad is trying to assemble some sort of toy. "You guys get Levi something new?"

"We stopped at the Walmart on the way back," My mother interrupts, reaching for a frying pan under the stove. "Of course your father and Levi found some sort of Lego kit to build."

"This one is supposed to be three-dimensional." My father adds, handing the directions to Lexie as Levi takes a seat at the table.

"Should we pick something up for dinner?" I ask, wondering how long it will take for Wade to get out of my bedroom. He's being quiet enough upstairs, but I don't want to give a chance for anyone to hear him climbing down from the side of the house. "I could go to Libby's."

"I have some chicken marinating in the refrigerator." Mom reaches above the stove for a bottle of oil. "I thought you could make a salad and we could make up some of Lexie's potato salad recipe."

"Sounds great," I admit, immediately going to the refrigerator to grab some potatoes I picked up the other day. "Lexie, I can chop them if you wanna make your recipe."

"Sure," She agrees from the table, before telling Levi to go clean himself up. I can feel my heart beating begin to slow as I grab some red potatoes and realize we will be in the kitchen for a while.

"Romaine lettuce good for the salad?" I ask, reaching back into the vegetable drawer.

"Of course," my mother responds, as she fills the pot on the stove with water. "And Evie girl?"

"Yes?" I answer as I take a few items to the counter.

"You should probably let Wade know that your father hasn't reinforced the trellis on the side of the house in years, so climbing out your window isn't that safe anymore." She says it so confidently that I feel my stomach drop. "And ask him if he wants to stay for dinner."

I hear water shoot from Lexie's mouth before she bursts

into laughter, but I don't laugh. I don't even know if I react before my mother keeps speaking and my cheeks just get warmer. "Baby girl, his car is in the driveway, your makeup is a mess, and you look, well...."

"It's so obvious," Lexie practically cackles from her seat at the table, kicking her legs.

"I... I haven't seen Wade. He's probably working on something down by the barn," I keep lying.

"What's obvious?" Levi asks before my father pushes his chair out and quickly begins to slide pieces back into the box he had already removed.

"Come on Levi, let's go work on this in the living room so they can get ready for dinner." My father quickly packs up and hands Levi his water bottle. "More space."

Levi quickly shrugs without question and follows my dad out of the room. I think about walking out with them and running back to my room, but my mother is leaning against the counter with a hand on her hip. I don't know that walking out would do me any good. Lexie is at the table, recovering from her laughing fit. "Oh this is funny."

"Lexie, your sister obviously didn't want us to know that she had a boy in her room or what they just did. Be nice." My mother smirks, before looking back at me. "If you're too uncomfortable at this moment to invite him to dinner, at least go check and make sure he made it outside okay and be a lady. Tell him you will call him later."

I try to mentally talk my skin into normalizing instead of being tomato red as Lexie begins laughing again. I pinch the bridge of my nose, kicking myself as my mother begins to join in on the laughter too. They are amused with themselves. I should have at least run a makeup wipe over my face or put a sweater on. I don't know what the sweater would have done, but maybe it would have made my skin look less...glowy. I take a deep breath and walk to the back door, because I assume Wade has made it outside. Broken trellis or not, he spent a lot of his youth climbing in and out of my bedroom window. It probably would have been better if we had just come downstairs and I said he was helping me clean up my makeup that fell. Something would have been better then coming downstairs and looking like this. I wasn't playing it cool, because my mind was still trapped in the bedroom with the man I've spent most of my life wanting. The man I start to wonder if I could have.

Chapter Twenty

Now

Wade

The drive out to the lake had been uneventful through a bunch of two-lane roads and morning fog. Levi wasn't used to being up so early and fell asleep the moment he was buckled in the backseat. Evie quietly sipped at her coffee along the drive as we talked. Not about anything too intimate, because of Levi, but there was something about it that felt peaceful. Her infectious giggle still hits me right in the gut, and I'm reminded her smile is enough to set my world ablaze. When she and Levi walked out of the house this morning, I rolled my eyes. She still managed to wear a long flowery sundress and some tennis shoes that looked like the tags had just been cut off. I asked her how new they were and she said she had them for years. I call bullshit. The dress was to make a point, but she insisted on telling me that she had shorts underneath. I should have known the moment that I told her no dresses, that was exactly what she would wear. Her stubborn ass wasn't going to walk out in old clothes. Still, dress or no dress, that girl can fish. It's kind of funny how I know she hasn't put a worm on a hook in at least a decade, but she knows what she is doing. Levi even held up the bait to try and tease her with it, but she just took it from him and pretended she was going to eat it before he was the one who was grossed out. I guess you can take the girl out of Alabama, but you can't take Alabama out of the girl.

I've come up to the spot where we sat all of our stuff for a moment to check a work email. I have a client who had a pipe burst the day before construction was set to begin and now there is more to handle. Now, she and Levi are down by the edge of the water and she's helping Levi with something inside of his tackle box. I haven't really been able to see her as an aunt in action and I must admit I kind of love watching it. She's gentle with him and often gets down to his level, even though she's already pretty short. She adores him and that just makes me adore her even more than I thought possible. I try not to focus too much on the other things happening between us for a few reasons. First, Dawson would probably mock or kill me. She's getting into my head again. I'm ashamed to admit how much my head wanders when I am with her. It felt good to be one with her, like she was some sort of puzzle piece I was missing. I try not to think about how much smaller she felt to me. The small bit of baby fat from our teens was gone, along with so much more. Now, I get why Nancy seems to be pushing food at her. She's not weak, but she's different. It pains me to wonder how much she still has a wall up, even if she seems to be relaxing against it a little. It was like no matter how good it felt to be with her, I could tell she's been through hell. When I kiss her, there is a familiarity but also something else between the two of us that can't be denied. We've been desperate for each other. Sometimes her lips kiss me like she's begging for something. Maybe, she needs someone to tell her it's okay to stay. To come home in every way possible. And I want her to, but I know there is more to this story and that is what makes it complicated. That is what shifts my focus. She lives in New York City and her life is different now. I have no idea if she wants a life in Alabama anymore. It's been what worries me the most. She's experienced love during her time away, even if I didn't. Albeit, it was different according to her. Evie is beautiful and funny. Her giggle is contagious and I should have known she wouldn't be single forever. Some guy was going to try and steal her away. To be honest, I don't know how well I can handle her heart also being with someone else. Dead or alive. I want to believe that I can live with it, encourage her feelings and embrace when she needs to miss this man. He isn't a threat. I don't know that he ever was, but there is something inside of me that gets angry all over again. A bitterness that I don't like. Maybe it's the knowledge that she had feelings for someone else and I was left feeling like no lady would ever compare. Maybe it's that I know there is a small bag in her purse and a letter with my name on it. Something she still hasn't given me. I'm not sure she ever will. Maybe just maybe, it's because someone got to love her, be in her heart while I was looking to get something out of my system. Something I couldn't get out of my system until I was with her again. Her. She was stuck in my system. I'm jealous of a dead man. Who the hell says that? Who the hell admits that they feel rage towards a guy that no longer walks the earth? Why can't I just be happy that the most beautiful woman in the world is looking up at me right now, smiling. Why do I feel so much anger and pain at the thought of how frail she looked to me? I doubt anyone else would think she was until they ran their fingers along body and felt the difference. I felt the difference. She's absolutely perfect in every way, yet I felt ominous and angry while running my hands over the bone I could feel in her shoulder or along her back. Make that two dead men I feel angry towards. My father started all of this. I'm angry for what he did. I'm still angry that she went through with it. I meant what I said to her in her bedroom. It didn't matter the cost, losing her was no longer an option. The option ceased to exist when I saw her gently wake up Levi this morning when we pulled into the parking lot at the lake or the way she wouldn't let him start fishing until she put sunblock on him and made him wear the hat Lexie packed.

I watch as Levi points to a pile of dirt and rocks and goes over there to explore. He's not close to the water now, so she dusts her hands off on her dress and begins to walk over to me. I give her a light smile, tossing a bottle of water to the side. "Why didn't you come back?"

"I figured Levi was kind of over the fishing," I laugh weakly as she moves to sit down, smoothing her dress over her legs. "He usually gets bored after a couple of hours."

"Well, he is six," she giggles as Levi begins to jump on a pile of mud. I don't say much, I just watch Levi and the way he's so used to playing on his own. He's a great kid. Absolutely hilarious and I think about how much fun Dawson and I have had being in his life. I know he knows his aunt well. At least she made an effort in his life no matter what the case. She stops giggling when I look at her and I see the smile fade before she looks at me. "So, Levi just said something interesting."

"Yeah?" I ask, handing her a bottle of water from the cooler. "What did he say?"

"Well Lexie told him we used to be boyfriend and girlfriend and that made him ask a lot of questions. Wanted to know why we aren't together," she explains, picking at the detailing in her dress. I guess I was never prepared for something like Levi learning Ev and I had a past, because it kind of feels like the wind was knocked out. Up until now, I kind of assumed everyone in this town knew. Even if it was before his time, it's just another damn reminder. "I wasn't sure what to say. Can't really tell a kid it's a little complicated. I just told him it was a long time ago."

"That it was," I mutter, picking a blade of grass off my knee and tossing it away from the blanket. I can feel her eyes on me, but I shift my eyes back to Levi. He's climbing on another mound of dirt, far away from the water. I hear her let out a sigh before she begins fidgeting with her dress.

"You're quiet." She comments, her voice quiet to keep it between us. "Did I do something down by the water? Is it because I made fun of the tiny catch you made? It was cute."

You're perfect. That is the problem.

"No. I just didn't sleep well last night," I lie. I slept amazing because she was with me for most of the evening. Then I reach over to her hand, squeezing it tight. She didn't do anything. Everything has been great. Still, I think I might be realizing that a lot happened in those twelve years. I don't know how easy it is to accept it all.

"I could stay tonight," she says, looking back at Levi who is trying to stick the fishing pole in the mud. "Levi, use a stick instead!"

"He's going to be a mess," I chuckle, doing my best to try and push down anything that resembles doubt.

"Lexie will be home when we get back so...she can deal with it. I think it's my job as his aunt to let him get all messy and fill him with sugar," she giggles, reaching for her own phone out of one of the bags she packed. Last night felt different. In a good way. A taste of what life could have been. She came over with her laptop and we both worked with the game on in the background, until I couldn't keep my hands off of her any longer. I always knew Evie was smart, but as she worked and tried to create a list of something she might want to do, I realized she's crazy intelligent. I guess you forget a lot of things when time passes. It bugs me that I forgot little details like that. "I'm thinking of starting a website. Maybe a blog."

"A website?" I ask as she scrolls through her phone. I

assume she's in her email, but I'm not sure.

"I was thinking a lot about what Harbor said and she's right. So fashion and makeup companies send products, but don't advertise to every woman. I mean, we think we do, but we don't. Sometimes the product just isn't for that woman, but what if I made a website? Makeup and fashion for every woman. I'm still early in the brain process so I don't really know what all of this means yet." She explains, the tone in her voice shifting. "I don't have an exact idea of what I can do about it, but I think I might stop by Libby's one of these days and get her perspective."

"Careful, she may tell you she uses something in the fryer for skincare," I tease, working to distract myself. Evie scrunches her nose, and it takes everything in me to not to lean over and kiss it. "You sound excited."

"I am," She smiles, sliding her glasses off. "I'm just waiting for my boss Linda to email me back to set up a time to talk about it. I have to see if it fits into what Glam and Simple wants to do."

"Why does Glam and Simple have to have a say in it?" I question as Levi grabs a small twig to investigate something on the mound he was just standing on. "It's your life. Not theirs."

"Nothing I just...I mean I have a job. I was just supposed to get away for a little while and maybe create an idea," she answers, but I see a hesitancy in her voice. Like maybe she feels uncomfortable sharing this much with me. I don't push her. It took too long to get to this point. To be relaxed together. Although I don't feel that right now. I know what it has taken me to get to this point, even if I am struggling. "Whatever I do has to help Glam and Simple."

"Does it? Because I thought you wanted Manhattan to be temporary," I quiz. She bites her lip, looking back out at Levi. "Ev, I know we were practically kids when we made plans. You said you wanted to do something that helped women and…"

"I work for a company that helps women." Evie's tone shifts, her voice sounds sad like I've disappointed her. "Eventually I have to go back to New York. Make a living."

"Selling lip gloss?" I suggest, though I don't like the way it comes out. Immediately I feel like backtracking my words. I see her face fall and immediately I regret what I said. "I didn't mean it like that."

"How did you mean it?" She asks point blank. I open my mouth but the words aren't there. "Because, I do more than just sell lip gloss which if I did…would be just fine. I have a whole team I lead and I report to the company's owner. So, if all you think I do is wear lip gloss and gush over the gossip column, you're wrong."

"Ev," I interrupt her, running a hand over my messy hair. "I'm sorry. It's getting hot, I didn't sleep great…I'm just in a mood."

"You don't have to be an ass," she says, pulling her knees to her chest. She's right. I didn't have to be an ass. She is trying. She's making an effort. She gave me answers I had needed. Not all of them, but she's tried. She's letting a wall come down and I am blowing it, because I haven't gotten over the past.

"You're right. I'm being a major ass." I want to wrap my arm around her, but Levi is close by and I know we still have a lot of questions between us. Different ones, but still questions. "I know you're smart and you have a career that is impressive. I'm just being moody."

"I'll say," she groans, sliding her purse into her bag. She holds out the bottle of water I had given her and she has a sheepish smile as she offers it back to me. She doesn't stay mad for long, but I do feel a sense of guilt for the lip gloss comment. It's the second time since she's been back that I made a harsh dig at her job and it seems unfair no matter what has happened.

Love in Haven

"I'm going to go see Levi."

"Ev." I reach for her hand before she pushes herself off the ground and lets out a loud groan. "I'm sorry. I'm a grade-A grouch."

"You are." She rolls her eyes, before dropping her head back. I can see her release the tension from her body and slides her hand into mine. "Come on. Let's go stop Levi from completely getting messy."

"I think it's too late for that," I chuckle as I gesture to Levi who has mud all on his legs. I toss the water bottle on the blanket and look down at it. I place a hand on the small of Evie's back as we walk towards Levi and she doesn't push away so I know it's possible that she's ready to move on. We stop and watch Levi explore. He reminds me of what it's like to be a six-year-old boy, obsessed with the dirt and making more messes than staying clean. "I think it's time to toss you into the lake to clean you off."

"I'm discovering," Levi says proudly, reaching into a small pile on the ground. Levi holds a long feather up in front of his face as if he's found gold on the banks of the river. "Aunt Evie...look what I found."

"Wow," Evie exclaims, reaching for the fishing pole that was tossed on the ground.

"I think it belongs to a bald eagle!" Levi claims as he pushes his hand out, holding the white and gray feather out proudly.

"Maybe," Evie grins, reaching for Levi's blue sunglasses that are covered in dirt. The feather very clearly doesn't belong to a bald eagle, but she doesn't tell him that. She steps down the bank and dips the sunglasses in the water to clean them off. "Levi, I think you're better at fishing than Wade."

"I am," He says confidently as he jumps onto another pile of dirt. Then he looks up at me and breaks into laughter.

"Really, kid?" I toss my hands up, shaking my head. I

didn't catch anything to rave about this morning, but somehow Evie and Levi managed to catch something impressive. I swear Ev is in cahoots with nature somehow. The way even in her city style, everything about the scenery around her compliments her. "I'll have you know, I have caught plenty of fish. Big ones. For the record books."

"I know. You're very manly," Evie exaggerates before she pats my back as she walks around to the mud pile, kneeling down with Levi to examine some rocks that Levi earlier announced to be fossils. The kid cracks me up, but watching him with his aunt sends me into a million thoughts I wish I could control. I wonder if Levi fears her leaving. If he knows this is temporary. Is it something he's used to or is he going to be left feeling a void like the rest of us? This is the longest she's been around throughout his entire life. "Levi, I think we need to clean up a little and get heading back."

"But I want to look for more fossils," Levi groans, picking a thin gray twig up off the ground. "What if I find a bone from a stegosaurus?"

"I am sure you will," Evie smiles warmly, before dusting off her dress with her hands. "But right now Wade owes you an ice cream and me a sweet tea."

"Of course I do." I walk up behind her, placing my hands on each of her sides. I probably shouldn't. We're out in the open and while it isn't a busy day at the lake shore, there are people around and a few of them are Haven locals. I can feel Evie stiffen, my lips moving to just behind her ear. "I owe you something else after we drop Levi off."

"Wade," She gasps, pushing my hand away as quickly as I put it there. She shakes her head as she walks away from me, but I can't help but smile when I see that her cheeks turn red. Every doubt I have, for just a split second, becomes less of a bother. The smile and the cheeks kill me. I would do anything for her. I've done everything for her. I've travelled hundreds of miles only for her to completely shut me out. I'm a man standing under a forest of trees with her and her nephew, wondering what the hell I am doing. Yet soaking up every second just for a sign of flushed cheeks or a smile. "Levi, I got some good photos of that one fish you caught. Grandpa will be so excited."

"Do we have to go back?" Levi groans, wiping at his eyes with a dirty fist. "I want to fish some more."

"Yes, we do." She says, handing over his tackle box and pole. She reaches for ours which area propped up against the tree and we make our way back through the dry grass to the area where our blanket is set up. The rays from the sun are hot against my neck as I lean over and fold up the oversized blanket that Evie tossed in my Jeep this morning. Levi is no help at this point, but he's finding ways to entertain himself as we finish packing up our spot and I can't help but notice Ev has grown quiet. It's my fault. I am the one who made another dick move comment about her job. I did it because I was angry. At her, at me. As we finish packing up our things, she and Levi begin to walk ahead towards the SUV. I watch as she giggles, her smile big as they talk between the two of them. I don't try to figure out what about, I just watch her. Begging myself for some sort of answer. For some way that I can move past it all and fight for her. Her time will run out here and all I can feel my pride focus on is that some other man has part of her heart. I reach for my keys, unlocking the door before Evie opens the back of the Jeep. Levi climbs into the back seat as I meet up with Ev. "Hey, what's going?"

"What do you mean?" I ask, sliding the faded Igloo cooler into the back before taking the fishing poles from her hand. Evie looks down at her feet, before crossing her arms. "I told you. I'm tired...hot. Nothing is going on."

"Okay..." She breathes and tosses the tote next to the fishing poles. "If you want, I can just stay home tonight. If you want to rest or whatever. I mean there is no reason we would be required to hang out together. I mean we don't have to do anything. If you're not wanting to spend time around each other."

"I want you to come over," I say quietly as Levi slides his headphones on, I don't fight my urges and I wrap an arm around her waist. "Let's just cook dinner and relax. We can find a movie to watch. No pressure."

"We can do that." A warm smile appears on her lips, and I sneak a quick kiss to her cheek. The only thing clear in my mind, is that I don't want her to think I don't want her. I spent over a decade wondering if I had loved her enough. If I had done enough to let her know I wanted her more than anything in this world. Even in my fits of anger this was true. Which is what makes everything else all that more confusing. I pull my hand from her waist, before closing the back of the car. Evie goes to the passenger side as I let out a deep breath. I'm not going to pretend to understand or think about what is going on in her head. She seems a bit more relaxed than when she first arrived in Haven and the relief that her family feels isn't lost on me. Hell, I feel relieved. But I know a few times having sex and some intense makeout sessions didn't fix the things between us. If I even know what it would take to fix it. If I know her at all. The Evie I know was a teen girl without a major care in the world. Hell, I'm a different man too. My thoughts freeze as I hear her call my name from the passenger window and I pull myself out of my thoughts to come around the driver's side. The truth is, I love her. I never stopped loving her and, in my pain, I ignored it. I had done what I could to try and stop, but I couldn't. This woman is who my heart will belong to until the day my last breath leaves my body. The problem is, I don't know what to make of it and I don't know that she feels it too. I can worry about all of that shit later. For now, I just want to drive home with her next to me, while we answer as many questions about the world that Levi throws at us.

Chapter Twenty-One

Evie

Then

New York City

The rain abrasively hits against the window of this shady motel in the Bronx. It was the cheapest I could find that still had a room available. It's too soon to move into FIT, but New York was the only place I could think of to go to in a hurry. After all, it was still the plan. I spoke to Mom and Dad tonight, even Lexie for a moment. Somehow, after an hour they finally let me off the phone and stopped insisting that they fly out to talk some sense into me. They promised to only come during freshman move in week. Mom thinks I've lost my mind a bit, getting cold feet or having some sort of breakdown. Dad seems to think I'm going through a phase and says he is putting extra money in my account. He doesn't have to, but he's not asking me for a reason why I left either. Lexie's the only one who has cursed me out. I deserved it too. She said Wade hasn't eaten or slept since I left. That he was driving himself crazy, but said he wanted to give me space. Then she said he'd left town. Telling not a soul where he's gone. She confirms what I already know. I've done this to him. The truth is that they're all wrong and I don't know if I am alive or dead. If I told them that, they wouldn't understand. My hair is wet, clinging to my shoulders as I strip my clothes off from walking several blocks in the rain for some takeout that the front desk girl told me was the best Chinese food on this side of the Hudson. I could have taken a cab, but something felt better about the walk in the rain. Maybe it was the simple reminder that there is blood pumping through my veins. It answers the question, *am I alive or dead?* I look at the takeout bag on the nightstand. A white plastic bag with a red, 'thank you' printed all over and covering a paper brown bag. It smells really good, but makes me nauseated at the same time. I haven't eaten today and that reminder makes the tears come again. I want to go home. I need Wade.

I feel a sob escape my lips with a cough that has snuck its way in there. I need him. There is no want. He is why I breathe, but right now I don't know how I can fix this. I've already left. His father has won and I've destroyed him. I cry as I strip the wet clothes off from the rain, knowing I can't sit in them the whole night. Although the brutal case of something doesn't sound so bad right now. Maybe then I could sleep and not cry over Wade.

I go to my suitcase, flip it open, and find his sweatshirt. It's wrong of me to put on his sweatshirt after what I did, but I did it for him. I wouldn't feel this way if I had it my way. If I had been given a choice. I've worn the sweatshirt every night that it has tear stains and I need to go to a laundromat, but don't have the energy yet to be the crazy lady crying as the washer spins. I slide the oversized fleece over my body before reaching for a pair of his gym shorts. I've always had a sweatshirt and some of his clothes, but before I snuck out of his bed, I grabbed two more things from the hamper. I double roll the shorts, but then I hear the phone ring. It isn't my cell phone, instead it's the old rotary phone on the nightstand. It doesn't stop as I walk across the room, so I quickly pick it up. I can hear the sound of the lobby and some cabs outside, so I finally mutter out some words. "Hello?"

"Um hi. This is Veronica from the front desk." A woman's voice I recognize is on the other end. She's the tall girl I see on my way in and out. The one who looks at me as if I'm the saddest person on the planet. Maybe I am. "There is a man who says he is looking for a girl named Everleigh Goode. His name is Wade—"

"I don't know him," I cut her off quickly with a lie that pierces right through my heart. I try to listen for him to say something, but I just hear the same noises as before. "I'm not here."

"Got it. Thanks Sheila," she answers confidently and the line goes dead and I don't even care that she pretended terribly that she was speaking to someone by a different name. It doesn't matter, I'm drowning in tears. I fall back into the bed. My hands fall over my face as I sob into them. If I have any neighbors in this motel, they surely hate me or are questioning my sanity. All I do is cry. I pull myself up from the bed, wondering if I can see through the rain out my window. The off chance that I can see him, to see he's alive and breathing for my own eyes. Surely, he'll be okay. Maybe if I could just see him.

I push back the musty old curtain, peering down at the sidewalk in front of the building. I can still see pretty well through the rain from four stories up. I sniffle as I see a woman pushing a stroller, two men moving a carpet up the block and then I see him. I see him stop in front of my building, squat down, and hold his head in his hands. It's too much. I want to run down stairs and tell him I'm sorry. I want to tell him everything. Maybe now he'll listen when I suggest running away. We don't need the plan. We can have a new plan. A new life. Nobody will ever make me stop loving this man. I look back at the door to the hotel room. I can do this. I need to get to him. I look back at the window and he's standing now, looking at his phone. He's still there. I run towards the door, not even caring that I am wearing the slippers I was walking around the hotel with. I discard the security lock and let the door close behind me as I hear my heart pounding like a drum through my ears. My pace picks up when I see the sign for the stairs, pushing the door open and running down as many flights as I can until I am at the ground level. I don't even look back as I run into the lobby, looking everywhere. Veronica seems to have left her post, so I run towards the front and out onto the sidewalk. "Wade!"

I spin around, but I don't see him anywhere. I can't see any sign of any direction he went towards and I can't even recall what he was wearing. Like the universe is holding me accountable to do the right thing. Telling me to give up and let him go to Boston. He'll get over me, but I won't get over him. I spin around again, in hopes there is some form of kismet energy that will send him back to me. I wait, leaning against a stone planter, but he doesn't come. The rain is starting to get heavier and I'm not ready to take his sweatshirt off. He's not coming back. And that is that.

Chapter Twenty-Two

Evie

Now

If someone had told me twenty years ago that the deep country town of Haven, Alabama would host a Beer and Wine Festival, I would have laughed in their face. That is way too modern and hip for Haven. Sure we have boutiques, but that is different. Haven doesn't do anything like a beer and wine event. But here I am, walking up a road with vendors every couple of feet and people walking around with drinks in their hands. Every hotel within thirty minutes is booked solid. It's a three-night event in the town and Wade asked me to meet him here. My parents are home with Levi while Lexie goes to Mobile to visit a friend of hers that had a new baby girl. I have no doubt they'll all be here on one of the other nights.

Walking down Main, I get a text from Wade. He's running a few minutes behind and then he sends me the picture of a dog covered in dirt. Apparently someone up the road from him must have had a dog get out and he's going to take it home before he comes over. He hasn't been moody since the other day at the lake. In fact, he's been perfect. So much so that I find myself lying in my bed wishing he was there. I'm not used to that feeling and I hate the guilt I feel. But I can't get myself to stop. There is something that happens when I am with him. Like a part of me can't stop smiling and when I am with him, I just can't stop myself from grabbing his face and kissing him. Almost an involuntary reaction. Which makes me wish he was here now. Which is fine, I can check my work email until he gets here. "Evie?"

I look up to see Harbor from the boutique walking up to me, wearing jeans and a baseball cap. "Hey!"

"I didn't expect to see you here!" She exclaims, her thick southern accent hangs in the air. It definitely sounds like a Louisiana accent. "Word on the street was that you usually don't stay in Haven too long."

"I'm on a bit of an extended trip, I guess," I say, immediately regretting it. I don't really know what I am doing at this point, but whenever I try to bring it up to Linda, she just brushes me off and says to take all of the time I needed as if this wasn't something she forced on me. "So, the shop is closed for the night?"

"No, I have two girls working tonight from the high school. One is eighteen and I am letting her test out closing," Harbor shrugs. "Besides, I don't know how much longer it will be open."

"Why is that?" I frown, as Harbor looks around, her eyes surveying the crowd. She does it for so long, that I actually start looking around in case I am missing something. It's just a bunch of people, enjoying this so-called Haven nightlife.

"The owner, Hilly, wants to sell at the end of the year." She looks back, her tone deflated. "I think she kind of bought the store on a whim and started a company, but she doesn't even come in at all. She lives three hours away. I guess now that she is getting older, she realizes it's not something she wants."

"That's too bad," I say, because I really mean it. I really enjoyed shopping at Hilly's, and it's such a great store to have in Haven. Fashion, some makeup products and all of the southern charm.

"Not sure, but I am hoping someone buys it and has a passion for it." Harbor communicates, lowering the bill of her cap. "It is such a beautiful shop with so much potential."

"It really is," I agree, but I struggle to think of anyone who lives in this town that might understand its potential. Before I can try to search my brain anymore, I see Wade begin to approach us. "Hey!"

"Hey," he grins, walking up with his newly cleaned jeans and a flannel buttoned except for the top few. He comes to my side, almost putting his hand on my back but then drops it quickly as if he thinks he better not. He probably shouldn't with some of the most aware crowd, but I miss his touch. "Hey, Harbor."

"Hey, Wade," Harbor greets him with a subtle wave, until she looks between the two of us and her grin widens. I can see that we definitely gave ourselves away just by our stupid grins when we see each other. "You know...I'm going to go visit Libby's stand. I heard she was sampling her rhubarb pie. Stop by the shop this week Everleigh. We just got in some new items and I swear they are to die for."

"I will," I promise as Harbor jumps forward and hugs me real quick. I wasn't expecting it, but then again I should have. I'm fully aware of where I am.

"Alright," She lightly waves as she backs up. "Bye Wade."

"See ya." He waves as Harbor turns back towards the crowd and disappears into it. I feel bad that the store is going to be in such limbo and may end up closing. It seems so silly to be bothered by it, but Harbor seems to really appreciate some of the things I do and she is a good employee for a company like that. Before I can dive into any more thoughts, Wade yanks my hand and begins walking. "Come here."

"Wha–where are we going?" I ask, struggling to keep up as he pulls me across the street and onto the sidewalk. I expect him to stop, but he doesn't. He's racing down the sidewalk, squeezing my hand. I want to remind him he's asking me to do this in peep toe wedges. "Wade."

"We're almost there." He says, turning sideways to avoid running into some guys walking by. When we reach the end of the strip before we would have to cross the street, he yanks me to turn left.

"Okay, I don't mean to sound like city folk, but I am wearing very expensive shoes that aren't made for running." I gasp as we reach the end of the old brick building. We're close to where a few employees park and the dumpsters. "I–okay now I am weirded out."

"Climb." He gestures up and I realize he's pointing to an old fire escape ladder. I look down and see a few milk cartons stacked up. He must be crazy.

"No way." I shake my head and begin to turn around, but he grabs my hand. "Are you insane? Those are wooden cartons and I am not scaling the side of a building."

"I am not asking you to scale the building. I am asking you to climb and trust me." He says, then gestures to the ladder. "I'll be right behind you."

"If this is how I die, I will personally come back and kill you," I groan, unsure if this is something I want to do. He's so confident, that it makes me want to trust him. The truth is, I would trust him with my life. Isn't this a part of that? I give him one more concerned glare, before he takes my hand and I step up on the carton, grabbing the thin metal of the latter. It's pretty sturdy for something so rusted, but I step onto it. I look down at him as he holds onto the carton's, keeping them steady as I lift my last foot off of them and onto the ladder. I used to do crazy things like this all the time, so why am I freaking out? Then, I feel a hand grab my ass. "Damn it, Wade!"

"Sorry, you're wearing a dress and it was too tempting," he claims as he begins to climb. "Somehow, I feel like two of us shouldn't be on this ladder at once."

"Then get off of it!" I shout, climbing a bit faster as I begin to fear that somehow no matter how stable this ladder is, it might not hold up. I am not dying next to a filled dumpster. Or any dumpster for that matter. I make my way to the top and look down at Wade. "Now what?"

"Climb onto the roof, Crazy," he shouts, only a few steps below me. "Hurry or I'll start shaking this ladder."

"You're an ass!" I shout, stepping over the last step and over the small part of brick ledge. When I get to the other side, I am relieved to have my feet planted on the ground. Or roof. Depending on how you look at it. There are a lot of little walls that cover things like the HVAC and I see a door to my right. "Are you kidding? There is a stairway from the inside, Wade!"

"That's not nearly as much fun." He casually speaks as he makes his way up and over the ledge. He dusts his hands off, before wrapping his arms around me. I can't help but close my eyes for a moment, letting my beating heart catch up for a moment as I lean against him, quickly forgetting that he just made me risk my life. "I have a surprise for you."

"Wasn't the surprise climbing a fire escape that's older than my parents?" I ask, as he reaches for my hand again, this time walking beside me. When we reach the other side of the roof, we stop. It takes me a moment, but there is a blanket, a bottle of wine on ice and an old picnic basket. Actually, the same picnic basket I used to bring with us when we were younger. "What is this?"

"I was thinking. Why not have all of the great parts of a

wine festival and enjoy the sunset?" He explains, walking in front of me and taking his phone out. I can't see what is on the screen, but he scrolls a bit before sitting the phone on a doc that's plugged into an extension cord. "I have cheese, wine, and music."

"You do?" I question as I step closer to the blanket and Wade moves to sit on the ground. He holds his hand out, his smile widening which just makes the stubble on his chin look damn sexy. I give him another suspicious look, but I take his hand and lower myself to the ground. He lets go of my hand, reaching instead for the bottle of wine as I look out at the sky. I know I have seen the sunset and even sunrise from a rooftop in Haven before. Still, there is something that feels like it's the first time all over again. Wade hands me a glass, before pouring himself one. "So, I guess Hilly who owns Hilly's...wants to sell or close the shop at the end of the year."

"What?" He frowns, reaching inside the picnic basket. He takes out two separate trays, One with cheeses and crackers, the other with fruits, nuts and even some chocolate covered strawberries. "That's too bad."

"Right? It's such a nice shop," I frown, as he sits up, pressing a kiss to the side of my head. "Anyway, it's a shame."

"It is," he confirms, pushing my hair behind my ears. "That store brings a lot of traffic into Haven in a really good way. It actually won an award last year from the Chamber of Commerce."

"Maybe Hilly will sell to someone local," I sigh, repositioning myself into his chest. I think briefly for a moment about what I would have done to the shop, but decide to shift my focus to the man currently breathing on my neck. "How was your day?"

"Good," He breathes, kissing the side of my neck. "Even better now."

"Even after nearly letting me fall to my death?" I giggle, placing my hand on his knee.

"I would have given my life before I ever let anything happen to you," he sighs, wrapping an arm around me. I close my eyes, letting him breathe me in as I try to think for just a moment. Try to memorize what this feels like and tell myself that soon I have to go. I don't think this would work if I left again and truthfully, I don't know that I deserve him. I try to tell myself to imagine my world if for a moment, I could go back. Back to him, back to the life I always wanted. I wonder if he could support me when I need to mourn and miss Daniel. I know it would be a lot to ask, but I think if anyone could do it, it would be Wade. My mind wanders to a million places it hasn't before. The sky is changing, the colors turning shades of rose and orange. It's becoming more ethereal as each second passes. Thoughts that come into my mind as he clutches my face, tilting my head back. He presses his lips into mind and everything washes away. I don't want to think. I don't want to worry what will come of us when I leave. I don't want to question if I want to throw it all away and leave him. I don't want to consider moving back to Haven. I just want to be in this moment, kissing this man that still gives me that stupid butterfly feeling. "Ev…"

"Yeah?" I pull my lips away, my fingers rubbing the lip gloss away from his lips.

"I love you," he whispers, and I feel everything in my body flash freeze. My body must stiffen, because he drops his hand and immediately straightens up and I am forced to sit up. "You don't have to say it. You don't have to say anything."

Idiot, you love him too. Three words.

"I um…thank you?" I say as a question, then shake my head. I can't say it yet, but the truth is I want to. I need to say something else, because he looks disappointed. I put my hand on his face. "Don't think I don't want to. To say it. I just…it's a lot. I need to…"

"Ev." He puts a hand out, moving his other hand over

mine on his cheek. I can see a little bit of panic in his eyes and I want to tell him I'm sorry. I know it's hurting him. I want to tell him its too soon to say that, but is it? There is a part of me that wants to run, but I can't find it in my heart to do that. Not to him. Not to me. "It's okay. I kind of just blurted it out. I mean I meant it, but I understand. You don't have to say it. It's okay."

"But I don't want you to think…" I begin, but he stops me, grabbing my hand and kissing it. He kisses it desperately as if he's trying to stop me from fleeing, I won't.

"Ev, it's okay. I promise," he nods and forces a smile on his lips. In a way that tells me he's sure, even if it did hurt. I know he wished something else would have happened when he said it and I do too. But it would have been wrong. Wrong to not know what I wanted to come from it. Wrong, because I don't know what would happen when I returned to New York and wrong, because I can't stop living with the guilt. "I just want us to enjoy our time. I said what I needed to and we can move on."

"Okay," I nod hesitantly, as his lips lean forward to lightly brush mine. He kisses me for reassurance, telling me we can brush it under the rug. He still loves me. Lexie was right. I feel the same way and it hurts. It hurts even more, because I wish I had it in me to say it. I wish I knew saying it would fix it all. I deepen the kiss, pushing him onto his back because I don't want to think anymore. I don't want to panic either, but I don't want him to think I don't want him either. So I want to make love to this man on this roof and let him know for now, I want him. I need him to know just how much I want him.

Chapter Twenty-Three

Wade

Now

Living on one of the old back roads in Haven has its benefits. There isn't a ton of traffic, but the sound of cars driving by against the dirt road is one of my favorite noises. I came home from one of my new build jobs, took a shower, got dressed and grabbed a beer. I've taken to my new favorite spot in one of the two rocking chairs I bought at a country tractor shop the other day. I checked in on Forest and Nancy's house today, even though my team has a good handle on the remodel. Truthfully, I use any chance I can to stop by and see them. Nancy made me one hell of a BLT. Of course, I didn't even have to ask.

Now that Ev is there, I stop by even more and her family doesn't do anything to call us out on how close we've gotten again. In fact, I get the idea that they're welcoming it. Her mother told us about a new restaurant that opened in the next town over and suggested we 'make a night of it.' I shift my eyes to the road as a cattle farmer's truck drives by and I sip from the bottle. I love these roads, but they don't distract me from a few of the things circulating in my head. I know that something is changed or maybe returned to the same with Evie, but I may have gotten carried away. I got cocky. I told Ev that I loved her. Truthfully, I hadn't meant to tell her when I did. It just kind of spilled out. I had realized it a while ago, but I was going to keep it inside. I wasn't sure that I wanted to even say it, but then she was there on that roof and I just said it. There was still too much to be worked out between us and hell, I knew neither one of us was ready for that admission. Judging by the look on her face, she was pretty panicked and thrown off by it. I could see it in her eyes, but I didn't want her to run or panic. And for a split moment, I thought maybe she wanted to say it too. For a split second there was a look in her eyes, but then again it's been a while since that word floated between the two of us and she said 'thank you.' *Thank you.* Like I gave her a bottle of water. The truth is though, no matter how much I meant it, it wasn't the right time. I'm not mad that she couldn't say it. Not when I was having my own doubts about whether or not I could ever fully be okay having another man's shadow between us. I don't know why it bothers me. I wish it didn't. In a way I am grateful for him. He kept her somewhat happy for some time and seemed to have taken good care of her. Sure, she didn't love him the same way. It just stings a bit and my pride starts to rumble. Although, it doesn't sting as much as saying I love you and not hearing it back. I don't know what I was expecting when I said it. It just came out of my mouth, because she was in my arms, we were on a roof in Haven and I couldn't stop. I meant the hell out of it.

The whole moment has been replaying in my head, my fingers scraping against the stubble on my chin as her rented Ford SUV comes down the street. I can't help but grin as she pulls in next to my Jeep, parking crooked like she always has. "I am going to have to paint lines for you to learn how to park!"

"Shut it!" She shouts from her car, powering it off. I stand up, sitting the nearly finished beer on the unfinished wood table between the chairs and walk down the steps. Her window is down and her hair is pulled back as I approach the car. "Sorry...texting Lexie back."

"What does she have to say?" I wait for her to finish, before reaching my head in, for a quick kiss from lips that taste like cherry.

"You taste like beer." She smiles, pulling her lips away.

"I have one inside with your name on it." I say, reaching my hand in to unlock the door before pulling it open. Ev is wearing a plain white t-shirt and some plaid shorts with tennis shoes. I love it. I love her dresses and everything else she wears, but there is something about this. God, she's perfect. "Burgers sound good?"

"Yeah," she says, holding her phone close as she tosses her bag on the floor of the car. Finally she gets out, her eyes still focused on the phone. I close the door behind quickly scooping her over my shoulder and her hand slaps my back. "Wade!"

"You were moving too slow," I say, rushing up the steps. I bypass the new rocking chair and table and push open the navy-blue front door. I can show her the table I built later. I put her down when we're in the unfinished entryway of the house.

"You could have just said hurry up." She breathes, standing on her tiptoes to give me a quick kiss. Definitely cherry. She confidently pats my chest and walks by me and heads into the kitchen. The sight of her so casually walking the halls of this house is enough to send me into overdrive. I've spent a great amount of time in my life trying to picture moments like these. It's the life I wanted on the hardest nights when I would try to fight through the pain, sometimes just trying to imagine that life might one day work its way out got me through. I'll admit I had lost hope, built a wall of anger and assumed all the chances were gone. But moments like these are telling me that it might have been worth it. Where she walks through this house, because it's hers too. I want her to tell me what fixtures and colors it needs. I didn't care about finishing it before, but now I know for sure. I want her here with me. The house isn't done because it was waiting for her. "Wade!"

"I'm coming," I breathe, running a hand over my mouth. When I walk into the kitchen, it does nothing to slow my thoughts. She's got the double door refrigerator open, leaning over to examine its contents. "Do I want beer or seltzer? Oh, you bought bologna!"

"Well, you're the only one who drinks seltzer," I comment, walking up behind her as she picks the cranberry lime hard seltzer. "And yes, I bought bologna and other groceries."

"Look at you doing the whole adult life thing," She giggles, walking over to the farmhouse sink and rinsing off the can. "Do you want to try this one? You haven't had the cranberry lime yet."

"I don't drink that stuff," I say, walking back to the refrigerator for a new cold beer.

"Not true, you drank half of mine last week," she frowns, rinsing a can off in the sink. "The coconut mango."

"Yeah, you didn't like it and I have a pretty serious 'no drink left behind' rule. It was actually pretty weak." I laugh as she pops the can open. I smile as I stand right in front of her and she takes a drink. "I talked to your Dad today."

"What did Forest have to say to you?" She giggles as I put my hands under her arms and lift her up onto the marble counter. I bite my lip as she wraps her arms around my neck. Focus.

"I was telling him that we should all take my new boat out next month to the lake. It doesn't arrive until next month, but I think it could be fun." I suggest, using my thumb to wipe a little bit of the seltzer that got on her lip.

"That could be fun," she says quietly, stiffening in my arms. I press a kiss at the corner of her mouth. Maybe burgers can wait.

"It could be," I chuckle as she pulls her lips away from mine. "Anyways. Next month. Boat day."

"I'll have to see," Evie's expression falls, as she sits her drink on the counter next to her and her body language changes. She looks more nervous. I shouldn't have done it. Maybe making plans like that with her family was a bit much for now. Hell, she's not ready to talk about a lot of things. It's hard not to fall into old habits, no matter how long it's been.

"What's wrong?" I frown as she abruptly breaks our connection, pulling her arms away. I wasn't expecting that, but I step back and lean against the counter. I don't know what's happened, but her giggles are long gone.

"Wade, I spoke with Linda last night," she sighs, looking at her phone as it rests on the counter.

"Okay." I frown at the mention of her boss's name. "What did she want?"

"Well, nothing exactly. We just needed to talk over some things," Evie answers, but she doesn't make eye contact with me either. "We talked and we went over some stuff that I have worked on since I have been working here in Haven and together, we decided that I would return to the office next week."

There it is.

"In New York?" I quiz, shifting on my feet. She looks uncomfortable, the bouncy demeanor evaporates as if she was hoping for it not to come up tonight. As if she wanted to be free of the conversation. Hell, now I wonder if she even wanted to tell me in the first place. "So, you're going back for a meeting? Or staying?"

"Wade, I live in New York," she says it as if she's reminding me. As if I have forgotten where she was. "I have a job. I'm going to New York, because I'm going back."

"Oh," I respond, the immediate feeling of disappointment hitting. I have a million questions soaring into my mind as she sits across from me. "So, that's it? You're leaving again?"

"Yeah." She bites her lip nervously.

"And what about Haven?" I ask, immediately questioning my stupid decision to tell her I loved her. That was an idiot move. I pushed her away as soon as she began to return home to me. "What about us?"

"Wade...I really liked spending time with you," Evie bites her lip back, nervously running her hands over her outer thighs. No. I feel something when she says that, that feels like a stab in the chest. Like we were just two people who maybe went on one bad first date. "But you had to know that this was a visit. I don't belong here."

"That's bullshit and you know it," I groan and put my hands on my waist, standing straight up. She does belong. She belongs here, in this house. She belongs in Haven more than she could possibly belong anywhere else.

"Wade, my life is in New York," she counters, but she can't look me in the eye anymore. She's been made uncomfortable, as if she is stunned by my lack of enthusiasm for her departure. There is no way that deep down this is what she wants. It isn't an assumption. I know this woman and I know I messed up. I told her I loved her. She needed more time. She needed us to work through everything. She needed more time in Haven. "My job...it's all there."

"Does it make you happy?" I blurt out my question, because the only good reason for her to just leave is that it fulfills her. That it's truly what she wants to do and surpasses anything she could ever gain from Haven. It doesn't. She and I both know that. "Is it so fulfilling that leaving Haven is the only option?"

"It's not about that," she rolls her eyes, which just elevates the annoyance I'm beginning to feel from that stab to the chest.

"Then what's it about?" I shrug, unwilling to just accept her casual answers. "Is it because I told you that I loved you?"

"Wade, you telling me that you love me isn't going to make me pack my bags," she breathes, but doesn't continue. The only thing clear is there is no mistaking how she looks like she wishes she weren't having this conversation. I feel the same way.

"But it won't make you stay," I point out, shaking my head in shame. Evie doesn't say anything, she just keeps her hands on the counter top, still unable to look at me. I don't want to fight with her, but I can feel how angry I am. Maybe it's the realization that this is happening again. "So you're just going to do what you did last time? Pick up your bags and bolt from Haven?"

"That's not fair," she warns, cautiously eying me as I can feel the anger hit. Not fair? "Wade."

"When the hell was any of this fair?" I snap, the temperature in the room rising. "I never got a choice the first time, I don't get one now. The only difference here is you can't blame my father for you running away this time."

"Are you serious?" She quizzes, tilting her head at me as if she's going to give me one more chance to fix what I said. Questioning if I really meant to snap at her like that. To be honest, I'm not sure. "You can't possibly be serious right now. How can you bring your father up and act like this is in any way like that?"

"That's exactly what you're doing right now," I say confidently, before pacing to the other side of the kitchen as I question if I may be losing my cool too quickly with her. "So, what was it? Were you going to wait until I fell asleep again and slip out in the middle of the night or were you going to wait until you went home in the morning?"

"I can't believe you," She scoffs, shaking her head as she hops off the counter.

"What is there to believe, Ev?" I snap, throwing my arms up. "I'm only asking if you want to repeat history."

"You're being ridiculous!" She shouts, raising her voice as if I've done something wrong by being upset.

"Am I? Because it seems like something you should have brought up with someone you like spending time with," I groan, repeating those words back to her without any hesitation. I know my temper is revving up right now, but I don't want to calm it. I want her to put thought into what she's doing. Into what she's walking away from. Again. "Ev, you're not even fully happy with that job."

"You know nothing about my job!" She shouts, truly showing how angry and defensive she's getting too. "You just mock it. Are you happy with your job?"

"I love my job! I followed my dreams, Ev," I shout back at her. The only part of the dream that didn't come true was this house.

"Yeah, because I left! You're angry for a choice I made when I was eighteen but it got you all of this!" She gestures around the room as her voice cracks. "It sucked and I wish it had never happened, but I could never live with knowing that there was a chancer none of that would have come true if I had been selfish. You have the house you wanted."

"No," I bite, shaking my head. "You don't get to act like this was all selfless. I wanted this house for us. Without you in it, it's just a hollow building with rooms in it. I never wanted this damn place if you weren't in it. I only built it, because I needed to see it. I had to see what it looked like. You don't get to pretend like this was all selfless."

"Do you really think it was easy for me? That I didn't spend every day regretting it?" She argues, her eyes turning red as she bites back her anger. "If you only knew what it had been like, Wade. And how the hell do you know that I wasn't up all night last night, weighing every option of what could happen when I go back to New York? That it's been going through my head the last couple of weeks. Hell, I even contemplated if I could convince you to come to New York with me next week until you and I could figure out what any of this meant."

"Like hell you were," I throw my hand up, something deep inside of me urging me to shut up but I just keep going. "You want me to hop a plane, go to New York and sleep in a bed that you slept in with another man. In the same apartment you shared with him."

"Then don't!" She shouts, shaking her head in disbelief. "I honestly didn't think you'd be threatened by a man who isn't even living anymore. Let it go, Wade."

"Really? It sounds a little bit like you're the one who can't let things go! He's gone, Ev!" I snap, my body tightening as I realize it's really gone too far. My hand falls to my side as I find myself thinking of a way to undo my words. Evie's stiffens as she drops her arms to her side in defeat. I feel guilty for crossing a line, perhaps showing just how weak I am. "Now I didn't mean it like that."

"Oh wow." She turns to the counter, expressionless as she reaches for her phone again. "How did you mean it?"-

"Not in a way that was as bad as it sounded," I respond gruffly, my head falling. I don't look at her. I want to, but I can't for the moment. "Ev, I just…"

"You should really stop talking now," She snaps and I finally look up as she leans towards the island, with her elbows on the marble. She rubs her eyes in circular motions with her long fingers. "I don't really know what you want me to say."

"I don't really know either," I concede. Neither one of us says a word, but there is a hollowness between the two of us. We don't know the other's next move. I want to beg her to stay, to tell her that I have faith that the two of us will be just fine, but the anger is still coming out on top. "I guess I thought after everything my father did and the things that have happened and changed over the last twelve years, I thought maybe it was time that you and I really figured our shit out. I never counted on my dad or a fiancé that wasn't me being a part of the story."

Evie pulls away from the counter, straightening up as she runs her fingers over the lines within the marble. She looks deep in thought, like she's trying to make sense of something. Hell, I just want her to say something that makes sense to me right now. Something that makes me think we're both still standing in this kitchen for the right reasons. I watch as she contemplates something deeply and takes her fingers off the island. Her eyes are filled with tears and I want to grab her. I want to tell her I'm so angry, but that loving her is worth it. That I would take a hundred more years of pain if it meant she was mine forever. "I guess that makes two dead men who have taken us down."

"Everleigh," I whisper, my voice hitching in my chest as her hands fall to her side and she almost robotically turns away. As I begin to walk towards her, Ev walks to the front of the house and I feel desperate to tell her she needs to stay. That we can get through this. None of this would have happened in the last couple of months if it wasn't meant to work. "Ev, stop."

"Wade." She walks, holding a hand up. "Did you really think this was a good idea? I mean maybe twelve years was too long. A lot of things have changed and…"

"Has it? Because I just think you're scared. You were scared then and you're scared now," I argue as we both stop in the hallway. She spins around and before she has a chance to say a word, I continue. "I think you're afraid of starting over and finally getting to live the life you want. I think you feel guilty, because even if you didn't love him the way you wanted, you feel like it's wrong to be with the man you were thinking about the whole time. Like somehow, you're disrespecting him, but you're not."

I wait as her eyes are fixed on a spot on the wall, the small crease below her forehead showing up like it does when she's thinking or serious. She's still here, in front of me but she doesn't say a word. She doesn't move or rush out either. Maybe I'm angry or just really frustrated, but I realize this is my only chance to fix this. "Ev, I'm struggling. I admit it. Yeah, maybe I feel a little threatened by him. Okay? And I know making this work would be really hard. Whether you're here or in New York, but there isn't a moment in my life that I can think of where I wouldn't fight for you if you'd let me."

"Please," she bites before shaking her head furiously. Her cheek is wet from a few lone tears that have slipped by as she tries to hold her gaze. Finally she breaks from that spot on the wall, but her eyes are haunting. "Wade."

"Ev, I love you. I mean it, but if you don't think you love me or you just don't feel like there is a future for us, then leave," I say hesitantly, as the words individually stab at me. "But if you think there is a way that you and I can figure it out and make this work, let's go talk. I promise I'll figure it out so that you're the happiest woman on the planet either in New York or Haven."

I replay in my head what bitterness and anger had led me to say just minutes ago. The truth is, the idea of living in the same place she shared with another man feels like a deal breaker. The idea made me angry, but as my rage battles with what I feel for this woman, I can't give her an ultimatum and I can't let her leave without knowing everything I would still do for her. The only mother to my children and she's hanging on by a thread. "Ev, we can do this."

I wait feeling embarrassingly desperate for something to happen. For her to say something. Silently I berate myself for getting angry. We can figure this out. This isn't the same as last time but in some ways it is. She's willingly leaving me behind. "I'm sorry."

She's sorry?

"I'm leaving," she whispers softly before she slowly backs up. I'm frozen in place as the distance between us grows. It's when her hand meets the doorknob at the front door that I feel anger win again. This damn woman is running away.

"Everleigh." I speak loudly, stepping forward. She looks back at me, the pain she's feeling painted across her face as I speak, protecting myself. "If you leave, you're saying this is over. That there is nothing left between us in your eyes. I can't chase after you."

She looks back at me, her grayish blue eyes giving insight to just how broken she was this whole time. So broken she's decided a life of loneliness and a lack of fulfilment is what she'd have over a new journey. Leaving me. I can see she's thinking something, but instead of letting me try and read her thoughts she steps out of the house, closing that navy door behind her. Forever. *No.* I rush forward as my heart rate picks up, pulling the heavy door open as she runs down the steps of the house and towards that stupid SUV. I know she's heard me step onto the porch but she just urgently makes her way to the car, unlocking the door and refusing to look back. I don't chase her, even if I want to. She knows I can't. Not again. Everleigh Rose operates with urgency as she closes the car door, turns on the ignition and does everything in her power to get the hell away from my house. If I wasn't mistaken, it was the break up, twelve years in the making. The final goodbye. The final door closing as I watch the love of my life leave me for good.

Chapter Twenty-Four

Everleigh

Now

I don't usually hear too much from the outside when I am in the Glam and Simple high-rise offices. At least I don't recall it. It's been a while since I've looked out the window of this office. I don't even remember if I ever spent much time admiring the view from this high. Normally, everything is going nonstop and I don't notice the world outside until I find time in my day to go get a salad. However, today the rain hits a little harder and I find myself staring as each droplet hits the window. I can see down to the street, ant sized people with umbrellas, yellow cabs, and I wonder if I really have it in me to go be among them at any time. I've been back in New York for almost three weeks and I feel like a shell of myself again. It's my own fault. I made the choice to leave without truly weighing my options. I made a decision for Wade and myself. I blink quickly as the rain falls instead of tears. Thank God. Linda and Kyra are already on my tail, trying to figure out what happened. I know they've spoken to Lexie and Mom. I've learned they're too nosy to take 'nothing' as an answer to what happened when I was in Haven.

So, instead they just look at me like I'm a sad and pathetic puppy walking around. Maybe I am, because I can't stop thinking about him.

Wade.

He's everywhere I go and absolutely nowhere. I see him when I close my eyes. It's like he's right in front of me, praying I'll say something different. I see him when I'm asleep and every other moment of my repetitive days. He hasn't tried to call and I haven't tried to call him, and if I did, I am pretty certain at this point he wouldn't answer.

A few nights ago, I went out with Kyra and Linda for drinks and I very nearly called him the moment I walked in the door. Begging him to come to New York, because I just needed him. Begging him to let me cry and be confused and to not hold me accountable for not having a clue on how to do any of this. But I knew. I couldn't let myself be that week no matter how tipsy I was. It was probably all of the Chardonnay on a stomach that has barely eaten a thing. Linda insisted that she and her driver drop me off instead of me finding my own way home. That familiar feeling of having him ripped out of my life was consuming every breath I take. I don't know how to measure it, but I think this time hurts even more and it's all my fault. I can't let Daniel go or forgive myself for the things I have done in the past so I would rather be miserable. Staring at a window, relating to the rain that is now aggressively hitting the window. I relate more to this torrential downpour than I do anything else.

"I think Linda's call is running late." I hear Kyra's voice and I can see out of the corner of my eye she's joined me at the window.

"It's with Wallace from Saks," I say quietly, finally shifting my gaze from the window to my platinum blonde friend. "They're combing over the final details.'"

"I can't believe Glam and Simple is going to have their own counter at Saks and Macy's." Kyra grins ear to ear and I can't help but smile a little too. Although, based on her look, it isn't as enthusiastic. "Ev, talk to me."

I haven't spoken to the ladies about him, but I know they suspect or know based on what conversations they have had. I don't try to find out what they know and despite how often they meddle, they haven't tried to push me into talking. They just do what they can and I appreciate that. "Kyra, there is nothing to talk about. Did Linda get the samples for the counter marquee? I can call Jerry..."

"No, stop. Forget the damn work for a split second." She puts a hand up forcefully in front of her. "You're a mess. I've seen you struggling before, but this...you're in love with him."

"Who?" I ask, dryly.

"Wade. The guy you were at the bar with when you were drunk on the phone. You said he was a friend or whatever, but I never knew you were ever engaged to someone from your hometown." She reminds me as her voice struggles to stay quiet, but she and I both know that a reminder was never needed. She looks around, keeping her voice quiet. "Lexie told me about you guys. How you guys kind of picked up where you left off."

"It wasn't like that," I murmur as my jaw tightens as I turn away from the window and head back to my little desk area. I don't want to look at the rain anymore as I wait for Linda. "Have you heard anything from printing?"

"I handled printing." She waves my comment off as she hops onto my desk, nearly knocking over some of the pictures. I lock my eyes on my inbox, checking to see if any new emails have come in that I can handle before she keeps talking. "So this Wade guy...."

"I would prefer we don't talk about the Wade guy," I state quickly as Kyra's face tightens up and she nods slowly.

"You're in luck. I have a meeting with Ricardo, so it's just you and Linda," she nods, patting her hands on her legs as the door to Linda's office opens and our design team walks out. I look at Kyra and she shrugs. "Maybe she's too busy to try and talk about your personal life."

"Thank you," I groan, pushing up from my desk as I reach for my planner and a ballpoint pen that is closest to me. Linda appears at the door of her office, waving us to come over and I swallow the anxious feeling that refuses to subside. I want to bring up an idea I had, but I'm not sure if I'm ready. There is so much floating in my head as I walk with my black pumps to her office. "Good morning, Linda."

"Evie," she nods, ushering me into her office. She closes the door behind her as I take a seat I take every day across from her chair. I hear someone come to the door and she has a quiet exchange with them and I'm pretty sure it's Kyra. I don't look back, but when she closes the door she confirms it. "That was Kyra. Just filling me in one something about her meeting."

"Sure," I breathe, but I question silently if she's told her not to talk about Wade or Daniel or even Haven.

"I'm sorry it's been so busy since you got back that we haven't gotten a chance to catch up about your time away," she sighs, sitting down in her chair as she opens her leopard blazer. My mind goes to what Kyra could have said, but I just tap my foot nervously as I wait for her to get situated. She clasps her hands together on the desk and stares at me. "So, how was Haven?"

"Fine," I reply quickly, opening the pages of the planner in front of me. "I stayed in contact on all of my tasks so that I wouldn't miss a thing. I approved all of the samples to print and the final candidates should be here tomorrow for your final approval. Also, I spoke with Berta in Poland and she's getting you the images of—"

"I don't want to hear about the work, Everleigh," Linda insists, leaning back in her chair. "I need to know that you're alright. You barely say a word, you work until it looks like you couldn't possibly handle any more and now I'm not convinced that sending you away was the right choice or maybe you came back too soon."

"I'm fine," I bite quickly as my voice raises unintentionally as her eyebrows shoot up, letting out a deep and tired breath. I "Sorry. I'm okay. Just a little tired."

"How are you sleeping?" She quizzes and I feel my eyes roll which isn't recommended to do to your boss, but when your boss is your friend who you know is trying to meddle. "Are you using our eye patches? You have bags. I have some samples in my file cabinet if you're out and don't want to run to the marketing storage."

"I'm sleeping fine," I reply, holding my hand up. "In fact, I was hoping we could discuss an idea I want to approach. That I think you should entertain."

"So, what you're saying is you're not going to confide in me like your socially ironic therapist?" She asks, her shoulders falling in actual disappointment as if she was fully ready to grab a pen and paper and get to work. I pull papers I printed earlier from the back of my planner and slide her a copy. "Damn. Okay."

"It might be a little different then what we're known for," I whisper nervously, brushing off anything I'm feeling as I put a hand over my nervous stomach. Linda takes the page and slides on her thick rimmed reading glasses. I don't know if they're for show or if she really needs them, but they look good.

I bite my lip nervously as Linda reads the prepared information that I have given her. She stays quiet, tapping her pen against the desk. For a moment, I feel different. Like I'm sharing this important idea with her and there maybe is something good that could come from it. Like maybe I am coming back to make a difference. "I thought maybe we could branch into a small boutique where we sell our products and clothes. But instead of just having limited sizing and styles, we appeal to a wide variety of women. No woman fits just one style...at least not the average woman."

"And you think a variety of fashion and different price points would work?" She holds the sheet, up, gesturing to the middle section. "Finding solutions for every lady?"

"Yes," I nod nervously as she slips the paper over again, examining it from top to bottom. Her eyes locked on the last few words. "I know it would basically be adding a whole other wing to the business and it would take a while, but I think it would be huge."

"I love it," Linda announces abruptly, letting the paper fall onto her desk and for a moment I don't think I've heard her right. "It's fresh and innovative. It ultimately expands to clients a business like this one wouldn't normally attract."

"Really?" I ask as I feel my eyes go wide. She loves it. All of that time back home did nurture some sort of good idea. Thank god I ran into Harbor who really seems to be into things like fashion and makeup. We should have spent more time together, because we really clicked and enjoyed a lot of the same things. "I think it could be really good for business."

"Evie," Linda looks up at me apologetically and lowers the paper with the plan on it. "It is a really great idea and I could see it working in a boutique setting or another business, but..."

"But what?" I frown as she offers the paper back to me. I accept it, but I still don't know what she means. Another business? "It's perfect for Glam and Simple."

"Evie, we're launching in Saks. Neiman Marcus and Bergdorf's have set up meetings next week," Linda explains proudly. "I love the idea, but it isn't for Glam and Simple.

That's just not our journey right now. We're in the big picture. Big time. I mean, we have a meeting with Gigi Hadid next week to be our new cover model. Which wouldn't have happened without you, by the way."

"Right," I breathe, the disappointment and feeling of harsh rejection slamming me right into my chest. How can she love the idea but shut it down so quickly? Immediately the first feeling that comes back is the idea that Haven was a bad idea all along. I left feeling more broken than I arrived, and the only idea that was fueled by passion was just basically said to not be good enough. "Sorry."

"Why are you sorry? It's still an amazing idea. It just isn't for Glam and Simple," Linda shrugs, eying me. She closes her notebook in front of her and slides the glasses off of her face. I can tell she wants to say something, but I don't know if I want to hear it. I turn a page in the planner, signaling that I am ready to move on with our meeting, but she doesn't take the hint. "Evie. You started here as an intern for an up-and-coming company that wasn't even certain it was still going to be open a year from then. I was lucky to have you and I'm still grateful that you're here at the top."

"Linda, it's fine," I assure her. I respect her and if it's not right for her company, she has a right to say so. I love the idea, but maybe it just wasn't meant to be for me. It wasn't an idea that was going to work. "Did you want to go over last month's marketing numbers?"

"No, I want to discuss your career," she answers abruptly as she leans back in her seat, running a hand through her perfectly wavy hair. "As in, are you happy?"

"How do you mean?" I ask, my brows furrowing as my stomach sinks.

"You came here wide eyed and bushy tailed, ready to work," Linda explains, gesturing towards the rest of the office.

The office that, when I started, had only a quarter of the employees. "But you started with a passion about clothes and shoes. I'm forever grateful you took a chance at an internship with my company, but even in your interview you were clear that fashion had your heart."

"But I also told you I was really intrigued by cosmetics and this company," I remind her, but I almost feel like I am pleading for my job. "Are you firing me?"

"Firing you? God, no." Linda sits up quickly in her chair and pushes her hair back. "I'm not a complete idiot. I would never fire you. You're spectacular at your job and one of my best. I just don't want you to rule out ever doing something else if you're passionate about it. You have an eye for this industry, but I know you have unused talents in other areas. Don't walk away from something or turn your back on it, just because you're safe here."

I know she wants me to marinate on that thought for a moment, but my head is a messy and screwed up place. There isn't any more room to question where I am or what I'm doing. I can tell she doesn't understand that, so I just smile and nod. "So, should we get started?"

Linda examines me, before she begins looking at the marketing numbers from the previous month so that we can approve the budget for next month. It fills me with relief that we can go back to work and stop questioning whether I am alright or doing the right thing. The right thing is so long gone, I don't know what it is anymore. It shouldn't have to be this complicated. I realize that. I know that in my head, I'm struggling maybe even more than I was before I went to Haven. In that fine line between guilt and heartbreak. There is guilt for Daniel. Like I spent so much of my time with him wanting someone else that I didn't appreciate just how good he was to me. That I didn't love him until his death the way he deserved. That my love for him was present, but not the way it should have been. Not in a way that made us healthy for each other.

    Then there is mammoth sized mass weighing me down for Wade. Twelve years he went without an answer as to why I abandoned him. To why I was so weak and scared. The guilt I feel for coming back and letting myself get too close when I knew I couldn't give him what he wanted. I can't give myself to him the way he deserves, not when I don't know why all of me wanted to, but then I felt like it was wrong. Like I owed so much to someone else. What if he was who I owed it to all along? What if I'm using one person to hide from another? What if Linda's right? Maybe there is another life I'm supposed to explore and I'm not because being lonely feels like the repayment for choices I have made. What if the happiness I felt in Haven wasn't just because of Wade? I felt like a person in Haven. A feeling I haven't had since I left.

Chapter Twenty-Five

Wade

Now

The taste of bourbon hits my mouth as I begin my third glass of the evening. The taste of rich oak and a little bit of honey hit just right. It was a long day with visits to several of my job sites. Except one I should have stopped by, but I didn't. I haven't stopped by the Goode's home remodel since Everleigh left town. Thankfully I know they're in good hands with one of my head contractors and I can credit how busy work has been. Business is going really well and I've had to hire even more onto my team for a project in Mobile. So I can blame it on how busy I am and not go by their house. The truth is, I don't want to be there. I feel like I set myself up when she was back here. I credit myself with being a manly man who acts big and tough, but the truth is I have the softest spot for that woman. It was a hold I quickly realized I didn't want her to let go of. If she had said let;s jump, I would have been right there with her. She was whiskey and I was addicted. She showed up and off the wagon I fell. Now, I'm back on earth and she's gone.

After the fight in the kitchen, she left. She showed she

wasn't ready to fight and I just let her leave. Looking back, I flew off the handle way too quick. I got angry and said a lot of things I shouldn't have. Things that would make her believe staying wasn't worth it. Things that might even make her think she wouldn't get the support she needed in her life. I said things I would trade anything to tuck back away. I spent two days after that, locked in this house just trying to figure out how to fix it. Then Dawson came by. I guess I was kind of surprised by what he was saying. I thought he would tell me to let her go, to chalk it up to a brief hookup with an ex, but he didn't. After I told him everything I said, he told me he had been afraid of this. That I might not be able to see past my own pride, to be the better man. To be the man she needed. He had his concerns about her too, but we're both his friends. He had concerns that I would be so unable to look past her being with someone else, that I would fail to realize it was never about that. That she would never forgive herself for the past. He said he was rooting for us like we were two crazy kids and maybe we were. What he didn't say was that we were damaged goods. *Ego* and *pride*. Those were the two words he said to me before he stepped off the porch and went back to his truck.

My ego. My pride.

Maybe he was right. Maybe I wasn't trying to view this in any other way than having the love of my life back. Maybe I was trying to pick up where we left off without considering how much has changed and how much we've grown. And now ego and pride conspired and I ruined this. I was right about one thing though. I can't chase her. Not this time.

I take another swig from the glass, swallowing the amber liquid that doesn't burn as much anymore as I see two narrow headlights slow when they approach my driveway. I don't even bother to look at whose car it is. I'll let them surprise me. That's the beauty of bourbon. You kind of just stop caring. When the car door closes, I look up to see Nancy Goode with her shoulders dropped, holding an oversized tote. "Oh, it's worse than I thought it would be."

"Good evening," I nod as I try to straighten up in the chair, but I can tell she's already seen the liquid in the glass next to me. I'm not drunk, but there is something about seeing someone like Nancy Goode that makes you want to be on your best behavior.

"You haven't been by the house recently so I thought I should stop by and bring you some food," she announces proudly as she holds the tote up for me to see before making her way up the front porch. "I see you have a drink already, so why don't you try some of the spaghetti I put in here?"

"I'm still sober," I respond defensively, but she pulls the other rocking chair I had pushed out of the way back next to mind and sits down.

"Sober people don't start off talking to people by telling them that they're sober," she replies as she bends over, taking a container from the bag and then also pulling out a plastic fork. "The spaghetti is the only thing still warm. It just got off the stove with the garlic bread."

"Ah, garlic bread," I breathe as she pulls out some tin foil. She opens it quickly to hand me a piece that I stick in my mouth as I pull the lid off of the spaghetti. I missed her cooking. "Sorry, work has been crazy. Is Ty treating you guys well?"

"Ty has been absolutely amazing. He knows his stuff," she answers confidently as she sits the bag on the ground and lets out a deep breath. "Of course, the remodel has nothing to do with why I am here. And I think you know that."

"Of course, you had to bring food." I gesture to the bag before tossing back some more of my drink. I ignore her eyes that I can feel right on me. "Care for a drink?"

"Oh, no thank you," she waves, shaking her head. "And

don't mind if I overstep a bit, but how about we make this one the last for you tonight?"

"Right," I scoff, clutching my glass. I know she's here to talk, but frankly I don't want to. "How can I help you, Nancy?"

"I know you're distancing yourself because of Evie and I'm sure it's just because you need time." She speaks softly, in that tone that mothers use when they don't want you to feel like you're in trouble, but they still need to talk to you anyways. Once upon a time I remember it from my own mother. God rest her soul. "And I understand it."

"She left you too," I mutter, giving into the food and dipping a little bit of the garlic bread into the spaghetti, dampening it with red sauce. "Again."

"Maybe, but this time she checks in," Nancy sighs as if that's supposed to make this better. Clarifying that I might be the only one she really left this time. "Usually she keeps her conversations simple. Mostly asks about Levi or what I made for dinner, but it's something."

"Lucky you," I huff, twirling the spaghetti around the plastic fork. I have no interest in eating, but even I can't deny the smell. I would rather focus on the food instead of the conversation.

"Wade, when I asked you at Forest's retirement party, to try, I didn't know what I was asking you to try and do," Nancy begins speaking, lightly rocking in the other chair as she looks out at the gravel. "I was hoping for anything, something, that would show my baby was ready to be home. She was ready. I think she's still ready but...well that isn't happening yet."

"She sure as hell bolted like someone who didn't want to be home," I argue, stabbing at the meatball to break it off while she tries to have a conversation with me.

"I wouldn't say that. I knew you looked at her the same way you used to," Nancy responds almost candidly. "No, this visit was different for a million reasons and none of them were the reasons I expected. A lot changes in twelve years, but I didn't count on her looking at you with the same eyes she did as a seventeen year old girl. Everything she made me believe was that she had been able to move on, but that she was just scared to see you. Even when she was angry."

"Yeah, well apparently old habits die hard," I remark, rubbing the stubble on my face. I don't think I've shaved more than once in the last few weeks, but it's kind of growing on me.

"Maybe," she answers, letting out a light sigh as we both watch the lightning bugs occasionally flicker in front of us. We sit in silence for a bit as I chow down on dinner. I sure as hell missed Nancy's cooking. I wouldn't tell Libby, but I think if Nancy opened a restaurant, it would give the diner a heavy run for its money. Thank God, Nancy has never shown an interest or people would be forced to choose sides. "You said Evie has to want to be fixed and I told you that I believe she does. Didn't I?"

"Yeah," I scoff, poking the fork at the dish with no actual intention of grabbing a specific piece. "Are you admitting you were wrong about that now? I promise I won't gloat."

"Not at all," Nancy chuckles lightly as it's clear she maintains that stance. "I just didn't know it would take the both of you to fix each other."

"I didn't need fixing," I object. I spent years loving Everleigh Goode. That was never in question.

"Really?" She challenges, reaching for the glass of whiskey between us and holding it up as I look away. "What glass is this for the night? For the week?"

"It's not like that," I immediately argue. I'm not having this discussion.

"I see," she dismissively laughs as she gestures to the bottle. "Wade, you're not Ridge. The angry and drunk lifestyle doesn't suit you and it won't help you with my daughter. When she comes back, she's not going to love what you've done to yourself. She's going to worry."

"Worry? That's not like Evie to worry about who she hurts. Your daughter left, Nancy. Now, I don't know about you, but I'm not chasing after her this time," I reply, reaching over to take the glass from her. Evie leaves when Evie gets scared. "She's gone. She chose New York over Haven."

"Maybe for now, but she'll be home," Nancy confidently speaks as she reaches for the cap of the bourbon bottle. I'm tempted to nod towards my glass so she knows to fill it before she closes up shop, but I think she might slap me if I tried. "Wade, people only run away from home, if they're scared. They return home because it's the one place they know they'll always belong. The one place that no matter what, they can fit into when they return."

"Poetic," I laugh dryly. I look out at the drive in front of me. At the green yard on the other side of it. The land I've stared at a million times, questioning if I had been a fool to build this place. I spent most years believing Evie would never see it with her own eyes. "So where does Everleigh fit in your theory?"

"With you." Her mother says this so casually, as if it's a no-brainer. Like it's so easy I can't possibly question it. Maybe at one point it was. I open my mouth to speak and tell her she's got it wrong. Except, Nancy takes it as her cue to keep going. "It isn't a theory. It's the truth."

"Nancy, if you came here to get me to go to New York and bring Ev home, I won't. I won't try that again." I shift, placing the glass dish of spaghetti on the table between us. "I told Evie I won't chase her again. I won't."

"No matter how much you might want to?" Nancy challenges, as I can feel her examining my face. I've grabbed my keys a million times since Evie walked out of the house. I flew off the handle and I had chances to go after her again. A buried sigh escapes as I contemplate what is coming next. Nancy surely isn't going to go until she believes she's gotten her point across and I'm not sure what I think that is. Still, she's not done. "Wade, I'm not asking you to do that. She'll be back. I told you this time was different and I meant that. She'll be back. I don't know exactly when, but she will."

"Oh?" I ask, a bitter laugh escaping my lips. I don't even try to entertain what she's said. It's not worth it. I shift uncomfortably in the rocking chair, wondering if I have the guts to tell Nancy Goode that I don't want to talk anymore.

"She's going to come home, Wade." Nancy's voice gets quiet as she looks pensively out at the road. Maybe she's just being optimistic. "Wade, when my daughter comes back to you, she's not going to be too happy to find you this way. You need to clean up. Sober up. Shave. You're better than this."

"Nanc—"

"You're not your father Wade," Nancy cuts me off, pushing herself up from the chair. She walks across the porch, before turning around and crossing her arms. "When Everleigh returns, and she will, she doesn't need to see him. She'll need you."

"You have a lot of faith in her," I say as Nancy picks up an empty bottle near the steps. She doesn't say anything about it, but just tightens the lid and tucks it under her arm. "I didn't drink that in one night."

"Wade, I ask that you clean this place up by the time my daughter makes her way home to you," she requests, examining the rest of the porch, but I know for a fact I managed to throw away any other bottles or they're inside. "I know the fact that she's been gone and engaged to another man can't be easy. Not when you two had the history that you had. That's outrageous to think that it would be easy for you. I myself, have spent so much time wondering if you two could move on from it.

Especially, when she's going to hold another man's memory close to her heart until the day she leaves this earth. Then I figured, you were wise enough to know that you're her future. That respecting him just means you two get to be together until you take your last breath. That it will get easier when you learn she doesn't love you any less and it will just make her love you more."

Nancy leans against the railing, looking out at the acres on the Tenant land. I got it for a steal after George Tenant died and his daughter from Tallahassee was eager to get rid of it. When I bought it, I remember wondering what Evie would think of it, secretly hoping she'd come home. It was a time when I was desperately wishing I could change things. I want to tell Nancy the truth. That I had Evie back and ruined it. That I could have been her biggest supporter with what she needed to do in New York, but I can't and a part of me thinks she already knows. She knows Everleigh told me she was going to New York and I did everything I could to push her out of Haven. Ev didn't have to tell her a thing. "Nancy."

"Wade, it doesn't matter Honey. Don't you get it? Twelve weeks or a few years doesn't matter. What you two said to each other before she left you that day doesn't matter. What matters is when she comes home or when you guys can finally make the decision to accept all of the other bull." Nancy stops me as she turns around leans against the rail, her hands in her pockets. "What your father did to my daughter or how you two hurt each other doesn't matter. What matters is there are four extra bedrooms upstairs and unfinished touches in this house. She's going to come home. I know she will, and your life is going to start, *really* start, and it's going to be worth every second."

"You seem really sure about that," I chuckle apprehensively. I look down at my worn work jeans. A little dirty and distressed. Nancy does sure have a way with words and a part of me wants to believe her. Maybe I do. Maybe, I am the man she thinks I am. The man I wanted to be. Nancy straightens up and heads to the stairs and lets out a deep sigh as she stops. "What?"

"Evie left this on my dresser. I didn't notice it until the other day because she sat it behind my wedding photo, and I was a little behind on dusting." Nancy turns around, reaching into her jeans pocket. She takes a small folded up paper out of her pocket. "It was in a little white bag that had her grandmother's ring in it. I guess she felt like she needed to hand the ring back after all this time. Well, there was this envelope in it and it has your name on it."

"What?" I frown, my breath hitching in my chest as she holds the distressed folded paper in front of me. The same envelope I found in Evie's bag when she left it in the Jeep. I unfold it for the second time, this time noticing the envelope has been opened. I cock my eyebrow and look up at Nancy.

"Okay fine. I read it," she reveals, waving her hand up in the air. "But so should you, Wade. You won't ever question where her heart is again. She's coming home to you. It might be an old note, but you won't ever question anything again. It's beautiful."

"You think I should read it," I breathe, my thumb rubbing over my name. I had fought reading it before, but now that it's open and Evie isn't here, I think I need to.

"I'm going to leave you to it. Read it when you're ready." Nancy clasps her hands together, leaning over to press a soft kiss on the top of my head. Then she puts her hand and fixes my hair. "Your father was a rough man. A hurt man. You know you were never any of those things he said you were, Wade. You deserved better."

"Thank you," I breathe, with the sound of another car passing down the road. "I suppose Forest is expecting you back home soon."

"Lexie and Levi," she says, waving her hand off again. "Forest had some business out of town to tend to. I imagine he'll be home in a day or two. Anyways, I should get going. Levi is saving some popcorn for me."

"Night, Nancy," I wave, letting out a deep breath as heat lightning sparks in the distance.

I want to say something else before she turns and walks down the steps of the porch. I try to form some sort of statement to ask a question, but I can't. Nancy looks back at me as she steps down onto the gravel and paints a slight smile on her face before she walks towards her car. She's pleased with our talk today. She did most of it. I watch as moments later, she pulls out onto the narrow two-lane country road.

When her car is out of sight, I look down at the envelope. I want to read what is in here, but I can't right now. I have the same feeling I did in the truck that day. Why a note? What can it say that might change things? Why is her mother so confident? I just can't open it right now. Not when I'm still pretty deep in the bourbon. Not if Nancy is right about it. Not if I am going to get myself out of this hole. I'm still angry. Still hurt. It's still raw. But what if Nancy is right? What if Evie really is coming home and what if she isn't gone for twelve years? What if I had stayed calmer in the kitchen that day? What if I had gone with her? Why was I so stubborn? I pushed her away first this time. I put all the blame on her again and now I am still angry. Maybe the letter will help with that, but I don't know. Nancy is right about one thing: I'm not Ridge Beckett and I am not the same man I was when Evie left the first time. I need to sober up. I need to be the man Nancy Beckett knows I am. The man Everleigh deserves to come home to. If she comes. I need to be the bigger man, a better man.

Chapter Twenty-Six

Evie

Now

The microwave annoyingly chirps three times and the smell of butter and salt break me from staring out of the window of the apartment. I sit my fresh glass of golden prosecco on the window sill and walk over to the kitchen, careful not to bump any of the cardboard boxes that I have managed to pack. If I have realized one thing since I made my way back to New York, it's that I have no use for staying in this apartment. It's a haunting reminder of Daniel and it only took me four years to realize that I didn't want to be in this space. I don't want to pass his clothes every morning as I pick my own out and I don't belong here. I called his family, surprised that they even answered for me. I invited them to come go through his things with me and his father asked that I donate the clothes. It's respectable, I guess. To want to give them to those in need, but I thought they would want to go through his things. He quickly asked me to do it myself and keep what I wanted before he hung up. It was brutal in a way, but I did it and only kept things I knew I could fit in a box. A box to remind me of him when I needed it. My fingers burn as I open the bag and steam releases, dropping it on the counter. "Shit. Ouch"

I do it every time. If it isn't some sort of metaphor for my life, I'm not sure what is. Doing the same thing, knowing how much it hurts. I shake my head, not wanting my mind to go back to Haven. The truth is, it hurts the same exact way when I left the first time. Maybe even worse. I'm painfully aware that this time feels even worse, which somehow makes it easier to try and pretend it doesn't. Or maybe it's that my whole life feels up in the air. It's been a couple of weeks since I shared my idea with Linda and she politely stated it wasn't right for her company. I respect that, and she's probably right. Except, I wasn't expecting her to love the idea so much or send me a list of contacts for people that I could talk to. I didn't expect that she and Kyra would see how much I missed Haven. Even if I tried to tell myself I was happy to be back. The reality is, I miss Wade. Too much. There has been a part of me gone since I was eighteen. For a little while, that piece of me was back and I was whole again. It was just going to be too hard and here I am. In a city I love, but don't belong in.

I grab my prosecco from the window and sit the popcorn on the other seat of the couch. The remote is around here somewhere and I figure I'll just watch some *Law and Order: SVU*. Watching Olivia Benson destroy some creep is a lot more entertaining than being alone with my thoughts. Before I can locate it, though, there is a knock at the door. Chances are the doorman or someone from the building administration is bringing me my packages. I ordered more boxes from Amazon and it should be kind of heavy. I open the metal door, but it isn't anyone from the front desk. It's my father. I can feel the breath escape my lips as soon as I speak. "Dad."

"Surprise," he shrugs innocently, pulling both hands from his jean pockets. I can feel my jaw has dropped a little as I step out of the doorway and my father steps onto the dark wood floor, looking around. It isn't a large entryway, so there isn't much to examine. Still he finds the light switch and flips it off and on real quick. I don't know why he's here, but he's already showing an interest in my electrical work. He flips it again, before giving it a nod of approval and turning around with his arms out. "A hug for your old man? I took the afternoon flight."

"I... sorry. I wasn't expecting you. Hi." I let out a laugh, feeling a little bewildered as I wrap my arms around my father. He's here. In New York. I can count on one hand the number of times my father has come to New York. All of those times, he put himself to work fixing something. Last time it was my dishwasher. He thought it was crazy that I was going to wait a few weeks for a maintenance man. Still, he smells like he always does. Familiar and like him. Like a little bit of his aftershave and mint from the gum he chews. I didn't realize I missed him so much, because I just keep hugging him tight and he lets me. I must eventually go on too long, because he pats my back and I pull away. "What are you doing here? Mom didn't say you were coming."

"Would you believe me if I said I was in the neighborhood?" He asks, flipping the light switch in the hallway to examine it. I don't roll my eyes like I normally would, because I actually feel just as relieved as I am surprised that he is here.

"Maybe if you were coming from Hoboken," I laugh weakly, pulling my hair down from the scrunchy that had it piled on top of my head. "What are you doing in New York, Dad?"

"Well, I figured it's been a while since I've popped in here and checked if anything needed fixing," he says, reaching out into the hall for an old Wilsons Leather duffle bag that my Mom bought him for Christmas one year. "I thought if it was okay with you, I would stay the night, head back to Alabama tomorrow."

"There are tools in there too, aren't there?" I ask, gesturing to the worn leather bag.

"Only the basics," he answers proudly, patting the bottom of the duffle, before walking ahead of me down the hallway. "I bought batteries for your fire alarms too, but...you're packing?"

"Yeah," I breathe, as I stop and cross my arms. "The lease is up at the end of the summer."

"Well, I have to say I am glad." My father waves his hands as he marches over the windows, taking in the view. "It's too big of an apartment for one girl...and way too high up. What if the elevator power goes out? Or if there is a fire and you have to get out quickly?"

"Dad," I hesitate, but follow him. His hands are braced on the window sill, checking how sturdy it is. I know he wasn't just in the neighborhood and I know he didn't just come to fix or inspect the architecture. Forest Goode doesn't operate that way. I cross my arms as he turns around. "Did Mama send you?"

"Everleigh Rose, I am here on my own authority," he announces, bracing his hands in front of his body defensively. "I am here completely on my own. Scouts honor."

I eye him suspiciously as he moves to the large black sectional Daniel and I had settled on several years ago, taking the bowl of popcorn and holding it in his lap. "So what are you planning on doing once you leave Buckingham Palace?"

"No idea," I answer honestly, plopping down on the other end of the couch. "I assume I'll find another apartment. Maybe I will try a new part of the city. Move a little further from the office or something."

"Is that what you want to do?" He asks, popping a few pieces of fresh popcorn in his mouth. I'm still a little stunned, I guess. I wasn't expecting anyone to be here tonight, especially my father who is now looking quite relaxed as he sits so comfortably in my apartment. My brain is playing catch up, because my father literally travelled over nine hundred miles just to walk in and eat my popcorn. "What?"

"I'm sorry." I place my hand on my temples, pacing to the window before I turn around and drop my hands. "Did you come here to try and get me to come back to Haven?"

"Yep," he says, before digging back into the popcorn. "Why would you ruin this with chocolate chips? At least use real M&M's if you're going to sweeten it up. Big New York girl, but you're skimping on the chocolate."

"First of all, it's Ghirardelli chocolate and you didn't answer my question," I groan, placing my hands on my hips.

"Yes, I did. I said 'yep' to your question about if I was trying to get you to come back to Haven. I am. But, not because your Mother asked me. Because, I think you and I both know where you want to be," he reassures me, looking so proud of himself as he crosses one leg over the other. "So are you coming or are we going to have one of those heart to hearts?"

"Dad, I know what you're trying to do, and it isn't that simple," I assure him, taking a seat on the other side of the couch.

"The choice itself *is* that simple," Forest Goode says so confidently that I don't think he believes for a moment that there is another choice. "It's 'go to Haven' or it's not. It's very black and white."

"Dad…"

"Let me finish." He holds a hand up, waving me off. "Now, where it gets complicated is that you're choosing grieving over living. Daniel is worth grieving for. He was a good man to you the majority of the time."

"Dad he—" I start to speak but my father gives me another look, one I've seen before. The one when he would come down on us as children for interrupting him when he was trying to explain something to us.

"You can pretend he was a saint, but he wasn't," my dad

argues, despite always being kind to Daniel. I've never heard him say anything like this and I have to admit it burns a little. "I won't challenge what he meant to you, but he wasn't right for you. You two seemed like friends, not someone you would marry. Sure, he was a good man, just not the right man. You deserved someone that you could be your full self around. A relationship isn't for one person to be themselves, it's for both people to be. Friends are meant to spend time with, but not forever. He wasn't even a best friend, because you were very buttoned up around him. There was no shine in your eyes. There was only one side of you when you were with him and that's okay. For friends. Acquaintances. Not for the man you would spend the rest of your life with. So, mourning him is fine. Acceptable. Quitting your life and not spending forever with the man you love? That's wrong."

I sit there in silence with him for what feels like several minutes. Stunned. Quiet. I never knew my father felt this way about Daniel. Acknowledging he was a good man, but believing I wasn't myself around him. Then I try to think about the couple my father saw when we were around. I try to think of an instance where I could prove him wrong. I can't. I can only think of Daniel being Daniel. Sure, he was fun, but he was a little bit buttoned up. It was just who he was and maybe because of his family. I think of his smile. A smile that I have to admit I still love when I think about. Then I think about us. The things I never did around him. The things we did for fun. The only part of that girl from Alabama that came out was when he would go to the occasional football game either in Tuscaloosa at Bryant-Denny Stadium or when the team went to another city. He liked sports, so he didn't mind going. I can feel the sadness spread across my face and I think my father can see it.

"You were the love of his life. You shouldn't feel guilty about that. He left this world, happy because of you. That meant everything to him," he explains, sitting the popcorn in the middle of the couch. "And maybe he was your world at the time or maybe he wasn't, but you owe it to yourself to recognize that he completed his mission in his life feeling loved and well...that's pretty damn important."

"What makes you so sure of that?" I question, wondering why I don't feel immediately better if he is right.

I can't easily figure out the look that comes across my father's face as he shifts, sliding his leather jacket off of each arm and carefully hanging it over the side of the couch. He adjusts his flannel top, leans back and clears his throat, before pinching at his chin. "Dad?"

"Her name was Becky. I was a sophomore at Murphy when she was a freshman," He begins, crossing his arms. "We dated until the summer before my senior year. I was just a scrawny guy and she still paid attention to me. Had the prettiest blonde hair you'd ever seen. A real blonde. Anyways, right before my senior year I decided I wanted to be cocky. I thought I knew everything there was to know about life. So I broke up with her. Broke her heart."

"I mean, you were in high school," I comment quietly, frowning as I realize just how serious he still is. I've seen my father sad at funerals. He's a strong man, but he has feelings. Still, I don't know why he's telling me about his breakup. "She had to know—"

"Let me finish." He echoes defensively, holding a hand up. Something tells me that I don't know how this story goes. That I wasn't supposed to ever know how this story ends, because I can see a familiar pain in my father's eyes. "It was just a week after classes started, when she was dropping a girlfriend off at home. Caught a bad storm on her way back and missed a stop sign. She died immediately."

"Oh my god," I breathe, the words falling away from me

as my father searches his fingers with a doleful look of pain on his face. He's staying strong, but it's crystal clear how sad this story is now. "I... does Mom know?"

"Your mother saved my life." He says, shaking his head as if to shake off some of the heaviness. "I was weighed down by guilt. For years. You get that from me, baby girl. Your mother met me and she told her girlfriends that night in Tuscaloosa that she was going to marry me. Well, little did I know, she was right."

"But you felt guilty? About Becky?" I ask, shifting in my seat, wanting to know more. How could I have gone all of these years and never known my father lived this too. "How did you..."

"When I met your mother, I completely ignored her." He manages a weak laugh and shakes his head. "I mean, she was so nice to me and I just blew her off. Then one day, she told me she liked me and asked me when I was going to ask her out."

"What did you do?" I ask curiously.

"I told her I couldn't be around her anymore," He responds confidently with a little smirk before reaching for a piece of popcorn. "Then I felt bad about being rude. So I drove to her house and I told her everything about Becky."

"Okay..." I say, impatiently waiting for him to tell the rest of this story. How he could go from telling my mother to get lost to marrying her. "So what happened?"

"Well, it took time for her and I to work things out, but she was patient with me. Every year on the anniversary since the first year we were together, she goes with me to Becky's grave. You actually share a birthday with Becky." My dad looks up at me and a weak smile forms on his lips.

"Becky and I have the same birthday?" I ask quietly, my heart broken a little for my father. "Was that hard? When I was born?"

"No." He smiles, reaching across the couch for my hand and squeezing it but quickly releasing it. "I was nervous that day. We already had one little girl at home and I was praying you were going to be a boy. God."

I can't help but laugh, knowing already that my father prayed I would be a boy. I've heard this a million times, but I know he loves being a girl dad. He was meant for it. I don't take it personally, because I know where his heart is. But I never knew the significance of my birthday. He looks back down at his hands, twisting his finger over his ring. "When your mother and I looked at you, the first thing she said was, 'she shares her birthday with Becky' and that was when I knew without a doubt, your mother respected that. Your mother wanted me to remember Becky and she wanted to help me. To this day we argue over what flowers are best to take to Becky's grave."

"You guys still go?" I ask, silencing my phone. Lexie's calling, probably to ask if I know Dad is coming to New York.

"We used to go once a year, now we've been going twice a year since her parents passed away. She was an only child and she deserves to be remembered." He smiles weakly, silencing his own phone that begins to buzz. "It's Lexie."

"She called me too," I roll my eyes, tossing my phone into my lap. I think of all the times my parents have said they went to Mobile or have taken a trip and wonder what were the times they went when we didn't know what for. As if it was something special between them. Then I think how beautiful it must be that they honor a woman's memory they have no responsibility to. Or that they increased how often they go, knowing she had no family to keep visiting her grave. I see the sentimental smile on my father's face as my phone rings again. Lexie. I groan loudly, answering the phone. "Lexie, what the hell do you want?"

"Evie, it's Mom!" Lexie screams into the phone before bursting into a cry as I hear Levi in the background, begging to know what is wrong. My stomach drops as I see the color drain from my father. He heard Lexie.

"Everleigh, what is going one?" My dad jumps up, nearly spilling the popcorn.

I shake my head, indicating I don't know, but I struggle to find any words. I hear the phone shift and then another familiar voice. "Ev, it's Dawson. We're on the way to the hospital. Nancy had some sort of attack and fell. We don't know much else. EMT's took her."

"Oh, God," I gasp, my fingers over my lips. In a second, the entire world stopped. The breath is sucked out of my father and I as I realize Lexie's cry will haunt me forever no matter what the outcome. We have to get home. Now. I can see my father already dialing up the airline. Flight or car, we'll be home tonight. He will find a way. I know by the haunting look on his face. I quickly tell Dawson that we're coming and to call me as soon as they know something. Anything. Then I selfishly try to remember every last second of the last conversation I had with my mother. We talked about Haven and she brought up Wade and I don't remember it all. I don't even remember if I told her that I loved her. Who doesn't remember something like that? My father yells at me to grab my driver's license for him to give to the agent, something about how they have a flight we can get on if we can get there in two hours. His bag was never unpacked, but I packed nothing. I reach for my wallet from my bag, quickly pulling out the driver's license before running to my room. I have to pack. My father's world can't come crashing down for the second time. My world can't come crashing down again. I need Haven. I need Wade.

Chapter Twenty-Seven

Wade

Now

This has been the night from hell. Actually, it was safe to say morning too. It's currently sometime after midnight I've been home for about two hours, but I can't sleep. This has probably been one of the worst moments of my life and I feel like I have had some bad ones. Not long after Nancy left my house, I got a call from Libby telling me that Nancy some sort of accident and was being flown to the hospital in Birmingham. There wasn't a second to think. I had to get there now. I was able to get through to Dawson who was nearby after having picked up Lexie and I caught a ride with them. I can't remember the last time my heart raced as quickly as it did when I found out. Lexie was a mess and that was hell to see. She finally calmed down when we spoke to the doctors. Nancy had a mild heart attack at home. She was at the top of the stairs when it happened and it caused her to fall. She broke her wrist and ankle on the way down. She'll be in the hospital for a bit. Between the heart attack and the surgery, she will need on her wrist, she'll be recovering for a while. It could have been so much worse. Lexie and Evie could have lost their mom tonight. I don't know if either one of those girls would have been okay if something worse had happened. Seeing them was awful.

I was with Lexie on the way to the hospital, but I didn't see Evie until about twenty minutes before I left. It was the second time I wasn't mentally prepared to see her, but I felt my chest sting the moment she walked in. Messy hair, eyes red from crying with Forest by her side. Our eyes caught for a moment and then the nurses directed them all into her mother's room. I guess she and her father were able to rent a car quickly and thank goodness for that. It wasn't long after that Dawson went to head out that I said I would go with him. We didn't talk much during the hour-long ride home. Between the shock of the evening and being completely exhausted, we didn't have it in us. We're relieved. Nancy is going to be okay. She's going to have one hell of a recovery, but she's tough. She's going to get through it and she has a ton of help. I've already told Lexie, Dawson and I will be there every step of the way, but she knows that. Nancy is our family. She's taken care of us during some of the hardest moments in our lives and we'll do the same for her. It isn't a question.

As the rain begins to beat against the kitchen window, I pray silently that the girls make it back from the hospital safely. Forest will stay the night with Nancy. I know he won't leave her side, but the girls will need to go home at some point. Libby came to pick up Levi once she could close the diner early and she was going to take him back to her place for the night. It's moments like this that I feel grateful for this small but mighty town. Haven is full of helpers and there is something about moments like these that remind you that you need them. I twist open a bottle of water as thunder rocks the house. I almost feel too tired to go to bed, but I am going to have to let my guys know I won't be working tomorrow. Sometimes you just have to take a day and that's what I need. At some point, I'll need to catch some sleep. Dawson is even calling out, advising his staff to move appointments.

I think about Ev for a moment. How scared and small she looked at the hospital. Her guard was down, terrified of what was to come. Terrified of what she was going to see. I don't ever want to see her that scared again. If I ever get to see her. I want to see her. I want to tell her I read the letter and that I can do this. That all of this being apart any longer is stupid, but I know it wasn't the time. Maybe it won't be the time. Maybe she doesn't want it to be the time anymore. I would understand after our last conversation. I didn't exactly make fighting for us a selling point. I let her leave, thinking I could and would never be a man who handles what she's been through. I threw in the towel. I gave up. Like my father. Nancy was right, I'm not Ridge Beckett.

Then I read the letter and I'm a little nervous to even admit it to myself, but I cried by the time I was done. Nancy said it would tell me everything I needed to know and it did. It told me more. There is a whole world out there, but it's just Everleigh and I. Hell, I love that woman. More than I could love anything or anyone else. Well, I can think of few anyone's I might love pretty close to as much. But that doesn't ever happen unless I fix this. I have to. When I saw her tonight, I wanted to grab her. I couldn't. Not there. Not then. At some point I will fix this. If it means I move to New York, I'll do it. I don't care. If she wants to move to the moon, we'll pack our bags. I know it's excessive, but I chuckle to myself. She names it, I'll do it. I lean over, putting my elbows on the kitchen island as the storm rages outside. I rest my head in my hands, knowing I should try to get in bed. The morning will come quickly and while I won't be working, there is a chance Forest or the girls will need something and I insist on helping them. I could order some breakfast from Libby's or go over and cook something. I'll figure that out in the morning. I straighten up, my body protesting in exhaustion as I stretch my arms out. I grab my water and walk to the other side, flipping the kitchen light out when I hear a knock at the front door. I frown when I try to peak at the windows from the kitchen entryway. It's not quite blue hour and the porchlights are still the only thing I can really spot so I walk closer and put my hand on the doorknob. I toss my head back, taking a deep breath. I'm exhausted. They pound at the door again, so I let out a deep breath and swing the door open.

Evie.

Evie. She's right in front of me, her body drenched in the rain that is pouring from the sky, her hair so wet some of it is sticking to her face. For a moment, I think maybe I've already started dreaming, but then she gasps.

"I want to come home," she declares, raising her voice over the rain as she uses her wet sleeve to wipe at her eyes. She's still in her clothes from earlier and I know she never tried to go to bed either. "I want to live here. With you."

"I want to live in this house. Our house. I want to change the doorknobs; I really don't think they match. We were wrong about those, and we made the book a really long time ago, but I want to be with you," she says, before shaking her head. "Damn, it's cold."

"Oh. Come inside," I say quickly, stepping out of the doorway as she comes inside, the water dripping everywhere. I'm still a little stunned, but I run to the pile in the dining room space and grab a blanket I ordered from a dark brown box. I quickly rip away the packaging. "Ev—"

"I'm not done talking," she says, refusing the blanket at first, pulling her jeans down and kicking her clothes to the side. "I'm getting the wet clothes off, I'm not stripping. I need to warm up, because I have things to say."

"Totally understand." I hold my hands back, trying to

ignore her body as she undresses. Thank God for the exhaustion or else I wouldn't believe this moment was real. When she finishes, she takes the blanket from me and wraps it around her body. I don't even care about the sopping wet clothes in a pile. Nothing matters. "Better?"

"Much," she nods, before turning to face me. Her hair is still dripping. "Wade, you were right about one thing. I belong here. With you. I can figure out a job here. Actually, I have to, because I just called Linda and told her I quit. Because I want to be here. With you."

"You...quit?" I ask, hesitantly, not sure if I heard her right.

"Well, I kind of quit. I'm going to work here for a while, but eventually I want to do something new, and she supports me, which is why I can work here until I decide what I really want to do." Evie's speaking so fast, I can barely keep up, but I can feel the smile on spreading onto my face. "It was her idea that I work from here instead of just quitting. Probably a good idea, but I'm staying in Haven. Well, kind of."

"Kind of?" I frown as a weak, but hopeful smile grows on her face.

"I have to move out of my place by the end of summer," she answers, bouncing slightly to indicate she's still cold, but I'm still stunned. I can't stop looking at her. She wants to come home. She wants home to be with me. "I thought maybe...we could stay in a hotel but you could help me move and meet Linda and Kyra. They want to meet you. I'm sure Dawson or Lexie could help if you don't feel comfortable..."

I don't give her another chance to speak. The letter told me everything. Her standing wet in the rain on my front porch tells me so much more. I kiss her as hard as I can before she can get another word out, because I don't think I could wait another second. She kisses me back, her hands moving to my hair and neither one of us is worried about the soaking wet clothing on the floor or her hair. A second later I feel her hands on my chest, pushing me away as she stands in front of that damn perfect navy door. "Wait."

"Yes, ma'am," I say, pressing my forehead against hers, the back of my fingers brushing water droplets from her cheek. Strands of her hair are wet beneath my fingers. "I love you, Evie Goode."

"I love you too, Wade Beckett," she says, smiling as she presses her nose against mine. There is a realization between the two of us that we have to move. Either for her to get dressed or for sleep. She presses a soft kiss against my lips, leaving mine a little wet and she slides her hand from the back of my neck. "I'm really tired."

"Me too," I respond, kissing her nose before pulling away. I look up the stairs to the door to my bedroom and extend my hand. "Let's go to bed."

"Let's." She smiles, holding the blanket up as I lead her to the bedroom. Our bedroom. In the house that isn't just mine. I can tell she's freezing, but I don't plan to find her clothing. I don't plan anything else, other than to hold her under the blankets, in our bed. Then we'll sleep. Probably for hours. That's all I really want. When we wake up, we'll tackle the world. I decide in my head, in this moment, that I've never been happier than right now. The home I built from a book, a teenage dream is real. The only woman I ever wanted is here with me. Home.

Epilogue
Evie

Forever

The light tunnels through the trees in a way that only an Alabama sun could when it starts to lower into the evening. The days in Bama can be burning hot, full of humidity and torturous rays, but when the night begins to come the temperatures lower and I'm reminded of why I love it here so much. Of why I missed it. Of why it's where I belong. Summer takes a little longer to go away. This isn't the Midwest; it still feels like summer. I can hear the music coming from the barn as I walk towards the pond on my parent's land, sliding my four-inch heels off as I get closer. I have an soft blanket tucked under my arm, ready to prevent grass stains. Ivory designer pumps weren't made for the ground here and maybe Wade was right, I should change into some sandals before I go back to the barn. I'll get them on my way back in, for now I want to enjoy that moment when the fireflies begin to come out and the air gets a little breezy. It reminds me of chasing the fireflies around as a little girl, begging my mother for an empty mason jar or something to keep them. Little did I know, it wasn't that easy and my mom would quickly distract me and let them loose.

My mother has been doing so well since the heart attack. She's using a cane now. It's better than the crutches she was on before. Mostly, because she was still trying to chase Levi around with them. She's a fighter and her doctors are so happy with her progress. Somehow, Dad has convinced her to let him help out more in the kitchen. We got lucky. When I received the call from Lexie, I had no idea what I was going to witness when I got back to Alabama. I just knew two things: I needed my mom and I needed Wade. Which is why I didn't want to waste another moment being without him. It turns out that I wasn't alone in that feeling. I came home from my mother's a week later to Wade in one of the spare bedrooms, on one knee. He wanted to ask me to begin our life together in the room he thought one day might be a nursery. I cried way harder than I ever thought I would. Given everything that had happened and how bummed Mom was to be in the hospital at the time, I told her first. When I told her I wanted to plan a quick wedding, I thought she was going to be angry, but it didn't. Nancy Goode has never been so excited. She immediately went into planning mode and decided it was going to be a 'late' summer wedding. Heat be damned.

I stayed with my parents last night and it was a little bit like old times. We watched our favorite movie as a family: *Beethoven*. My Dad cries every time. It was the first time Levi got to see it and it was special to be a part of it. Now he wants a dog and Lexie is going to have her hands full if Dawson has anything to say about it.

"You fulfilled your mission, Mrs. Beckett," I hear Wade's voice and I swing around, holding my dress up a little to prevent it from getting twisted. When I see him, he holds up a bottle of champagne and two glasses. "You looked damn good doing it."

"You don't look too bad either," I giggle, opening the plaid blanket and spreading it out in front of the pond. I would put it on the dock, but if my mother saw the bottom of this dress get messy, she would kill me.

"Levi asked me where I was going, so I had to slip him twenty bucks to keep quiet." Wade laughs, sliding onto the blanket and leaning back so I can cradle in his arms. Immediately my eyes fall closed as he wraps his arm over me and I realize I won't want to get up from this spot.

"He's a good kid." I giggle, as I reach for the bottom of champagne and frown when I realize it's already open. "Really?"

"I had to make a quick escape. It would have been too hard to locate a new bottle," he shrugs, handing me the glasses to fill up. "This one will do."

"Fine," I pout dramatically, pouring us each a glass. I can't help but giggle as it still manages to bubble over and a little bit drips onto my dress. "Don't tell Nancy I got champagne on my dress."

"I think you're good." He laughs, taking one of the glasses. I put the bottle down and hold up my glass. "Okay, but no more big toasts. I think we've had our fair share today."

"Agreed," he nods, before a smile spreads across his face. The first few buttons of his shirt are unbuttoned and I have never felt more in love. "To us."

"To us," I grin, before we both take a sip. Wade told me last night that the wedding would be crazy busy, but that he wanted us to steal a moment for each other and I am glad we did. I smile as he kisses the top of my head. The truth is, I didn't feel alive. Not until I was back in his arms, and when I left and returned to New York, I felt even more lost. Ever since I moved home, I feel like I have unleashed this person that spent twelve years trying to come to the surface. I miss the city sometimes, but all I do is tell Wade and we make a trip. As it turns out, Wade really likes New York. Especially the pizza and sporting events. Broadway not so much. But he'll go for me.

"I have a wedding present for you." He interrupts my thoughts as he slides a square blue velvet box in front of me. "And you can't hate it."

"I can't hate it?" I giggle, taking it into my hands. "Is it a new bottle of champagne? This box is kind of small."

"Just open it." He teases, kissing the top of my head. I take a deep breath and pull the box open. A single silver key. My first thought is the house, but I have a house key. I look up at him and he urges me to sit up. I pull my body from his, turning to face him. "It's a key to Hilly's. I bought the business from Hilly. So, you'll have to change the name, but the shop itself and the stuff currently inside of it is ours. Well, yours."

"What?" I breathe, as I feel the shock come over my body. A shop. Hilly's. I look up at him, words gone from my head. "You bought me a shop. A whole store."

"I talked to Linda, Kyra, your mom, and Lexie," he says nervously, his fingers pushing hair from my face. "We figure you can run it as a shop or a website. You can do whatever you want with it, but it's yours babe. Make your ideas come to life and if you don't love it, we'll turn around and sell it."

I can tell he's waiting for me to say something, but I'm pretty sure I am still stunned. So happy, but shocked. I manage for a smile to spread across my lips as I finally speak. "Wade...I love it."

"Thank God," he says, pulling my lips to his, my hair falling into his face. "I just wanted you to do something you want to do. It can be anything. You tell me and we'll make it happen together. Anything except a Broadway theatre."

"You're ridiculous," I giggle, kissing my husband again. Coming back to Haven hadn't been my plan until Linda and my family got together and pretty much made me. Running into Wade was the last thing I wanted. There had been so much pain there, I thought there was no possible way this life would ever happen. Now, I'm sitting on my parents' land, no longer worrying about how clean I keep this wedding dress. Wade Beckett is mine. He was always mine. It wasn't always easy to return home. It was painful and forced a lot of uncomfortable truths to come out into the open. But every night when I walk out of our bathroom and see him up in bed, watching Sports Center, I can't help but feel like I am right where I was always going to end up. Right at home, in love, in Haven.

Acknowledgements

I can't believe it's finally time to see this book on paper! There was a point where I wasn't sure that this would happen. Actually, there were several points. It's so exciting that we're finally here! Of course, I have to give a thank you to so many important people.

Thank you to my editor, Savannah! You are such a rockstar and I am so grateful that I trusted my baby with you! Thank you to Lorna and Lynn for an amazing interior and cover.

Thank you to my LSM girls for rooting for me and cheering me on. Tiffany- thank you for reading this book and giving all of your amazing feedback. And for being excited for book two!

To my grandmother's. Grandmother Betty, thank you for asking about my book every time you talk to me. Grandma Elena, thank you for reading and doing the first round of edits for my book. It meant the world to me. Grandma Karen, thank you for my love of old movies and love stories. One of my favorite views growing up, was finding your head buried in a Danielle Steele novel.

To my family littles: Sam, Noah, Sebastian, Amelia, CJ, Little Tommie, Maddie, Max, Zach, Jaclynn, Ireland, Addie, Leon, Audrey and Hadley. If you can dream it, you can do it. If someone says you shouldn't try, don't listen.

Mom and Dad, thanks for always supporting whatever crazy idea I throw out into the universe. You are the best parents for a dreamer like me. To Justin, Kirsten and Alyssa, for being so supportive. I am also so grateful for so many friends and family who have read this book, supported me or given feedback on questions about titles and storylines. I love you all!

Milton Keynes UK
Ingram Content Group UK Ltd.
UKHW040630111223
434160UK00001B/54